I0608994

Copyright © 2020 by Edwina Fort

Author Edwina Fort P.O. Box 346 Keithville, LA 1047 www.authoredwinafort.com

Mean Tucker/Edwina Fort. – 1st edition ISBN

# Acknowledgments

As always, first and foremost I would like to thank the Heavenly Father, who has once again provided me with a chance to sow. Gardening is what I was born to do. Where would I be if I could not plant seeds? I would like to thank my friend, Daina Mckay, it was she who first gave me the courage to dream. I would also like to thank my husband and my children for learning how to live around my crazy. I would like to thank my team, who has also learned how to coexist with my swings. Crystal girl...where would I be without you? And last but certainly not least, I would like to thank my fans. Y'all keep the fire lit under me lest I get negligent in my responsibility. For that, I am eternally grateful.

# MEAN TUCKER

## Part 1 & 2

### EDWINA FORT

# Mean Tucker Part I
## NAPTHALI AND FREE'S TALE

## Prologue

### Free

IT WAS ALMOST OVER. I was almost free from this hell known as high school. No...I take that back. I was almost free from this hell known as Aldshore, Michigan, my house, my so-called family, high school, and most importantly, Naphtali Tucker Pelletier, who was a real-life sociopath who everybody called Tucker, but I called Mean Tuck.

I looked up the name Tucker once because that's what I did. I stayed hidden in the library most times with my nose stuck in a book. It was the only safe place, the only place the Beautiful Ones will never travel.

Anyway, I looked up the name Tucker and would you guys believe it is derived from an old English word in the 7th century that meant *tormenter*?

What's the irony? That's exactly what he was, my tormenter.

And no matter what I did to try and avoid him, he always found me because he was psychotic and tormented me to the cheers and encouragement of his posse that the whole school referred to as the Beautiful Ones, because there was not an unattractive one to be found in their midst. And he, the most beautiful of them all was their king.

He was not only their king, he was king of the whole damn school, the golden boy of the small beach town, captain of the football team, adopted son of the Mayor, and if you let everybody in this town tell it, the next best thing from the Second Coming.

Now me…

Well, I was nobody. I was born in Detroit. My mom was a black hippie, who loved life. She loved it so much she named me Free, but she also loved drugs and ended up overdosing when I was in eighth grade. Her death almost killed me. She was the best mom in the whole world and now she was gone.

Anyway, my estranged father, who I hadn't seen since I was a baby, showed up to the funeral and informed me that I was moving to Aldshore, a small beach town off Lake Michigan, known for its wealth, to live with him and his new wife, who had twin daughters from a previous marriage that were my age. Apparently, my dad had married up. Neither he nor my mom was from money, but my dad's new wife surely was.

Although they lived in a huge mansion, they'd given me a small room in the basement. Angie, my dad's wife was not happy with the fact that he'd shown up with a strange kid to tarnish her pristine reputation.

I was her charity case and she never let me forget it.

And because my dad in all sense and purpose was also a charity case, there wasn't much he could do to help me.

I mean, don't get me wrong, he was a well-known psychiatrist in the area, in fact, that was how he and Angie met. He was her doctor, but his notoriety was nothing compared to hers. She was what was known as Black royalty. She came from old money.

This whole town was full of Black royalty. And like I told you, sitting at the very top was the Pelletier family. Word is, Mayor Pelletier and his wife had tried to have a baby for many years, but couldn't. So they'd sent a scout out to find them the very best specimen to adopt and they'd found Tucker.

LOL… I don't know how true that is, but Tucker is a very fine specimen. Every girl at school fancied themselves in love with him. And for the life of me, I couldn't understand why someone so gorgeous and so popular always went out of their way to hunt me down and then torture me.

You know what…scratch that. I *do* know why. It's because he's a psychotic sociopath, who I was sure suffered from multiple personality disorder. Something about me had triggered something in his brain and now he didn't feel complete unless he was causing me misery. And although I've spent many hours wondering what I could have possibly done to gain the attention of someone like him, I'm still at a complete loss.

It's not that I thought I was ugly, I wasn't. It's just that I wasn't perfect like the Beautiful Ones. I wore glasses that I had to tape up because I didn't have the funds to replace them. Angie won't buy me another pair and she won't let me get a job so that I can buy myself another pair, because

God forbid anybody sees any of her daughters, including her little charity case working a real job.

So, I walked around with thick duct tape holding the left side of my frames together. I didn't have long straight hair like my stepsisters. Both Layla and Laureen spent hours at the beauty salon every week.

Not me, Angie was already paying a fortune to house me and send me to this fancy school. There was nothing left for amenities like clothes and beauty salon appointments. All my clothes were Layla and Laureen's hand-me-downs.

But I didn't mind not going to the beauty salon, because I actually loved my hair. In fact, I thought it was my best feature. It was my mama's hair, thick and curly. I fought with it each morning to get it in a ponytail. And by noon each day, most of it was escaping my ponytail to frame my face, making me look like my mom.

Like I told you guys, my clothes were Layla and Laureen's hand-me-downs and they made sure everybody in school knew it. So yeah, I couldn't figure out why Tucker made it his mission to seek me out and torture me every day. There was nothing special about me.

And trust me, I did my very best to avoid him.

The two classes he and I had together were the two classes I was doing the worst in. I always came late, because it wasn't safe to be early and I always made up an excuse to leave early, because it wasn't safe to leave late.

I didn't go into the lunch room...

Goodness, in the four years of me attending this school, I can count on one hand the times I'd eaten lunch in the cafeteria and those times had been the most tortuous.

My freshman year, he'd sat his beautiful chocolate,

athletic frame down at my table and then while staring at me with a gaze that held me hypnotized, proceeded to eat my whole lunch. But what made it so bad is that I didn't realize the whole cafeteria was laughing at me because his gaze had me completely paralyzed. I couldn't believe that Tucker...the Tucker that was king of this school, even in freshman year, was sitting at my table and not only that, he was looking at me.

It wasn't until he'd finished eating my lunch, stood and walked away from me that I blinked, coming out of the trance he'd put me under to realize that everybody was laughing at me, including my two stepsisters, who were both one of the Beautiful Ones.

Tears came to my eyes as hot embarrassment washed over me. I got up and ran from the cafeteria and didn't re-enter it till my sophomore year. This time, I'd gone in with my new friend Rachel. She was a freshman and like me, she wasn't rich or a part of the in-crowd. Her mom was a well-known prostitute, so she too suffered from bullying.

But her tormenter was Jackson, Tucker's right-hand man and best friend...and a golden boy in his own right. His daddy was the town's sheriff, so he knew all about Rachel's mom and her home life and he teased her about it endlessly. Several times he'd made her cry.

Anyway, on the first day of school, she wanted to go into the cafeteria to eat lunch. I thought enough time had passed since the last debacle, so maybe it was safe. Boy was I wrong. I'd been pointing something out to her as we passed Tucker's table, not paying attention and right as I passed, he shot up from the table into my path, causing me to crash into him.

It was like hitting a brick wall. I flew to the ground

hearing my glasses land somewhere by my head. My books and papers went everywhere. But that wasn't the horrifying part, I'd been wearing one of my stepsister's hand-me-down skirts that was slightly too big for me and the skirt flew up to my waist. Chaos erupted. I was on full display from my belly button down.

I could have died when Tucker's eyes landed on my white underwear. I swear it seemed like time stood still.

I heard my stepsister Layla, the oldest twin yell, "Look, she's wearing granny panties!" In a state of shock, I scrambled to try and gain control of my skirt and pull it down.

That moment was so unreal. The whole time my hands that were extremely clumsy in my shocked state were trying to gain control of my skirt. The look in Tucker's gaze as he looked at my dark brown legs and belly button was throwing me for another loop.

I'd never seen hunger in the opposite sex's eyes towards me before, so seeing it for the first time was a bit of a trip and seeing it in none other than the famous Tucker's eyes had to be the biggest shock of them all. I had gotten the skirt down, but because I'd pulled too hard, my belly was now exposed.

Nobody was paying attention to him, they were all laughing and pointing at me. But I was watching him, I saw him get an erection. And he didn't try to hide it from me, which really made it all the more mortifying.

Rachel bent down and pulled down my shirt to cover my belly and then helped me up. Tears of embarrassment were blinding me. With trembling hands, I put my glasses back on so that I could pick up my books and papers. Rachel helped me.

Still on my hands and knees, I'd retrieved every paper

but my literature report. I recognized the black Jordan that stood on top of it and dread filled my being. Without looking up, I pulled at the report, but it didn't budge.

Dear God, why does he have to torment me so? Slowly my gaze rose up the powerful bow-legs encased in the black designer jeans that probably cost more than everything I have in my closet. The bulge was still there in his pants and I wondered if anybody else had noticed. My gaze continued up to a lean waist, farther up to the massive chest and finally to a face too beautiful to belong to such an ugly individual.

I pulled at the paper, letting him know I needed him to move his foot.

"Say please…" Even in his sophomore year, his voice had been extremely deep. Tears came to my eyes. I didn't want to say please to him, I wanted to get a gun and shoot him.

"Please…" I told him with trembling lips, so embarrassed I was thanking God for my dark brown skin.

He didn't move his foot right away. Instead, his eyes swept over my face. The muscle ticked in his jaw and I wondered in that moment what he was thinking. My peers still laughed and cracked jokes about my grannie panties behind me, but he didn't seem to notice. It was something else going on in his psychotic mind.

His hand lifted as if it was going to caress my face, but he must have caught himself and lowered it. Then mercifully he moved his foot…

Oh God! That was so humiliating. And I'd like to tell y'all that was the most humiliating thing to happen to me, but then I'd be lying.

Junior year was hard for me. It was the year my father

got killed by the brother of the woman he'd been cheating on Angie with. Long story...I'll fill you guys in on that later. But his death left me at the complete mercy of Angie and my evil stepsisters.

The one good thing about it was that I'd found out he'd left money for me to go to college, which was perfect because Angie had told me more than once that she wasn't paying for me to go.

Anyway, so my dad died. Although there wasn't much love lost between us, it was still a little hard. But then junior year also meant I had to take swimming in gym. And as if God was just not in a giving mood, that year I had gym with Tucker, thus beginning my showing up for class late and leaving early.

However, one day, that didn't work out for me. I'd entered the empty gym, because you had to walk through it to get to the locker rooms and then the pool. But it just so happened that Tucker and a few of his friends were also late and had entered the gym at the same time.

Because my mama didn't raise no fool, I took off running towards the locker rooms, but I don't know why I did that because it was like a red flag to a group of bulls.

"Catch her a**!" Tucker yelled and they took off after me.

And as if that day couldn't get any worse, I had on one of Layla's old skirts that of course was too big, so when Jackson caught me, my skirt fell down as I went wild in his arms.

No, wait! That isn't the worst of it...

That day, I had on these cute little pair of Hello Kitty underwear that I'd found on a discount rack at Walmart. Jackson, who didn't know that my skirt had fallen, held onto my arms as I tried to pull them away from him so that I could pull up my skirt.

"Jackson! Let me go!" I cried.

"Okay..." he said before shoving me away from him, causing me to trip over my skirt and into Tucker's waiting arms. It was then he saw that my skirt had fallen. When his surprised gaze fell to my panties, Tucker's arms tightened around me as at that point, he was practically holding me. My feet were just barely touching the floor.

"Don't look at her!" he growled, sounding like he wanted to kill his friend.

Jackson held up his hands and turned and walked out of the gym. It was then when I saw that the other two boys that had been with them were also gone. The danger of being alone with him had registered somewhere in the back of my mind. But his possessiveness had me so confused, I had no idea what was going on. My adrenaline was pumping out of control.

Tucker eased me back down on my feet, in no hurry, pressing my body to his in a way that made me feel...I don't know, hot?

I instantly reached down to get my skirt, but he beat me to it, snatching it away from me. I stood frozen in horror, because the position he was in was quite scandalous. He was down on one knee in front of me. His face was so close to my center.

All my limbs had locked as my brain raced to try and process what was happening to me. Mean Tuck, the most popular boy in the world was on his knee in front of me, staring at my Hello Kitty panties. He'd just growled at his friend for looking at me...as if—

All thoughts fled from my mind when I felt his big

warm hands gently cupping my butt before he pulled me close, pressing his face into my center.

My mouth opened in utter shock, but when I felt him inhale, something else went through me, something I'd never felt before...

Arousal...

There in that gym Mean Tucker had awakened arousal in me.

"You smell so innocent. Damn, it smells good. I want to taste you..."

*What?!*

The sound of a door closing in the distance snapped me out of the lust-filled haze he'd so cleverly put me in. I stumbled out of his hands and snatched my skirt from him before scrambling into it. The whole time he stayed on one knee and watched me with his hungry eyes.

When I got back situated, he grabbed the front of my skirt and yanked me till I was back in front of him.

"Stop, Mean Tuck!" I cried trying to push away from him, but he wouldn't let me. He was so much stronger than me, my little shoves weren't even causing him to budge.

"Why are you such a f***ing d**k tease?" he growled up at me.

I looked back to see if someone had come in the gym so that I could call for help, but unfortunately they hadn't.

"Let me go!"

"Answer me..." He was still down on his knee holding me pinned to him.

"I'm not." My gaze went back to the door.

*Please, somebody, come in and help me. I was in the hands of a backyard bully!*

"Look at me, Free."

I couldn't...His eyes were too intense and they worked havoc on my soul. He was my bully. He should never be able to get into my soul. I shook my head and he shook me...

"Look at me!"

My gaze lowered to his and I nearly groaned at the look I saw there.

"Why don't you ever look at me? You look at Rachel and all the rest of your little geek squad rejects."

I was now clutching his big shoulders to keep from falling. "They're not rejects."

"Why do you care so much for them? You won't even f***ing look at me."

And then a thought hit me. Is that why he was always picking on me?

It's true, I had a small little group of friends. And yes, we were the rejects, but I did my best to make them feel special. No, we weren't the Beautiful Ones, but we were the smart ones. When we were together, we laughed and talked about stuff that we were interested in and we completely ignored the Beautiful Ones, something the rest of the school never did.

When the Beautiful Ones entered a room, everybody stopped to stare, especially if their king was with them.

Now here he was on his knee in front of me, asking me why I ignored him. Serves him right, someone should ignore him. He was used to things coming too easy for him. His looks coupled with his family's money had completely spoiled him.

However, he was wrong about me not looking at him. I'd done more than that. I'd *studied* him. It was safe to say he was the reason I'd chosen to pursue psychology like my father. Earlier, when I'd said he suffered from multi-personality disorder, I was not simply venting, it's true.

I don't think anybody else noticed it, but Tucker can turn his emotions off like a light switch. He becomes a completely different person when he does. I'd only seen this happen a few times and each time had been when he was fighting.

During sophomore year, another school had come to play us. Tucker and a member of the other team got in a fight. Something came over Mean Tuck and he ruthlessly beat that kid down. He beat him so bad that the coaches and other members of the team were afraid to get close to him to break it up.

When he was done and the kid was unconscious, he just stepped over the guy, leaving him bleeding on the ground and never even looked back.

Apparently, that guy was in a gang, because a few days later, he came back with some of his friends. They showed up thinking because Tucker was rich, he was going to be afraid of them.

Goodness, I'll never forget the look on his face when the change came over him. He wore an evil grin as they jumped out their cars yelling and posturing like boys their age do, telling him what they were going to do to him. They were yelling out the name of their gang.

Not impressed in the least, Tucker made eye contact with Jackson, who'd been leaning on the gate and then, I kid y'all not, Jackson and Tucker proceeded to whoop those guys' tails. And I can't prove it, but I think that Tucker and Jackson may have taken it a step further. A few days later, the bodies of some of the gang members were found with their necks broken.

Of course, being the sons of the mayor and the town's sheriff, nothing happened to Tucker and Jackson. The cops didn't even come and question them. He and Jackson were hailed as some kind of heroes for defeating a gang of boys by themselves. But when word got out that some of those same guys had been found dead, people started to speculate that it was Tucker and Jackson.

I don't know if he did it or not, but I know that the guy who he'd beaten up on the other team never came back with any more of his friends, and when his school played ours again later in the season, he didn't come with them.

I was convinced that the Tucker that beat up those guys is not the same Tucker that terrorized me. The Tucker that terrorized me was the one here before me. He cared about things, like whether or not I saw him.

That other Tucker, the Tucker I think may have broken those guys necks, didn't care about anything. He didn't show signs of feeling any emotion at all.

"I care for them," I told him, referring to his question about my friends who he and his posse referred to as the geek squad. "Because nobody else does. There are some of us whose life hasn't been all that kind to." And then I snatched away from him and walked towards the locker room.

I expected him to come after me or try and trip me...or throw something at me, but when none of that happened and I made it to the door that led into the locker room in one piece, I risked a peek back at him and was surprised to see him still on his knee where I'd left him watching me.

Senior year, he'd started invading my sanctuary... the

library. He would do things like snatch whatever book I was reading from me and toss it in the toilet or pour his soda all over it right when I'm at a good part.

I'd tried to tell Ms. Grey, the school librarian on him, but just like every other teacher here, she was completely enamored with him and wouldn't even begin to lift a finger to serve him with a disciplinary action.

He got away with murder, literally and figuratively. Because he'd taken the football team to state all four years and brought back a championship, the whole town loved him. I couldn't even call the cops on him because he was the sheriff's son's best friend.

I tried to tell Angie that I needed help because he was bullying me and she'd only laughed...

"Yeah right! The Pelletier boy is not thinking about you." She gestured toward me. "Look at you, what is there to think about? He's probably just picking on you trying to get one of your sister's attention. You know how boys that age are."

I wanted to laugh at that. Both Layla and Laureen have been trying to be Mean Tuck's and Jackson's girls for all four years of high school and probably before that, I wasn't here to know for sure. But because it was no secret that the twins and the rest of the cheerleaders got around, I don't think he looked at them as girlfriend material.

In fact, I don't think he looked at any girl here as girl-friend material because I have yet to hear about him having a girlfriend, although I've heard about him sleeping with girls plenty.

Nevertheless, Angie was no help. Although my mom had named me Free, I felt far from it. Mean Tuck held me prisoner to his cruelty and there was nothing I could do about it. As you can see, he can murder me and nobody would even bat an eye because he was the town's golden boy.

So I was biding my time. I just focused on keeping my grades up. The money my father had left me had gotten me an acceptance letter to the Grambling University. I was going for their Sociology and Psychology program. When I was done, I wanted to be able to help people like my mom, who had habits they could not break. Maybe I can help someone before they ended up dead like her.

Yes…I was counting the days before I was free of this hell that was my life.

Most girls dreamed of prom night. They sat starry-eyed and imagined how they would look in their beautiful gowns and how good they would look standing next to their princes.

Not me. I dreaded it and wouldn't have gone if Angie hadn't forced me.

"You only get one prom. Every girl should have those memories to hold onto." Then she handed me twenty-five dollars and told me to go shopping for what I needed.

*Twenty-five dollars…*

Lucky for me, Rachel is the thrift store queen. She often bragged about her skills. Although I was dreading prom night, she and I had fun shopping for it. We rode the bus to Michigan City and made a day of it.

"You know what's so bad? Right now, your stepmom and sisters are probably sitting in some fancy fitting room sipping champagne while they get fitted for the gowns," Rachel said as she and I looked through the racks at one of her favorite thrift stores.

I shrugged. "Angie once told me that she didn't owe

me anything…" I paused for a moment. "And you know what? She's right. She doesn't owe me nothing. Both of my parents are dead and really, everything she does for me is just from her good will."

Rachel rolled her beautiful eyes. Like her mom, she was what folks around these parts called an exotic beauty. I don't know where her people originated from, but she looked as if she was from the Pacific Islands somewhere.

If she hadn't been forced to wear her mother's scarlet letter, somebody like Jackson would be competing with the other boys for her hand rather than torturing her, because he knew nobody cared what happened to the town prostitute's daughter.

"Good will my a**. You're a modern-day Cinderella. You clean their house, do all the laundry, cook all the food…Put up with those twin demon seeds she calls children and the best she can do is hand you twenty-five dollars?" She shook her head. "Nothing good happens to people like her."

I know she was probably thinking about her mom, who's selfish careless ways had ruined many things for Rach…I don't want to tell you guys too much of her tale because I've heard it on good authority that she will be telling y'all her tale herself really soon…

So… No spoilers…

LOL… Anyway, we found the perfect dress for me. At first, I was a little worried because it was yellow and I don't think people wore yellow dresses to prom, but then I thought, who cares? The dress is beautiful and I wanted it.

It called to me. The yellow wrap dress looked so good against my brown skin. Once I moisturized really good, it was really going to make my melanin pop. I was a little uncomfortable with the split on the side that went up almost to my thigh. But Rachel said because it's a maxi dress, it will be perfect.

The dress was so long it will drag the ground even if I wore heels, so I didn't bother. We found some beautiful golden sandals with long laces that wrapped about my legs Roman style for only two dollars and fifty cents.

I went to Rachel's house to get dressed on prom night. I was the only one who'd ever been to her house because it really wasn't much of a house. They barely had any furniture and the few pieces they had were very dirty. Her mom did a lot of entertaining and it always smelled like a bar in here.

Rachel had two locks on her room door, but even that didn't keep some of her mom's friends out. Sometimes I snuck her in my room so that she could sleep safe, which wasn't hard to do because my room was in the basement and nobody really came down there.

Rachel was not ashamed to bring me to her house because she and I were in the same boat. Both of us were living our own personal hells, counting down the days till we could be free. Poor Rach still had a whole year left.

Anyway, I went to her place to get dressed so that she could do my hair and make-up. She braided my hair in two long braids and then wrapped them around my head like a crown, before weaving pretty yellow flowers in it.

She went light on the make-up because she said I didn't need it.

"You are so pretty, Free, you don't need any make-up... You already look like a chocolate baby doll." I smiled hugging her close. I loved Rachel. At that time in my life, she was the only person who cared for me.

When she was done, I stood in her mirror staring at my reflection in disbelief. Somehow, she'd made me look like a princess.

"Thank you so much, Rach, you worked a miracle." She playfully hit my arm.

"Yeah right, I think you're the only one unaware of how beautiful you are. It's the reason your stepsisters are so jealous of you."

I shook my head at that. Rach has been saying that since I've known her, but I didn't think it was true. Layla and Laureen had beautiful clothes and spent hours at the hair salon and nail parlor. They weren't jealous of me. I was the nobody that stayed in their basement, living off their charity.

Anyway, a group of my friends and I decided to go together since no one had asked us. We agreed to meet at Dillion's house and have a cocktail before we went. And although neither of us said it, we really were drinking some liquid courage.

By the time we entered the prom, we were all a little tipsy. And I'm not going to lie, I ended up having a really good time, even when the Beautiful Ones entered and even when their king entered looking extremely handsome in his suit with Tamesha Walker on his arm.

In fact, I threw my head back and laughed because I knew that both Layla and Laureen had hoped that it would have been them, but he hadn't chosen either of them. It made sense that he chose Tamesha, she was the most popular girl in the school.

Love Child by Diana Ross came on, it was one of my favorite songs in the whole world. Thanks to the four glasses of champagne I had, I didn't hesitate to turn around and face my friends, who cheered me on and I pretended to be Diana.

They laughed as I did a really horrible impersonation.

*You think that I don't feel love,*
*What I feel for you is real love. In other's eyes, I see reflected a*
*hurt, scorned, rejected.*
*Love Child, never meant to be,*
*Love Child, born in poverty,*
*Love Child, never meant to be,*
*Love Child, take a look at me.*

Although my friends laughed, they had no idea how much I related to this song... They had no idea that I was that Love Child...

*I started my life in an old, cold, rundown tenement slum.*
*My father left, he never even married Mom.*
*I shared the guilt my mama knew,*
*So afraid that others knew I had no name.*
*This love we're contemplating, is worth the pain of waiting.*
*We'll only end up hating the child we may be creating.*
*Love Child, never meant to be,*
*Love Child, by society,*
*Love Child, never meant to be,*
*Love Child, diff'rent from the rest.*

AT SOME POINT, I got lost in the song and hugged myself as I continued to dance...

*I started school in a worn, torn, dress that somebody threw out.*
*I knew the way it was to always live in doubt,*
*To be without the simple things,*
*So afraid my friends could see the guilt in me.*
*Don't think I don't need you,*
*Don't think I don't want to please you.*
*No child of mine'll be bearing the name of shame I've been*
*wearin'.*
*Love Child, never quite as good,*

WHAT WAS to become of me? Now that high school was practically over, my life would officially begin... I continued to dance to the song, completely lost in my head, however when my back came up against something solid, I froze and whipped around.

My hand flew to my mouth when I saw that I'd bumped into Tucker. He stood looking at me as if this was his first time ever seeing me.

"Sorry, Mean Tuck!" I told him before a giggle slipped through my lips.

But then I thought, why am I apologizing? He must have walked up to me, because I was still standing close to my friends, who all now watched him warily, like sheep who'd just spotted a lion.

His gaze flew up to mine. He must have just realized I was a little tipsy. "Do you know you're the only one at this school brave enough to give me a nickname?"

I thought about his words... It was true. I will never forget the day I first let the name slip through my lips. I was running late for algebra, freshmen year and he rounded the corner at the same time I did. I went around him, but he still took offense and knocked my books out of my arms.

I was so mad that I turned around and called him Mean Tuck... I wanted to tell him he was a Mean F*** but got scared and changed my mind at the last minute and Mean Tuck came out my mouth instead. I guess I've been calling him that ever since. But you know what was amazing that I'd just realized? He'd never stopped me. I mean, at any point and time, he could have been like, *don't call me that* and I would have been like, *you got it.*

"Yeah, but I'm not brave. You terrify me."

Wow! The champagne had the truth slipping through my lips very easily. I know tomorrow I was going to regret it.

He chuckled as his gaze continued to take me in. "You look really pretty, Free."

My mouth opened in shock, but then I closed it back. "Yeah right, what's the catch? You going to pour glue in my hair or trip me," I chuckled. "You going to try and rip my dress?"

As soon as the words escaped my lips, I regretted it. His gaze lowered to the tie in my dress. I froze when his hand grabbed it. One pull and my dress will open.

"Looks like the only thing I have to do is pull this string."

"Come on, Tucker...give her a break tonight," Dillion, the bravest of our crew said, taking a cautious step forward.

Tucker's gaze rose from my waist to look at Dillion. The frown that came upon his face was breathtaking.

"What?!" he growled, causing both Dillion and I to jump.

"Nothing, bro..." my very wise friend said taking a few steps back.

"That's what the f*** I thought." Then his gaze came back to me and his eyes softened again.

"What you going to do to keep me from pulling this string?"

"I—" at a complete loss for words I looked around for a teacher, but then he started pulling the string.

"What do you want me to do?" I cried, grabbing his big hand.

"Go for a ride with me."

"Ummm..."

He started pulling the string again. "Okay!" I squeaked.

With a satisfied smile on his face, he held his hand out to me. The hand I put in his shook. He led me out the gym past his date, who was steaming mad and the other Beautiful Ones.

"Where do you think you're going?" Layla asked me walking toward us, she was steaming too.

"Sit," was all Tucker said and I promise, she did just that.

I couldn't help the laughter that escaped my throat as he continued to pull me out of the gym. I looked back and she was still sitting, I laughed harder. I knew she was going to make me pay tomorrow for that, but I couldn't help it. He'd just ordered her to sit like a dog and she'd done it.

However, by the time we made it to Tucker's truck, all my laughter had died down as my nervousness came back. And let me tell y'all something about this nervousness, if it hadn't been for the champagne, it would be outright terror.

When he opened the passenger door, I pulled back a little, but he only turned and wrapped his big hands around my waist before lifting me into the seat. Then as if he feared I was going to try and run away, he reached over and secured the seat belt around me.

I thought about jumping out and running for my life as he rounded the truck to get in, but I must confess to being a little curious about this sudden turn of events. This was one of my last nights in this town. Graduation was tomorrow and I'd set up early enrollment at Grambling because I had a summer job with the campus library.

If everything went well, I pray I'd be able to keep that job throughout my time there. The pay wasn't bad and I would be surrounded by what I loved…books.

"You hungry?" he asked after he started the powerful engine.

I shrugged. "I can eat."

We drove a short way to Webster's Bistro. "Let's grab something to go," he said as he helped me out of his truck.

"I've never eaten here," I told him as I walked through the door he held open for me.

"What? I see your stepsisters and mom here all the time."

I chuckled without any humor. "Yeah…" was all I said, too ashamed to admit that Angie didn't bring me to eat here because it was too expensive.

She said stowaways don't get to eat fine dining.

"Yeah, what?" he asked as he handed me a menu.

Leave it to him not to let it drop. "Yeah, well…she never brought me."

He must have seen that he'd hit a nerve because he let it drop. "Okay, just order anything you want."

"Anything?"

He nodded with a grin on his face. "Anything."

And so I did. He carried two big bags in his hand when we left. He drove a short distance to the beach and then parked his truck. With a blanket tucked under one arm and the two bags of food in that hand, he held my hand with his other and guided me a little way down the beach. He led me to an area that was private.

"I didn't even know this place existed," I told him looking out at Lake Michigan. There was a huge moon in the sky casting a beautiful glow down on the calm water.

"Most people don't," he said as he laid out the blanket, putting the food on top.

There was a gentle breeze that blew my dress up around my legs as I walked toward the water. Wanting to put my feet in it, I untied my sandals and gathered my dress as I stepped into the cool water. A wave that was bigger than I thought washed up against me, splashing my front. Laughing, I ran out the water and back toward Tucker.

He lay reclined on the blanket watching me as he ate his fries. Giggling, I sat down next to him.

"What did you drink tonight?" he asked as I began to dig through the bag for my food. Really, it was all mine. The only thing he'd ordered was a burger and fries.

"Champagne."

"Who gave you champagne? That p***y Dillion?"

"He is not a p***y, he's a really nice guy."

He rolled his eyes. "Yet, here you are at the beach with me."

I paused in taking out my food. "What is that supposed to mean?"

"That nice guy sh*t is overrated."

I shook my head at him. "Why are you so violent?"

He shrugged looking out at the water. "I don't know, I think I was born this way."

I took a bite out of one of the grapevine rolls I'd ordered, it was so good. Before I could toss the rest of it in my mouth, his big hand came over mine and took it away from me, popping it in his instead.

"Nobody is born violent," I told him frowning at him.

"I was…"

"Hmmm…" I didn't argue, maybe he was.

I forked up one of the big meatballs I'd ordered and took a bite, closing my eyes and moaning at how good it tasted.

That damn Angie's been holding out…

I lifted my fork to finish the meatball, but before I could put it in my mouth, Mr. Man reached over, taking my fork and put the rest of the meatball into his.

"Mean Tuck, really? Why don't you just get your own?"

He chuckled. "Yours taste better."

I looked down at the plate of meatballs. "They're literally coming from the same plate."

"Yeah, but yours taste better."

And so, we continued to eat in silence, me taking a bite of food and then feeding him the rest. Once I got full, he pushed the food to the side and then he just sat there or more like reclined there, looking up at me.

My nervousness was back. I knew what he wanted and I think I may have wanted it too. What a way to spend one of my last nights in this town. Angie said that a girl should be able to take the memories of her prom night with her forever.

I don't think I would ever forget this… Naphtali Tucker Pelletier, the most popular boy in the whole town was lying with me on a private beach, looking at me as if I was the most beautiful girl in the world.

He reached up and took my glasses off my face.

"So, what are you going to do after graduation?" I asked out of pure nervousness.

"My dad's good friend is the deputy administrator for the Drug Enforcement Administration. He recruited me when I was like twelve. I'll be leaving for the academy the day after graduation."

"Wow, the DEA," I said as he gently pushed my shoulder back until I was lying flat on the blanket in front of him. "I thought that you would do something like become a famous football player."

He shook his head as his big hand came to rest flat on my stomach. "Not enough action for me."

I drew up my left leg and the split in my dressed opened so that my leg was completely exposed. His gaze followed it.

"Your skin is so pretty. It's like fine spun chocolate."

I smiled, that was the nicest thing I had ever heard him say. "Thank you."

His finger played with the string to my dress and my heart began to accelerate. This thing was getting ready to happen. He and I both were leaving town after graduation, we may never see each other again after that.

*But this is the guy that has bullied you for four years straight.*

That was true…But this is also the guy that has starred

in a number of my dreams that left me hot and wet and panting for something that I knew deep down in my heart that only he could give me.

"I ummm..."

For the first time since I've known him, he sounded nervous. I was confused about that. I know for a fact he was no virgin like me. I'd heard many stories of him screwing some girl in back of his truck, or at someone's house...

So why was he nervous now?

"Do you have a condom?" He looked up at me surprised. But then a grin settled on his face as he reached in his pocket and pulled out a condom.

"Okay..." I inhaled. "Untie my dress..."

The look of joy that settled on his face was like a kid in the candy store. He took his time pulling the strings and then gently opened my dress.

I bit my lip as he stared down at my body. Today I wore the one cute panty and bra set that I owned. It was the color of bubble gum.

"I knew you were going to be beautiful," he whispered before his head lowered and he kissed my stomach.

I gasped as a wave of pleasure washed over me. He moaned as he continued to open-mouth kiss my belly. When he hooked his hands inside my panties and pulled them down my legs before stuffing my panties in his pocket, I had to ball up my hands to keep from stopping him.

Nobody has ever seen what he is looking at...Well, outside of my mom when I was younger, but nobody of late.

"So beautiful," he whispered again before his head

lowered. But this time it was not my belly button he was tonguing.

I stared up at the beautiful night sky, clutching the blanket in my palms as he brought me to peek for the very first time in my life. When I came apart, I cried out his name...

Minutes later, I heard the crackle of the condom wrapper and then he was there over me...

"I'm so sorry, baby, but this is going to hurt a little."

When he filled me for the first time, my mouth opened to cry out, but his mouth covered mine as he consumed my cry.

He didn't move again for a while. He just lay there, letting me get accustomed to his size as he continued to kiss me.

His kisses were so drugging that it wasn't long before my hips were moving underneath him. This time when he filled me, my cries that filled the night were those of passion. When my world shattered for the second time, tears came from my eyes.

Breathing heavily, he rolled to his back pulling me so that I lay on his chest. Very gently he kissed the top of my head.

"Thank you for seeing me, Free..."

Those were the last words I remembered before I drifted to sleep. I did it with a smile on my face. My tormentor and I had ended our relationship on a good note. After this, I think I can forgive him for all the hell he'd put me through.

However, the next morning when I woke up, I was lying alone on the blanket. I closed my dress as I sat up looking around. Like a fool, I sat there waiting for him to come back. After about twenty minutes, I had to face the fact that he'd left me on the beach.

My house wasn't far from here, just a short walk, but still…he'd left me after taking my virginity, like I was some cheap whore or one of the groupies that was willing to put up with or do anything for him.

A strong sense of humiliation washed over me. Last night, he'd made me feel as if I was different. I laughed bitterly… I am such a fool.

My bully had won. This is by far the most painful thing he's ever done to me.

For the first time since I've known him, I felt hate.

I hated Naphtali Tucker Pelletier with my whole heart and soul.

# Chapter 1

## TUCKER'S BACK

### Free

THIS MORNING I woke up to a cloud hanging over my little house, although it was sunny and bright outside. My mother would have said the aura is off. My grandmother, whose little book house I now call my own would have said, God was getting ready to shake up my world. I think by the end of this day, I would have deduced that they both would have been right.

I know many of you are wondering why I call what used to be my grandmother's home before she passed but was now mine a book house, and I will come back to that. For now, I must tell you how this turned out to be the worst day of my whole entire life.

Actually, it began last night. Dillion, my boyfriend for the last four years, was supposed to pick me up from my office and take me to dinner, a dinner where I was more than positive he was going to propose to me. I know this because I found a ring in the nightstand next to his bed the last time I spent a night at his place. No, I wasn't snooping. I was actually looking for a cord to charge my phone and I knew that he kept an extra one in that drawer.

Anyway… He never showed up to get me, didn't call or anything. I waited there at my clinic for nearly two hours before calling for a cab, angry with myself for leaving my own car at home, thinking he would actually be here to pick me up.

Of course, when I made it in and tried to call him and got no answer, my mind started having thoughts of him being in a car crash or getting mugged. The Endurance Clinic was in a rough neighborhood. He probably pulled up to get me and somebody jumped in his car and drove off with him.

After about the third time of trying to call him and still not getting an answer, I bit the bullet and called his mom to see if she'd heard from him. Now, let me tell you guys something, his mother hated me. No, I don't mean a gentle dislike. I mean hated me… would run me over with her car if she could or step over my burning body and dump a glass of water on the ground across the street kind of hate.

So needless to say, the conversation was very painful.

"Hello," *Her well-polished voice came from the other end.*

"Hello, Mrs. Collins. I was calling to see if you'd heard from Dillion. He was supposed to pick me up from work tonight, but he never showed.*

"Who am I speaking with?"*

I rolled my eyes. See what I mean? *"It's Free, Mrs. Collins. Dillion's girlfriend for the last four years and one of his best friends for the last fourteen."* She knew damn well who I was.

*"What kind of name is Free?"*

I exhaled; this wasn't the first time she'd asked me this. In fact, it wasn't the fiftieth time she'd asked me this. My mother, God bless her heart, thought she was doing something empowering by naming me Free Spirit. But what she'd really done was curse me with the burden of always having to overcompensate to prove to my colleagues and others in my field that I and my studies were to be taken seriously. It was one of the reasons I no longer told people my first and middle name. If I didn't know that it would break my mother's heart if she was still living, I would have changed it years ago.

My colleagues called me Dr. Roberson and the few associates I had just called me Doc. However, the two people I could honestly call friends insisted on calling me Free, Rachel, because she's known me as Free forever and ignored all of my requests for her to stop using that worrisome name.

And Oaklee… well, Oak is just Oak. It's really hard for me to try and determine why she does any of the things that she does. When you guys meet her, you will understand what I mean by that. With that being said, I could not demand for Dillion's mom to call me Doc or even Dr. Roberson for that matter, it was just too formal. So instead, I had to put up with her abuse.

*"It's the name my mom gave me,"* I carefully explained to her. I wanted to add to the bane of my existence but thought better of it. She would not understand.

*"Hghmm..."* Although I wasn't standing next to her, I would bet my last dollar she was holding her little nose way up in the air.

*"I called my son about an hour ago, and he said he was in the*

35

*middle of having dinner with a really good friend of his. She sounded beautiful."* And then she hung up the phone in my ear.

I felt like someone punched me in my stomach, but I convinced myself it was foolish to feel that way. I did not put it above Mrs. Collins to lie to me in order to hurt me.

Hmmm?

Why does she hate me so?

I'll give you the quick version. Basically, when Dillion and I were younger, we used to talk about how we were going to save the world. I was going to med school to become a psychiatrist to provide people who couldn't afford good healthcare to help fight their addictions. And he was going to med school to join Doctors Without Borders to help the people in war-torn countries that the news doesn't report on.

Mr. and Mrs. Collins found out about our plans and threatened to not pay for his schooling if he decided to go through with such a foolish notion. In the end, he gave in and promised them that he would not give away his services for free. I did pre-med at Grambling, made it to the dean's list, and then got accepted into Morehouse School of Medicine, which was a major accomplishment in my opinion.

However, the Collins didn't see it that way, especially since Dillion got accepted into Harvard. They've always felt like he was slumming it hanging out with me. Of course, they were nice to me until they found out I was Angie's charity case. Then they wanted him to end our friendship instantly. They assumed I'd been the one to put the Doctors Without Borders idea in his head and doubled down on their efforts to get rid of me.

I think they exhaled a long sigh of relief when we graduated, me going to Grambling and him to Harvard. However, they didn't count on us bumping into each other ten years later at a medical convention and hitting it off. When he brought me home to have dinner with them four years ago, I thought Mrs. Collins was going to have a stroke. She sat sour-faced the whole evening.

And for the life of me, I can't understand why. Yes, I run a free clinic for addicts in the Oakwood Heights area. Yes, I was barely receiving funding for it and was struggling to keep the lights on, but that had nothing to do with Dillion. He'd done them proud and was well on his way to becoming one of the highest paid neurosurgeons in the Detroit area, which was quite impressive for two reasons. One, he's pretty young to have blazed such a trail and two, he's black.

I am extremely proud of him and although our busy schedules leave us only a little time to spend together, I try and tell him that as often as I can. Anyway...that is the gist of the Collins' hate. They believe their son is slumming it with the likes of me.

So, I'd convinced myself not to feed into her words. Yes, it's possible Dillion had forgotten our dinner date and was having dinner with a colleague. It's happened before. And yes, it's possible said colleague was a female. No big deal in our field. Right?

Right...

Except, last night before I went to bed, I got a strange call from Angie.

"Free, I need you to come by the house before you go into your little clinic."

I exhaled. Between Angie and Mrs. Collins and the rest

of their little crew of snobby hens, I'd had my fill of the black elite.

"I can't, I have an appointment at eight-thirty."

"Well, cancel it!" she snapped. "Your sister and Dillion have great news to share with everyone. And I also had my accountant cut a check for you and your poor little drug addicts. An associate of mine informed me you are once again at risk of losing that dump. Can't have my name attached to an eviction for God's sake."

Normally, I would explain to her how shallow and degrading her words were although I knew I would be wasting my breath. I'm a doctor, it's my job to help the mentally unstable, so I press on. However, she said two things that prevented me from going there. One, she had a check for the clinic. As much as I hated accepting money from her because it caused me to be beholden to her, when all I wanted to do was cut her and her evil daughters out of my life, I was still very grateful for it.

Without her nearly monthly donations, the doors to the Endurance Clinic would have closed a long time ago. Because it is a private practice and I can't technically call my facilities a rehab, we don't qualify for the many grants and government assistance programs set aside for such establishments. Thanks to the 2010 Affordable Care Act, most rehabs in the Detroit area now qualify for compensation for the treatment of patients with Medicaid.

But since the Endurance Clinic is not a rehab, but a psychiatric office, Medicaid refuses to cover it. It's a damn shame! This city would rather invest in prisons and jails than helping the people overcome *Post Traumatic Slave Syndrome*, a study done by one of my role models and a woman whose astounding work has helped me to stay the course and continue to fight the good fight, *Dr. Joy DeGruy.*

Oh guys, if you haven't listened to Dr. Joy speak, you are missing out. Go to YouTube and check out one of her lectures on Post Traumatic Slave Syndrome, you will not regret it. It will shed light on so many things.

Anyway, I digress… Needless to say, funding has been one of my biggest struggles. There are a few grants we can obtain, but not nearly enough for me to keep the lights on, let alone pay the other two doctors that I have on staff what they truly deserve. And the truth is, without Angie's monthly donations, I wouldn't be able to pay them much of anything.

So yeah, the fact that she was saying she had a check for us would get me to cancel my eight-thirty appointment. The bonus is that for the first time, I didn't have to go to her and beg for the check, she'd actually called me and offered it. It must be my lucky day.

The other thing that caught my attention was that she said one of the twins and Dillion had news to share with everyone. I smiled, did that crazy man enlist one of my sisters to help him pull off this proposal? Awww! Shucks! How romantic… I went to bed with that smile still on my face.

The next morning, I woke up and took extra care getting ready for work. It took me nearly an hour to flat iron my hair each day, and I was thinking strongly of just chopping it all off. When I was a girl, I wore it long and thick in its natural state, because it reminded me of my mom. Now that I'm a woman, who understands life a little better, I try to do things completely opposite of my mother.

And although I haven't quite gotten my nerves up

enough to cut my hair or perm it for that matter, I made sure to flat iron it every day, so that I could pull it all back into a nice sensible bun. That was me, Sensible Free.

Instead of putting on my brown tweed skirt suit that I normally wore on Mondays, I put on the navy blue one. It was a special occasion after all. It wasn't every day that the love of my life proposed to me. I partnered that up with my silk blouse with the navy-blue flowers. This one tied at my throat, giving me a nice flirty look. And instead of going for my black flats, I decided to be daring and wear my black penny loafers with the two-inch heels.

By the time I got to my old house, I was practically percolating with excitement. However, when I walked through the door, my steps came to a halt when I saw Laureen and Dillion sitting on the couch extremely close together, holding hands.

Angie was leaning over the arm of the couch next to her, holding Laureen's other hand in the air so that she could get a better look at the ring on her daughter's finger. The diamond on it caught the morning sunlight just right to cause momentary blindness.

Can you guys guess what ring she had on her finger? If you guessed the ring I'd seen in Dillion's drawer the other night you would be right. But what I couldn't figure out was why the hell she had his ring on her finger.

And why the hell were they holding hands?!

The smile was still on my face because I think that maybe I was in shock. "What's going on, guys?" I asked, trying to wrap my mind around what I was seeing. Dillion had yet to make eye contact with me. Instead, he looked off somewhere past my head.

"Don't just stand there, Free, come and congratulate

your sister," Angie admonished me, turning Laureen's hand so that I could see the ring better *as if it was necessary.* "Dillion proposed to her last night at dinner and she said yes! Isn't that great?!"

Have you guys ever been punched in the stomach really hard? You know that moment right after the punch, but right before your brain registers what happened. So, you're just standing there for that split-second wondering why you can't breathe. If you have, then you understand how I'm feeling at this moment.

My gaze flew back to Dillion. Using a finger, he pushed his glasses back on his face while chewing on his jaw. I knew that move. He did this whenever his mother hissed her vile venom at me and he pretended he didn't hear so that he wouldn't have to say anything against his mommy dearest. The Snake!

*Okay, Free...*

Okay... I exhaled, blowing out the negative energy that was invading my body.

This won't cause me to fall. I have conquered so many obstacles. This is just another one to overcome. Looking like a black Paris Hilton, Layla sat in the high back Victorian-style chair in front of the fireplace, her cup of coffee was lifted halfway to her grinning mouth as she waited for my response.

Laureen wore a look of triumph as she held her hand out so that I could get a better look at the ring. There was a mirroring look on Angie's face. And Dillion...the coward still looked at the creepy mask over the front door that had been there ever since I was a little girl.

My wicked ass stepmother and her two sniveling demonic daughters were waiting to see me break. They've been trying to break me since I first walked through this door at twelve, like forcing me to wear the twins' hand-me-downs to school while they told everyone about it. Or making me wake up at the crack of dawn to make their breakfast and prepare their clothes for school.

"It's the least you could do", Angie would say, seeing as to how I was freeloading off of them. She called it my way of giving back. Many days I cried in my bed downstairs, but never once in front of them and I wasn't going to start now.

I ran my hands down my blue tweed skirt, welcoming the scratchiness of the material against my palms. And then I put that smile back on my face.

"Yes, congratulations!"

The look of disappointment on Laureen's face and the one of surprise on Dillion's made it all worthwhile. "Have you guys set a date?"

"Wow! Are you really not upset she took your ma—" Layla began, but her words came to a halt when Angie cut eyes at her.

"Please, Layla, don't be obtuse. This is your sister's special day. We will not cry over spilled milk!"

*Keep that smile on your face, Free! Don't you dare run across this floor and claw that crow's eyes out. Come on, little sista, just hold on a little while longer. Get the check and then you're free.*

You see what I mean? Beholden... Now I understand why she offered the check instead of waiting for me to come begging.

My gaze went back to Dillion as Laureen went on and on about their wedding plans and how she wanted me to be one of her bridesmaids. The coward was still avoiding my eyes. He reached up and loosened his tie, chewing fiercely on his jaw. I know by now he was tasting blood.

I'd always thought Dillion was handsome. No, he wasn't Mean Tuck handsome. He didn't have the strong jawline and muscled shoulders, that beautiful chocolate skin, or the confidence. Dear God, he didn't have the confidence Mean Tuck had in just his baby finger. Dillion is cute in a gentleman kind of way, the kind of guy that was supposed to be safe, you know.

But as I stand here and watch him cower behind my sister, I've realized something about him that has bugged me for a while, he has no testicular fortitude. At first, I thought I felt this way because Tuck had ruined me for other men and I was determined not to allow it. But now I know I felt this way because Dillion was the kind of coward that was okay with hiding behind a woman's skirt.

*What a turn off...*

Laureen and the other Beautiful Ones picked on us all through high school. Was he really too blind to see that she was only interested in him because he was making a name for himself in the world of medicine?

So many things were beginning to make sense. His and my schedules have always been very hectic, but we managed to make time for each other at least once a week. He would either spend the night at my place or me at his. But for the last three months, he's been canceling on me, claiming he's been called into work for some emergency or another.

Because I've become like a mad hound trying to find funding for the clinic, I barely paid any attention to it, secretly appreciating the fact that he was not available because I'm always so tired and am never really in the mood to have sex with him.

Until today, I'd been ashamed of that fact. The bitterness in me wanted to tell Laureen just what she was getting into with the mama's boy. He blamed our lack of passion in the bedroom on me. But I knew it wasn't me because I'd had a passionate night before... very passionate.

I looked at my watch. "Okay, sis, just keep me posted, I'm at your service. Angie, did you have that check for me?"

When I finally made it back to my car, I sat there for a moment and waited for the tears to come. Frowning my face up a bit, I tried to force them out. Surely after a four-year relationship, there should be tears.

I leaned my forehead against the steering wheel. *Please God, don't let me be broken forever... Please don't let my bully continue to win in my life!*

As many of you know, my bully took my virginity prom night. It was the most spectacular thing I'd ever experienced. His touch went on to plague my dreams for many years after that. I'd had a few boyfriends since then, but because they didn't make me feel like he made me feel, the relationships never worked because in my mind, they were lacking that spark, you know.

But then I realized I was sabotaging my relationships by comparing them to an oddity. Naphtali Tucker Pelletier is a freak of nature that should not exist on a planet with normal men. Why did he have to be the one to introduce me to passion? Now I was broken and felt passionless because no other man can compete.

The few guys I'd dated in college never got past second

base, just because I couldn't stand the feel of their hands on me. Dillion had been the first to make it all the way and that was only because I was determined to take my life back from that infuriating man. But I don't know what good that did. If I'm being perfectly honest with myself, I can admit that we didn't get intimate nearly as much as Dillion wanted. I've faked a headache on more than one occasion.

He thought it was because he'd taken my virginity and I was still getting used to having sex. Chuckling, I shook my head…poor fool.

The sound of my phone ringing from my purse caused the grin to leave my face. There was something wrong with me. I should be crying, not laughing…goodness.

"Dr. Roberson…" I said into the receiver as I turned the key starting the engine.

"Free, oh my God, I need your help!" Oaklee's frantic Texas drawl came from the other end.

I exhaled. "What have you done now?"

"It wasn't me! It was that bastard cop, Ashur! I was minding my business when he came along and decided to arrest me for no reason!"

There was what sounded like a scuffle. "Let me go, pig!" she yelled. "I'm going to press charges on you for harassment!"

The phone dropped to the ground and I could hear Oaklee yelling for help at the top of her lungs.

"Hello," Jackson's deep voice came from the other end.

"Jackson? What is going on?" I cried as I headed toward the police station. I was so glad I was still in the area and had not headed back toward the city.

He chuckled. "Doc, instead of having her work for you,

you need to think about taking her on as a patient."

"Jackson Carr, are you trying to tell me how to do my job!" I hissed.

He chuckled again. "No ma'am, I'm simply suggesting that you talk to your two friends and tell them they should think about making less waves in my town."

I clutched the steering wheel, wanting to curse. This bastard had some nerve. My two friends did nothing wrong but exist and he and his deputy, Ashur did all they could to make their lives hell. Jackson had been bullying Rachel since high school and Ashur had taken to bullying Oaklee when she moved to this town from Texas. They were the same tyrants they were back then, worse even...

"Sheriff, one could argue that Oak has a point. Why is it that Deputy Ashur is always around whenever my friend finds herself going a smidge over the speed limit?"

"First of all, let's not pretend speeding is all that Oaklee's into. She *finds herself* at the heart of every protest that happens in this area. Would you like to know where Officer Ashur found her this time?"

Chewing my lip, I contemplated telling him no. That damn Oaklee! She told me she was done with the protest hopping.

"Don't worry, Doc, I'll tell you anyway. She and three other people were picketing outside of Oldman Potter's hardware store, preventing customers from going in. Would you like to know why?"

"Why?" I muttered, knowing I was going to regret asking that.

"Because Mr. Potter doesn't carry any vegan paint. When Ashur brought the irate Ms. Oaklee in, I asked her if she is a vegan. Would you like to know what she told me?"

"What?" I mumbled, sounding like a sulking child.

"She said no, she's not even a vegetarian. When I asked why the hell she was protesting, she said it was the principle of the matter. So, I repeat, instead of being your secretary, she should be a patient. How long before you get here?"

"I'll be there in ten minutes."

Damn it! Oaklee was not helping me. This was my fourth time picking her up from the police station this month. Jackson was not going to keep bending the rules for us and not charging her with anything. Why can't the deputy just leave her alone? She rejected his advances and now he was torturing her. He'd given her several tickets since she moved to town and almost always seems to find a reason to haul her into the station.

By the time I made it to the precinct I had a headache from trying to concentrate on the cleansing tears I knew I should be shedding. My evil stepsister had just stolen my boyfriend, surely there were some tears in there somewhere.

And the fact that the station was overrun with single women did very little to ease the pounding between my temples. Mrs. Tiddle and her daughter, Martha nearly ran me down exiting as I entered.

"Sorry, Free!" Martha muttered as she and her mother, who was clearly very angry stormed past me. When I finally made it through the door my mouth dropped. Every desperate housewife and their even more desperate daughters on this side of Lake Michigan had found a reason to be here. It was a madhouse.

Poor Rasheeda, who manned the front desk for the sheriff looked like she was ready to go out of her mind.

Talking to her was a woman I recognized from childhood but couldn't remember her name. She was demanding an audience with the sheriff about her new neighbors whose son she suspected was breaking into her car.

Now for the record, Jackson and his super cute deputy, Ashur did attract their fair share of women, what with both of them being this small town's premier man flesh and all, but this was just ridiculous! I'd never seen it like this.

"Oh my God! What is going on around here?" I asked Rasheeda when I finally made it to the front of the line.

She exhaled and let her head drop on her shoulders. "Doc, just kill me now."

I chuckled reaching out to pat her shoulders. "Poor baby, your boss shouldn't be such man candy. Is he and Ashur parading around town with their shirts off again?"

The two of them and another one of their friends from high school, who was also one of the Beautiful Ones, signed up for the three-on-three basketball tournament to help raise funds for the Boys and Girls Club that wasn't too far from where Rachel lived when she was younger. And they nearly caused a stampede when in the second quarter, the three of them took off their shirts. Word spread like wildfire. I got wind of it all the way at my clinic that was in the city.

Rasheeda shook her head miserably. "Worse, Tucker's back…"

Three words…

She uttered three little words that caused my world to shift and feel as if the ground had been pulled from under me.

# Chapter 2

## A SIGHT FOR SORE EYES

---

*Didn't know what I had until I lost it. Didn't know I was blessed until I got a second chance to hold it...*

*Edwina Fort*

---

## Naphtali

I REMOVED the last box from the back of my truck before shutting the trunk behind me. The sound of Mobb Deep's *Survival of The Fittest* blared through the speakers, causing the streets to rumble. A few kids farther down the beach danced to it. However, standing on the deck next to mine was the dickhead I assumed was my new neighbor. He stood with his frail arms folded in a way that I guess was supposed to be intimidating. Judging by the frown on his f*cked up face, he had a problem with not only my choice in music, but the level in which I chose to play it.

"This is a peaceful neighborhood. Do you mind turning that-that… racket, down?!"

I grinned, impressed the little pipsqueak had actually worked up enough courage to try and reprimand me. Slowly, I walked toward him. I think now is a good time to introduce myself to my new neighbor.

The closer I got, the more my size became apparent to him. By the time I came to a stop in front of where he stood on his deck, his eyes had grown wide. You see, he was standing on a deck and I on the ground and he and I were looking at each other eye to eye; his eyes widened in fear, and mine frowned in anger.

"I didn't hear you from way back there. My music was too loud. Can you repeat what you said to me so that I can address it properly?" He swallowed as his gaze took me in fully. Afterward, a weak smile came to his face.

"I was just saying, welcome to the neighborhood."

The grin returned to my face. "Oh…okay. I could have sworn you had something different to say."

He shook his head rapidly. "No, no…just welcoming you to the Beachfront."

I gave him one last look, giving the man a chance to speak his piece. Wisely, he chose to remain silent. Chuckling, I shook my head as I crossed the sand to my place. However, when I got inside, it was to see that my best friend Jackson, the bastard, had not moved from where he sat with his feet propped up on my kitchen table, reading the magazine I'd just grabbed from the gas station during my drive back from VA.

"Really, man?! You just gon' sit here and not help me?"

I kicked the asshole's feet out of my way as I passed him with the box, carrying it into my bedroom for the next year.

Sh*t…what I was hoping was for the next year. Be just my luck this doctor is some asshole, egotistical bastard, whose Ph.D. has him thinking he's too smart to get these hands laid on him.

Jackson put his feet back on the table when I passed and continued to thumb through the sports magazine.

"Yeah, buddy, I didn't come here to do any physical labor. I'm on my lunch break…nobody works on their break, that completely defeats the purpose."

I shook my head. "Mutha f*cka! You said I'm going to come over and help you get moved in on my lunch break."

He chuckled as he turned the magazine to the side, getting a better look at the centerfold. "You're welcome, you ungrateful bastard…"

After storing the box inside the walk-in closet with the others, I walked back to the kitchen and took two beers out of the fridge, handing one to Jackson.

"You know I can't drink on duty," he muttered as he opened the bottle and drained half of it in one gulp.

I exhaled, taking the seat opposite him at the table. I really wasn't feeling this civilian sh*t. My captain thought I needed time to heal or some crazy bullsh*t like that. He thought two years of being undercover in the New York branch of the Carlota Cartel messed me up in some way. If he knew how troubled my soul really was, it would scare the hell out of him. The darkness that existed inside of me has been there for as long as I could remember. I joined the agency f*cked up. Nothing I saw in my two years with the cartel shocked me or moved me one way or the other. Each night, I went to sleep with no problem.

The captain didn't understand that this dark energy inside of me needed to be fed. And by him grounding me, he'd just made me more dangerous than I've been in a while. At least before, I was able to expend this energy on bad guys. Now, he'd placed me back amongst civilians and expected me to behave like a f*cking lap dog.

I know what I'm saying sounds a little wild to a few of you out there listening to my tale, but I don't know how else to explain this side of me. I needed violence. I needed to do damage with my hands, to crush, to smash...to destroy. And there were only two things in my life that have ever calmed that need in me.

One was the girl in the yellow dress, Free Spirit Robinson. I don't know what it was about her, but whenever I was around her, I felt peace. She was like cool water to my burning soul. The sound of her voice, the smell of her skin...her taste.

Her taste was so damn good, that although I only sampled it once, it still lingers in my memory like a sweet dream or my first car. Yeah... Free was so sweet. Hmmm... I wonder if she still in the Detroit area. Maybe I'll look her up while I'm here in town.

And as for the second thing that quieted the beast inside of me, why, it's the very thing the captain wanted to take away. Speaking of which, I patted my pocket, looking for the blunt I'd rolled earlier for after I got settled in.

I smiled when I felt it and eased it out of my pocket like it was a rare diamond. Very carefully, I lit it, taking a nice deep pull from the brown beauty, letting its essence soothe the rage. Son-of-a-b*tch captain, made me walk away from the best weed man in North America. Now, I was going to have to try and find someone that can compete here in Detroit.

Jackson slammed the magazine on the table. "Hey, asshole, you can't smoke that sh*t in front of me, I'm the f*cking sheriff!"

I chuckled, trying to hand the blunt to him. "Hmmm, taste that, *Sheriff* and step into my world."

Waving it away, he picked the magazine back up, opening it. "Get that sh*t away from me. That's why they fired your dumb ass. Daaaamn!" he said, turning the magazine to get a better look at page 26. I already know what got his attention. It was the same thing that made me buy the magazine.

"Is that Serena Williams??? My God, this woman looks good in a swimming suit! Maaan, if I ever got a hold of her thick ass, I swear, she'd be ready to marry me. I wouldn't rest until I made her come apart back-to-back, screaming my name at the top of her lungs... She'd be like, *Jackson! Oh, Jackson! I can't take anymore, Jackson! Pleaaase, let me co—*"

The sound of me choking cut him off midsentence. See, it was never good for somebody to say corny sh*t like this while I'm smoking because now, I was about to die from laughing at him with a mouth full of smoke. Pounding my chest, I had to put my blunt out to get myself together.

"What's so funny?" Jackson asked offended. And yeah, that sh*t just made me laugh harder.

"First of all," I said when I could finally catch my breath, "You wouldn't do sh*t for Serena Williams but end up being her b*tch 'cause she'd put that thang on you and have your pu\*\*y ass sprung. And second of all, I didn't get fired, bastard, I'm on vacation."

And with that, I relit my brown beauty to continue to enjoy my favorite pastime. Don't mind the way I talk to Jackson. He and I have been best friends since first grade, when we get together, we talk sh\*t... always been that way.

"Vacation?!" he asked sitting up in the chair, planting his feet on the floor. "Is that what your delusional ass is calling that? Mutha f\*cka, you got fired! Wake up, bro and face reality."

I looked at the tip of the blunt as I held that sweet smoke in my lungs. F\*ck Jackson, he didn't know what he was talking about. The captain wanted the doctor to tell him I was clean and that there was no problem, and that f\*cking doctor was going to tell him I was clean and that there was no f\*cking problem. I grinned, we can do this sh\*t two ways, him signing that report the way I tell him voluntarily, or me crushing his broken hand between mine as I force him to sign the report the way I tell him.

Either way, after this year was up, I'll be back on the force and I will still be enjoying my favorite pastime.

Period...

"What is your parents saying about your *vacation*?"

I shrugged. "Sh\*t. Of course, my mom is happy I'm home. Tried to get me to stay at the house since they'll be leaving soon for their European tour and are going to be gone for half the year. My dad tried to get me to go and see a psychiatrist he'd heard was the best. He still thinks I'm on leave to recoup from being undercover in the cartel for two years."

Jackson chuckled. "I can't believe you have to go to rehab."

I shook my head. "That's f*cked up, ain't it? You ever heard of somebody going to rehab for weed?"

"Stop b*tching," he grumbled, continuing to look through the magazine. "Rehab for you rich kids is just another day at the county club. Which one are they sending you to? Palm Springs?"

"Psss! Yeah right! Them cheap bastards sending me to some sh*thole called the Endurance Clinic in the heart of the f*cking hood."

The smile left Jackson's face as he finally looked up from the pages in front of him. "Wait, the Endurance Clinic in Oakwood Heights?"

I nodded as I exhaled a mouth full of smoke. "Yeah…why?"

The asshole stared at me looking dumb for a minute before he held his head back and barked with laughter, slapping my damn table as he did it.

I kicked his chair nearly sending him toppling backward. "What's wrong with you, mutha f*cka?! Hitting my sh*t like that…"

This f*cking house was costing me a grip. I paid extra to get it fully furnished. Nothing in this b*tch was cheap. And he was banging on the table like he was crazy. After about a minute of gut-wrenching laughter, he finally got himself together.

"Nap, what's your doctor's name, man?" he said, wiping away tears.

I frowned at that dumb bastard. What the hell did it matter to him? "Dr. Kimble? Why?"

He didn't respond, just shook his head as he drained the rest of his beer, that knowing grin still on his face.

I narrowed my eyes at him. "Why, J?"

"No reason, just curious, that's all." His phone went off at his waist, after checking the number, he stood. "Time for me to make my way back to the station."

"Jackson!" I called after him. "Why you ask?" This bastard knew something that he wasn't telling me.

He opened the door, but before he exited, he turned and looked at me in a thoughtful way. I was instantly suspicious. Jackson didn't do thoughtful.

"I've always wanted to ask you a question. You remember that girl you use to obsess over in school? The pretty little shy one with the glasses?" He snapped his fingers. "What was her name?"

"Free," I said as I studied him through the smoke I exhaled.

"Yeah, Free…" He smiled thoughtfully. "What was it about her that did it for you? She was shy and used to wear those big, ugly glasses with the duct tape on them. Yet, anytime she was around, she had your complete attention. I could never figure it out."

"That's 'cause it wasn't meant for you to figure it out. It's none of your business. Now I got a question for *you*? What makes you bring up Free? Is she still in Detroit? Is she married?"

The bastard grinned evilly at me. "You know, I've been thinking, one of the things that helps *drug addicts* on their road to recovery is support from their friends," he continued without answering any of my questions. "And since I'm your best friend, I think I'll try and make my way to the Endurance Clinic from time to time to check on your progress and support you any way I can."

Leaning back in my chair completely relaxed, I pointed at him. "That would be great, buddy, but when you leave Mayberry, can you take the Andy Griffith getup off? It can't be helping you with the ladies."

He looked down at his sheriff uniform. "What the sh*t are you talking? The ladies find this uniform irresistible. My refrigerator is full of casseroles and dishes from all the little mommies with fantasies of f*cking the sheriff."

You see what I mean? This bastard was so damn corny. He left out of the door to the sound of my laughter.


FREE


"FREE, don't hang up! Please! Just let me explai—" Rolling my eyes, I hung up the phone before pressing the intercom button.

"How can I help you, boss lady?" Oaklee's chirpy southern voice came from the other end.

"Didn't I tell you I was not accepting any calls from Dillion?"

"Yes ma'am…" she responded, the sound of her typing away at her computer bleeding through the line as well.

"And yet, I just hung up on him for the tenth time this week."

"Wha—" The line went dead before the click clunk of her red cowboy boots crossing the wooden floor came seconds before my door flew in. With an astonished look on her beautiful face, she plopped down in the chair on the other side of my desk.

"Are you kidding me?! What the hell is wrong with that man? How in the hell is he going to stalk you after proposing to your sister? I swear, a young lady called and asked to speak with Dr. Robinson. He must have had her call and then took the phone from her. You know damn well if I knew it was that scum, I would not have pushed the call through."

I shook my head as I continued to read through the file of yet another one of Dr. Kimbell's patients. I only had seven minutes to study it before said patient was due in my office.

"Why does he keep calling you?"

My gaze met hers. "I have no idea. Do you know he tried to come by my house last night?"

Her mouth dropped. "Noooo! What did he say?"

I chuckled. "I didn't answer the door. Please! As if I would..."

"I told you, he's going to try and have his cake and cookies too."

"I think what you meant to say is, he's going to try and have his cake and eat it too." I corrected her, chuckling. Oaklee was always quoting sayings, but she never got them right. No, not once... However, I think she may be right about Dillion's motives. He'd not stopped calling me since he and Laureen announced their engagement last week.

The first time he called, I'd foolishly answered the phone. Honestly, I don't know why. Maybe because I needed closure. But what I got was him apologizing profusely and begging me to allow him to come over so that he could explain to me face to face about what happened.

Of course, I said no, I didn't want to see him. I only wanted to know why he'd lied to me all that time and was seeing my sister behind my back. God! How low can you go?

Amazingly, he blamed it all on me. Accused me of being cold to him, while she was loving and welcoming. I couldn't help but laugh in his ear. Laureen was many things, loving and welcoming were not one of them.

In the end, I told him he was entitled to his opinion of me. But I'll be honest and admit for most of that conversation, I had more important things on my mind, like the fact that Rasheeda had told me that Mean Tuck was back in Aldshore.

My goodness! I've never ran so fast. I practically snatched Oaklee, threw her in my car, and hightailed it back to the city without looking back. No way I wanted to risk running into him. I tried to tell myself I was being ridiculous and no longer had to run from my old bully, but some habits were hard to break. Not only did I run, I told Oaklee, who lives right outside of Aldshore not too far from Rachel's mom's place, that she was going to have to find another way home that night because it was no way I was risking going back there.

However, the part that bothered me most was that I still couldn't get Tuck off my mind. I couldn't help but wonder how he'd changed after nearly fifteen years. Was he still deadly handsome or had age uglied him? Was he still mean? Tucker the boy had been intimidating as hell. What was Tucker the man like? And although I hated it, I couldn't get that night he and I shared on that beach off my mind either. He'd been so gentle with me, touching my body in a way that made me feel like a piece of silk.

When I hung up with Dillion that day, those tears I'd been trying to squeeze out finally flowed. Whether I was crying because my boyfriend had left me for my sister or because my bully was back in town, I couldn't tell you. All the hate, rage, and although I really hated to admit it, lust I felt for Tucker resurfaced. But I did cry, and when I got home that night, I baked a pound cake, because I bake when I'm emotional. And then as I ate a salad, I cried again, because although I'd baked that delicious smelling cake, I couldn't eat it. Thanks to the fact that I am twenty pounds overweight; I'm on a stupid diet.

I exhaled as I looked back at the file in my hand. "Like I said, I don't know why he keeps calling me, but outside of telling me where he and his fiancée are registered, he has nothing else to say to me."

Oaklee chuckled, shaking her head. "Is that witch really asking you to be in her wedding?"

I nodded... "Yep, it's going to be held in Vegas in three months, the bridesmaids' dresses are peach and cream. Mine has a great big ugly bow just above my butt."

She snagged one of the apples I kept in a bowl on my desk for my patients, taking a loud bite out of it. "I can't believe you're going to go through with that. I would tell that b*tch to kiss my ass."

"You already know I looked for a way out. But Angie threatened to close her checkbook permanently if I so much as hinted to the fact that I couldn't be in my precious sister's wedding, bringing eternal shame and embarrassment to the family."

By the time I was finished talking, Oaklee's mouth was hanging open, showing off her bite of half-chewed apple.

"What the hell?! Is she even real? That heffa is a reptile! Rach has been saying that since day one."

That made me laugh. Rachel has been saying that about Angie. She was convinced my stepmother was of the devil.

"How in the hell does she expect you to stand there while that baby iguana marries your man? God, Free, why do you put up with their abuse?!"

I sighed. "You don't know how much I wish I didn't have to. Sometimes, I feel like walking away from all of this, just so that I can truly be Free."

Although it shamed me to say those words, they were true. After my mom died of an overdose, I became obsessed with the notion that I would never let another beautiful soul die from the evil clutches of opioids. I really had good intentions when I started this whole thing, but now, it was beginning to feel like a noose around my neck. The burden of carrying this clinic was heavier than I'd expected.

It was killing me... and yet, I was too far in to stop now.

Oaklee reached over and took my hand. "You're always sacrificing for everybody else, but nobody's doing anything for you."

Once again, her ability to read me had taken me by surprise. It was one of the things that drew me to her two years ago when she showed up on the clinic doorstep looking for a job. Well, that and the fact that although she was my secretary and one of my best friends, she was also what we in the industry called an off the record patient. She was a patient that didn't know she was a patient.

No, she didn't do drugs or anything like that. Oak's an adrenaline junky. She suffered some things in her childhood that made her feel powerless, so now, she seeks to take her power back through protest. I know that sounds strange, but it is a thing. Oaklee is addicted to the rush she feels in the heart of a good protest. It's her way of taking back control, and the more violent the protest is, the better.

I would go into detail, but I hear Oak is going to be telling you guys her story, so I don't want to spoil anything. But trust me when I tell you, you're going to laugh and cry...and yes, you're going to want to rage against the system...just like Oaklee.

"Damn, you even have to come and get me from jail all the time," she continued. I gently squeezed her hand, the last thing in the world she needed to feel is guilt.

"It's no worries, sweetheart. I don't mind at all. If not for you, there would be no laughter in Rachel's and my life. You remember the time Asher arrested you for protesting outside of the Mabesko cookie factory?"

She nodded as her beautiful face broke into a smile. "Those bastard's cut the chocolate chip ratio to cookie dough by thirty percent!"

Laughing, I shook my head. "I don't even know what that means, but it sure in the hell was funny."

Rachel and I still laugh about that till this day. Poor Asher had his hands full. How a chocolate chip protest ended in violence I will never know. But there was video of Oaklee screaming her head off about how the cooperation beast is ruining everything, her red cowboy boots in the air as she tried to kick and buck out of Asher's arms. And the poor bastard who was completely obsessed with her wouldn't let any of the other officer's touch her, so she was truly his headache.

I was about to address the time she made Asher so mad that he took her out on his boat and threw her in Lake Michigan, but right then, Dr. Ross stuck his handsome head in my office, informing me that Dr. Kimbell's twelve o'clock was here.

"How are you holding up?" I asked him.

Dr. Kimbell fell and fractured his spine two days ago, so he'll be off for the next few months, leaving his caseload to be divided between Dr. Ross and me, who were both already swamped down with our own caseloads.

He exhaled, rubbing the back of his neck. "I wouldn't dare complain when I haven't heard a peep from you." He smiled and Oaklee and I were both reminded of how handsome he is.

I chuckled. "Well, let me make it easy for you…" I put both of my hands up by my head. "I'm going craazzzzzyyy!"

He laughed for a bit before growing silent. I could tell he was trying to think of the best way to say something.

His gaze came to mine. "Do you want to grab a bite to eat after work?"

The smile left my face. *Wow! Please don't do this to me right now, Nate. Don't do this to our relationship.*

I cleared my throat. "Um, I don't think that's a good idea," I said very carefully, not wanting to hurt his feelings.

However, I saw that I failed when the light left his eyes as he nodded. "Yeah…yeah, of course. If you need me, I'll be across the hall," he muttered as he turned and walked out of my office pulling the door closed behind him.

Oaklee waited to hear the sound of his door shutting

before her gaze shot to mine. "I told you he wanted you! I told you! I told you!" This she said while doing a little silly dance in her seat.

I rolled my eyes. "Please, I am so done. I just want to get me a cat and grow old alone."

She frowned. "Oh, stop talking foolish, Free. What's wrong with Dr. Ross? He's a nice guy..."

"Yep, I'm done with nice guys too. You see where the last one got me." And on that note, I told her to show my next patient in.

By the time three o'clock rolled around, I was ready to cry. Because I had to cram extra patients into my day, I'd not left my office all day, not even for lunch. Rubbing my back that was sore from sitting in my chair for so long, I made my way to the water machine, taking a moment to get a drink before it was time to see my last patient.

*Goodness, I couldn't wait to get home and soak in a long, hot bath.* As I was walking back with my cup in hand, I passed Oaklee coming from my office.

"I showed your last patient in, he's sitting on the couch." She was doing something funny with her eyebrows that caused me to frown at her.

"Are you okay, Oak?"

She giggled like a schoolgirl. "Wait till you get a look at the hunk of man that's in there waiting for you. I bet you'll start rethinking your vow of celibacy by the time you're finished with him, honey."

Shaking my head, I put my hand on her shoulder. "Sweetheart, if he's here, it's because he's addicted to drugs. No matter how handsome a man is, it is never wise to date one with such a nasty habit. Until he gets clean, he will always put his drug first. Remember that..."

And then I turned to head into my office. I didn't even glance at the man on the couch as I walked toward my desk to retrieve my notepad. I hate to say it, but I never really saw my patients as anything but very sick individuals who needed help. I've never been sexually attracted to any of them.

I turned the cup up to steal one last sip of water before the thirty-minute session ahead of me.

"Well, well, well...If it ain't the girl in the yellow dress."

The sound of that deep voice caused all the water I'd just taken inside my mouth to coming spewing back out all over the wall in front of me. I whipped around and my mouth dropped at the sight of the chocolate Adonis sitting on the couch with his powerful arms thrown across the back. He sat up, bringing his elbows to rest against his knees as he studied me before lifting one side of his mouth in a sexy grin.

"Hey, beautiful."

"Mean Tuck..." I gasped.

# Chapter 3

## THE SILVER LINING

*If Given The Chance To Exact A Little Revenge…Would You?*

### Free

I DON'T KNOW how long I stood there staring at him with my mouth agape. *Sweet Baby Moses!* This man looked so damn good! My gaze went from his boot covered feet to the top of his gorgeous head. And yes, I had the answer to my question. Tucker the man, was a hundred times more intimidating than Tucker the boy had been.

He stood and my eyes only widened at how big he was. The muscles he now sported were hard and seasoned, not the new round ones of youth.

With a grin on his face, he took a few steps toward me and that was what snapped me out of my stupor. Muscle memory had me taking several steps back, nearly knocking my award off the wall in my haste to put space between him and me.

"Oh my God! What are you doing here?!" I cried as the panic I felt made my heartbeat sound loud in my ears.

He chuckled. "Damn, Free, you're looking at me like I'm a monster or something." This he said while holding out his hands in the way that one would when trying to calm a frightened kitten.

*Is he serious?* "You *are* a monster! The monster of my childhood! I still have nightmares!"

He slightly tilted his head. "Yeah, about that…I'm sorry for picking on you like that. You know how sh*tty little boys can be."

My mouth dropped again. "Are you kidding me?! You think you can just waltz in here and give me that bullsh*t apology and I'm suppose to what? Forgive you?" He chuckled again, which was very irritating. What was with all the laughing?

"I mean…yeah."

I exhaled, running my hands down my tweed skirt, welcoming the scratchy feel as I regained control over my emotions. I am no longer the little girl that had to put up with his crap. I am a doctor, dammit! And even if it killed me, I was going to act like one. I held my head up in a way that would make Dillion's mom green with envy.

"How can I help you, Naphtali?"

He studied me for a second, trying to read my frosty demeanor before he too exhaled, rubbing his hand down his head.

"I think I'm your three o'clock. Your receptionist said

my doctor had an accident and that you will be taking over for him."

I blinked at him, trying my best to keep my composure. "You are aware that this is a clinic for drug addicts, right?"

As I asked my question, I took the time to study him a little closer. One of the things that separated me from most of the other doctors in my field was that I refused to profile my patients. Everyone was different and had a unique story.

With the expensive boots, name-brand jeans, gold chain, and watch, at first glance, Tucker didn't come across as one who spent his money on opioids. But now that he'd brought it to my attention, there was something different about him.

He felt more chill and laid back and he was doing a lot of smiling and grinning. When he was a boy, I rarely saw him grin...for anything pleasant at least. I saw him laugh at Jackson while they made fun of each other, but not for much else. He'd not stopped smiling since I walked in. My gaze went to his eyes, and yes, there was a slight tint of redness to them.

He put his hand to his chest. "My captain forced me to come because I may smoke a joint from time to time."

My eyes narrowed. I'd been doing this long enough to know when one of my patients is lying to me.

"A joint?"

He held up his fingers to show me how small. "Just an itty bitty little joint."

"Itty, bitty, little...Mm-hmm...will you excuse me for a moment?"

I forced myself to take normal steps as I exited my office. But as soon as the door was closed, I hurried to

Oaklee's desk and snatched her out of it by her arm, pulling her into our little kitchen, shutting the door behind us.

"Girl, what's the matter with you?" she asked as she took in my panicked expression.

I put my hand on my chest, trying to calm my racing heart. "Oh my God, Oak! Do you know who that is in there?!"

She grinned. "Yep, my future baby daddy if I'm lucky."

I shook my head at her as I tried to catch my breath. "No...No, you don't want him. He's a real bastard!"

She put her hands on my shoulders like I'd done her earlier. "Calm down, Doc...and tell me what's going on."

I pulled her over to the table and took a seat. "Okay, you remember hearing Rachel and me talk about the guy that used to bully me in high school?" Her eyes hardened as she nodded her head.

"Well! That's him! That's Mean Tucker!"

Her mouth dropped. "That's the guy?"

"That's him and you gave me his case." I stood. "I can't do this! He's going to have to go!"

She grabbed my hand, snatching me back down. "Oh no you don't! His agency is paying good money for him to be here. He's joined the list of rare clients that can afford to pay full price. We need him, you can't turn him away."

I chewed on my nail, a habit that I'd not done since high school as I pondered over this. No, we didn't turn away clients that could afford to pay full price for our services, but there was no way in hell I can counsel Mean Tuck. I would be a nervous wreck all the time and wouldn't be able to focus on anything the man says.

When I was a girl, I couldn't be in a room with him

without being hyper-aware of his presence the whole time. Picking up a folder from the table in front of me, I began to fan myself. Goodness! My body was already responding to his nearness. I felt hot all over...this wasn't going to work!

"Fine, I'll just have to give him to Nate!" I said slamming the folder down on the table.

Oaklee gave me the side-eye. "Really? After you shot him down? Now you're going to ask him for a favor. Yeah, that's a good look. Plus, he's already loaded down. He has a three o'clock in his office." She shook her head. "I'm sorry, Free, you're going to have to put on your big girl shoes and go and face your fear."

"Big girl *pants*," I corrected her.

She frowned at me. "What?"

"Big girl pants. The saying is put on your big girl—You know what, forget about it."

What did it matter how she said it? She had a point. I felt tears burning the back of my eyes. What I was doing right now was completely unprofessional and went against the oath I took to help people who struggled with drug addiction. But God, this was Tuck... My tormentor! It was too much to ask of me to help him. I hated him! He'd broken me and ruined me for other men. He was the reason I have yet to have a successful relationship.

"Pluuuussss," Oaklee continued as a devious glow came into her eyes. "What better position to be in to get a little revenge." She was actually rubbing her hands together like every evil villain in the cartoons.

I'm ashamed to say my being did not instantly reject her words and against my better judgment, I asked...

"What do you mean?"

She pulled her chair closer to mine. "Obviously, you

didn't have time to go over his file. He's on temporary leave from his agency because he can't let go of Mary Jane." Hmmm, so he was telling the truth. He was really here for marijuana.

"Whether or not he is reinstated will be contingent on your prognosis." When I still failed to see how this will put me in a position to exact revenge, she exhaled loudly.

"Don't you see? It's you who will determine if he gets his job back!"

"Ohhhhhh! No, Oaklee...I couldn't do that! Absolutely not!"

My goodness! What was wrong with my friend? How could she suggest I do such a thing? Just the thought of me stooping to a level so low was unheard of. To think she wanted me to use my power over him to repay him for all the dirty, rotten, and extremely embarrassing things that he's done to me. Of course, I would never do such a thing...

However...

I've had a horrible week, so I'll be lying if I said that the thought of torturing my childhood bully wasn't causing me to feel a hell of a lot better. As a matter of fact, the longer I thought about it, the more appealing it became. No, I really mean it! Something amazing was happening inside of me. I felt years of frustration at the injustice of being a victim come rushing to the surface like an erupting volcano.

"My guess is, you can get him to do just about anything if he thinks it will get him back working. Just imagine, you can get revenge for all the cruel pranks he played on you when you guys were kids. Whatever you can think up." She balled up her fist.

"Make his ass pay, Free! Do it for all the downtrodden. Do it for all the times the oppressor has railroaded the innocent, taking away their voice, cloaking them in a shawl of darkness. Snuffing out their light-"

I put my hand on her arm, stopping her. "Calm down, Che Guevara, I'll do it."

The level of excitement that shot through her was contagious. For the first time, I was experiencing the rush she felt whenever she was in the heart of a protest. And it felt great! I had Mean Tuck at my mercy!

Oh my God! I had that bastard at my mercy!

The fact that I could lose my license if it was ever discovered that I was even thinking about doing something like this to a client that trusted me to help them overcome their problem, didn't darken my disposition.

And before you guys start shaking your heads at me, saying what I'm doing is cruel, let me remind you of cruel. Two weeks after that incident happened in gym class, where I'd been trying to run from him, and my skirt fell down. I'd made an excuse to leave swimming early, like I always did so I wouldn't get caught by Tucker.

I went to the locker room and peeled out of my wet swimsuit before hurrying through a shower. When I got back to my locker to get dressed, I saw that my lock had been picked. Getting a bad feeling, I opened it to discover my clothes missing.

When I turned around, Tucker was leaning against the wall, watching me with my clothes in his hand. Clutching the towel to me, I rushed him and tried to snatch them from him.

"Give me my clothes back!" I cried with real tears in my eyes. I was so tired of him picking on me.

He held them up and away from me so that I had to stand on my toes while pressing against him to try and get them. Now keep in mind, the whole time, I only had one of the little thin school towels wrapped around me.

"Say please," he growled before wrapping his other arm around me, holding me to him.

I bit my lip because I didn't want to say please to the bastard. He was always doing that, forcing me to beg him.

"Say please or I'm going to throw your clothes in the shower and turn it on, and you'll have to walk around the whole day in just that towel."

Of course, I knew that was crap, I would get dry clothes from somewhere. But the thought of anybody seeing me in only my towel was horrifying, including the gym teacher, who I would have to tell in order to get dry clothes.

"Please, Tuck…" I muttered, staring at his chest.

"I didn't hear you."

My gaze came up to his. "Please!" I spat through clenched teeth.

"Well now, that wasn't nice at all. Now you've got to give me a kiss."

My mouth dropped. I'd never kissed a boy before. I shook my head. "No!"

He shrugged and began to head toward the shower.

"Wait!" I cried, clutching his arm. He leaned back against the wall and I stood on my toes and gave him a quick peck.

"What the f*ck was that? Naw, that ain't going to do it. Kiss me like you love me or I'm tossing your clothes."

I still stood there in his arms staring up at him like he'd lost his mind. "But I don't love you, I hate you."

"Well, you better pretend that you do or your clothes take a dive."

I was freaking out. My bully was forcing me to kiss him, and I had no idea what I was doing.

"I've never done this…" I muttered, not knowing why I was giving him of all people that kind of ammo.

He shrugged again. "You got to start somewhere."

Nodding, I inhaled before I stood on my toes and wrapped my arms around his neck. With his arm that was still wrapped around my waist, he pulled me closer, so now it was just his chest against mine, holding my towel together. I was praying he didn't realize that because the bastard would surely exploit that had he known.

Very carefully, I brought my lips to his. What started off as an innocent exploration quickly turned to something else. He began to coach me through the kiss, telling me what to do with my lips and my tongue. It didn't take me long to get the hang of it and then I don't know what happened. One minute I was standing in front of him on my toes kissing him and the next, we had somehow turned and it was my back pressed against the wall and he standing in front of me, pressing all his hard muscles against me. The sound of the bell ringing is what drew us apart.

"You kiss horribly," he grumbled, handing me my clothes. "You're going to have to practice more often."

Now outside of the fact that his insult hurt my feelings, after that day, he proceeded to corner me and steal kisses all the time, always ending every one of them with an insult. By the time I graduated, I knew I was a professional kisser, thanks to him. Some days, he kissed me so much my lips were sore when I went home.

Anyway, like I was saying, don't feel sorry for Tucker. Instead, cheer me on and let's let the games begin!

Dammit, now it was *me* sounding like Che Guevara...


Naphtali


*WHAT HAD HAPPENED to the girl in the yellow dress?*

I mean, don't get me wrong, Free was still fine as hell, but she wasn't the girl I remembered from high school. Now, she was all...Pent up. Tweed skirt, tight bun, penny loafers. She looked like that sexy schoolteacher you fantasized about unraveling.

Damn! And she hated my ass. But what really hit me harder than it ever did was her fear. I mean, don't get me wrong, when I was a boy, I saw her afraid of me all the time, but my dumb ass didn't have enough sense to do something about it. But now...now, I couldn't stand to see that look in her eyes. I didn't want her afraid of me, I'd changed.

Well... At least I'd changed as far as she was concerned. When I was younger, I didn't know how to deal with my strong feelings for her and the fact that she thought I was a piece of sh*t. Often times, I was angry that I desired someone way out of my league. Free was so different from me. She was smart and kind, and I was just the piece of sh*t jock that wanted her to be kind to me.

And what did I do? I picked on her and lashed out, trying to get her to notice me. And now, she hated the very ground I walked on. No doubt, she was out there telling her people that she refused to see me.

I grinned as I rested my arms on the back of the couch. Too f*cking bad, she wasn't getting rid of me.

What? Did y'all think I'd changed that much? Ha! Yeah right... Now that I'd found my girl in the yellow dress again, I think I'll keep her. The first thing I had to do was show her that she could trust me and didn't have to be afraid of me anymore. I don't care what it took, I will show her that I'm not her bully anymore but her lover. And then, we'll see what we can do about replacing the look of hate on her face with pleasure.

Yeah...sh*t, I got an erection just thinking about unraveling her. First thing I would do is take that stiff ass bun out her hair, freeing it. And then, I'd tear that tweed skirt from her body and run my tongue--

The sound of the door opening brought my thoughts to a halt. I shifted on the seat, adjusting myself so that she couldn't see that I was standing at attention for her.

"I'm so sorry to keep you waiting," she said, bringing her little notepad and her cup of coffee to the psych chair that sat off to the side of the couch I sat on.

I smiled. "No worries. I thought you'd gone out there to try and get rid of me."

She chuckled, shaking her head, although she had yet to look me in the eye. "No, I wouldn't do that. You need help and I'm a doctor. So, let's talk about it."

"Should I lie down on the couch?" I joked.

Her gaze came to mine. "If you like..." Her voice was still so very soft. She had the perfect voice for being a psychiatrist.

"So, you told me earlier that your boss has you here because you smoked an itty, bitty, little joint from time to time. Is that correct?"

"What happened to you, Free?"

My question caught her off guard, for a moment before she got herself together, it caused her to be ruffled. I smiled, realizing another reason I picked on her. I liked to see her ruffled…it was sexy.

She cleared her throat. "I'm sure I don't know what you mean."

"In school, you were so…so, Free. Now, you don't seem happy. It's like you're weighed down." She looked at me as if she was seeing me for the first time, until her iron composure that I was beginning to hate settled back in place.

"Tucker, if we're going to do this, I'm going to need you to stay focused." She stood and walked toward her desk to retrieve a file. My gaze fell to her hips and that luscious behind. That was something that had changed since school. Free had thickened up nicely.

"Now, it says here that my recommendation is what's going to be used to determine whether or not you'll be reinstated on the force. Is that correct?"

I exhaled. "Yeah, my captain tripping hard. I tried to tell him nobody comes to rehab for weed."

"You do understand that this is not a rehab, right? We're a mental wellness clinic. We believe that the addiction is defeated here." She tapped her head with her little finger.

"But that's just it. Can you really call marijuana an addiction? It's herbal…"

She wrote something down on her pad before she spoke. "Well, tell me this, if it's not an addiction, then why haven't you quit, seeing as to how it's come in the way of your job performance?"

I held up my finger. "First of all, I can quit whenever I like. As you know, I can be an asshole sometimes. The weed helps me not to be, that's all..."

She tapped her lip with her pen and I damn near growled. This woman was so goddamn sexy, I was finding it hard to focus. She had to know she became the *making love to my psychiatrist* fantasy of every man that sat on this couch, watching her do her thing.

I inhaled sharply as that thought stirred that mean son of b*tch inside me. Instantly, my hand twitched for a blunt. You see, that was my secret. Weed kept that killer inside of me chilled the f*ck out.

Now y'all know...

"The part that concerns me is that you speak of marijuana as if it's a fix for a problem. And if that's the case, then it's something that you are dependent on, very much like an addiction."

I shrugged. "Yeah, I understand that, but I wouldn't look at it that way. Really, it's quite simple. Marijuana affect my mood and makes me a kinder person. I don't understand what the big deal is."

She was back to writing on her little pad. "Okay, I think I understand where you're coming from and how to help you so that at the end of your suspension, we can get you reinstated with a clean bill of health."

Damn, this was breezier than I thought. Must be somebody up there smiling down on me. Who knew Free Spirit was going to be my doctor for the next year? But I can tell you what, she will be in my bed in the next few weeks. I can already tell she was going to be a tough nut to crack, which is why I'm giving it a few weeks instead of a few days. But make no mistake about it... I was going to be f*cking my psychiatrist very soon.

"Alright, Doc, what you got?"

"By you only having an issue with marijuana and not anything stronger, I don't think we need to have the private one-on-one sessions. For my clients with mild addictions or those who have overcome their previous addictions and just need a little encouragement to help them stay the course, I have a group meeting that meets every other Tuesday. I'm going to sign you up for that."

Well, that took some of the wind out of my sails. I was looking forward to our private sessions.

"And if it's being a kinder person that attracts you to marijuana, then we're going to work on helping you be kinder without it." She smiled and I licked my lips because I wanted to kiss her so f*cking bad.

"How does that sound?"

I held up my hands. "You're the doctor."

"Good...also, I would like for you to go and adopt a kitten before we meet again."

"Say what?"

She bit her bottom lip. "A kitten, a baby cat."

"Yeah, I know what a baby cat is. Why the hell would I go and adopt one?"

"Mr. Pelletier, let's get a few things understood." *Oh, so now I was Mr. Pelletier.* "At the end of this year, your agency is going to want my recommendation about whether or not you should be reinstated on the force. I want to say yes, I do. But if you give me a hard time and question my methods, I'm afraid I'm going to have to tell them no. Please don't make me out to be the bad guy."

I exhaled, she had me there. F*ck, I had to do what she

said for more than just that reason. I didn't want her to look at me like the bad guy because I was trying to get her into my bed, and I needed to kill the images she had of me as a f*cking bully.

"But I'm not really a cat person...you know?"

She nodded. "I do, but we're trying to awaken the kindness inside of you without marijuana. So, adopting a pet is a very good start."

I smiled. "Okay then, I'll adopt a dog."

"Yeah, it's just that in my opinion, cats are kinder creatures, and they're definitely cuter."

"Cuter?" I might as well put on a f*cking tutu and start doing fairy flips. What the hell...

She nodded with a big grin on her face. "Yeah...Cuter."

"And when you give your kitty a name, try and tap into your inner sensitivity when you do. So that every time you call him or her, you're reminded that yes, you are a kind person in here." She tapped her chest.

I nodded. *Give my cat a p*ssy name...got it.*

"And then, bring him or her to the meeting and introduce it to us."

"Come again."

She smiled. "We'd like to meet your inner kindness." What the hippy kind of sh*t... I have never in my life heard of this kind of therapy.

"Okay, let me get this straight. You want me to go and adopt a kitty. Give it a bullsh*t ass name—"

She began to shake her head at me, clearly upset. "Please, Mr. Pelletier, refrain from using such language. It's not bullsh*t, it's kindness. Remember...that emotion we're trying to get you to feel without the help of marijuana?"

I nodded. "Oh, so sorry...please forgive me. I mean a

kind name." The smile was back on her face. "And then bring the mutha fu—" I cleared my throat. "The kitten to the meeting and introduce it to a bunch of crackheads?"

Her mouth opened as if I'd slapped her. "Tucker! This is a no-judgment zone. You don't want anybody to judge you, do you?"

"Well, that all depends. Is there anybody else here for weed?"

She began to sputter, nice and ruffled. "That's beside the point. We don't use the term crackhead inside of these walls."

I held up my hands. "My fault. Dopies…"

She shook her head. "We don't use that either."

"What am I allowed to use, Doc?"

"Thank you for asking. If you must call them something, then call them *fellow patients in need of a helping hand like myself.*" And then she was back to smiling at me.

"So yeah, I'm not going to say that. So how about I just call them people."

"Perfect!" she gushed.

"You want me to adopt a kitty, give it a kind name, and then bring it here and introduce it to people with drug problems?"

She nodded. "Yeppers!"

"Hmmmm," I said as I sat back on the couch.

"What are you feeling, Naphtali?"

My gaze came to hers. "Honestly?"

"Yes, honestly."

"I feel f*cked up. I don't want to adopt a f*cking cat; I hate cats. I definitely don't want to bring the little mutha f*cka in here and introduce it to a room full of f*cking crackheads."

82

"And yet, this is my request, and I am the one who must sign on the dotted line to get you reinstated. So technically, you have no choice."

"Exactly," I growled.

"And how does that make you feel?"

"What? The fact that you've taken away my choice?"

"Yes."

I thought about her question, trying to examine my f*cking feelings. "It makes me feel…Helpless."

For a minute, it looked as if glee danced in her eyes before her ever so dependable resolve settled back in place. She wrote something down in her notepad before her gaze came back to mine.

"But Doc, it's not good for me to feel helpless."

She swallowed as she began to chew on her bottom lip again. "And why is that?" she asked so low if I wasn't watching her mouth, I wouldn't have heard it.

"Because when I do, a ruthless mutha f*cka awakens inside of me." She had no idea just how honest I was being. But then she said something that surprised the sh*t out of me.

"Come now, Mean Tucker. Surely a little kitty cat won't cause that other side of you to awaken. In fact, you can rest assured that the random acts of kindness I have planned for you will make sure that the other side of you stays asleep."

# Chapter 4

## THE BOOK HOUSE

Free

BY THE TIME I closed the clinic on Friday night, I was so tired it took all the strength I had to put one foot in front of the other as I headed to my car. Tomorrow, I was going to sleep till noon, no matter how much my body protested staying in the bed so long.

"Free..."

A scream froze in my throat as Dillion materialized out of the shadows next to my car. I put my hand on my chest, trying to still my racing heart.

"Dillion, don't do that! You scared the heck out of me! Why are you skulking in the shadows like some kind of crazy man?"

He grinned as his gaze took me in, lingering on my breasts. "Why haven't you taken any of my calls?"

I shook my head as I took my keys out of my purse. "Why would I?"

"Because I love you and you love me."

"What?!" I looked at him as if he'd lost his mind. "Love? Is that what you call cheating on me with my sister? If that's love, I don't want to have anything to do with it."

I went to try and put my key in the door, but he moved so suddenly blocking my way, he frightened me. I took several steps back.

"Move!" I growled.

"Wait! You have to hear me out first."

"I don't have to do anything, I've heard enough!" I went to take a step toward my car, but he moved back in my way.

"Angie is forcing me to marry Laureen! You have to know I would never willingly give you up for her," he blurted.

I folded my arms. "Well, your story sure has changed. What happened to it being my fault and you going to her because she was warmer and made time for you?"

He shook his head. "Lies! I didn't expect you to block my calls and refuse to see me. I thought my words would make you fight for us."

"What the hell did you think was going to happen? That I was so desperate that I would be your side piece? Is that it? You want me to ignore the fact that you're engaged to my sister and continue to welcome you in my arms?"

He raked his hands down his face as he began to pace. "You know how forceful Angie can get. Her firm writes the grants for my hospital. She threatened to pull the Pullman grant from us if I didn't agree to the marriage."

"The Pullman grant?"

That is a huge grant, one that helped to fund a lot of the

bigger hospitals in Michigan. I'd been trying to get Angie to consider the Endurance Clinic for it for the last two years. Of course, she only laughs and tells me not to get ahead of myself, while keeping me on the hook with the smaller grants she does get for us.

He nodded before gesturing toward the clinic behind me. "Just like she's been threatening the grants that are keeping this place going. She has it in for you, Free. She wants to take away anything that makes you happy. You can't let her do this to us, baby!"

I put my hand to my chest. "*I* can't let her do this?! *You* were the one who agreed to that marriage."

"What choice did I have?!" he cried holding his hands out to the side of him. "My ass is toast if word got out that the hospital lost the Pullman grant because of me. No hospital in the state will hire me on after that. I would be totally blackballed."

I too began to pace. Dammit! What did I ever do to Angie? Dillion was right, she hated me, and I didn't know why. Ever since I first stepped foot in her house, she's gone out of her way to belittle me, embarrass me, and make sure I always knew my place. And now, she'd sunk her evil fangs into Dillion.

I wanted to oust her, to report her the Federal Trade Commission, but who knew how far Angie's reach went. My guess is it was pretty far, which is why she was still able to go on her reign of terror without anybody putting a stop to it. As far as I knew, it was only one other family in these parts more powerful than hers and it was the Pelletiers. And, well, you can see who their protégé is... Mean Tucker.

"What are we going to do?" Dillion asked, causing my steps to come to a halt.

I looked up at him and for the second time in a matter of days, his weakness disgusted me. I could never imagine Mean Tucker saying something like this. That thought had me putting my hand on my head. Dammit! There I go comparing another man to Naphtali.

Goodness...

It was just too much for one night. My mind and body were exhausted and I just couldn't think clearly right now. I held my hand up, stopping him from saying whatever it was he was opening his mouth to say.

"Just give me some time to think. I'm too tired right now... I'll figure something out when I get a little rest."

My answer must have been a satisfactory one because he nodded and moved from in front of my door. I didn't hesitate to open it and get in.

"When will I hear from you again?" he asked, holding the door open, preventing it from closing. Wanting to be away from him, I opened my mouth and lied.

"I'll call you tomorrow."

He smiled and leaned in the car to kiss me. My whole system rebelled at such an act and I nearly fell into the back seat backing away from him.

"What are you doing?!" I cried.

"Giving you a kiss goodnight, what does it look like?"

I frantically shook my head. "We're not there yet!"

Oh, y'all! He was really freaking me out! I just wanted to get away from him. He didn't move back right away. Still leaning all the way in my car, he stared at me for a moment.

"Don't let her split us up, Free. We're destined to be together."

I felt sick to my stomach. Had he always been this weak? Why hadn't I noticed it before now? Just wanting to get this over with, I nodded.

"Okay, but you've put a lot on my plate tonight. I need to process everything."

Finally, he began to step back. "Yeah, of course. I'll talk to you tomorrow. Goodnight, sweetness."

When he shut the door, I exhaled. Not wanting to run the risk of him changing his mind and coming for my door handle again, I started the engine and got out of there. As I drove home, I pondered over his words. Could it be true? Had Angie threatened to stand in the way of Dillion's hospital getting the Pullman grant?

*Could she even do that?* I know she could wreak havoc with a small private practice like mine, but could she really cause trouble for a mega hospital like Dillion's. Michigan General was no small-fry and although they like me, depended on several grants along with patient insurance to keep their doors open, they had some of the best doctors in the world on their staff.

*Surely, Angie's reach didn't go that far.* Then again, maybe it did. I remember when I was fourteen and Angie, my father, and the twins had been invited to a small fundraising dinner for President Clinton. Of course, they left me at home, because Angie said dinners like that wasn't for the children of hippy whores. She would never allow their image to be so tarnished.

Anyway, the twins gushed for weeks about what it was like to have dinner with the Clintons' daughter and how she'd asked them about a pair of shoes they both owned, and how Angie had later sent her a pair, which she wore at her father's second term inauguration.

I've seen Angie destroy powerful people. Maybe Dillion had a point about being afraid. But still, he could have warned me that this was happening, instead of allowing me to get sucker-punched with it the other day.

When I made it inside my home, I kicked off my shoes right there at the door and collapsed on the couch. I wanted to go upstairs to my bed, I really did, but I was too tired to go any further. I think I will just lie here for a few moments and then drag myself up to the shower.

Yeah, that was a good plan...

However, when next I opened my eyes, the sun was shining bright through the window. I sat up on the couch and looked at my watch.

"Ten-thirty...Wow!" I didn't remember closing my eyes. You ever been so tired your body just shut down on you? I think that's what happened last night.

Actually feeling rested, I stretched on the couch like a cat. That thought brought a smile to my face. When I was a little girl, my mom would tickle me while I stretched, calling me her little kitty cat.

I missed my mom. She was such a good woman, so kind and loving. She dedicated her whole life to giving to those less fortunate than her, which was amazing because she wasn't rich, not even close. But she had a giving heart and didn't mind sharing her last piece of bread with someone that needed it.

Still sitting on the couch where I crashed, I looked around my home and exhaled. It's time for me to explain the book house to you guys. The book house belonged to my father's mother, who was also a psychiatrist. I'd never met her. She was killed by one of her patients when I was three. I don't think she was a very good woman, but I'll tell you more about that in a sec.

My father never sold her home. In fact, he didn't do much with it at all. I found out when my dad's will was read that the house had been passed down to me. At first, I didn't think anything of it. At that time, I hadn't planned on coming back to Michigan at all.

But after I'd finished my last year of residency, it became clear that I could save money by living in the house that I already owned, which was how I ended up back here. Granted starting a private practice in the Oakwood Heights area had been fairly easy, due to all the programs that had been set up to bring life back to Detroit. And yeah, a lot of that, Angie had begrudgingly helped me with.

Anyhow, when I first stepped foot inside the old home, it was to find books everywhere. Nearly every wall was a bookshelf filled with them. The basement and the attic were filled with boxes of books. I've been trying to go through them all just to make room for other things, like furniture. Obviously, my late grandmother didn't care about things like that. Most of her medical journals I kept, but I've donated a lot of the other books to the local libraries.

Because my work schedule is always so hectic, I'm moving at a slower pace than what I'd like. But I've managed to work my way through the basement, first floor, and the second floor with only the attic still left to do.

I pulled myself off the couch and up to the shower, after which I dressed in a pair of jeans and a button-up shirt, preparing myself to begin my journey through the attic, where most of my grandmother's personal medical records were. I'd intentionally saved the attic for last, the things that I'd found in those records so far had been frightening.

She'd been a psychiatrist for the United States Army during the time of Vietnam. I'd read through a few of her case studies already and was completely horrified by what I saw. My grandmother worked under a doctor named Baxter Silva, who specialized in behavior science. They worked with a group of soldiers that had returned from the war with severe cases of PTSD.

My goodness, the things they had put those soldiers through were the things of nightmares. I told myself just to toss the files in the trash, but because I'm a glutton for pain, I have to know what came of the studies. So, with coffee in hand, I headed up to the attic to begin my journey into the deranged mind of Dr. Baxter Silva.

———

THE SOUND of my phone ringing brought me out. I looked at my watch and was surprised to see that it was nearly 4:00.

"Wow!" I'd been so drawn into what I was reading, I didn't even notice that my stomach was empty and protesting loudly.

My grandmother had kept all these records behind her boss's back. More than once, she wrote that if *they*, whoever they were, knew she was documenting the things that she had, she would end up dead. And from what I'd read so far, I can see why. I'd seen movies with stuff like this happening but would have never thought these things could happen in real life.

I was just reading the case file of a female patient that was code-named Daisy. She was their youngest patient at only sixteen. Daisy's parents had brought her in to see my grandmother because she told her parents that she'd been having visions about the end of the world, and they thought the child was losing her mind.

However, bringing her in to my grandmother was the worst thing they could have done for their daughter. Dr. Baxter and my grandmother put that poor girl through hell—

The sound of my phone ringing again brought my thoughts to a halt. Oh well, I will have to pick this up later. I will fill you guys in on whatever new information I find out, although I'm a bit afraid of what else is in the file. I just pray Daisy made it out alive.

Anyway, I quickly shoved the files to the side and hurried downstairs. Because I was still thinking about Daisy, I forgot to look at the number before I said hello.

"Hello…"

"Hey, beautiful…"

I nearly groaned at the sound of that deep baritone coming from the other end. My knees gave out and I collapsed on the bed as all thoughts of mind control, LSD, and Vietnam fled my mind to be filled with the image of a chocolate Adonis.

"Hey!"

I could have kicked myself for how breathy that sounded. Clearing my throat, I tried again.

"How did you get my number?"

Naphtali chuckled. "The phonebook."

I grinned. "You got my cell phone number out the phonebook?"

"Listen, Doc," he said, clearly changing the subject. "I got bigger problems. I'm out here trying to do what my doctor suggested and I'm running into roadblocks."

"What kind of roadblocks?"

"Well, nobody will allow me to adopt a kitty because they think I'm going to go home and cook it or some sh*t! I kid you not. I went to three different shelters and every one of them are being ran by captain save a damn cat, that takes one look at me and instantly shut it down. The last one I went to threatened to call the cops on me for cruelty to animals."

I put my hand over my mouth so he wouldn't hear me laughing at him.

"I told the crazy cat lady, I am a f*cking cop and pointed out the fact that I couldn't be cruel to an animal I didn't even have yet. Do you know what the psycho told me?"

I cleared my throat again so that he couldn't hear my laughter. "No, what did she say?"

"She said she was pressing charges for whatever future cruelty I had planned. Can you believe that sh*t?"

"No, I can't. That's crazy…"

"Yeah, it is. If you want this thing to happen, then you're going to have to come and get the f*cking cat for me. I'll meet you at Coney Island over there on Lafayette. All that cat shopping has made me hungry."

And then the phone went dead. I stared at it for a moment, trying to figure out what the hell just happened. No way I was going anywhere with him. I turned on my phone to call him back but then paused.

Was this his way of trying to get out of my little torture show? Did he know that I would refuse to go with him, so that he could say, *well I tried?*

"Oh, I don't think so, buddy!" Nothing will stand in the way of my revenge. I grabbed my keys and headed out.

Twenty minutes later, I pulled up at Coney Island to find Mean Tucker dressed in black jeans, a black t-shirt that hugged his muscled body beautifully and a pair of Timberlands, leaning against his truck with his ankles crossed, waiting on me.

Gracious, the man could have been posing for a photoshoot with how good he looked standing there. I glanced down at myself and wished that maybe I would have changed into something else. I still wore the clothes I'd put on to clean the attic. My hair was still in the bun from yesterday, but because I hadn't touched it up, more than a few strands had escaped to frame my face. Dang it! I have to look like something the dog dragged home.

"I didn't think you were going to come," he said as he watched me approach him. His gaze slowly raked over me, making me more conscious of the fact that I looked a mess.

I grinned. "I bet...but here I am. We don't want anything to stand in the way of your success, now do we?"

He chuckled as he held the restaurant door open for me. "Yeah, whatever. Let's grab a bite to eat first."

As soon as I walked into the restaurant, my stomach started doing happy flips. Unfortunately, I was going to have to disappoint it because there was nothing and I do mean nothing on this menu that didn't go against my diet.

"What can I get for you?" the cashier asked.

Tucker shoulder bumped me. "Doc, go 'head and order first."

95

I narrowed my eyes at him. Although he didn't shoulder bump me to the point that I fell down like he used to do when we were younger, it was enough to remind me how big of a jerk he was.

And...

I don't know, for some reason, that took away a little of the nervousness I felt about being here with him, made it feel more familiar if that makes sense. I rolled my eyes at him and looked back toward the menu.

"Do you guys have salads?"

"Yeah, we got the Coney Salad, you want any meat on it?"

I shook my head. Coney Island was known for their fatty meats that taste like heaven but added the pounds instantly.

Tucker turned to face me, leaning his back against the counter. I had to stop myself from doing the cowardly thing and taking a few steps back. This position brought us closer than I was comfortable with. And let me tell you, having his complete attention like this always made me feel like my insides were going to turn into jello. I felt warm all over.

"Come on, Doc, order some real food. When did you turn into one of those girls that nibble on carrot sticks in front of the sexy guy?"

I held my head back and had a really good laugh at that. "Sexy guy? What sexy guy? The only thing I see is my childhood bully."

He put his hand on his chest. "First of all, I've changed. You can't keep bringing up the past. I've been born again."

That made me laugh even more. "You've been born again?"

With a sexy grin on his face, he nodded. "Hell yeah, I have. I'm a new man. I've turned over a new leaf."

I narrowed my eyes at him again. "I don't believe you."

"That's okay. I'm going to show you. I'm so gentle these days they've threatened to fire me from the force for my gentle nature when handling the drug dealers. Can you believe that?"

The casher eyeballed Tucker before making a sound in his throat that said he clearly didn't believe it. And neither did I. Biting my lip to keep from grinning too hard, I shook my head.

"No, I can't believe that."

"Wow, Freebie...You're really hurting my feelings." My gaze came to his and for a moment, I was drowning in his intense gaze. This new Tucker was a threat to my system. I was prepared to deal with the jerk from high school, the boy that I grew to hate. However, that was not who had come back. A man had returned, and I must say that I don't quite know how to handle him.

He'd called me Freebie. I didn't think he remembered that name. During senior year, we took a class trip to the zoo with our little buddies, the kindergarten class from a neighboring school. We had to take them around and show them a good time. My little buddy couldn't get my name right, so instead of calling me Free, she called me Freebie the whole time.

And of course, Tucker heard her calling me that and he started calling me that for the rest of the school year. I don't know what possessed me to put my hand on his massive chest and pat it, but that's exactly what I did. And yes, it felt as good as it looked.

"Something tells me you'll be alright."

He put his hand over mine, holding it to his chest and I gasped at the unexpected feel of his warm palm covering mine.

"I pray I'll be alright. Come on, let's order some food, I have the munchi—" he caught himself. "Ur, um... appetite. I have a very big appetite."

My laughter escaped my lips before I could catch it. "Oh my God, Tucker! Are you high?"

His gaze went to the cashier, who was now openly eavesdropping on our conversation, before coming back to mine. "Me? High?"

Instead of answering my question, he began to order a bucket load of food. By the time we sat down at the table, the only thing I could do was stare at it in amazement. He had three chili-cheese dogs, that was spilling over with toppings, an extra-large order of chili cheese fries that was big enough to feed a small army, a corn-beef melt, and a large chocolate shake that all looked mouthwatering. Sitting in front of me was the sorriest salad on this side of heaven.

"Wow! That doesn't look good at all." He muttered dryly.

I shrugged. "It doesn't matter. I'm on a very strict diet, and what you have in front of you looks like it should come with a defibrillator."

He shook his head as he lifted the corn-beef melt that oozed with cheese and took a massive bite before closing his eyes and groaning as he chewed.

"Strict diet you say?" His gaze fell to my pathetic salad. "That looks like a bland disaster. Kinda like yo' boy... Dillion."

My fork paused on its way to my mouth. I couldn't

help but wonder if he'd heard that Dillion and I dated. Even though he's been throwing digs at my ex since high school, I opened my mouth to argue against what he'd said but changed my mind. Why the hell would I stick up for Dillion's cheating behind now? Instead, I ate the bite of salad and yeah, he was right, it was a bland disaster. But I'd rather go blind than admit it to the likes of him.

I pointed my fork at him. "This looks like self-control. Maybe you should take notes."

He held his head back and barked with laughter before surprising me by lifting his sandwich to my lips.

Turning my head, I waved the heavenly smelling temptation away. "Get that thing away from me!"

"Come on, Freebie, take a bite. You know you want to taste my *beef* girl." And then he rubbed his sandwich against my lips.

Chuckling at his vulgare play on words, I shook my head. "No! I don't!"

"One little bite won't hurt your strict diet. What are you even dieting for? You look amazing."

*Don't you grin, Free…Don't you dare!*

"And I want to remain that way, so get your *beef* away from me!"

"Not till you have a taste… Just one."

So yeah, this new playful Tucker that was obviously the result of him smoking marijuana, wore me down until I finally took a massive bite out of his beef. And Oh-My-Goodness! It was the best tasting thing to ever touch my tongue!

"And you have to taste the dog," he said, bringing the chili cheese dog to my lips. It smelt so good. I guess one little bit won't hurt.

I am so ashamed of myself. After opening Pandora's Box, I ended up falling deep into the rabbit hole and didn't come out until I'd consumed a chili-cheese dog, half of the beef melt, a good number of fries and half of the chocolate shake that had been made with real chocolate ice cream.

When I was done, the only thing, I could do was sit back in my chair and unbutton my pants. I can't remember the last time I'd been so full. Tucker sat across from me. He too sat back in his chair staring down at the empty plates on the table.

"Damn, Freebie! I sure hope your counseling skills is better than your self-control. Sh*t, you had to have gained at least 5 pounds. Shame on you for breaking your strict diet like that."

My angry gaze shot across the table at him. The jerk had the nerve to wink at me before he erupted in laughter. I don't know what happened to me. One minute I was sitting there in control of myself and the next, a screech of rage left my lips before I was up and out of the chair chasing him out of Coney Island.

When he saw me coming for him, the bastard's eyes widened before he flew out of the chair, laughing at me the whole time.

———

"THAT ONE RIGHT THERE. That's the one," I said, pointing to the homeliest kitten I've ever seen in my life.

Both Tucker and the young lady from the animal shelter frowned at me in confusion.

"Are you sure you don't want this fluffy gray one?" she asked, gesturing to the little button of joy that sat next to the baby tabby cat that looked as if it had been in a knife fight.

"Yeah, you sure we don't want the gray one?" Tuck asked from where he had his big hands resting on his knees as he too leaned over to see inside the cage.

I shook my head. "Nope, we want that one."

His frown grew. "Doc, that kitten look like it should be enrolling in your drug program. I don't think it's a good idea for two addicts to be living with each other. He looks like he's going to try and introduce me to harder stuff than just herb."

Laughing I hit his shoulder. Oh, my goodness! Tucker on weed was hilarious. "Stop being silly. There is nothing wrong with this little fella."

The lady pulled him out of the cage and plopped him in my hands. Poor kitty really did look beat up. One of his little ears pointed down and the other pointed off towards the right. He had two different color eyes, a blue and a green one. And he had a patch of fur that stuck straight up on his head, giving him a little mohawk. But what made him so bad was he didn't play and move around like the other kittens, he just sat in my hands staring at me. And I swear it looked as if he frowned.

"I love him!" I cried.

"Good, then you keep him," Tucker said, trying to walk away.

"Not so fast, Mr," I told him, grabbing his big hand and plopping the little booger down in it.

"Say hi to your new best friend. This little fella is going to be the beginning of your journey to tapping into your sensitive side, so that you can become a kinder individual, without marijuana."

Tucker lifted his hand until he and the little kitty was eye to eye. I had to bite my bottom lip to keep from laughing. I'd never seen a kitten so serious. The little fella didn't fidget or anything. He just sat on his hind legs in Tucker's big palm, staring at him as if he was boring him.

Naphtali pointed at him. "I don't want no trouble out of you." And then the kitty opened his mouth and made a sound that was almost as ridiculous as his looks.

Tucker's stunned gaze came to mine. "What the hell was that?"

"Yeah…so, that's the way he meows," the young lady said before she handed us the adoption papers.

After we left there, I went with Tucker to get supplies for his new friend. The whole time, I was in tears laughing at the two. We discovered something else about the kitty; he was a bit of a grouch. If we jarred his box too much, he let out one of his obscene meows. If we moved too fast or laughed too loud, he meowed.

I was curious to see how he and Tucker were going to get along when Naphtali's high wore off and his mean self had settled back into place.

Tucker and his new grouchy little friend walked me to my car. "Don't forget to give him a sensitive name. I want you to really show me that you're capable of tapping into that side of you. And then bring him with you Tuesday and introduce him to the others…oh, and if you come high to one of the meetings, that's an automatic fail."

He frowned. "I wasn't aware we were being graded."

"Of course you're being graded, silly. I can't have you being a bad influence on my other clients who are serious about their recovery."

# Chapter 5

TRUE NATURE

---

## Naphtali

THE VERY FIRST moment I knew I could feel anything outside of anger and lust, was when I first laid eyes on Free. Her sisters had made sure to tell anyone who would listen that she was a charity case and from the poor side of the tracks.

At first, I didn't give much thought to her, but then she walked through the door of my geometry class, clutching her books to her chest, biting on her bottom lip, and for the first time in my life, I felt my heart beating and blood rushing through my veins. I sat hypnotized as the teacher introduced her to the class. She was simply beautiful. No make-up or fancy hair, no sparkly long nails or any of the other things the girls at school spent their daddy's money on. Her skin was the color of rich deep chocolate, smooth and clear...and I found myself wanting to touch it, to see if it was as soft as it looked.

But she gazed right past me and continued to do so no matter how much I put myself in her way. It was only in those times when I was in her space that I was allowed to feel something other than rage. And yeah, I forced her to look at me...I needed for her to see me.

I was desperate...

As a kid, I thought that anger was the only emotion I was able to experience. For the life of me, I was incapable of feeling anything else. I had parents, but I didn't know how to love them, and I doubted if they ever truly learned how to love me.

I can't really remember the day I was adopted, my earliest memory was of my father telling me to make him proud. He made sure to remind me quite often that he and my mother could have left me at the agency and taken home a different kid. The more I achieved, the more he rewarded me with material things.

He and I got something of an understanding. I made sure he looked good as the mayor and he made sure my pockets stayed fat. Hell, that was good enough for me; who needed the kind of parents who loved you unconditionally when you had the kind of parents who paid you for being exceptional? I excelled at everything I did.

However, my mother was a different story entirely. Whereas my father was open about the fact that I was his trophy, investing in me because I made his household look good, my mother perfected the art of pretending that she really cared. And I'm not a complete dick, I appreciate her effort.

The truth is, I think she could sense what lives inside of me and it scares the hell out of her. But she wants to be a good mom, so she pretends that it doesn't, although I know better.

*I can't say that I blame her though…*

What lives inside of me scares the sh\*t out of me too. It's been there for as long as I can remember. I feel it pacing back and forth inside of my flesh like a caged animal, constantly looking for a way out.

The more I keep it inside, the angrier it becomes. And because I ain't no b\*tch, the angrier I become. My whole life has been battling it, trying to prove my dominance over it, but sometimes I fail. And during those times, people die.

I'm able to control it enough that we've never killed an innocent, but not enough to stop it from taking out anyone that it believes is a threat. It kills without hesitation, without a single thought of mercy. Its disregard for human life is unparalleled.

The first time I killed a man, I was ten years old. My dad and I were driving home from a pizza joint where my team had been celebrating a win. We stopped at a light on 67th street and a man slung open my door and pointed a gun at us, telling us to get out of the car.

When we got out, he took my dad's suit, shoes, wallet, watch, and wedding ring, then he told him he was jacking his Benz. When he finally turned my way, that was the first time I could remember feeling the change coming over me.

*"Take that chain off, lil nigga!"* He sneered pointing his gun at my chest. My dad was standing there in only his underwear, the look he gave me was clear as day. He wanted me to f\*ck this dude up.

*"I ain't giving you sh\*t,"* I told him, feeling dead inside.

In the moment, I hated my father. I hated him for

telling the monster within me that it was okay for him to have me. I hated him for not doing sh*t and ending up standing there in nothing but his f*cking drawers. But most of all, I hated him for what he did afterward.

*"What you say to me, lil nigga?"* the man said before he took several steps toward me.

I don't know where I learned to move like I did or how I became so fast, but one minute I was standing there and the next, his gun was in my hand and I was pulling the trigger, only to realize there were no bullets in the gun. But that didn't stop the killer inside of me, he'd been awakened, and it wanted blood.

I took the pistol and hit him in the throat with it, crushing his Adam's apple. And after that, things went black. When I came to, I was standing over several dead bodies, their blood dripping from my hands. My father was balled up in a fetal position, looking at me as if I was a monster.

Apparently, the man hadn't been alone, and when his boys saw what was happening to him, ran to his aid. I don't remember killing any of them. When my dad saw that I was back, he stood from the ground with pride in his eyes. And then he said something that chilled my soul,

*"You are by far my best investment. Me and you, son, we're going all the way to the top!"*

He told me not to worry about the dead bodies, he would make sure no one ever knew it was me. And it was that night that a precedent had been set.

He went on to cover up every killing done by my hand. He never said it was wrong, he never tried to get help for me. He never even tried to get me off the streets. He just put more money in my bank account while patting me on the back, letting the world know that I was his son, and he was so proud of my prowess.

But what he doesn't know is if this thing inside of me could exist without me, it would kill me too…without hesitation, which is why it is and will always remain my biggest enemy. And as soon as I figure out how, I was ghosting the mutha f*cka…without hesitation.

Although I haven't yet found what can kill it, for now, I managed to stumble across something that can cause it to chill the f*ck out.

Weed…

Smiling, I picked up the cigar to bust it open. Who the f*ck was I kidding? Gunja helped *me* to chill the f*ck out as well. It quieted the rage inside of me that had nothing to do with my other personality.

I guess you can say I got high for the *both* of us…

A hiss came from the cage across the room.

"Hiss all you want, devil cat; you're not getting out of that cage," I told the little demon seed as I rolled my blunt.

And before you mutha f*ckas get on me about jailing the little hellion, let me tell y'all something. That kitty is a bigger asshole than me and my other personality put together.

I brought the little bastard home and let him out of the cage, he looks around my pad as if he wasn't impressed before copping a squat and taking a huge piss on my Armani rug. The first time I chalked it up as nervous jitters. So, I cleaned up his little spill and then set up his litter box like Free had shown me. The little bastard scratched around in the box before sauntering back over to my rug, squatting and taking a massive crap on it. The whole time he did it, he gave me a look that said, *what the hell you gon' do about it?*

"*You sh\*t on my rug one more time and your ass is going in the cage for the rest of the night,*" I told him, giving the little mutha f\*cka fair warning. He must not have cared for me reprimanding him because he hissed at me before swatting at my feet with his claws.

I set up his food and water bowl. He took a few sips of the water, sniffed at the food and then turned and looked me dead in the eye before tipping it over on the floor, letting out one of those annoying ass meows.

"*Man, if you didn't like the food, all you had to do was say something,*" I muttered as I cleaned up the third mess from this little dude within hours. I jumped in the shower and when I got out, it was to see him copping another squat over my rug. He waited until I walked out and made eye contact with him before letting go of another round of kitty poop.

"*That's it, you little sh\*t!*" I picked him up and put his little ass in the cage. Do y'all know he meowed all night? At one point, I had to turn up the TV to try and drown him out. When that didn't work, I gave up and let his little ass out. He ran under my bed and hid for the rest of the night.

However, as soon as I walked out of my room this morning, it was to find his ass squatting over my rug, waiting to make eye contact and then letting go of another round of his little *f\*ck you* donation. Let's just say the little bastard has been in the cage ever since, and he ain't coming out until it's time to introduce his ass to the crackheads.

Now, I just needed to think of a name for his ass. And as I settled back on my couch to enjoy my morning med stick, I did just that. By the time it was time for me to head out for my meeting, I'd had no luck with coming up with anything suitable. When thinking of the little terror, the only names that kept coming to mind was asshole, dipstick, son-of-a-b*tch, lil mutha f*cka… But I'm sure none of those names will help get me close to my goal, which is winning over the doctor's heart. So, by the time I pulled up to the clinic, I decided to just wing some sh*t.

I was already good and irritated because I was more sober than I liked to be. Thanks to Free's little threat, I didn't have my mid-evening smoke, which meant I was back to feeling the animal pacing back and forth inside of me.

"Hey, Nap! Wait up, we'll walk in with you."

*Jackson!*

Dammit! My irritation level just tripled. I turned around surprised to see him and Asher getting out of Asher's truck. Neither of them was dressed in their uniforms, which meant this was a social call.

"What the hell are you assholes doing here?" I grumbled as I walked through the doors of the clinic.

"We were in the neighborhood and decided to drop by and support our boy. Bumped into the doctor yesterday and she told us about your weekly meetings and said we were welcome to come to support our best friend in his journey to recovery. What do you have there?" Jackson finally paused, looking down at the cage in my hand.

I stopped and glared at him. "Why, nosey mutha f*cka?! Why don't the two of you get the f*ck out of my business and go home!"

Asher grinned, throwing his arm around my shoulder. "Why would we do that, buddy? We're here for you."

I opened my mouth to tell them to f*ck off, but my words died in my throat. The doctor, dressed in another one of those pinned up tweed suits that made me want to savage out and rip it off her body, stepped out of the meeting room and smiled at me. That was all it took to make my thoughts get muddled and shot to sh*t. Had she done that more often in high school, I would have been putty in her little hands.

"Hello, gentlemen, you're just in time." And that voice... It was soft and sweet. She had the kind of voice that could soothe a wild beast. I know, it's always had that effect on the one that lived inside of me.

"Welcome, fellas," she said to Jackson and Asher, shaking their hands. "It is so nice of you to come out and support your friend in his wellness journey. Please have a seat in any of the chairs off to the side. The inner circle of chairs is reserved for my clients."

"Thank you so much for inviting us, Doc, I wouldn't miss this for the world," Jackson told her as he and Asher scurried into the room like two rats. Coming to a stop, I frowned down at her.

"Oh my... is somebody feeling a little grumpy?" She used the same voice someone would when talking to a naughty child. That sh*t only made me frown more.

"Why the hell did you invite those assholes? What kind of AA meeting allows outsiders in?"

She gently touched my arm and all the anger I felt seeped out of me like air in a balloon, not to mention the fact that she smelled edible; it was a mixture of vanilla and grapefruit.

*Hmmmm...Grapefruit*

"Okay, so first, this isn't an AA meeting," she spoke to

me like I was slow. Maybe I was. That's what the f*ck this woman did to me. She turned my mind to sh*t because when I was around her, all the blood left it and rushed to other parts of my body.

"And second, you'll find that I don't run my clinic like other doctors run theirs. My methods are a bit unconventional, a luxury I opted for when opening a private practice." Her little hand moved to my chest and I damn near growled. I think the doctor liked touching my chest because she always found a reason to, even though sometimes I think she does it unconsciously.

"I'm going to need you to trust me, okay?"

Like a big ass lump on the f*cking log, I nodded. "Okay."

*Damn! This girl had me wrapped around her little f*cking fingers.*

She smiled. "Okay, now go ahead and take a seat in one of the available chairs in the center of the room. We'll get started in just a moment."

Placing the cage on the floor by my feet, I sat with my back to Jackson and Asher. I didn't want to look in their dumb ass faces while I was forced to go through this sh*t. Instead, I looked around at the other sappy suckers in the group and wasn't surprised to see that they were all men. No doubt, they all put up with this sh*t for the same reason I was. Speaking of that reason, she came inside the room and shut the door behind her.

"Good evening, everyone. I hope that you guys have had a successful week in your war against the enemy."

She sat in one of the chairs across the circle from me and crossed her legs and everything else faded to black as I zoned in on those thick thighs of hers. Damn! I couldn't wait to taste her again. She'd given me her virginity on prom night and I've never forgotten the feel of her heat wrapped so tightly around me or her taste. I was a boy then and didn't really know what to do with her. But now I'm a man with a man-size appetite and I couldn't wait to get a hold of her ass.

I shifted in my seat adjusting myself. Sh*t, I was getting a f*cking erection just thinking about it. Only Free can cause me to get erect with just the thought of her.

"Tucker!" she said, bringing me out of my lusty thoughts.

"Hmmm..."

The sound of chuckling coming from behind me brought me all the way out of my thoughts. I sat up a bit in my chair and cleared my throat. "What was that? I didn't hear you..."

She gave me one of those smiles that one would give a mentally incapable individual. "I asked you if you can stand and introduce yourself to the group."

F*ck! How did I know she was going to say some sh*t like that? "Yeah, I was hoping to maybe sit this round out. You know, until I get comfortable with everyone."

"How about we show you how it's done. And then when we're finished, you can give it a try. This is a safe place; nobody is going to judge you here." She gestured to the guy that sat a couple of chairs to my right.

"Gary, why don't you begin."

Gary was the nervous type, always looking for the next big thing. In my field, I've seen them all. If I had to guess, his drug of choice is cocaine. He needed a drug that could keep up with his ambition to have the next big record label, or real-estate franchise, or whatever it was that will help him get rich quick with the minimum amount of know-how.

He stood and gave a nervous glance around the room, his gaze lingering on me. No doubt, his spidey-senses were tingling, something about cops and addicts…they can sniff them out like they can their drug of choice.

"My name is Gary. I'm the CEO of Sexy Baby Records. My fast life requires many hours of the day and night, leaving me little time to rest. I was introduced to cocaine ten years ago and I've been riding the white horse ever since. However, thanks to Dr. Robinson, I've been clean for the last year."

The other fourteen men in the circle clapped for him as he took his seat.

"Remember, Gary, your recovery has nothing to do with me. You made up your mind that you were taking control of your life… You made that decision, Gary, so, let's give you a round of applause. You are the true hero."

My gaze went to Jackson and Asher when they started f*cking clapping again. Both of the bastards were sitting in the back with huge grins on their faces, enjoying the hell out of themselves at my misery. And on it went, one sappy ass story after another. When it finally got around to me again, I was fighting to stay awake.

"Okay, Tucker…It's your turn."

I tried to give her a look, pleading with her to move on, but she wouldn't…she had her sweet hooks in me and she wasn't letting up.

Exhaling, I stood. "My name is Naphtali. I'm a cop." As soon as I said that, all the other *clients* sat up on instant alert.

*Good, you bastards, that's what the hell you get for boring me out of my f\*cking mind.*

"I don't have an addiction, I'm here because—"

"The first step to recovery is having the courage and the strength to admit that you have a problem," some dickhead said from my left. My angry gaze shot to his, he inhaled sharply and sealed his f\*cking lips.

"Like I was saying before this—"

The doc clearing her throat brought my sentence to an end. "This is an open circle. I try and encourage you guys to encourage each other. Quincy was simply stating a well-known fact. The first step to recovery is admitting you have a problem. Please continue…"

Dammit! I was f\*cking up…I'm supposed to be different from the dickhead she knew in high school. Okay, let me try again.

"Thank you for that, doc. Of course, you're right." My gaze went to Quincy's b\*tch ass. "Sorry about that, little buddy." More chuckling came from behind me and I was one step from picking up my chair and hurling it at my two bastard friends.

Quincy smiled and nodded. "That's alright. We're here for each other."

I take that back. I was one step away from picking up my chair and hurling it at this douchebag. *Damn! I was beginning to sweat. This sh\*t was going to be harder than I thought.*

I cleared my throat. "I have a problem with weed."

"WEED?!" an older guy who was missing a few teeth cried out. "Don't tell me you in here for some mutha f\*ckan WEED!"

"Papa C! What is our policy about judgment?" Free admonished the older fella.

"Yeah, I know, baby...but this mutha f*cka in here talkin' 'bout he had a problem with weed. That ain't no mutha f*ckan problem! I got a problem! I used to be the daddy of fifty hoes. But because I couldn't let go of the rock, neighboring pimps stole each one of them. Now, everybody call me the broke pimp. Ain't that some sh*t?!"

The broke pimp had Free good and ruffled. She went on to admonish him about his language and the way he was making me feel.

"Naw, I'm good. I agree with my man," I told her, then went on to give him some dap, 'cause sh*t that's the same thing I'd been saying. Out of all these saps here, Papa C was my favorite so far.

"Alright, young blood, it ain't no thang," he said before he settled back down in his chair.

"And who do you have with you today?" Free said gesturing to the terror's cage at my feet, getting this sh*t show back on the road.

My hesitant gaze lowered to the cage. "Who? This guy?"

She smiled. "Yes, that guy."

I rubbed my hands down my face, really wanting to skip this part. This f*cking cat was the devil. Who knows what it's going to do when I open this cage? He seems like the kind of bastard that would hold a grudge.

"Hey, doc, can we skip this part? I'm not real comfort-able...you know?"

"I know, sweetheart, but this is a part of your healing. The only way to get comfortable with something is by doing it. So, take your time, we're here for you."

I could feel Asher and Jackson boring holes in my back. I bet they were loving this sh*t. I reached down and grabbed the cage. *F*ck it! Let's get it done!*

"This is my pet kitty, I named him Grapefruit. He's ummm…" I cleared my throat again. *Sh*t!* I was sweating. "He's ummmm, helping me tap into my sensitive side to help—"

Before I could finish, the two mutha f*ckas behind me exploded in f*cking laughter. My gaze shot to them. Both of them were laughing so hard they'd fallen over to the empty chairs next to them.

"What the f--?!" I looked back at Free, waiting for her to say something to them or at the very least to kick them the f*ck out. When she didn't do anything but sit and wait for me to continue, I gestured toward them.

"Is this what we're doing then? We're allowing the supportive guests to laugh at the sensitive clients with the conditions?"

Her gaze went behind me to Asher and Jackson, who were both wiping tears from their eyes. "Fellas, do you mind not laughing at Naphtali's vulnerability? Grapefruit is a really good friend and support system for him. Let's not make him feel bad for embracing that."

It took the f*ckers a minute, but eventually, they got their sh*t together. "Okay, you're right. We won't laugh at Tuck's Fruity-" Jackson began, but couldn't finish because he was still f*cking laughing at me. I swear, when this was over, I was going to kick both of their asses.

"Grapefruit, punk! His name is Grapefruit!" I growled, but that only made the assholes laugh harder.

Free's beautiful eyes came back to me. "Go ahead, Tucker, let us meet Grapefruit."

After shooting one more murderous glance behind me, I opened the cage. As I was reaching in, a horrible screeching sound emitted from it before a small, hand-size furball with claws shot out of it straight at my face.

"Arrrggghhh! Sh*t!!!" I yelled as it then proceeded to use those razor-sharp claws, trying to shred me to pieces, moving faster than I could see, circling my head, neck, arms, and chest.

FREE

OH! God! Give me the strength! I can't believe what I was seeing. This is so worth it. If I lose my practice tomorrow, seeing my bully get his butt kicked by a baby kitten was well worth it. Now I can die happy.

I wish you guys were here to see this with your own eyes. I know I will never be able to do it justice trying to describe it. Mean Tuck was yelling and doing this little jerky dance as the kitten sheathed his claws in another piece of his flesh. He was knocking over chairs and everything as he tried to get Grapefruit off of him.

"Shoot this mutha f*cka, J!" he yelled.

My mouth opened in a laugh that I could not let go of in front of my patients. And dear God, it was killing me. No, I'm serious, I was getting ready to die...I couldn't breathe!

Help me! Oh my God!!!! Help Meeeee!!!!

My gaze went to Jackson and Asher, but I don't know why I did that. The both of them were laughing so hard Asher had fallen out of his chair and Jackson held up his cellphone recording the spectacle Tucker's big self made trying to dislodge the angry little kitty. But he was laughing so hard there is no way that will be good footage.

I'm a doctor, I can't laugh in front of my clients…But help me, I need something or I was going to die.

Papa C handed me one of the files from the desk next to him. Desperately, I reached for it, holding it up in front of my face, so that nobody could see the tears coming out of my eyes as I tried but failed to hold in my laughter.

"Damn, player! You need to get yo' sh*t together." Papa C told Tucker as he tried to see the best way he could help him. Papa C was the only one not laughing at him, everybody else was in tears.

Tucker snatched off his shirt, trying to get to the kitty that had somehow worked its way underneath it. He wore a gun holster over his tank top. When I saw him reach and grab his gun, I made my move.

"Come here, Grapefruit." I cooed to the kitty, plucking him off Tucker's back, sheltering him in my arms.

"Put him down, baby, I'm going to shoot it!" Naphtali yelled aiming his gun at him. I turned around so that my back was between them. The little furball burrowed into my arms shaking badly.

"Put your gun away, you're scaring him."

Tucker looked at me as if I'd gone crazy. "Scaring it?! Do you see this sh*t?!" He held out his beautifully muscled arms that were now covered in about a hundred little red welts.

Jackson and Asher were laughing so loud they were drowning out Tucker's heavy breathing. Jackson was asking for a ventilator. I know the feeling, I had to get out of here before I blew.

"I'm going to take the kitty to my office until things cool down." I hurried out of the room, if I looked back at Tucker, I wasn't going to make it. As soon as I closed my office door, I collapsed on the couch and had a really good laugh.

Oh my God! I haven't laughed this good in a long time. Grapefruit had cuddled up next to me and nodded off, his fight with Naphtali tuckering him completely out. It's official, this kitty is my favorite being in the whole world.

It took me about ten minutes to get myself together. I left Grapefruit napping on the couch as I made my way back into the meeting room. Everything seemed back to normal...Well, as much as it could get.

Tucker had put his shirt back on and now sported a few bandages on his face, neck, and arms. My other clients who sat in the circle with him stared straight forward, no doubt afraid to laugh at him now that the kitty wasn't occupying his time.

However, Jackson and Asher did not share their fear and still quietly laughed amongst themselves. Both of their heads were bowed as they looked down at Jackson's phone. Every now and again, one of them would throw their heads back and chuckle, only to catch a mean glare from Tucker.

*Okay, Free, you can do this without laughing. You are a professional.* I ran my hand down my skirt, using the roughness of the wool against my palms to help keep my mind off what I'd just seen.

"Alright, now that everything is back to normal, our hour is almost up. But before we go, you will need to pick your support buddy."

His irritated gaze came to me and I almost lost it. I had

to press my lips together to keep from laughing.

"Support buddy?"

Poor baby, he was afraid of what I had in store for him next. Now, this is the point in the story where you should insert the evil laugh, because hell yeah, I had plenty in store for him.

However, this wasn't a part of it. "Yeah, a support buddy is someone you can call to talk you off the ledge. You find yourself wanting to smoke, you call your support buddy. They will be your strength and talk you down. Some of our support buddies have formed great friend-ships. Sometimes they just go for a walk with each other or maybe to the bar for a little drink. Maybe they catch a show…" I gestured to Melvin and Ryan.

"Melvin and Ryan catch the baseball game together from time to time."

Both Melvin and Ryan quickly looked away, not wanting to make eye contact and I instantly got a bad feel-ing. And although something told me to not press the issue, I forged on.

"Now, who has room in their group for Naphtali? I know many of you may look at marijuana as no big deal, but that's the furthest thing from the truth with someone who desires to quit smoking."

When no one volunteered, I started calling on people. "George, how about you and Douglas?"

George's nervous gaze went to Naphtali, who looked up at him and growled. He shook his head rapidly. "Ummm, no, doc, I don't think that's a good idea. Douglas and I just learned how to tolerate each other. We don't want to sully the waters by throwing in another person-ality too soon."

"Okay, well how about you, Papa C?"

Instead of answering my question, Papa C followed with a question. "Say, baby, how about you be his support buddy? Can't you see his big ass makes everybody else nervous as hell? What you want to do, be the reason most of these mutha f*ckas start doping again?"

It was now Tucker who wore a grin. "Papa C, I think that's a great idea," he told him, doing that little fist bump with the older man. Out of all the folks in this group, he would take to the ex-pimp.

"It ain't nothing to it, young blood."

I rolled my eyes before shaking my head. "No, I'm sorry. That's not going to work. The traditional way of doing that is to have the patients be there to support the patients."

Tucker's intense gaze settled on me. "Yeah, but didn't you just say, you don't do things the conventional way?" He gestured to Jackson and Asher, who were now all ears in back of him.

"Isn't that why you let these two assholes in?"

Papa C chuckled. "Well damn, doc, I think he has you there."

Crap! I think he's right! There is no way I can speak my way around this without looking like a huge hypocrite.

*I am so screwed!*

"I mean, yeah, it's no big deal. I can be an ear when you need one."

Tucker's grin turned evil. It was the grin of my nightmares. It was the grin he'd worn on his face every time he tormented me.

"Indeed..." was all he said.

*Oh God! I am so screwed...*

# Chapter 6

## THE DAISY REPORT

Free

*APRIL 9, 1972*

*I MET with Daisy today for two full hours. Her parents are worried that her depression is going to lead to a suicide attempt. Tuesday night, they found her in bed clutching her stomach in intense agony, yelling that the labor pains have begun. When I questioned if it was possible she could be pregnant, they both strongly denied it, seeming to be convinced Daisy is still a virgin. I suggested her parents take her to get examined for sexual activity to err on the side of caution. Daisy's gynecologist confirmed her hymen is still intact.*

*When I questioned Daisy about her behavior three nights ago and what she meant by the labor pains have begun, she responded with her typical answer, that she doesn't remember saying it or even being in pain.*

*There has to be a way to crack through the barrier she's erected. I'm just somehow overlooking it.*

*APRIL 11, 1972*

*DAISY IS LOSING weight at a rapid pace. She refuses to eat unless forced and her parents fear that she will not survive to see her seventeenth birthday. Her parents are also concerned about the bookbag of supplies they found in her closet. They said it appears as if she is planning for a camping trip.*

*When I asked Daisy about the bag, she said she had to be ready. I wanted to question her further but decided against it. Patience is needed if I'm ever to build trust between the two of us. It is a slow journey but one that is growing.*

*Daisy is by far the phenomenal of my career. It will be my studies of her that will finally get me noticed by Dr. Baxter. I just know it!*

*APRIL 27, 1972*

*TO MY DISAPPOINTMENT, Daisy seemed happier today when her mother brought her in to see me. Although I'm not proud of this, I administered her 20cc's of phenacetin to encourage the imbalance between the cholinergic and serotonergic mechanisms in Daisy's brain, thus causing her to feel depressed again.*

*May God forgive me. I know this is wrong, but the last thing I need is for her parents to believe she is on the mend and reduce our session time. I cannot lose my hold on Daisy. If my suspi-*

cions are correct about her, she could be the missing link to help us discover exactly what happened to the 7$^{th}$ Special Forces group on the night of Feb 22, 1969 in the Saigon jungle.


MAY 6, 1972


DR. BAXTER HAS REJECTED my studies on Daisy and believes them to be a waste of time. I doubt he even gave them any real thought. If I was a man or better yet a white man, he would have welcomed my research. I don't know who the bigger oppressor of the black woman is, our own black men or white folk…

No!

I can't give up, I believe so strongly in what I've found, that I'm willing to stake my whole career on it. One day, Dr. Baxter will see and then he will reward me greatly for it.


MAY 14, 1972


I AM GAINING Daisy's trust. For the first time, she's opened up to me and spoke about the man with no shoes that visits her in her dreams. I believe this to be the same man that visited the 7$^{th}$ Special Forces group on the night of Feb 22, 1969 in Saigon, the night Sergeant Major James Bennet Law was changed.

I have yet to make the connection between Daisy and Sergeant Major Law, but I believe that if I work with her a little longer, she will help us to understand what happened in the Saigon jungle on the night of Feb 22.

• • •

*MAY 18, 1972*

*DAISY'S BRAIN seems to be fighting the side effects of the phenacetin, thus making her parents feel as if she has become a normal teen. They've already decided to cut back our sessions to once a month. I offered to see her free of charge, but they're more worried about the stigma that comes with having a daughter who sees a psychiatrist places on their family.*

*I can't allow them to take her away from me. In fact, I need to somehow get them to sign over their rights temporarily, just long enough for me to break Daisy's mind.*

*I've been following the work of Dr. Fields. He's administered small doses of LSD to a group of soldiers that caused them to go into a suggestive state, a state in which thoughts and desires can be applied. I think this may be the key to opening Daisy's mind completely.*

*The negatives: A) She's only sixteen and will more than likely develop a dependency on the drug.*

*B) The damages done to her brain will be irreparable*

*THE POSITIVES: A) I will find out who the man with no shoes is and be able to relay that information to Dr. Baxter, helping to solve some of the mystery behind Sergeant Major Law's physical abilities.*

*B) Maybe even find out that Daisy is the perfect candidate for impregnation with Sergeant Major Law.*

*JUNE 11, 1972*

. . .

*AFTER ADMINISTERING small doses of LSD to Daisy and planting thoughts of suicide in her head. She finally made the attempt. As predicted, her parents phoned me the next day. I told them that they had called at the perfect time. There is a trial of a new drug that is said to be able to help get rid of depression permanently.*

*God, I can't believe they bought that. If there had been another doctor around, they would have instantly called me on my BS. But because Daisy's parents are amongst the uneducated, that went over with flying colors. The same day, they signed a waiver, admitting Daisy into my custody for the next year.*

*I almost feel bad for what I'm about to do to her. But as Dr. Baxter always says, a few will have to be sacrificed for the overall good of the many.*

————

"I HATE HIM, SO MUCH!" Rachel growled as she collapsed next to me on the couch.

I was so tired I didn't bother to move my legs out of the way, which meant she was halfway sitting on me. However, if she was as tired as she looked, I don't think she cared. I don't know about her, but for me, it had been a long week. All I wanted to do was crawl in my bed and sleep the weekend away.

Last Sunday, I found a box of tapes in the attic of short recordings my grandmother did, documenting her studies on Daisy. So instead of coming home after work and sleeping all week, I've been up through the night listening to them. There are hundreds of them., each one ghastlier than the one before.

I can't believe I came from the loins of a woman so evil. The things she did to that innocent girl, whose parents trusted her with her wellbeing was past horrifying. And I have a bad feeling what I heard so far is just the tip of the iceberg.

"If he was standing in front of my car, I would just step on the gas and run him over. God! Why does the man have to plague me so? What did I ever do to him?" Rachel whined, drawing me out of my thoughts.

"What did he do this time?" I muttered, already half asleep as I lazily drew my fingers through Grapefruit's mohawk. His gentle purring wasn't helping me stay awake at all.

As you guys can see, I still had him. I didn't think it was wise to send him home with Tucker after what happened last Tuesday. Plus, I was in love with him, I wouldn't give him back if Tucker asked for him.

Anyway, Rachel called for an emergency girl's night, and since she was temporarily staying with her mom and Oaklee's place was the size of a closet, my house was the designated bachelorette pad.

"That bastard came into the shop, sat his arrogant ass in my chair, and demanded service."

My head was resting against the back of the couch, I chuckled without opening my eyes.

"Free!" Rachel cried, startling me awake. "Did you hear what I said?!"

"Oh my God, Rach! I heard you...you don't have to yell at me!"

Oaklee stuck her head out of the kitchen. "Do you guys want to do watermelon margaritas or strawberry?"

"I don't care, just make sure you clean up behind your-self, I'm too tired to do anything in there tonight."

"Why do you bother to ask us about the flavor? By the time you're done, the only thing we taste is tequila anyway," Rach told her.

Oaklee thought about her words before shrugging. "You know what? You're right...watermelon it is." And then she disappeared back into the kitchen.

"What did you do after he sat in your chair?" I asked, knowing she wouldn't let me rest about this until we went into a full-blown Jackson bashing session.

She exhaled, resting her head against the back of the couch. "You know I'm a perfectionist. I gave him the full treatment, washed his hair, cut it, massaged, and moistur-ized his beard. By the time I was done, he was purring in my hands. I should have slit his throat then."

The 'he' she's speaking of murdering is Jackson. Their hate for each other went back to high school. Poor baby... she'd suffered from Jackson's bullying a lot worse than I had from Tucker. Tucker bullied me because he was a grade-A psychopath. Jackson bullied Rachel because he blamed her mom for his parents divorcing during sopho-more year.

Rach had managed to escape his cruel intents after she graduated by leaving town like I did. But after going through a horrible divorce two months ago, ended up back here in the very town she'd thought she would never see again, sleeping in the very bedroom she hated more than Jackson. She and I were two peas of a pod.

But at least she and her mom were getting along better these days. Even still, Rach is working around the clock at the beauty shop to be able to get her own place as soon as she can.

"Why didn't you just refuse to serve him?" I asked.

She sucked on her teeth. "Please, that would be all the excuse Kathy needs to get rid of me." Kathy is the lady that owned the beauty shop she worked at.

"God forbid anyone upset her precious sheriff. If I wasn't bringing in the most clients, she would have already gotten rid of me. That just show you how the Most High works, she behind my back talking with all the rest of them heffas up there, and I'm the only one that ain't never late with my booth rent."

"What's her problem anyway?" Oaklee asked as she carried three frosty glasses brimming with watermelon margaritas into the living room as well as a pitcher with the left-over mix. *Goodness, it was going to be a long night.*

I sat up to take my glass and Oaklee took that as an invitation to squeeze herself between us on the couch.

"The crazy b*tch is jealous because Jackson is harassing me and not her."

I took a sip of my drink and cringed. "Good God, Oak! How much tequila did you use in these?"

She grinned. "Enough..." Her gaze went back to Rachel. "So, she wants the sheriff to harass her?"

"Girl, all these heffas imagine themselves in love with the Beautiful Ones."

Oaklee frowned. "And let me guess... Ashur was a Beautiful One as well?"

Both Rach and I nodded our heads. "Yep, he ran with them."

She sucked her teeth. "That's his damn problem...he

assumes I should be impressed with that. And because I'm not, he's decided to make my life hell."

Rachel waved her hand. "Consider yourself lucky. Free and me have been suffering with this crap for a long time, and I'm damn tired of it! We're not kids anymore! Who the hell does he think he is? I'm tired of him charging me for the sins of my mother." She angrily shoved her straw in and out of her drink.

"I mean, I get it, she split up their family. That's got to be tough. But why not place the blame solely on her shoulders? Or better yet, blame his dad who was going behind his mom's back sleeping with my mom. He forces me to wear her scarlet letter and that sh*t ain't fair. Kathy shouldn't worry that I'm attracted to Jackson, however, she should be worried that I might take my gun and shoot him with it!"

Because I was trained to pick up on certain things in speech patterns, I had to ask...

"Should I be worried that this is your third time threatening bodily harm on the sheriff since you got here?"

Her gaze came to mine. "I don't know, should I be worried that you've set out to humiliate one of your patients for a vendetta?"

I blinked, not prepared for such a rapid comeback. "I don't know what you're talking about."

"Oh, give it up! Oaklee already told me what's going on. She told me what you did to Tucker last Tuesday at the support group meeting."

"Oak!" I screeched. I distinctly discussed the importance of keeping my plan between her and me. I could lose my license if it ever got out.

"What? I didn't tell anybody else," she said hiding her smile behind her cup.

Rachel lifted the pitcher of margarita mix off the coffee table and poured us all a refill.

"You care to explain yourself? That is so unlike you to jeopardize your practice in such a way. So unlike you to take a risk of any kind as a matter of fact."

My mouth opened, insulted. "I take risks!"

Both she and Oaklee laughed at that, insulting me more. "Please, Free, the last risk you took was adding a spoonful of white sugar to your coffee a month ago."

Even though I didn't show it, Rachel's words hurt my feelings, mainly because they were true, but partly because there was a side of me that even my friends couldn't see. To this day, Rachel didn't know that I'd allowed Tucker to take my virginity prom night. And neither of them understood how brave and yes, risky it was to open a psychiatric office in the heart of the ghetto and try and tackle mental health among poor black folks, who had been trained their whole life to think of such things as taboo.

I took a deep drink from my cup before I spoke. "You want an explanation?" She nodded. "Okay, here it is. Last Tuesday, I watched the guy that bullied me all through high school get his ass handed to him by this kitten."

I scooped up Grapefruit from where he'd fallen asleep in my lap. "And I can't tell you how much of a healing that was to me."

Smiling, Rachel took Grapefruit out of my hand and snuggled him. Just a really quick side note, I've discovered that my kitty loves women, but will not tolerate men. Believe it or not, he already has an alpha personality and really wants to be the only male in his environment.

Isn't that amazing? LOL!

Before we could enjoy our second cocktail, my phone rang. Because I've been dodging Dillion's calls like the plague, I made sure to look at the number before answering it.

"Dammit! It's Angie." The smile left both of my friends' faces.

Rachel shook her head. "Don't answer it, she's calling to mess up my evening."

Hitting the off button, sending the call to voicemail, I tossed my phone back on the table. "You may be right. Too tired to deal with her anyway." But no sooner had I said that, my phone was ringing again.

I exhaled; Angie was on the warpath. Knowing there was no way around this, I answered.

"Where are you, young lady?" she hissed in the phone, sounding very upset.

"I'm home." I wanted to add, *where else would I be*, but thought better of it.

"Your sister's bridal party meet-and-greet dinner starts in twenty minutes! You were supposed to be here at the restaurant to help the servants get everything set up!"

How many times had I heard Angie say those words? *Free, you need to help the servants clean this and cook that. Free, for tonight, maybe you should dine in the kitchen with the servants.*

I don't know why she still pretends that I am anything other than a servant to them. Putting my drink down, I looked at my watch. *God, I really didn't feel like moving off of my couch.* But I know if I didn't, Angie would go out of her way to make my life and the life of my clients hell.

Who has a bridal party meet-and-greet dinner anyway?

I know all of those heffas and they know me. Hell, they were all Laureen's sorority sisters, so it wasn't like they didn't know each other. Who the hell was being introduced?

I exhaled…Angie has always been this way, just doing the absolute most. She looked for any excuse to rub her wealth in someone's face. Tonight, she wanted all of Laureen's sorority sisters green with envy. I've seen it too many times. It's like making people envious of her and her daughters get her high or something.

"Okay, I'll be there in twenty minutes."

"But wait! It starts in twen—" I hung up. I'll just pretend I thought the conversation was over. No way I was coming to be her f*cking servant. She can kiss my ass!

"Dammit! I knew she was going to do this!" Rachel said placing Grapefruit back on the couch. "Why did you answer the phone?"

"What? Would you had preferred for her to come to the door? Because you know that was coming next."

Oaklee sucked on her teeth. "I hate that woman."

"Yeah, join the party," I muttered as I pulled my already tired body off the couch.

"It's not worth it," Rach said shaking her head.

"What's not worth it?"

"The clinic. The funding for it… It's not worth what this woman puts you through. Your cause was and is a noble one. You've done great things for the less fortunate. But look at you. You're always tired because you're under-staffed and overbooked. You're always stressing out about how you're going to pay for this or that. You were almost free of Angie, but because of politics and red tape, now you're at her mercy even more so than when you were young, living under her roof. It's killing you, Free. It's wearing you down."

Tears burned the back of my eyes as I slid my feet into my penny loafers, but I didn't let a one of them fall. Crying wasn't going to do any good. And this was the story of my life anyway.

Rachel didn't understand the force that drove me, even more so now that I've found out my grandmother was the devil incarnate. The whole world is suffering because there are more people taking than there are giving. I'm not alright with that. God just didn't make me that way.

"Yeah, well, somebody has to do it." I pinned her with my gaze. "If not me...then who?"

When after a moment she couldn't answer my question, I grabbed my car keys off the table.

"You guys are more than welcome to crash here. I'll talk to you in the morning."

———

"I'M SO sorry you and Dillion didn't work out... But it's good he and Laureen were able to find happiness, huh?"

I smiled as I chewed on the stiffest romaine lettuce I'd ever tasted. It felt like it was shredding the top of my mouth.

"Yeah, good thing," I muttered to a Laureen look-a-like. In fact, all twelve of the bridesmaids outside of me were Laureen look-a-likes. I remember when she and Layla pledged Sigma Phi Rho, the both of them took great pleasure in telling me that the sorority would never pledge someone *like me*.

I could then sit and wonder why Laureen would then

go out of her way to have someone *like me* in her wedding, who was clearly the complete opposite of her and her friends and not to mention the small fact that I am her future husband's ex. But then I would be wasting my time because I already knew the answer. Everybody knew the answer.

Angie and her offspring wanted to see me suffer.

They've always wanted me to suffer. And just like I've always done, I refuse to give them the satisfaction of knowing that their little antics were getting to me. So I smiled at Tracy just like I smiled at her other friends who gave me their condolences for getting my boyfriend stolen by my sister and pretended that it was no big deal.

But deep inside, I was wishing with all my might to be anywhere else on the earth than here, especially when Angie dressed to the nines in a cream Lela Rose guipure lace dress, sashayed over to the table she'd stashed me, in back of all the others.

"Free, can you be a dear and run along and let Chef know we're ready to set up the dessert buffet?"

I exhaled before lifting my wine glass and taking a sip. "No, I'm not going to do that. However, I'm sure one of the lovely waitstaff of this exquisite establishment would be honored to do so. We know that someone with your impeccable taste would never grace a venue with waitstaff that is not of the topmost echelon of waitstaff."

Yeah, I know…It sounded just as stupid to my ears. But I've had years of dealing with Angie, trust me, she basks in any compliment sent her way. Typical narcissistic behavior.

The trick is to speak to her in a quiet calm voice without a lick of attitude in my tone while giving a very sincere look.

"Careful, little sister, one would think you were feeling bitter about Laureen's happiness," Layla said sliding next to her mother. Now Layla on the other hand, has always been an instigating snake.

I smiled. "Oh no, big sis, I'm overjoyed that Laureen has found the love of her life. What Dillion and I had was clearly a four-year phase. Good thing we figured it out before it got too far gone. I would prefer to see Laureen happy than live in misery."

B*tch!

"Will you have a date for the rehearsal dinner or shall I put you down for one," Angie gushed with a devious smile on her pretty face.

"How soon will I have to let you know?"

"Preferably by the time the invitations go out."

I nodded. "Got it! I will let you know by that time…"

And because God is merciful, my phone chose right then to light up, signifying that I'd just received a text.

"Excuse me," I told them as I hurried away from the table.

*The Bully: Help, Doc, I'm on the ledge. I have a Bob Marley size spliff and I'm trying to talk myself out of lighting it. I need you! Meet me at the old pier. Please come quick! I---can't---hold on----much---looonger!"*

I put my hand over my mouth to hide my smile. He is such an asshole. But right now, he's a lifesaver.

*Me: Hold on, buddy! I'm on my way! Whatever you do, don't light the Bob Marley size spliff!"*

When I turned back to the table, the smile was gone from my face. If Angie had one inkling that something had actually made me laugh, she would set out to change that.

"I'm so sorry, guys, a patient of mine is on the ledge. I

have to go and talk him down." Angie's eyes flashed with anger, but I ignored it as I grabbed my purse from the chair I'd been sitting in.

My gaze went to Laureen's friends who sat at my table. "So sorry, duty calls."

"No, I completely understand. My husband's a doctor. He gets called away all the time." Kristy, or was it Mary, said.

"Lay, can you give my apologies to Laur?"

"Really, Free, this couldn't wait till after the dinner's over," she snapped instead of answering my question.

"No, sweetheart, you can always guarantee most emergencies happen at the most inopportune times. Bye, guys... I'll see you at the rehearsal dinner." As I hurried away, I could feel Angie's hateful gaze boring a hole in my back.

# Chapter 7

DANGEROUS SITUATIONS

---

*Fighting The Enemy In Him Was Easy, It Was Fighting The Enemy Within Myself That Posed The Problem...*

---

## Free

I'D BEEN SO desperate to leave the bridal party meet and greet dinner that I'd readily agreed to meet Tucker at the old pier. But as I stepped out of my car in the parking lot that was empty of every vehicle except mine and his, I realized that I may have put myself in a very dangerous situation.

This is the same abandoned stretch of beach where he'd taken my virginity prom night. I had to forcibly swallow the anger that tried to bubble up to the surface at the painful memory of that. But there was another feeling I was surprised that I needed to fight. It was the same feeling I had that night.

*Anticipation…*

It was something in the air. The moon set full and big over Lake Michigan, casting its beautiful glow on the water, just like it did the night Tucker made love to me. Yes, there was definitely something in the air.

The buzz from the crickets seemed gentle, their song soothing rather that antagonizing. Although I was on the lake, there were no mosquitoes or flies buzzing around my head. A gentle breeze blew, causing my silk blouse to caress my overheated flesh.

Panicking, I put my hand on my car door. I had to get out of here. No way I could do this. But right then my phone rang from my purse nearly scaring the heck out of me. With hands that shook, I took it out and was not surprised to see that it was Naphtali.

"Hello." I pray he didn't hear the fear in my voice.

"Come on, Freebie, I'm waiting for you, baby. Don't be a scaredy-cat." Dammit! Even his baritone sounded especially good tonight.

"Where are you?" I asked, my hand still on my door.

"Down here by the boat."

Standing on my toes, I looked down the pier and my mouth formed an O when I saw Tucker standing there looking edible next to a beautiful boat. As magnificent as the boat was, it paled in comparison to the powerful bowlegged brotha that stood next to it. He lifted his hand and casually waved me to him.

My teeth bit down harder on my lower lip. The alarm system inside my head was blaring loudly.

*Danger! Run, girl! That chocolate Adonis down there is*

*dangerous. The last time you were here with him he'd been a boy. He ain't a boy no more! You go down there, he's going to get you! Run!*

No way was I supposed to be here in this moment with my enemy.

No way!

"I'm not doing it..." I didn't care how much of a coward I looked. It was better to be a coward than to go down there and be conquered, at least that was my motto. Taking my phone back out of my purse, I pressed the green call button by his name.

I could see him shaking his head chuckling as he answered his phone. *Please, Tucker, have mercy on me and let me get in my car and drive away.*

"Hey, Doc."

"Hey, ummm, something just came up. I'm going to have to talk to you and drive, is that okay?"

"Sure, Doc." He casually reached into his pocket and pulled something out of it before sliding it between his lips. Seconds later, his handsome face lit up as a flame touched whatever it was in his mouth.

"What are you doing?!" I screeched. At this point, my nerves were a wreck.

"Nothing..." I could hear him inhaling as he spoke.

"You know I can see you, right?"

He chuckled. "Then hurry up and get in your car so that you can't."

I felt like throwing a tantrum like a child. "Tucker! That defeats the purpose!" Yeah, I was whining.

"Well, Doc, I told you I was on the ledge. You said you would be here to help me, but you wasn't, so now I'm smoking. Sorry, I'm just not that strong."

"Fine! If I come down there, will you put the joint out?"

"Mmmhhhmmm…," he muttered slowly before sending a cloud of smoke in the air. Like the devil, I could feel him studying me through the smoke.

*Okay! Okay… you can do this. You are a doctor. You took an oath to help people like him. You're going to go down there and just have a little chat. Give him a few words of encouragement and then you're going to leave.*

*Simple!*

*But what you're not going to do, and I mean absolutely not, is sleep with him! Not going to happen! I don't care if you haven't been sexually fulfilled since the last time he touched you or that there was a great chance the man Tucker was a way better lover than the boy Tucker had been.*

And the boy Tucker had not been bad, let me tell y'all…

*No! That is beside the point! You're going to go down there and be a doctor and not a hoochie.*

I nodded my head as I wiped my palms down my tweed skirt. "Got it!"

And with that, I squared my shoulders and made my way down to the pier. I felt strong. I felt like I could do this. All I had to do was remember the pain of him taking my virginity and then abandoning me.

Yeah! That did it….

That did it for all of seven seconds. The closer I got to him and the more of him I took in; I was beginning to have serious doubts. He stood there looking mouth-watering in a pair of gray jeans, gray boots, and a gray tank top that left all those beautiful chocolate muscles on display.

Goodness! Whew! Okay…stay focused.

"Doc, what's going on? You're looking more tense than

usual?" he asked when I got within hearing distance. But his slick behind was still taking pulls off that joint.

"I thought we had an agreement, I come down and you put out the joint."

"Yeah, but you're not here yet," he said with a grin on his face as he blew out a mouth full of smoke. Narrowing my eyes, I closed the gap between us.

Holding out my arms, I hissed. "I'm here."

He grinned again, but it was the grin the wolf wore when he spotted Little Red coming with her basket.

"Yes…you are." His gaze raked over my body as he inhaled one last mouth full of the joint before tossing it. "A deal's a deal…" When he spoke, smoke escaped his mouth.

"Well, since you've smoked already, I guess you don't need me."

He reached in his pocket and pulled out a blunt before his sexy gaze came back to mine. "I need you, Freebie."

*Dear God, give me the strength. This man should not be this gorgeous…*

I held out my hand for the blunt. Casually he lay it in my palm. Without looking away from him, I slung it into the water.

"Now… what can we do to take your mind off getting high?"

He was giving me that wolf grin again. I returned his smile as I folded my arms waiting on him to say something that was going to make me turn around and march right back to my car.

"Fishing."

*Ooookay…not what I expected.*

"Fishing?"

"Yeah, I like to fish to take my mind off things. You fish?"

I shook my head. "Never."

His mouth opened in surprise. "You've never been fishing, Freebie?"

Because he was high as a kite, his tone of voice was actually pretty goofy and made me chuckle. And yeah... relax a bit. I don't know, he just didn't feel that dangerous while he was high. It's the darnedest thing.

"No, I've never been."

"Well...we have to do something about that." He put his hand on his stomach and bowed a bit. "May I invite you to a late-night fishing trip?"

"Can you fish at night?"

"Sure...it's the best time." My gaze went to his boat. Like him, it was big, dark, and beautiful, all sleek lines and gold trims.

"You're going to think I'm joking, but I've never been on a boat either."

He shook his head before holding out his hand for mine. "We have to do something about that, please allow me to escort you aboard *The Naphtali*."

I chuckled. "You named your boat after yourself?"

"Actually, my dad named it when he gifted it to me on my seventeenth birthday."

"Your dad bought you a boat when you turned seventeen?" I asked as I took his hand and allowed him to escort me onto it.

He chuckled. "All that glitter ain't gold, Free."

My gaze rose to his. The doctor in me wanted to explore that statement. But then I reminded myself that this was my bully and I killed the impulse. I will never allow Tucker to hurt me again. He's hurt me worse than anybody else in the world and he won't get another chance.

So, instead, I turned away to look around the beautiful gift he'd received on his seventeenth birthday. I wasn't lying to him; I'd never been on a boat. I didn't have that kind of childhood. My mother managed to keep a roof over our heads, which was amazing, considering her addiction. But we didn't have much money for anything else, which a lot of times included food. If my father and Angie went out on a boat, they'd never taken me. And by the time I was in college, I was too busy trying to graduate with honors to do anything fun.

"What do you think?" Tucker asked me as he guided me around, giving me a little tour of the place.

"It's lovely!"

The cabin resembled a luxury studio that was big enough to house a king-size bed that sat up off the floor on a dais. Whoever decorated really had an eye. They kept with the black and gold motif of the boat, from the expensive bedding to the couch...even the kitchen cabinets were made of black wood. I wonder if it had been decorated like this when he was seventeen. It seemed kind of mature for a teen.

Just outside the sliding doors of the cabin was a deck with a small dining area that overlooked the water. I stood looking out at the moonlight on the lake as he prepared the boat for sailing. When he was finished, he took my hand and led me up a set of stairs to the helm.

"Wow!" I cried as I watched him start the engine. "You're the captain too?"

"I'm the captain too, baby."

"And have you been driving boats since you were seventeen?"

"I've been steering boats since I was fourteen."

"Oh, my goodness! That's amazing…" I gave him a playful punch in the arm. "I did not know that about you, Mean Tuck."

He chuckled as he turned the big wheel, guiding us farther out into the lake. "Oh, Freebie, there are so many things you don't know about me."

I took the time to admire his powerful profile as he drove. I bet there were a lot of things about him I didn't know.

"How does one get to know their bully?" I didn't mean to ask that out loud.

His gaze came to mine. "By seeing him…"

I opened my mouth to ask him what the hell he meant by that. It's something he often said when we were kids. But I changed my mind. I didn't want to know. I didn't want to see him. I wanted to torture him to help myself heal and then I wanted to see him leave after this year was up.

I walked over to the railing and looked out at the beautiful night as he drove, holding my head back to let the wind whip past my face, wishing I could let my hair down. God, it's been a long day.

Heck, it's been a long week… Who was I kidding? I've had a long life.

At some point, it was supposed to get easier. As a child coming up in Angie's house, I thought that my life would somehow get easier when I became an adult and was no longer under her tyrannical rule, but it only got harder. Just one damn problem after another.

Rachel said the stress was killing me. And maybe she's right, stress is a hell of a thing, and worked havoc on the body. But at this point, I didn't know how to live a life without it.

Naphtali

SHE WAS SO DAMN BEAUTIFUL. She took my breath away. I watched her lean on the rail holding her head back, enjoying the breeze and wondered what she was thinking. No doubt she was stressing over some sh*t.

The girl in the yellow dress had been replaced by a tense doctor. As God is my witness, when she steps foot off this boat tonight...or tomorrow, she was going to be good and relaxed. I would make sure of that.

Hell, I can use some unwinding myself. I wasn't lying when I told her I was on the ledge. I may have been lying when I told her I was fighting with myself over smoking though.

I got a call from my captain today. After inquiring about my drug counseling and telling me the whole team was missing me, he dropped a bomb in my lap.

"Hey, Nap, keep your eyes open. Marcellus's kid brother, Rau was spotted in Miami yesterday. I've got eyes on him, but my sources say he's here inquiring about his brother's death. You need me to send Harry to Detroit to wait the year out with you?"

"Naw, Cap, don't do that to him. What kind of partner would I be to force him to live this hell out with me?"

"Hell, my ass. I saw a pic of your doctor. The team has

a wager going of how long it's going to take you to get her in bed."

"Wow! I leave and everybody stops working. Don't you bums have better things to do than to be snooping around in my love life?"

"Wait! Love?"

"Bye, Cap..."

"Wait, kid, did you say love?"

"Bye, Cap..."

"Hey, pay up! The kid's in love... I told you it was bound to happen," I heard him say before the line went dead.

Shaking my head at my squad's immaturity, I hung up the phone but sat for a minute, thinking on his reason for calling. Marcellus was a mean son-of-a-b*tch that died at the hands of the Bully. During the two years that I spent undercover with his gang, I'd seen some sick sh*t. These bastards are the kind of mutha f*ckas that skinned niggas before wrapping their bodies in barbwire and hanging them in their grandmother's front yard like butchered meat just to make an example out of them. In America and Argentina, they were known for their brutality.

For two years, I walked in the form of the Bully. It was the only way I was able to get in as deep as I did. Evil recognized Evil. Marcellus loved my alter. For the first time, he'd met a mutha f*cka more ruthless than him. But in those two years, I was scared to death that I was going to lose myself completely.

It felt too good walking in the Bully's shoes. It felt good not giving a f*ck. But there has always been something inside of me that told me the Bully was f*cked up and I had to keep fighting to hold onto my humanity. In those two years, I had to get away every now and again to allow myself to be me, if only for a few days.

And now the captain said Marcellus's kid brother was here from Argentina asking questions. It's not that I was worried that they would find me. With the things they'd seen the Bully do, they would never suspect me of being a cop, so they will never think to look in that direction. But I still didn't like taking any chances. The cartel had a way of finding sh*t out.

Tomorrow, I was going to holla at Jackson and Asher; I needed more eyes on Free. Now that she was back in my life, if anything was to ever happen to her, I'm afraid of what I would become. I'm afraid of what would be released into the world. There would be no coming back for me because I wouldn't rest till every member of their family met the same fate. EVERY F*CKING MEMBER!

———

FREE

"OH, my goodness! I can't believe you've caught another fish!"

We've been sitting on the deck at the back of the boat for a little over an hour. And in that time, Tucker had already caught two fish. After driving us out farther into the lake, he killed the engine and prepared both of our poles with bait before situating them in two slots that he'd built at the back of the boat so that we can fish hands-free. But it seemed that the fish only liked his pole because they hadn't so much as grazed mine.

He chuckled as he unhooked the fish from the bait. "It's because you're sitting up there so stiff. The fish can sense your anxiety."

"That's not true...is it?"

He nodded before gesturing towards me. "Look at the way you're sitting up there, no way the fish are going to come anywhere near you. You have to relax. Why don't you come down here and sit by me?" He patted the spot on the step just above the one he sat on.

It was true, I felt a little stiff. He'd taken off his boots and rolled up his pants so that his feet and legs could hang in the water. I sat in one of the chairs at the little table still fully clothed.

He patted the step again. "Come on, Freebie, kick off your shoes and put your feet in the water."

"Naw, that's okay. I have on tights."

He frowned. "What the hell...What are you, six? Tights? And what the f*ck is with the penny loafers?"

I looked down at my shoes. "What's wrong with my loafers? They're reliable."

Chuckling he shook his head. "I take that back. You're eighty..."

"Am not!"

He nodded. "Yeah, you are...You're an old square."

I told myself I wasn't going to let him get under my skin like he used to do in high school, but I was failing miserably. His words were upsetting me, mainly because they were reminiscent of something Rachel said earlier.

"Just because I wear tights and penny loafers doesn't mean I'm a square!" I hissed.

"Well, prove it. Come down here and put your feet in the water."

I slammed my empty beer bottle on the table and stood, kicking off my shoes. "You think you're so cool..." I muttered as I reached under my skirt and rolled my tights down my legs.

"News flash! I never thought you were that cool!" I continued. He turned so that he could have a better view of me taking off my tights. Lifting his own beer bottle, he drank deeply as his heated gaze followed their journey down my legs.

My body responded to his look in a way that took my breath for a moment. Too late I wished that I hadn't let him bait me into doing this in front of him. Straightening my skirt, I folded my tights and tucked them in my shoe.

"There...not square at all!" I told him as I sat on the step just above him and eased my feet into the water. But it was so cold I screeched and pulled them back out.

"It's cold!"

"Here, let me help you."

His big warm hand wrapped around my right foot and he pulled it over his leg into his lap before lowering it into the water. I screeched again and started to jerk it back out, however, he started doing something that caused me to pause.

Oh my God! He was rubbing my feet!

"What are you doing?!" My voice was laced with panic.

"Rubbing your feet."

"Why?"

"Why not? Just chill and let me warm them for you. Or are you too square to chill?"

I frowned at him. "I know how to chill."

"Well then, chill..."

"Fine..."

151

I sat back and forced myself to appear relaxed, but then something happened. After about a minute of him massaging my foot, I really began to relax. And after two minutes, I was in heaven. My feet had been sore because I'd been on them all day, and now...and now...

*Oh God! It felt so good.*

He was really good at this. When he pulled my other leg into his lap and began to massage it, I closed my eyes and moaned.

"Mmmmm, that feels so good, Mean Tuck."

His hands stopped and my eyes flew open. "Why did you sto—" I began, but my words came to the halt when I saw the look on his face. I'd done something wrong.

"What's the matter?"

"Are you f*cking kidding me?" he growled.

I tried to pull my legs out of his lap, but he wouldn't let me. "What did I do?" I asked instead.

"You can't moan like that and say that sh*t and then just expect me to remain on good behavior."

I bit my lip to keep from smiling. "What are you talking about?"

"Really, Free, you think it's safe to play games with me?"

"Okay!" I laughed. "I'm sorry...I won't do it again."

He grinned. "You won't do what again?"

"I won't moan and say how good what you're doing feels."

"Hmmmm....we'll see." And then he went back to rubbing my feet.

I stared at the side of his head. "What does that mean?"

"Shhh...enjoy the massage."

He thinks he's so slick. But my feet hurt too much not

to sit back and do what he said. The way I figured, rubbing my feet was the least he could do to pay me for all the hell he'd put me through.

"When's the last time your man rubbed your feet?" he asked as he drizzled another handful of water over my right foot before wrapping his strong hand around my sole and massaging it.

I was feeling so good at this moment that I didn't want to ruin it talking about Dillion, so I didn't answer him.

"Answer me, baby," he urged me gently. I exhaled, leave it to Tucker to push the envelope anyway.

"If I had a man, do you think I would be here letting you rub my feet?" I muttered, feeling more relaxed than I've felt in a long time.

"What's up with Dillion old p*ssy ass?"

I chuckled. "Nothing at all…He's marrying my sister in a few months."

"That dude has always been a b*tch. I hated his ass in school."

It was true. Mean Tuck picked on me, but sometimes it felt that he was trying to kill Dillion. Senior year, I'd mercifully been spared of having gym with Naphtali, but that year, Dillion had not been so lucky. Tucker fractured his arm the first week during a game of touch football. He told the gym teacher he forgot they were just playing touch football and thought he was in football practice.

All the students that saw Mean Tuck tackle Dillion said that he'd hit him so hard, they thought Dillion had died. He laid on the ground unconscious for a full minute before the gym teacher could revive him. And then there was the time Dillion and I were walking down the hall and Tucker had come out of nowhere to catch a football that Jackson threw to him. His back slammed into Dillion, sending him flying across the hallway to crash face-first into the lockers. He'd broken his nose in the fall and had to wear a nose brace for nearly a month.

"You still love him?" Tucker asked as he continued to work his magic on my feet.

I thought about his question. *Did I still love Dillion? I know that I should.* Up till a few weeks ago, I thought we had a pretty good relationship. It has crossed my mind that I should be more broken up about the fact that he was marrying my sister, but I wasn't. And I'm afraid the reason is because I never really loved him.

"No…I don't think that I do," I told him, shaking my head.

"Good, I would hate to have to f*ck him up."

Before I could address him, my fishing rod jerked. My eyes flew open as I reached for it to prevent it from being snatched into the water.

"Oh, my God! I caught something! What do I do?!" I cried as the rod began to jerk like crazy.

"Reel it in, bae!" Tucker said as he reached over and helped me reel in my line.

I was so excited I could barely sit still. When we finally got it reeled in, I was amazed by the size of it.

Tucker whistled. "This bad boy has to be about five pounds…Good job, Freebie! I'm proud of you, girl."

With a huge grin on my face, I clapped my hands together. I was proud of me too. "What kind of fish is it?"

"Smallmouth bass," he said as he got busy taking the hook out of the fish's mouth.

"What are we going to do with it?" I was now on my knees with my hands resting on his shoulder, subconsciously hiding behind him from my huge fish that was wiggling angrily in his hands.

"We're going to cook it."

My mouth opened in shock. "Cook it?!"

"Yeah…"

"I don't know how to cook a real fish."

He looked back at me with a grin on his face. "What kind of fish do you eat if not real fish?"

I punched his shoulder. "You know what I mean. I don't know how to clean it and cut it…"

He jerked his head toward the deck. "Come on, I'll show you how."

Disappearing in the cabin, he reappeared a second later with newspaper in his hand that he laid out on the deck before pulling a pocketknife out of his jeans. Squatting down, he began to scrape the scales off the fish. Being careful to keep my skirt decent, I sat down on the deck floor next to him.

"How did you learn how to do that?" I asked, completely fascinated by what he was doing.

"After my dad gifted me with this boat, I practically lived on it. This stretch of beach has always been my favorite place. One night I got hungry and decided to go fishing. After I caught the fish, I realized I had no f*cking idea what to do with it. So, I watched a YouTube video."

*A YouTube video!*

I blinked at him before erupting in laughter. I had not expected him to say that.

"Oh my God, Tuck. I thought you were getting ready to say something deep like an old man sitting on a log floating in the middle of the lake showed me how."

He chuckled, shaking his head as he began to gut the fish. "Nope...Good old-fashioned YouTube."

He was so efficient with what he was doing that I just sat in silence watching his strong hands flex as he scaled and gutted all three of the fish. He reminded me of one of the surgeons that worked at the hospital where I'd done my clinicals. I forget his name, but whenever he performed surgery, I would watch his big strong hands, fascinated that they were able to move so efficiently.

"How do you touch the guts and organs without gloves?" I asked.

"Awww, you don't need gloves. It's just a little fish blood." He picked up a hand full of the bloody intestines and tossed it at me.

I screamed at the top of my lungs as I tried to prevent the bloody organs from ruining my clothes, but in my panic, ended up only making it worse and getting fish guts all over my blouse and skirt. There was even some juice on my face and glasses.

I sat there staring at him with my mouth opened in shock. He wore a look of amused horror on his face.

"Damn, Free! I'm so sorry...You were supposed to catch it, not play volleyball with it and get it all over your clothes."

"What is wrong with you?! Why are you such a jerk?!" I screeched, close to tears.

He shook his head fighting to hold on to his laughter. "I don't know why I did that. There is something wrong with me, I think you're right. You've been right all these years."

All that he said while laughing, and of course it took the sincerity away from his apology. I looked down just as a heart dropped down my blouse to land in my lap. Right on the verge of tears, my gaze came back to his.

"Oh no, baby, don't cry," he said shooting to his feet, helping me up. "Here, you can take a shower while I cook the fish for us. I'm so sorry, Freebie. I am a jerk…it's true."

He led me into the cabin. "I'm going to make the best fish you've ever tasted."

That made me chuckle. "Can you cook?"

"Oh yeah, on our days off, all the fellas on my team come over to my place to watch the game and eat some of my famous chili." He stopped at his dresser to take out clothes for me.

"Will you look at that," I told him, still very angry he'd just ruined my nice clothes. "All this time I thought your only talent was destroying things and beating people up."

Yeah, that was a low blow and outright mean, but I didn't care. He always seemed to bring the *best* out of me.

"Damn, Freebie…that hurt my feelings," he said as he began to crowd my space. For every step he took forward, I took one back until the door prevented me from going any farther. I sucked in my breath as he came to a stop within inches of me. Our chests were nearly touching. As if they had a will of their own, my eyes lowered to his lips. Memories of all the times he'd grabbed me and ravished my mouth in high school came to mind and all the anger I'd just felt melted away to be replaced by something else.

Those were dangerous thoughts…them paired with his delicious smell and muscled strength standing so close were affecting my body in a way that had those alarm bells ringing. *I wonder if he could feel my heart racing.*

His gaze took its time roaming over my face, studying it like he used to do when we were in school. This was the same way he looked at me that day in the cafeteria when my skirt flew up. No man has ever looked at me this way.

No...not one.

When I was a girl, I didn't understand this look. But now that I'm a woman, I knew—no, better yet, my body knew what this look meant. His hungry gaze settled on my lips and I nervously licked them, wondering if he was going to kiss me. And then I wondered if I would stop him.

I gasped when he reached up and used his big finger to gently wipe fish guts off my cheek. "Yes, I'm really good at smashing sh*t. But if you take the time to see me, you may just find out I'm a brotha with many talents."

His arm circled my waist, pulling me against his strong body while his other hand went to the knob on the door behind me, opening it.

"This is the bathroom, take your time. Yell if you need anything." And then he stepped back, removing his arm from around my waist. I felt the loss instantly...and I didn't like it.

He took several steps back still holding my gaze captive, another thing he's always been able to do since high school. In his eyes, I saw things that his lips would never say. And it was only when he turned to walk out of the cabin, breaking the eye contact that I was able to blink or even breathe for that matter.

# Chapter 8

## HE'S FULL OF SURPRISES

Free

"MMMMM! Tuck, this fish is so good."

He chuckled. "See? There you go moaning again."

"I can't help it. This really is the best fish I've ever eaten."

It was, guys. I can't believe he can cook this well, as a matter of fact, I can't believe how relaxed and content I felt in the presence of my nemesis. After taking a nice long shower to wash off all the fish guts the maniac threw on me, I slid into the pair of sweatpants he'd given me and the t-shirt. Of course, everything was too big, but it was comfortable.

When I walked out of the bathroom, the heavenly scent of the well-seasoned dish that greeted me took me off guard. Needing to see with my own eyes that yes, this was Mean Tucker, bully extraordinaire and an all-around asshole standing at his stove creating art. I carefully approached him.

He was sautéing what looked like bok choy with onion and red peppers…fresh garlic.

"That smells heavenly," I told him.

"Thank you. Go ahead and grab us two more beers out the fridge, this is just about done."

I grabbed the beers and brought them out to the table on the deck. Shortly after, he followed with the plates. Between the beers, the foot massage, the hot shower, the comfy sweats, and the good food, I was feeling like I was actually winding down from a hectic week.

After we finished eating, neither of us was in a rush to move, we just continued to sip our beers, enjoying the lake. I can see why this was his favorite place when he was younger. I remembered when he first brought me here, I was surprised because I didn't know this little hidden gem existed.

*Wow, what does it mean that he brought you to his getaway pla—*

You know what…What does it matter? I quickly shut that voice off. Subject change please…

"Okay, now I'm curious. What other hidden talents do you have?" I asked him instead. The man was continuing to surprise me. That fish he'd just made could have been showcased at a 5-star restaurant. I truly only thought he was good at one thing…brutality. Who knew he was a well-rounded brotha?

He turned to me with a lifted eyebrow. I laughed…his mind had gone straight to the gutter. There goes the Tucker I remembered. And as to prove my point, he licked his lips as his eyes lowered to my lap.

"Not that, dirty man, I already know you're good at that..." Too late I snapped my lips shut.

*Oh*

*My*

*God!*

*I can't believe I'd just said that!*

Taking my glasses off, I wiped away an imaginary spot with my napkin to cover up my embarrassment. Damn beer had me speaking my mind too freely...

He grinned. "You know I'm good at what?"

"I'm not answering that," I told him, easing my glasses back on my face. "You know what I meant. What other talents do you have that's not X-rated?"

He turned to face me fully, the devious look still on his face. For some reason, it felt like this position brought him closer. I didn't make eye contact with him, instead, I continued to look out at the water. I'm telling you guys, I am so glad for my dark skin because I was blushing like crazy right now.

"Which one of my talents did you enjoy best that night? 'Cause I can assure you, I've improved a great deal. Was it when I kissed your lips or your neck?" As he spoke, his hungry gaze fell from my lips to my neck. "Was it when I ran my tongue across your bellybutton, enjoying the texture of your soft skin."

He leaned closer. "Or was it when I spread your legs and buried my face in between your---"

"Tucker!" I squeaked stopping him. And of course, the fact that he'd ruffled my feathers amused him greatly.

Chuckling he relaxed back in his chair. Against my will, my eyes lowered to his muscled abs that looked amazing in that gray tank top.

"Alright, little Freebie, I won't pick on you. Hmmm… what other talent do I have?"

"And it can't be anything violent. We know you're good at that too."

He thought for a minute. "I can sing."

It was my turn to chuckle. "No, you can't."

"Yeah, I can…"

*Oh, this is exciting!* I scooted my chair closer to him. "Go ahead, let me hear something."

He gave me the side-eye. "Really? You can't just take my word for it?"

I shook my head. "Absolutely not. You know folks always lying about knowing how to sing."

He looked down at the beer bottle in his hand, and I could see him contemplating within himself whether he should sing for me.

"Come on, Mean Tuck…sing for me."

He lifted his beer and drained it before sitting up in his seat. "F*ck it."

I had to bite my lip to keep from cheesing. Although I was excited to hear him sing, there was a part of me that didn't think he could do it. Imagining him of all people carrying a tune was just not something I ever done.

He cleared his throat before turning to look at me, and then guys…he opened his mouth and surprised the hell out of me.

*It's like I missed the shot,*
*It's like I dropped the ball,*
*Damn, I'm sorry,*

OH WOW!

He *can* sing…

He can really sing and was belting out, Ruben Studdard's *Sorry* better than freaking Ruben Studdard. This song was my jam back in the day.

> *It's like I'm on stage,*
> *And I forgot the words.*
> *Damn, I'm sorry,*
> *It's like building a new house,*
> *With no roof and no doors.*
> *Damn, I'm sorry,*

SO, do you guys remember my defense strategy I told you all about when I was walking towards this boat? Yeah, well, those walls began to crumble brick by brick faster than I could catch them. He was singing to me. He'd chosen this song to tell me something he hasn't been able to. And Dear God, I wasn't going to make it.

> *It's like trying to propose,*
> *And I ain't got the ring.*
> *Oooh, damn, I'm sorry,*

STANDING FROM HIS CHAIR, he gently pulled me out of mine before wrapping his arms around my waist, bringing me closer. The whole time, his eyes held mine in that gaze that hypnotized me. I had fallen completely under his spell; whatever he willed, I knew that I would do.

> *But girl, I've apologized*
> *A million times before.*

HE HIT THAT NOTE! Oh, my goodness! He was breaking me down swiftly. This wasn't fair. It was not enough that he is the most beautiful specimen I've ever laid eyes on, but he had the voice of an angel. It wasn't fair.

> *So here it comes again, for all the wrong I've done.*
> *Here's one million one.*

WE BEGAN to sway gently to the song he weaved around us…

> *It's like stayin' out at night,*
> *Had way too much to drink.*
> *Damn, I'm sorry*
> *It's like you change your hair,*
> *And I don't say a thing.*

*Damn, I'm sorry.*
*It's like we're fallin' fast asleep,*
*With no kiss, and before we hit.*
*Yeah, I'm sorry.*
*And it's like I forgot your gift,*
*On 07 01 03.*
*Damn, so sorry!*

HE CHANGED the lyrics to July 1… That was my birthday. He knew my birthday.

*But girl, I've apologized*
*A million times before.*
*So here it comes again*
*For all the wrong I've done.*
*Here's one million one.*

HIS BEAUTIFUL VOICE trailed off and we just stood staring into each other's eyes. I was so gone, but the words he spoke next only sealed the deal.

"I DON'T CARE if it takes me apologizing for the rest of my life, I'm willing to do that. I just want you to forgive me, Free, I was stu—" I put my finger on his lips, cutting him off before standing on my toes, replacing my finger with my lips.

At this point, I was past talking. His singing had been my weakness and I wanted him. I wanted him to make me feel good. It had been so long since I felt good.

That was all the urging he needed. His big hands palmed the sides of my face and he took over the kiss, ravishing my mouth as if he was a starving man and I was his drink.

"Damn, baby, I've wanted to do that since I first laid eyes on you again," he muttered in between kisses. "I missed stealing kisses from you."

When his hungry mouth latched on to my neck, he awakened something inside of me that has lain dormant for fifteen years.

*Passion...*

I was not broken. Dillion called me cold, but there was my heat. There it was... And it was true, only Tuck could turn it on.

I wrapped my arms around his neck, bringing his lips back to mine. I know that I should be stopping this; it could be catastrophic for my career. Sleeping with a patient was the number one sin in my profession. Yet at this moment, I would risk anything to continue to feel alive. And the fact is...he is the only man that can make me feel this way. I wanted him so badly I was nearly climbing him like a tree. His masculinity was like a drug and I was addicted.

That night I learned something about myself. I am an *extremely* passionate woman, and I have needs that if gone too long without being fulfilled, turned me into something of a savage. I don't know if I pushed him back in the chair or if he sat down, all I know is I ended up straddling his lap, kissing his lips, his neck...

He pulled back and I think I may have growled at him. "Grrrrhhh!"

Biting his lip, he grinned in that sexy way that he does. I tried to kiss him again, but he only pushed me back a bit.

"Tucker!" This was too much. The bastard! How could he get my engines going like this only to stop? I swear I will never talk to him again.

"What do you want, Free?"

"I want you to finish what you started."

He nodded. "I will, baby. I promise to give you everything that you need. But I need you to do something for me first."

"What?"

"Take the f*cking bun out of your hair. I hate it..."

That made me smile as I reached up and pulled the pins out of my hair. "Why do you hate my bun?"

"It hides your hair. I've always loved your hair."

"Really? You sure did pull it a lot." Tossing the pins on the table, I pulled off the oversized scrunchie I used to keep it in a tight ball. As soon as I did, my heavy braid fell on my shoulder.

He reached up and helped me undo the braid before running his big hands through it, ruffling it up until it was a cloud around my head and shoulders. When he was done, he took my glasses off my face and placed them on the table next to the pins.

Sitting back in the chair he took me in. "There she is..."he whispered. "There's the girl that haunted my dreams for the last fifteen years. The girl in the yellow dress."

He brought his hand up and gently gathered a fist full of my hair in it before bringing his mouth so close to my ear the heat from his soft lips caused my eyes to shutter close.

"I'm going to pull your hair again, Freebie," he whispered before his fist tightened in my hair, it wasn't to the point of pain, but it did cause me to gasp. And that's when his mouth took mine and he kissed me in a way that made my toes curl.

I moaned, trying not to be consumed by him, but it did no good. He consumed me, and I willingly gave myself to him. I can't tell if it was he who reached for my shirt or me, but I can tell you it came off and my bra soon followed.

"Let me see...Let me see them," he said, pushing me back so that he could see my breasts. Embarrassed, I palmed them, hiding myself. I am a full-figured woman. My breasts were not how he remembered them in high school.

"Why are you hiding yourself from me?" he asked, frowning up at me.

"Why do you need to see them?"

He didn't answer right away. He just stared at me shaking his head a bit. "You still don't get it, do you?"

"Get what?"

"How much I desire you. How much I've always desired you... Don't hide from me, girl. I want to see every inch of you. Taste every inch of you..."

Biting my lips, I eased my hands away, allowing the plump globes to spill out. The need that appeared in his eyes ignited the fire inside of me. He carefully lifted my breasts in his strong hands, weighing them, squeezing them... a growl left his throat before his arm shot around my back, pulling me towards his hungry mouth. When his lips closed around my quivering nipple, I cried out as what felt like electricity shot from my breast to my center.

Clutching his head, I held him to me as his hands came to my waist and began to slowly rotate, causing my soft heat to rub against his hardness. The fire that he ignited was turning into a raging blaze in my core; my need was so intense it was blinding.

I can't believe that I was already so close. My muscles began to tense as my body prepared for a release, and right when I thought I was going to burst, his mouth pulled away from my breast with a pop and his hardness left the cushion of my warmth.

I wanted to yell at him, my fists were balled in his tank top, holding him to me. But he stood with me in his arms, displaying his strength and slowly lowered me to the padded part of the deck floor. My skin was so heated that I barely registered the cold of the cushion against my back. He came down to his knees over me and quickly snatched his tank top over his head.

My, my, my…

Tucker's body was a thing of art. I reached up to touch a scar on his muscled stomach.

"What happened?"

He looked down to where I touched. "Shot," was all he muttered before his hands came to the waistband of the sweatpants I wore, with one yank he had them off.

"Sh*t, Free…" he hissed, staring down at my moist heat. "I feel like I've been hungry for you forever…" Spreading my legs, he lowered himself over me. For the second time in my life, I found myself staring at a beautiful night sky as my world shattered into a million pieces.

I heard the crinkle of a condom wrapper and then he

was entering me. Tears burned the back of my eyes from the intense pleasure of his warmth filling me…stretching me. He proceeded to masterfully bring me to the edge again, then he would decrease his stroke before I could fall over, all while watching the sweet torture he was causing me play out on my face.

My nails clawed at his back and arms as I tried to urge him to put me out of my misery and let me shatter.

"Be a good girl Free, and come apart when I tell you," he'd, say easily controlling me with his dominating touch. I didn't recognize myself as I clung to him, calling out his name. I was completely wild and abandoned.

*I loved it!*

"What do you want, baby?" he whispered in my ear.

"I want to come!"

He grinned before taking my lips in a kiss that robbed my breath. "Say please…"

I know I growled at him this time. What was with him and making me say please…But then he slowed his stroke.

"Please!" I cried out.

"Your wish is my command…"

Whew, chile!!! When that man turned it on, he turned it on. A scream ripped from my throat as my world shattered in a way that made me wonder if I would be left handicap. Those tears that had burned the back of my eyes now streamed from them as I fought to come back to earth.

The both of us lay there on our backs, looking up at the stars, panting, me completely naked, and him in his jeans that were opened.

The longer I lay there, the more it became clear to me that I had just made a huge mistake. Not only had we just made our relationship more complicated, I could lose my license and my practice.

"I can feel you tensing up, Doc," he muttered. Sitting up, I reached for the closest thing to me, which was his tank top.

"I'm so sorry for this. You're my patient and I took advantage of you," I told him, putting his shirt over my head.

He sat up on his elbow and I had to force myself to look elsewhere. Like I told you guys earlier, this man's body was pure art.

"So, let me get this straight. You think that *you*," he said, pointing to me. "Took advantage of *me*?" I stood but had to grasp on to the table because my legs were shaking so badly, I thought they were going to collapse from under me.

*Goodness!*

"Yeah, Tuck. I'm your doctor. You're vulnerable. And I took advantage of that." When my legs became a bit steadier, I began to look around for my pants.

Naphtali still hadn't moved. He was trying to process what I was saying. "Hmmmm..." was all he settled on.

"Anyway, we can't do this again," I told him, gesturing between the two of us.

He thought about my words before muttering another, "Hmmmm..."

"What does *hmmmm*, mean? Please say more. I already feel horrible." It's amazing how much lust can cloud the mind. I can't believe I had sex with this man. This man that has always made my life complicated. And what have I done? Gone and made it more so.

"You want to know what I think?"

I nodded, desperately needing him to tell me that we are going to be okay, and we can pretend like this never happened.

"I think you look good as hell in my tank top. I think you've made me hungry again and now you need to feed me. I think... you should take advantage of me a few more times," he said before he moved so fast that a squeak of surprise left my throat.

One nanosecond, he was lying down there looking like the dark Adonis he is, and the next, he was up, coming for me. I didn't have time to scream before I was up in his arms and over his shoulder caveman style. Carrying me inside the cabin, he tossed me on the bed, I laughed as I fought the covers to sit up on my elbows. And as I took him in standing at the foot of the bed, I realized that I wanted him again too.

"Naughty doctor. I'm so vulnerable right now. Shame on you for taking advantage of me," he teased before he jumped on the bed after me.

Annnnndd, welllllll... I learned something else about myself that night. My body was completely incapable of telling Mean Tucker No...

In fact, it would fail to tell him no, twice more, once in his bed, and another time bent over the island in his kitchen; it was that time that took me out. I don't remember him carrying me to his bed or putting me under the covers. I vaguely remember the sound of the powerful engine starting as he steered us back to the pier, or the feel of him sliding under the covers behind me, pulling me into his arms.

However, the one thing I do remember was how good it felt lying in his arms, the same way it had prom night, only this time, I didn't wait for him to leave me the next morning. I slept for a few hours and then I eased out of his arms and his bed. Being careful not to make a peep, I dressed in the clothes he'd let me borrow and after grabbing my things, slipped off the boat.

And you know, guys, I didn't feel that bad. I thought I would after giving in to him twice more, but surprisingly I didn't. Rachel was right. It was time for me to do something for myself. Obviously, it has been a long while since I've enjoyed anything like I enjoyed Tucker's lovemaking. He was a master at it…making me want it every time.

The way I figured, if I promised not to do it again, there was no need to beat myself up. Everybody deserved to treat themselves to a triple scoop of sinfully delicious chocolate ice cream from time to time, right?

Right…

Yeah, I felt good. However, my joy fled like a thief in the night when I pulled up to my house and saw that Rachel's car was still there.

Dammit!

It was one thing to indulge in a guilty pleasure when no one can see you. It was another thing to have a flashlight shined on the situation. How in the world was I going to explain this? I am the sensible friend. I didn't do things like have one-night stands.

I looked at my watch… eight-thirty. Maybe they were still asleep. It was a really good chance if they drank that whole pitcher of margaritas. Oaklee's liquor hand was heavy.

As I put my key in the door, I felt like a teen sneaking back in after staying out all night. That thought made me chuckled as I eased the door open. However, the smell of coffee and something cooking sent the message that I was busted.

I inhaled. At this point, it was nothing I could do but own it. So, I boldly walked into the house, shutting the door behind me and headed for the kitchen.

Rachel sat at the table nursing a cup of coffee. Her hair that was always immaculate was all over her head. Yes indeed, she looked as if they'd drank that whole pitcher of margaritas. Oaklee stood at the stove scrambling eggs.

With my head held high, I walked past them both to the coffee pot.

"Well, well, well… Where have you been, young lady?" Oaklee asked, spooning the eggs into a bowl.

Grabbing a mug, I poured me a big cup of coffee. "Ummm, a patient of mine had an emergency last night."

"And was that patient's name *penis*?" Rachel asked.

"Don't be vulgar, Rach."

All this I said without turning to face my friends. I've yet to make eye contact with them. Instead, I stirred cream and sugar in my coffee. You see, I knew that when I turned around, they were going to lay into me. So, I might as well be prepared.

Once I had my coffee to my liking, I took a deep breath and then turned to face them and just like I figured, they both stared at me as if I was a stranger, Rachel with a frown on her face, and Oaklee with that little impish grin on hers.

"B*tch, you had a booty call!" Rachel dove right in.

"It was not a *booty call*."

"Oh yeah?" Oaklee asked. "Your hair's all over your head, you have the look of a woman that has been *well* satisfied…oh, and not to mention the small fact that you're wearing men's clothing. What would you call it?"

"Okay!" I told them. "So, I had a booty call…so what?."

Oaklee did a little dance of glee while Rachel shook her head in disappointment.

"Please don't tell me you gave in to Dillion, Free," she grumbled, managing to slam her coffee cup on the table without spilling a drop. "He's just living the life, f*cking both sisters. Now, all he has to do is get Layla to get on board and he'll be in pimp paradise."

My mouth opened in shock. "What?! Dillion?! Heffa, are you crazy?"

When she realized it wasn't Dillion I had sex with, her mouth snapped shut and the look of disappointment on her face was replaced by a grin that matched Oaklee's.

"If you didn't spend the night with Dillion, who did you spend the night with?" Oak asked as she took my hand, pulling me to the table.

I made them both wait as I eased down in the chair because yeah, I was a little sore, and scooped some of the eggs in my plate before grabbing a piece of toast. They were practically percolating with anticipation.

"Spit it out already!" Rachel yelled.

"Was it, Naphtali?" Oaklee asked.

When I didn't say anything, both of their mouths dropped. "It was Naphtali?" Rachel screeched. I took a bite of my toast.

"Oh my God! You spent the night with Mean Tucker!" She jumped out of her chair.

"How was it?" Oaklee asked.

Rachel sat back in her chair pulling it closer to mine. "Yeah, how was it?"

They were both leaning into me, ready to eat up my words. I thought about telling them none of their business. Buuutttt...I couldn't do that to my girls.

"It was..." My words trailed off as I closed my eyes, remembering how he'd bent me over the kitchen island with his hand fisted in my hair as he mercilessly brought me to a screaming orgasm.

"It was... everything."

"Woooow," they muttered, staring at the look on my face.

"Congratulations, Free!" Oaklee cried, taking my hand in hers.

"Yeah, baby...you deserved, *everything*," Rachel said, taking my other hand.

I nodded. "Yeah...I did."

# Chapter 9

## TELLING IT LIKE IT IS

*I ain't comin' at you with no disrespect*
*All I'm sayin' is that you damn well got to be correct*
*Because if you're gonna be speaking for a whole generation*
*And you know enough to handle their education*
*Be sure you know the real deal about past situations*
*And ain't just repeating what you heard on a local TV station*
*Sometimes they tell lies and put them in a truthful disguise*
*But the truth is, that's why we said it wouldn't be televised*
*They don't know what to say to our young folks*
*But they know that you do*
*And if they really knew the truth*
*Why would they tell you?*

*Gil Scott Heron*

_____

Free

*DAISY SEEMS to be taking the separation from her parents, who I will call Mr. and Mrs. Rose for the sake of their identity, well, although she did show signs of agitation the first few nights. My nurses contacted me and said she asked repeatedly for her bag from her closet at home. I asked Mrs. Rose to bring the bag to the hospital for Daisy's comfort. I will admit to being more than curious to see what was in it and why it was so important to her.*

*However, when her mom dropped it off, I was surprised to see that it in fact contained camping supplies: a small medical kit, a knife, rope, a small popup tent, a canteen for water, and a few protein bars. I thoroughly checked the bag for hidden compartments but couldn't find any. Needing to get to the bottom of the mysterious items, I scheduled to meet with Daisy the next day. To keep better records of our time together, I am going to be recording our sessions from this point on.*

JULY 21, 1972

*"I'M HERE WITH DAISY, how are you feeling?"*
    *"That's not my name."*

*"Remember when I said we were going to call you that, to protect your identity?"*

*"Oh."*

*"How are you enjoying your stay with us?"*

*"It's fine."*

*"Are the nurses kind to you?"*

*"Yes."*

*"That's good. I want to talk about your bag today. Nurse June did give it to you, didn't she?"*

*"Yes."*

*"You were really upset without it. Why is that?"*

*"I don't want to be like the five virgins. When it's time, I want to be prepared."*

*"Time for what?"*

*"When it's time to go home."*

————

## Naphtali

"Wait a minute... I can't go out there and say this corny sh*t. Those kids will chew my ass up."

Free scoffed, waving away my concerns. "No, they won't. Not all children are like how you were in high school. This is a new generation; they care about things like the condition of the earth and environmental changes. Trust me, this message will resonate with them."

I glanced at the teenagers filing into the auditorium. There was no doubt in my mind that more than half of them were gangbanging and that a good number of them were selling dope. Sh*t, we had to walk through a metal detector to get in this joint.

As if cued, a scuffle broke out between a couple of guys that the security guards who stood at the doors and in the aisles like prison guards quickly broke up, taking the culprits out of the auditorium with their hands behind their backs.

My gaze came back to Free. "Are you f*cking kidding me? These thugs don't give a f*ck about the environment!"

Her mouth popped open as if I'd slapped her. "Naphtali Tucker Pelletier, that is not fair. How can you judge a whole group of children off a few bad apples sprinkled into the bunch? That's the problem with this society, they treat kids from the inner city like dirt. They have voices and dreams...they just need somebody to believe in them."

I lifted an eyebrow. "Do it look like my name Mr. Clark?" Balling up the little speech she'd written for me to read, I tossed it in the trash. "I am not going out there saying that corny sh*t."

*Who the f*ck did she think she was dealing with?*

Yeah, I know, I'm in a bad mood, but it's her f*cking fault. First of all, I'm sober... She called me after successfully managing to dodge me for a whole week, which irritated the sh*t out of me.

With Rau here looking for the person responsible for his brother's death, it just wasn't safe for her. There is a very slim chance they will find me, and a slim chance is a risk I was not willing to take with Free's life, which resulted in Jackson, Ashur, and me fluctuating in keeping watch on her from a distance all week. Of course, I took the night shift, she's mine...don't need them watching her during those hours. What was irritating as hell about that is, I would have preferred keeping an eye on her up close and personal and then I wouldn't have had to bother my boys at all.

But her ass didn't return my call and when she did, it was to ask if I would speak to a few high school kids about the dangers of drugs. What with me working for the Drug Enforcement Administration and all...*Her words*.

Because my goofy ass thirsty just wanted to be close to her again, I agreed. Didn't think much of it until she told me where to meet her.

"Wait, hold up! That's Douglass High. More crimes happen in those halls than on the streets," I'd told her, not believing that's where she wanted to meet.

"I'm aware of that. What better place to deliver the message of the dangers of drugs?"

Like the pu**y whipped sap that I am, I agreed, although my spidey senses were warning against it. My first instinct was to smoke, but then I'm like, *I can't show up there high. Free would kill me*. And then there would be no talking her into coming back to my place tonight.

All week I've been craving her. The little tease gave me a taste of something I've always hungered for, only to pull it away. It was bad enough she'd snuck off the boat without waking me. She could have gotten hurt that morning; there were no eyes on her. Now, she's got it in her mind that the night we'd shared was just a one-time thing, and that she and I were finished.

Damn shame after all these years, she still didn't know what kind of mutha f*cka she was dealing with. If she thought that I was going to let her go, she was out her rabbit ass mind, especially now that her life may be in danger. But sh*t the truth is, I've wanted this girl for a long time, and now that I had... I just wasn't giving her up.

Period!

After prom night, every woman that I was with fell short. They didn't taste like Free or feel like her wrapped around me. The other night on the boat, I couldn't get enough of her. The only reason I'd let her sleep is because she'd literally passed out in my arms. But I wanted her again. And then when I woke up to find her gone, I was angry enough to break some sh*t. After I got control of my rage, I called her. Of course, she didn't answer the phone. So, I left her a message telling her to return my call.

I knew the game she was playing and because I ain't no simp, I didn't blow her phone up after that or show up at her job, but damn, I wanted to. I had to settle on watching her from a distance.

Naw, I ain't gon' lie to y'all, I'm worse than a simp. This f*cking girl has turned me into one of those creepy ass stalkers. A couple of those nights, I broke into her house and stood over her bed, watching her sleep and sh*t.

Yeah! I know…That's a busta move. But I needed to see her up close and make sure she was alright. She works so much and is always tense and stressing over something. I want so bad to take away all her worries, but I know she will never let me.

And for y'all out there listening to my sob story, don't clown yo' boy. You mutha f*ckas thought it was cute when old Eddie did that sh*t to Bella on that vampire movie. So, don't throw no shade at me for doing the same sh*t. And don't ask me how I know what happened in that simp ass movie… I just know. So, let's just drop the subject.

Anyway, when she called me this morning, I thought I'd won the f*cking lottery. But nooo…she wasn't' calling so that we could pick up where we left off and light another fire between the bedsheets, she was calling for me to come give a p*ssy ass speech in front of an auditorium full of snotty nose ass kids.

Damn... I should have smoked that blunt before I left.

"Now you listen to me, Mr!" she growled, stepping to me like she was 6'2 instead of 5'4. This made me smile a bit.

"You're going to take this speech." She held up the crumpled piece of paper that she snatched out of the trash. "And you're going to carry yourself out there and read it to those children. Or else..."

I closed the small gap between us, staring down at her. "Or else what?" My gaze fell to her lips and the only thing I could think about was kissing her.

"Or else I'm going to get on the phone with your captain. Are you aware that he personally calls me for reports on you?"

I lifted one side of my mouth in a grin. She said that sh*t like she really thought I could be controlled by my captain. But I went on and played her game because she looked so damn sexy right now being all bossy and sh*t.

"Yeah...so?"

"So..." she hissed, poking me in the chest with her little finger. "I will call your captain and tell him you're not being compliant to my program and I can't possibly see how I can give you a recommendation to be reinstated." Then she folded her arms.

My gaze fell to her enticing mouth again. As if she could sense my hunger, she licked her lips and a groan escaped mine. F*ck! This woman had me wrapped around her finger.

Ya'll want to know a little secret? This is how I know

she's meant to be mine. There has never, ever been another human being with this kind of power over me. For Free, I'll go out on this stage in front of a room full of mobsters and read this p*ssy ass speech.

I took the paper out of her hand, but I wrapped my arm around her waist, pulling her close.

"You wore your hair down."

Biting her lip, she grinned. "I did."

"Did you do that for me?"

She chuckled. "Nope...I did it for *me*."

"It's beautiful," I whispered before I took her lips in the kiss I'd been waiting all week for.

———

Free

*Good God! This man could kiss...*

Wrapping my arms around his neck, I lost myself for just a moment. His kisses always made me feel so desired. He made me feel like a superwoman that could conquer anything because a great man needed me.

I moaned when he deepened it, forgetting all about the fact that we were in a school. Mmmmm...how I've missed him this week. And I can hear all of your thoughts out there. I know you all are saying right now, why the hell did I not return his call?

Well, the answer to that is simple. One doesn't become addicted to a drug by doing a bunch of it all at once. One becomes addicted to a drug from all the *'just one more time'* samples they consume.

Yes, I wanted to call him every day this week and ask

him to come over and help me relax after a stressful day in that special way that he does. But I can't allow myself to become strung out on Naphtali! He's the only one in the world with the power to hurt me completely.

That thought gave me the strength to push him back.

"You have to stop doing that. I'm your doctor. I could get in big trouble if word got out that we slept together."

He frowned. "That's bullsh*t...I'm telling you now, I ain't trying to hear that sh*t, Free!"

*Hmmm... he must be sober.* Today, he felt very dangerous. It felt like the rage inside of him was barely being contained. Now I was rethinking my little prank that I'd planned. I didn't want to put any of the children's lives in danger.

*Surely, he wouldn't hurt a kid, would he?*

Hell yes, he would...I needed to abort this mission! "Hey, you know what? Let's just call--" I began, but right then, principal Kline joined us.

"Naphtali Pelletier! Man, it is an honor to have you here speaking to our children today," he said shaking a still frowning Tucker's hand. "In high school, I used to dream of hanging out with you fellas. You are a legend, brotha!"

"You attended Pendleton?" my grouchy companion muttered.

Mr. Kline let out a jolly laugh that only seemed to irritate Tucker more. "Come on, man, don't tell me you don't remember me. I was on the football team with you... Lil' Swift Kline?" He opened his arms as if that would somehow jog Tucker's memory. Poor guy.

Naphtali shrugged. "Naw...don't remember."

With a smile on my face, I reached up and gave his arm

a little pinch. Outside of his nostrils flaring a bit, he showed no other sign of even feeling it.

"Don't feel bad, Mr. Kline, he was King of the Beautiful Ones, his royal highness barely noticed me either." We laughed to try and ease some of the awkwardness, but Tucker didn't laugh with us.

He turned his head to look at me. And not just any look...The one that he does when it seems as if he is searching for my soul.

"Now Free, that's just not true. And I'm sure Lil' Swift Kline here knows that. If he went to school with us, he'd have to be blind not see that I adored you. For some reason, only you can't see that..." His gaze returned to the principal, who was watching us with his mouth hanging open a bit.

"Where do you want me?"

"Umm—" Like myself, Tucker's words had momentarily robbed him of speech. "Yeah, right this way."

Mr. Kline recovered before I did as I watched Naphtali head toward the podium and his doom, his words played over again in my head.

*He'd have to be blind not see that I adored you. For some reason, only you can't see that...*

Can't? As is present tense?

"Free! Did we miss Tucker's speech?" Ashur called, pulling me out of my thoughts. I looked up to see him and Jackson dressed in full uniform heading my way.

Smiling, I shook my head. "No, you guys are just in time. Come on, I reserved us a few seats right up front."

So I know most of you thought that just because Tucker rendered me completely helpless with his lovemaking the other night, I was going to abandon my plan to abstract vengeance for the suffering he put me through in high school.

Ha!

I wouldn't dream of it. You know, just to be honest with you guys, I think that some of Mean Tucker's qualities have rubbed off on me. Either that or this diabolical side of me has lain dormant all this time and now has decided to show its face.

It's possible I'm enjoying Tucker's misery a little too much. But for the first time in my life, I'm doing what's best for Free. And what's best for Free is making him see how it felt to be a victim. There was a little voice in the back of my head that warned that the pit I dug for my fellow man would be the one I fall in, but I ignored it.

Meanwhile, I am glad Jackson is here. At least I know that if things get too far out of hand, he will be able to stop Tucker from hurting one of the children.

*At least I prayed...*

So, you guys are wondering what I've planned this time...right? Well, let me tell you all about it as I rub my hands together with the sinister smile on my face... feel free to insert an evil laugh here.

Yeah, I know that was corny. But remember, I'm a geek and proud of it. Anyway, Mr. Kline asked me a few weeks ago if I would speak to the children during their drug awareness week. Of course, I agreed, but because things have been so hectic down at the clinic and I'd been so caught up in my grandmother's journal's on Daisy, I hadn't had time to put together a presentation.

Last night, I forced myself not to go up to the attic and to sit down and at the very least, write a decent speech. That was when the idea came to me. I had the perfect way to humiliate Tucker, so that he could see how it felt to have a whole school of children laugh at him.

When I called Mr. Kline and asked him if it would be okay for Naphtali Pelletier to speak in my place, he nearly fangirled on me before he could catch himself. At first, he didn't believe I'd actually gotten *thee* Tucker to speak in my stead.

And no, I'm not kidding, those were actually his words.
*"You mean thee Tucker from Pendleton?"*

I'd chuckled, still amazed that folks worshipped him the way that they did...and obviously still do.

*"Yes, thee Tucker from Pendleton."* It took me a little longer to convince him that it was true, but once I did, he was all for it.

So, y'all, sit back and enjoy the show...

"Let me get my phone ready..." Jackson muttered, queuing the recording setting on his phone. "Something is telling me I'm going to want to document this moment."

I bit my lip to hide my grin. "Absolutely, this was really nice of him to come out and speak to the children about the dangers of drugs."

Principal Kline walked out on stage and brought order to the room. It took him a full four minutes to get the children quiet.

"Douglass High, we are in for a special treat. A legend has decided to grace these halls to speak with you guys today. And you know..." He paused for just a second, once again fighting his inner fangirl.

"I just want to take a moment and try and describe what it was like to attend high school with this man." And then he proceeded to spend the next ten minutes bragging on Naphtali's many accomplishments.

From my seat, I could see where Tucker stood waiting to be called out on the stage and he was not happy with the fact that the principal was so starstruck. His fists were clenched and the muscle in his cheek twitched furiously.

Hmmmm… In school, folks worshipped Naphtali like a god. His father, the old mayor of Aldshore bragged on him to whoever listened. I often wondered if the reason he'd been voted into office for nearly ten years straight was because his son was so accomplished at nearly everything he put his hands to do and everyone wanted to be connected with him.

But now, I wonder had the esteem and the recognition Naphtali received always bothered him, or was this a new development. I never paid attention to his response to all the praise in high school, I just assumed he basked in it, because, well… who doesn't want to be loved by everyone?

Finally, Mr. Kline finished his introduction and told the kids to give a round of applause for Naphtali Pelletier. Of course, only about five kids actually clapped.

Tucker stepped to the podium and for a moment, he just sneered at the audience, but his frown grew when he saw Jackson and Ashur. When his angry gaze settled on me, I smiled and gave him two thumbs up.

*"You can do this…"* I mouthed, nearly breaking my jaw to keep my smile from turning into a chuckle.

He exhaled long and loud in the mic as he uncrumpled the speech I'd written for him. It was clear he did not want to be up there on that stage. Jackson held his phone up and pressed record.

"My name is Naphtali Tucker Pelletier and I'm an officer of the law." His irritated gaze shot to me for a moment as he let me know without saying a word how corny he thought that sounded.

I did grin then. If he thought that was corny, he hadn't seen anything yet.

"On the streets, I'm known as Mean Tucker because I—" He paused, and it took all I had not to burst. When his pleading eyes came to me, I gave him the signal to continue.

The muscle was back to ticking in his chin as he trudged on. "Because I'm mean when it comes to the war on drugs." All that he said like a little boy who was being forced to apologize to someone he didn't want to.

"Just like the birds soar high in the sky and the bees and butterflies buzz in the flowers, each of you are beautiful in your own unique—" his words faltered again.

Jackson's shoulders were shaking next to me from where he silently laughed…

"Man, sit yo' corny ass down!" someone yelled from the back before the auditorium burst out laughing. Tucker's gaze shot up to search out the culprit.

Mr. Kline, who still stood off to the side of Tucker, stepped back to the podium.

"Excuse me! We will not have that kind of disrespect. Officer Pelletier was nice enough to come and speak with us today. Let's show him how much we appreciate him by sitting quietly and listening to what he has to say."

When that managed to gain a little more control over the room, Mr. Kline stepped back so that Tucker could continue.

Again, Naphtali exhaled loudly in the mic before he began speaking.

"In this war against drugs, I would like for you guys to get mean like me. The next time someone try and pressure you into doing drugs, you should tell them no, and do something else instead." He frowned as he continued to read. "Like… paint a pretty picture, adopt a kitty cat…or write a poem?"

His gaze shot to mine. "What the hell, Free?"

But it was too late, the damage had been done, the auditorium was once again in an uproar.

"Get off the stage, clown!" the same culprit yelled, causing everybody to laugh again.

"Adopt these nuts!" someone else called, causing the crowd to go into another round of laughter.

"Sit yo' ass down, Officer Smiley!" the taunts continued. Mr. Kline made to step to the mic again to try and bring order to the room, but Tucker's arm shot out stopping him.

"Naw, I got it this time. Hey!" he growled, pointing toward the direction the taunts came from. "Let me reintroduce myself because I think you little sh*ts misunderstood."

Mr. Kline's mouth dropped. He began to tell Tucker something, maybe that he couldn't curse at the students, but Tucker's angry gaze settled on him and he decided against it.

*Good decision, bro.*

Oh my goodness, guys! I was in so much trouble. Tucker was pissed. This may have been a bad idea.

Oh crap!

"My name is Officer Will-F*ck-A-Kid-Up!" That brought the room to complete silence as hundreds of red lights from cell phones appeared in the darkness.

"Oh no!" I cried, using my hands to cover my face. My career was over. It was all over.

"Didn't think this one through huh, doc?" Jackson muttered as he too continued to record.

Tucker balled up the speech I'd written for him and tossed it in my general direction.

"Let me get real with you," he growled, looking angrier than I'd seen him in a long time.

*Dear God! I am so sorry...I didn't think this through at all. Lack of sleep could be the culprit. But Heavenly Father, if you're listening, please don't let Tucker's other personality come out and harm one of these children!*

"Nobody is rooting for you! Nobody wants to see you succeed! The system is set up so that you can fail. You are seen as a cancer. Is it because there is something wrong with you? Is it because you have nothing to offer to society?" He shook his head as it seemed as if he made eye contact with each youth there.

"No... it's because your potential scares the sh*t out of the powers that be. Your young minds are continually fed negative images of yourselves. It's in the movies, in the music, on your televisions. You're being bombarded with what they want you to be. Well, guess what." He sneered. "It's a trap. And most of you are falling headfirst into it. But I tell you from personal experience that you have the potential to fight it." He paused for a moment. "IT... CAN...BE...FOUGHT!"

He shook his head again as he gazed off toward the back of the room, his mind going somewhere that only he could see.

"But it won't be easy... Fighting what you've been programmed to be will be one of the hardest things you'll ever do. It's a lot of pressure. But you have to ask yourself, what is God trying to produce in us, that he would allow the kind of pressure that would crush others to rest on our shoulders?"

"What is your destiny?" His gaze roamed the audience before it settled on the funny guy that did all the yelling. "What is your destiny?"

He had the kid's attention. The look in his eyes reflected the one in Tucker's. They'd bonded on a level that I'd never understand. He'd managed to get through to them.

The kid shook his head. "I don't know…"

Tucker shrugged. "It's clear. Extreme pressure either crushes and you crumble, or you use your God-given strength and come out a diamond. And that, young people…is what they fear. They fear a world full of diamonds. Embrace the fact that life doesn't come easy to you. Embrace the fact that you're being molded to be a diamond rather than a noodle. And then go forth and shine bright like you were always meant to do. I'm out…" And with that, he turned and walked past a stunned Mr. Kline off the stage and out of the auditorium.

Yep! I felt like a piece of garbage. Absolutely! Jumping to my feet, I hurried after him. But on my way, I observed a miracle. The kid that had thrown most of the jokes at Tucker was the first to come to his feet and applaud. The rest of the children followed…the roar from their cheers nearly brought down the walls.

"Tucker!" I called as I ran out of the school. He was heading toward his truck. "Tucker, wait!"

He stopped but didn't turn around. I walked around

him until I was standing in front of him, blocking his way to his truck.

"I'm sorry." I felt so bad I couldn't make eye contact with him, so I just stared at his chest.

"Sorry for what, Free?" The fact that he didn't yell that at me only made me feel worse. I looked down at my nails as I picked imaginary dirt from them.

"I may have done that on purpose."

"Done what? Write that bullsh*t ass speech?" I nodded, still looking down at my fingers. *God, I felt like crap.*

"Why?"

"Ummm... I— payback," I whispered. "In trying to seek revenge for you bullying me, I lost my way and became the exact thing I was punishing you for being. I became the bully."

For a minute, neither of us said anything, and then he slowly closed the distance between us. I was a little afraid, but I stood my ground. I deserved whatever he does... what I did in there was horrible.

I'd been so focused on getting revenge on him that I'd not thought about the children. The speech I'd written for Tucker's embarrassment was in no way meant to benefit them. Principal Kline had given me the opportunity to have access to their minds for just a moment to instill an important message and I'd blown it. Thank God Tucker had enough sense to throw away that stupid paper and utilize that moment.

Tears burned the back of my eyes. How could I have been so careless with their lives? He put his finger underneath my chin and gently lifted it so that our gazes touched. Slowly he lowered his head and kissed me softly.

"It's okay... I had it coming."

I wrapped my hand around his squeezing it. "But what about the children? They didn't deserve that. How could I have been so careless with their lives?"

He grinned. "Don't be so hard on yourself. Something about me brings out the worst in you."

I blinked up at him before I erupted in laughter. "You know what? That is so true."

He lifted his other hand and brought it to my hair. "But I'd like to think there is something about me that brings out the best in you as well."

My gaze fell to his lips and that was all the urging he needed. This time when he kissed me, there was nothing sweet about it. It was the dominating kiss of his that always rendered me useless. And when he deepened it, I groaned, knowing that I'd lost this round and tonight I was his.

*One more taste of the Naphtali drug shouldn't harm me...*

# Chapter 10

FEEDING HER SOUL

---

*Love Takes Off the Mask That We Fear We Can Not Live Without, And Know That We Can Not Live Within...*

James Baldwin

---

### Free

IT HAD ALL BEEN A LIE!

All of it!

The kind, caring, considerate Tucker had all been a lie! He was still very much the bastard I remembered from high school. And the Beautiful Ones were still the mean, shallow, spoiled rich brats they've always been. And now I was stuck here in a mansion in Toronto, Canada in the middle of nowhere with the whole group of them.

And Tucker... well, Tucker was still their king.

The server that had given me my last three glasses of wine, came my way with more on his golden tray. He was the only one here at this party that was keeping me from freaking out. Anytime my glass got low, he managed to be here to hand me a refill of my liquid courage.

I don't know how he was able to see so well with the lights not only dimmed but tinted red. God knows I was struggling. Unfortunately, I'd decided to wear my contacts that had a lower prescription than my glasses due to the fact that I had a slight astigmatism in my right eye. In normal light, they worked just fine, but in this tint, I was all but blind.

"Thank you," I muttered, taking the glass of wine the server offered before handing him my empty one.

"You're welcome, ma'am."

Tears burned the back of my eyes when he muttered those words. Such simple words...yet they were the kindest ones I've heard all evening. I felt so out of place here. These weren't my kind of people. I felt like I was in a room full of vampires...and Tucker was the head vampire.

Needing to find a way home, I took my phone out of my purse and moaned when I saw I still had no signal. I wasn't joking when I said this mansion was in the middle of nowhere. Everybody that's here got flown in by helicopters. The massive lawn was littered with them. Apparently, this is how the filthy rich partied.

Honestly, I didn't know what good it was going to do if I had a working phone. It wasn't like I could call an Uber or for Oaklee and Rachel to come pick me up or anything like that. No... I was completely at the mercy of that bastard bully. It was his family's helicopter he and I had flown here on. And I doubted real seriously if I would be able to catch a ride with any of the other Beautiful Ones. Thanks to the fact that their king was upset with me, and Layla and Laureen were upset with me, they had all decided to ostracize me.

Yeah, that's right...Layla and Laureen were here too. The b*tches!

I felt like I was back in high school. But instead of hiding behind the bleachers, I was hiding in the corner of the huge ballroom like the wallflower that I've always been, where no one paid attention to me except for that really nice server who kept me supplied with liquid courage.

I swallowed a mouth full of wine. If I could just get drunk enough, I will tell all these bastards to kiss my ass and walk back to town if I had to. My gaze settled on Tucker across the room, he still sat where I left him in the V.I.P area, and although I couldn't make out his facial features, I could feel him watching me with his angry gaze. Layla was now glued to his side, flirting shamelessly with him.

I downed the rest of my wine, ready for something stronger. Don't get me wrong. He wasn't flirting back with her, but he wasn't stopping her from flirting with him. In my book, he might as well be doing the deed.

God! I don't even know what I did to make him so upset...

Maybe you guys can help me figure it out. First, let me get a stronger drink and then I will fill you in on what happened.

Sticking to the shadows, I made my way to the bar and eased into one of the chairs at the very end. After doing a quick scan of the room to make sure Dillion wasn't trying to corner me again, I ordered a Margarita with an extra shot of tequila.

Yeah, I know... Dillion is here too. It's madness! I felt like I was in the freaking Twilight Zone. But before I tell you what happened with him, I must start with yesterday morning.

———

*YESTERDAY MORNING*

"NO...DON'T GO," Tucker grumbled in his sleep, drawing me deeper into the circle of his arms. Only then did his breathing even out as deep sleep reclaimed him.

Well, okay... I guess I was spending the night since he'd just foiled my plans of easing out of his bed. I tried to test his hold again by moving back just a bit, but his arms only tightened, pulling me even closer.

Exhaling, I gave up and relaxed. I was so doomed. I am afraid I was in real danger of falling in love with this man. He was like a flower unfolding before my eyes, and each layer of him revealed is more beautiful than the one before.

Hearing him speak to the children today forever changed me. It was a harsh speech, but it was one that they would remember for the rest of their lives. Today, he shared a part of himself with them. When he spoke about fighting what you've been programmed to be, there was real pain behind those words.

And now I wondered what had happened to him. What was really going on with his other personality? Even in high school, I understood that he suffered from a genuine case of multiple personality disorder. But how bad was it?

The things I saw him do in school reminds me so much of what I've been reading in my grandmother's journals. I read briefly about the experiments her boss, Dr. Baxter Silva was doing on two soldiers, Sergeant Major James Bennet Law and Sergeant Major Albert Gaines, causing their minds to split in two. One frame of mind was that of a normal civilian, and the other a stone-cold killer. But I didn't get too far into her notes on that, because I stumbled upon her research on Daisy, and for some reason, have become completely consumed by it.

I don't know what it is about that case, but it calls out to me. The other day, I went to the store and bought a bag and a few supplies that I now keep in my car. In today's time, it's called a bugout bag. I don't know what they called them in Daisy's day. I know the fact that I'd gone out and bought a bag sounds crazy to some of you guys, but it was something about Daisy's need to be prepared that resonated with me. Something about that action jogs the memory of my own childhood.

I vaguely remember my mother keeping two bags in her bedroom closet. One for me and one for her, she'd said. But I was so young that I can't remember what the bags were for. And eventually, they got pushed so far to the back of the closet they were easily forgotten.

"Mmmmm, Doc. What are you thinking about? You're all tense again," Tucker muttered before he gently kissed my neck.

I smiled; how did he know how I felt? The man had just been fast asleep. In fact, he was still asleep. Gently, I ran my fingers through the soft curls of his low-cut fade, trying to lure him into a deeper rest. But it must have had the opposite effect because his innocent sleepy kisses on my neck turned hungry.

He shifted a bit, causing his very awake member to brush against my center that was still sensitive from our last lovemaking session that was just a few hours ago. A moan escaped my lips as my eyes drifted shut. Even half-asleep, Tucker had the power to cause my well-sated body to reignite for him instantly.

Clutching him, I gasped when I felt him enter me... stretching me. Oh God! I should stop him; he was half asleep and didn't think about protection, and I hadn't taken my birth control pills since Dillion left.

But...Mmmmm... It felt so good.

"You feel so good, Free. So wet...so hot. The best... I only want you, forever baby," he whispered in my ear before taking my lips in a kiss that wiped out all the resistance I even thought of having.

I don't know if it was because I was so sensitive or the sleepy words he'd muttered, but I didn't last long before my back arched off the bed and my nails dug into his muscled deltoids as my world shattered into a million pieces, only to be prolonged and intensified by the feel of his warm seed filling me.

He lay his head on my breasts and was back fast asleep almost instantly. I picked up rubbing my fingers threw his soft hair, massaging his scalp. And my last thought before I joined him in the blessed abyss was, *I wonder if he was even aware that we'd just had unprotected sex. And what the world did he mean by, he only wanted to be with me...forever?*

---

"A FRIEND of mine is having a party at his place in Toronto this weekend. Come with me..."

My gaze connected with his through his dresser mirror. I stood in front of it moisturizing my skin with his lotion after enjoying a nice long hot shower that he'd invaded and made love to me yet again against the stone of the shower wall.

He was insatiable. And what was really amazing was that I was discovering I was insatiable too. It's true with Dillion, I often had to force myself to get in the mood when he came by. But with Tucker, I was having no such problems, every time he reached for me, I was willing and ready.

Oh, and my question last night about whether he'd been aware that we'd had unprotected sex had been answered this morning in the shower. Now before I tell you guys how, I just want to first prerequisite it with a few things.

First, he surprised me with breakfast in bed. And it was a really good breakfast: pancakes, beef sausage, grits, and the prettiest, fluffiest, most tasty eggs I'd ever had in my life. And obviously, by now, you guys know that I'm the kind of girl that can appreciate a good meal.

Second, I'd brought myself comfort about the fact that we'd had unprotected sex by first remembering that his department had sent over his medical records in his file that I'd taken a good look at after only glancing at it the first day he showed up in my office. And they gave him a full examination every six months since he joined the agency, except for a two-year period where his records seemed to go blank but pick back up afterward. His last exam was three months ago, he was tested for STD's and all the tests came back clean. I'm just praying that in that three-month time, he didn't contract anything.

And as for me, not only did Dillion and I use condoms every time, but I'd also been to see my gynecologist since the last time he and I did anything as well.

Now… as for becoming pregnant, I did some quick math in my head. And I am more than certain I'm not ovulating… Once again, at least I pray. Just for the record, for everyone out there reading my tale, yes, this is extremely irresponsible. And as a doctor, I cannot in good conscience encourage this kind of behavior.

But as a woman, I can admit that I'm weak and I make mistakes. When he stepped into the shower and lifted me in his strong arms while entering me with a powerful thrust that stole my breath, I made another mistake because he'd done it once again without protection, and it never crossed my mind to tell him to stop. I welcomed the pleasure I received against that stone shower wall, just like I welcomed his warm seed afterward.

Oh God, I don't know why I'm so weak…

You know what? I take that back. I knew what my weakness was, it had been my weakness since freshman year. He sat behind me on the bed in a pair of gray boxer briefs and nothing else to cover that beautifully sculpted chocolate body, waiting on my answer about traveling to Toronto with him for the weekend.

"I can't," I told him as I slid my legs into my jeans.

He frowned. "Why?"

"We're trying to put together a job fair at the clinic next Wednesday for the residents in the Oakwood Heights community. I've found a few employers that's willing to hire felons and those without degrees. My goal is to present the people with opportunities they can be proud of, and a paycheck that will cover their bills. So far, I've found a few companies that have agreed to come out and show support, but not nearly enough. I'm going to have to spend all weekend trying to find a few more."

I shook my head. "And with Dr. Kimble still out with an injury, that leaves just Dr. Ross, Oaklee, and me to try and bring this all together, while still meeting with our patients."

He grabbed my hand, pulling me toward him before lifting me so that I straddled his lap. "Damn, Free, do you think you can save the world all by yourself?"

I smiled. "No...but I can do the best that I can."

He didn't return my smile. "How much can you do if you work yourself to death? What good would you be to the people if you're worn out? You have to take time for yourself. Trust me, I know." He shook his head.

"When the captain told me I had to take a year off, I liked to had lost my f*cking mind. What was I going to do for a year? I didn't know how to sit still...sitting still for me is—" His voice trailed off as he turned his gaze toward the lake outside of his bedroom window.

I gently turned his head back to face me. "Is what?"

"It's dangerous. With nothing to do, it gives me too much time to face myself."

"Why is that a bad thing?"

He chuckled. "Because I'm f*cked up inside that's why. But we're not talking about me. So, don't try and change the subject. We're talking about you, and the fact that you're trying to work yourself to death."

A little whimper escaped my throat as I lowered my head to rest on his shoulder. "I know...But I just have so much to do." He wrapped his strong arms around me and I welcomed the comfort they brought. And as if he willed it, a sudden feeling of tiredness came over me.

The truth is, I am weary. I would love to go away with him for the weekend, but I don't think I even remember how to do something like that. I can't remember the last time I took a break.

"I don't know if you noticed, but I've been on my best behavior. I haven't been a brute or a bully in anyway… although you just admitted to bullying me. But I'm a big boy, I can take it." His silliness made me giggle.

"So, I'm going to ask you to forgive me 'cause I'm getting ready to be a bully now. You're going to Toronto with me for the weekend. And you going to relax and have fun. That's final."

I sat up and looked at him as I thought about his words. I really could use a break. I could cancel a few of my clients Monday and Tuesday morning to see if I can get a few more companies on board for the job fair. Hmmm…So tempting.

"Where are we going to stay?"

He shook his head. "Let me worry about all that. Remember, stress-free weekend."

I bit my lip… "You may be the worst thing that ever happened to me."

He grinned, shaking his head. "Naw, baby, I'm the *best* thing that's ever happened to you. You'll see." This he said before he tossed me back into the bed. Laughing, I yelled as I tried to escape him… The man was insatiable.

———

TRAVELING to Canada wasn't new to me. With Toronto only being an hour away, it had been a get-a-way favorite of Angie's and my dad's. She used to take Layla and Laureen shopping there in the Fashion District all the time. And although she took me with them, she very rarely bought me anything from the fancy stores they frequented. Walmart or the twins' hand-me-downs was my lane and she made sure I never forgot it.

You know what? No! I forced myself to stop thinking about Angie. It would only ruin the great mood that I was in. At the time, I was so glad I'd let Tucker talk me into this, I've been smiling and laughing since I left home.

He came with me to my place so that I could pack a bag and call Rachel to look after Grapefruit for a couple of days. And of course, my kitty and Tucker clashed the whole time we were there. Tucker threatened to shoot him, and Grapefruit hissed at him, causing the big tough cop to squeak like a girl. Not ashamed in the least, his gaze came to me. "That cat is Satan." I fell out laughing. Oh y'all, it was amazing to see him being bullied by something so small. That is *so* what he gets.

Anyway, feeling like I was in a fairytale, he whisked me away to the airport after that to where his family's private jet awaited us. On the plane were a very nice pilot and copilot who introduced themselves to me, telling me if I needed anything, not to be afraid to ask.

"You know what?" Tucker said to me a little later from where he sat in the plush leather seat next to mine. They were so comfortable that although we'd only been in the air for about thirty minutes, with thirty minutes still to go, I was fighting to keep my eyes open.

With my head resting back on the seat, I turned to face him with a sleepy smile on my face. "What?"

"This whole time we've been together, I haven't had an urge to smoke once."

My smile grew. "Really?" He interlocked his fingers with mine, bringing our palms together before lifting our hands so that he could kiss the back of mine.

"Really...You take my mind off the things that cause the unsettling side of me to stir up. I just hope you allow me to do the same for you this weekend."

I looked around the beautiful plane. "You're already on the right track."

And it only got better from there. We landed on a private runway in Toronto in front of the most beautiful mansion I'd ever seen. I was completely floored when Tucker told me the house belonged to his family.

I knew that his parents were filthy rich. Goodness, Angie obsessed over them all the time. If they were having a party or something like that and she didn't get an invite, she would get extremely depressed, so much so that she would stay in her bed for days.

But I had no idea they were *this* wealthy. I've always been curious as to what a mayor's salary looked like. But according to Angie, the Pelletier's wealth stemmed from African gold mines. It is said that the mayor's great grand-mother was a Moroccan princess who married a wealthy Frenchman that moved his family from France to America in the thirties.

Because in that time, interracial couples were heavily frowned upon in the States, even filthy rich ones, they had a hard time finding a place where they were welcomed. So with nowhere else to turn, they ended up buying a town.

Aldshore...

Yep, you guessed it. Before it became the bustling beach town of the black elite, it all belonged to the Pelletier's. But although Tucker was a prince in his own right, and pretty much the heir to the Aldshore throne, he never acted like it.

I mean, yeah, he was mean, and now that I was seeing him through adult eyes, I'm beginning to suspect that there is a deep and twisted root to his behavior back then. But still, he didn't carry himself like someone who held the world in his palms.

Even now, I watched as he interacted with the staff of this castle of a house, who were all in a frenzy because they didn't know he was coming this weekend. He spoke to them like they were his equal, even agreed to catch the fight with one of the groundkeepers later if we were back from the city in time.

There was something different about him. It was hard to explain, he just didn't...fit. If that makes any sense. He was rougher around the edges than the other rich people in the neighborhood I lived in during high school. I will never include myself with them. Angie made sure to always remind me that I wasn't one of them and would never be, and I'm grateful for it.

Laureen, Layla, and damn never everyone else I went to school with, except for Rachel and the other kids who were there on the scholarship program, were extremely spoiled and pampered, and were completely clueless about what was going on in the real world outside of their little plush bubbles.

But not Tucker... He's never been like that. He's never tried to speak with fancy speech, like so many residents in

Aldshore. He never tried to dress in any way other than what he was comfortable with. And vice versa, whenever schools from the rougher neighborhoods came to play ours, he never tried to pretend that he was anything other than what he was.

"Are you hungry?" he asked as he showed me to our room for the weekend.

"Yes, I'm starv—" My words stalled as I got the first look at our room. "Woooww! It's beautiful!" This one room was bigger than my whole house, from floor to ceiling, I'm not kidding. I've never seen anything like it. If you add a kitchen, someone could live in this room. And it was gorgeous, life of the rich and famous gorgeous. No wonder Angie is always kissing Mayor Pelletier and his wife's butts.

"You like it?" Tucker asked, pulling me into the circle of his arms.

I grinned. "I love it. You know, if you keep spoiling me like this, I'm never going to want to go home."

The smile slowly left his face as his gaze turned into that one that cripples me. The intensity level of it always held me paralyzed.

"Promise?"

I opened my mouth, but no words came out. I wanted to tell him I was just kidding, but it was clear he was not. So instead, I blinked to break the spell he'd easily cast on me and forced myself to smile.

"So…what are we having for lunch? And please don't say anything heavy, I've already eaten two days' worth of carbs in those delicious pancakes you made for breakfast."

He didn't speak at first, just continued to look at me as if he was reading all of my secrets. I went to step back out of his arms, but he only tightened his embrace, holding me in place. The muscle ticked in his jaw, letting me know that I'd upset him.

"Since you can't make a promise to me, allow me to make one to you...." His intense gaze studied my face, my hair...my neck. "I promise to do whatever it takes to make you mine..." His whispered words sounded like a threat.

I know what you guys are thinking at this point, that maybe that is why he was upset, but I don't think so. After that, we would continue to have an awesome day. He took me out to lunch, we caught a show and made it back to his place to watch the fight with the groundkeeper, who's name I found out was Raphael, his son, and a few of his son's friends.

Talk about fun, we had a ball. Do you guys know that there is a theater room in Tucker's house?! Oh, my goodness! It was the best night of my life. We drank, we argued, we talked smack to each other. He and I got so drunk we had to help each other back to his room where we passed out fully clothed on his bed.

This morning I woke up to the surprise of my life. Tucker was gone, but laying on the bed next to me was a note that said there was a car waiting downstairs to take me for a day that was just for me, and that we would meet back at his place to head to the party together.

Ohhhh, guys! Never in my life have I ever experienced anything like it. My first stop was to have a beautiful breakfast at a little French chateau. It was quiet and peaceful, and for the first time in a long time, my mind was not bogged down with the long list of things that I had to do.

After that, I was taken to a spa. Okay, so this part of my story is a little embarrassing, but I'm going to tell you guys anyway because if we're going to discover what I did to upset Tucker, I'm going to have to be transparent with you guys.

I cried...

Yep, you guys heard me. A very nice young lady showed me to a dressing room where a big plush white robe awaited me. She told me to get undressed because I had several relaxation treatments planned for me.

The first was a facial. Have you ever gotten your face massaged? Oh, my goodness! I had no idea my face was tense until that young lady's talented fingers went to work. When she was done, I thanked her profusely with tears in my eyes.

However, it was the full body massage that broke me down. I lay on that table for an hour. And in that hour, the masseuse tore down my soul...swept out all my worries and rebuilt it. By the time she was finished, I felt like a new woman. As if she understood what I was going through, she placed her hands on my shoulders and gently whispered for me to take my time before softly closing the door behind her.

I lay on her table, balled in a fetal position, and quietly wept. She stripped away all my stress and I felt naked. Eventually, I got myself together and when I saw that woman again, I just hugged her. She must have been quite used to that because she didn't laugh at me or even stiffen in my arms, she just gently rubbed my back as I held on to her for dear life.

Whew! Okay, so after that, I was taken for a mani/pedi, and then to the beauty salon. By the time I made it back to Tucker's place, I felt like a noodle. I was so relaxed I felt rejuvenated. When I got back to work, I would have a burst of renewed energy.

Mrs. Barletta, Tucker's housekeeper informed me that Tucker was still not back but that there were a few packages waiting for me in our suite. I'm not going to lie, at that point, I felt like a kid in the candy store. No one has ever spoiled me. Everything I had, I worked hard for. Blood, sweat, and tears...

So of course, I was shamelessly soaking up being spoiled for the first time in my life, and after giving Mrs. Barletta a hug that pleasantly surprised her, ran up the stairs like a little girl to see what other surprises awaited me.

I threw open the door to find several boxes laying on the bed. I recognized the names on these boxes, all the names of stores Angie said were not for people like me. With a huge grin on my face, I crossed the floor and after climbing up on the huge bed, opened the first box.

I gasped when I saw the stunning yellow satin material inside. In wonder, I ran my hand across it. I've never in my life felt anything so soft. For a moment, I was hypnotized by the sheer beauty of the material, but only for a moment. With a squeak of excitement, I jumped out of the bed and gently lifted the dress out of the box. The yellow material unfolded like a magic cloth. I kid you not, it was so brilliant it shined golden in the dim lighting of the room.

Holding it in front of me, I walked to the mirror to get a better look.

"Wow!" I cried.

It was a wrap dress that would need to be tied together in the front, just like my prom dress, only this beauty would never be found on a discount rack. I quickly looked through another box and found a pair of golden heels to die for. And would you guys believe they resembled the sandals I'd worn on prom night? But where the straps on my sandals tied all the way up my leg Greco-Roman style, these shoes had one little tie that made a cute bow at the heel.

I lifted the lid off another box to find a beautiful yellow satin shawl, in another box were a pair of lace panties with the matching bra. Can you guys guess what color they were? Bubble gum pink, like the pair I'd worn prom night, only this pair did not come from Walmart.

*My God, how did he remember my outfit in such detail?*

He'd called me the girl in the yellow dress several times. Like mine, that night seemed to be seared into his memory. But if it was so special to him, why did he leave me all alone on the beach that next morning? I shook my head... No negative thoughts. Not tonight.

Instead, I opened one of the smaller boxes and cried out when the light reflected off a pair of yellow diamond teardrop earrings, nearly blinding me. With hands that shook, I opened the second box and was completely floored to find the matching yellow diamond tennis bracelet.

*What the world?!*

Alright, just let me think about this for a minute. I had a choice to make. There was no doubt in my mind that if I added up all that had been spent on me today, it would equal a staggering amount.

I've never owned anything like the items I held in my hand. It wasn't that I was cheap, it's just that I poured all of my money into the clinic and would feel absolutely horrible if I wasted it buying myself things like this, when there were children and adults alike who depended on the clinic for a meal once a day.

And let me tell you, that was a program I was struggling to hold on to. But thank God I've been able to manage thus far, although, I honestly didn't know how much longer I would be able to. Maybe if I—

No!

Worry-free weekend!

Right! So, anyway, if I'm ever going to have anything like the items I now held in my hands, it would have to be a gift from someone because as we've established, I would never buy them for myself.

Would it really be a horrible thing to accept these once in a lifetime opportunities, even if it is coming from a man that I should not be establishing this kind of relationship with and is planning on telling after this weekend was over, that we needed to end whatever this is we've started?

Yep, that's what I said too... This one time won't kill me. And if you really think about it, this is the least Naphtali could do, seeing as to how he tortured me when we were kids. How much is my pain worth? Surely, a pair of diamond earrings and the matching bracelet.

That bit of vain reasoning was all the convincing I needed. Standing, I stripped out of my clothes before carefully putting on each wonderfully amazing item he'd gifted me with.

Because I didn't want to ruin this beautiful dress with my red eyeglasses, I decided to wear my contacts instead, so glad I'd thought to pack them. When it was all said and done, I stood in the mirror staring at a stranger.

I swear the last time I felt this beautiful was prom night. The beautician had flat ironed my hair before curling it in an updo that left my neck exposed. She let a few curls artfully escape in a way that looked as if it had happened naturally. Because of the conditioning massage, my brown skin glowed almost as beautifully as the yellow satin that rested against it.

And these shoes…My goodness! They made my legs look long and graceful. I felt like a model. I did a little twirl in the mirror and cried out in joy when the dress swished beautifully around my legs like only satin could.

"The girl in the yellow dress."

The sound of Tucker's deep voice startled me. I turned to see him standing in the door looking delicious in all black. This man could have easily gotten a career as a model. He wasn't just sexy. He was the dangerous kind of sexy. Get a girl to make a complete fool of herself kind of sexy. Make a girl beg kind of sexy.

He looked good in jeans and a t-shirt. But tonight, he'd traded those in for a black button-up shirt and a pair of black slacks that molded against his muscled frame in a way that showed they had been tailored especially for him.

On his feet were pair of black Italian leather boots. Instead of the big gold chains he normally wears, he'd settled for a smaller one that nicely highlighted his dark skin. Outside of that, the only other jewelry he wore was a diamond stud in his ear and a gold watch that I was sure cost more than my house on his wrist. He held another jewelry box in his hand, this one long and thin.

I opened my arms doing another little twirl, mainly because I liked the feel of the satin material caressing my legs.

"How do I look?"

"You look…" His words trailed off as his gaze took its

time taking me in, all while he walked toward me as if he could not resist my pull. I had to fight to control my giddiness. I didn't want him to see the effect his approval had on me.

"Amazing," he finished, drawing me into his arms. He leaned down to kiss me, but I leaned all the way back.

"What are you doing?"

"I want a kiss!" he growled.

I shook my head. "I don't think so. You're going to mess up my lipstick."

It was something about what I said that really turned him on because another growl left his throat before he pulled me to him and completely ravished my mouth. The kiss was so hot, I damn near said, skip the party, you have to put out the fire you started.

When he lifted his head, he looked down at my kiss swollen lips and smiled. "Yeah, I like that sh*t."

I spun back to the mirror and to my horror, saw that he'd successfully smeared my lipstick in a way that made it seemed as if he'd had his dirty way with my mouth.

"Dang it, Tucker!" I whined as I picked up a napkin to try and repair my lipstick. It was then I felt the cold touch my neck.

"Whaaa" Stunned, I watched as he gently lay a yellow diamond teardrop necklace around my throat.

"Oh my God, Tucker," I whispered as I lifted fingers that shook to touch it. "Is this real?"

He chuckled. "Yep..."

I turned around to face him. There was no way I could accept this. If I did, it would send the wrong message. No one spent this kind of money on a friend, not even a friend with benefits.

I shook my head as I opened my mouth to tell him I couldn't take it, but he only dipped in and took my lips in another kiss that I was more than positive was ruining my lipstick again.

"It's yours, I'm not taking it back, so don't bother trying." He took my hand. "Come on, we're late."

That knocked the wind out me, so much so that when we walked out the side door to see the sleek black heli-copter sitting on a launchpad in the center of the yard, I couldn't do anything but stare like a deer caught in the headlights. My senses were being overwhelmed.

He told me as we flew that his friend's place was high up in the mountains and the drive took too long, the quickest way up was by helicopter. My face was pressed to the window as I stared down at the beautiful trees. And then the mansion came into view and amazingly, it was an actual castle surrounded by beautiful gardens.

As we were landing, we flew over what looked like a maze made of roses. "Is that a maze?" I asked pointing down to it, my curiosity good and pricked.

"Mmmhhhmmm, maybe if we have time, we can check it out. Not many people can find their way out once they enter."

I chuckled. "I wouldn't have a problem. I'm a bit of a puzzle fanatic. Haven't seen one yet that I couldn't solve."

"Is that a fact?" he asked as he helped me step out of the chopper onto the red carpet that had been rolled out for us to walk on so that we didn't have to step in the grass.

*Wow! Fancy…*

"Yes, my good friend," I told him. "That's a check you can take to the bank."

Bringing my hand to rest on his arm so that he could

escort me across the lawn, he chuckled again. "Alright, I might hold you to that."

I looked up amazed as several more helicopters began to land on the massive lawn around us. There were x's marked on the grass, showing them where to safely land. In front of them red carpet, each of them leading to a long strip that led to a massive stone stairway that was lit with candles.

The sun had just begun to set in the sky and several servers hurried around the ground lighting torches that cast a romantic glow on everything. Others held golden trays with champagne on them. I could hear the bass of the dance music coming from inside and strobe lighting bursting from the windows.

"So...this is how the very rich party, huh?"

His gaze came to mine. But before he could respond, I heard a voice that threw a bucket of cold water on my good time.

"Free... Is that you? Oh my God, Layla! Free is here..."

Crap!

# Chapter 11

## THE BEST OF BOTH WORLDS

*A double-minded man is unstable in all his ways…*

*James 1:8*

### Free

"LAUREEN, WOW!" I said with a smile so fake I thought my cheeks would shatter. "What are you doing here?"

*Dear God, if you're merciful, please take me anywhere else.*

"Oh, and look! Dillion's here with you." *Of course, he is…*

"Hey, Free," he bit out between clenched teeth, eyeballing my hand that rested on Tucker's arm.

"Why wouldn't I be here. These *are* my friends after all!" Laureen continued.

The expression on her face was clear. She couldn't

believe Tucker was here with me. During his bullying days, they had only seen him be mean to me. They never saw him grab me into the janitor's closet and kiss my lips till they were swollen, or sneak into the library and pull me behind the bookshelves where nobody ever went, attacking my mouth as if he was starved for it.

As far as they knew, he hated the very ground I walked on. Poor Laureen looked as if she swallowed a lemon. Meanwhile, Tucker was busy chatting with the other guy that stepped off the chopper with them. My guess is, he was Layla's date. But whoever he was, he and Tucker were good friends and hadn't seen each other in a while, they greeted each other with that one arm man hug.

He asked Tucker if Jackson and Asher were coming tonight, to which Tucker replied no, that they couldn't get away from the station.

"My question is what are you doing here?" Laureen insisted like the pest she is.

"Well, Laureen, obviously I was invited." I wanted to tell her it was a free freaking country and I can go anywhere I wanted but didn't want to start a fight in front of all these strangers. If that was one thing Angie taught us, was to keep our family dirt sealed behind closed doors. To the world, we were a happy family. Them the wealthy big hearts that took in the little poor orphan, and me the poor orphan who was more than grateful for their generosity.

Goodness! I almost threw up.

Layla finally joined us and I inhaled, preparing myself. Out of the two, she was definitely the eviler twin. When she realized it was me, her mouth popped open like someone slapped her. Her surprised gaze went from my

shoes to my dress, and finally settled on the diamond necklace around my neck...I could see her calculating the price
of each item as she went along. This was truly a talent that
only rich, spoiled people possessed.

The word *how* formed on her lips, but right then, Naphtali's arm came around my waist. When I tell you smoke
came from that sista's ears... She looked just like Wile E.
Coyote after swallowing a stick of dynamite.

*I guess she got her answer...*

"Hey, Free, funny bumping into you here." She nodded
at Tucker. "And with him, of all people."

"You ready," Naphtali asked when he finished talking
to the other guy.

"Oh yes!" I smiled and let him lead us away. Perfect
timing. I could feel all three of them boring holes in my
back.

"Oh my God, Tucker! You're not even going to speak to
me?" Layla cried after us.

He lifted a hand without turning around. "What's up."

Ryan, the guy that was hosting the party, who was also
one of the Beautiful Ones and had been a huge jerk to me
in high school, met us at the top of the steps. He must have
told his servers to notify him as soon as Tucker's chopper
landed.

"Bro! It's so good to see you! I thought you had forgot
about us little people back here." He joked as he and
Tucker clasped hands in the bro hug. My gaze traveled all
the way up to the towers of his castle. *Little people my ass.*

"Come on, man, you know I'll never forget my boys.
Just been hella busy. Finally got a little vacation time,"
Tucker told him, guiding me through the grand doors to a
huge foyer. Ryan's gaze finally fell on me.

"Wow! And who is this beautiful lady?" he said, reaching for my hand. Tucker brought his hand between ours, stopping them from touching.

"Mine," he growled.

"It's me...Free!" I said at the same time. If not for Tucker, Ryan would have been my main bully. But most times, Naphtali scared him away from me. I literally heard him tell him in high school to stay away from me, and that I was his to torture.

Ryan took in the glare on Tucker's face before he cautiously looked at me and grinned mischievously. He was the chuckle knucklehead of their crew. The practical jokester.

"Damn, Free! You looking good as hell! Bro, don't kill me!" he yelled, sliding out of Tucker's reach just in time, holding up his hands. We all shared a good laugh over that. I see he was still immature.

"Hey, man, when I heard you were coming, I had a VIP area set up, so that you can have a good time without everybody bombarding you. Once word spread that you're here, it's going to get crazy. Follow me..." He led us through the huge doors that led into what was clearly a ballroom that had been decorated to resemble one of those swanky nightclubs. We walked through dancing bodies to a little alcove that sat off towards the very back of the room. And sure enough, two big bodyguards stood in front of it, ready to stop anyone without clearance.

Tucker chuckled, shaking his head when he saw them. "Ryan ass was always extra." He said close to my ear.

"What? You don't trust these guys to keep you safe?" I joked.

224

"Pssst... Yeah, right. If the sh*t go down, I would probably have to keep *them* safe."

"Wow...I forgot how humble you are."

He chuckled before throwing my words back at me. "Truth is truth. That's a check you can take to the bank, baby."

Even though he was being vain, I believed him. If anything went down, like he put it, I would definitely roll out with him over the two fellas that stood at the entrance of this room.

"This area is for the Beautiful Ones," Ryan said as he showed us to a table that was clearly for the king. "But this table is for you and your beautiful lady. What can I get you guys to drink?"

And by him, he meant his waitstaff manager that followed him, ready to assist him in any way. My nerves were so frayed I was more than ready for a drink.

"Margarita, please..."

Now this is where you guys need to pay close attention because whatever happened to piss Tucker off, happened sometime after that.

Ryan's attempt to keep Tucker from being swarmed with people worked for the most part, but it did nothing to protect him from the Beautiful Ones and their immediate friends. All of them wanted to be next to him or to talk to him... even take pictures with him on their cell phones. It was madness. I couldn't imagine what would happen if not for the big guys turning everybody else away that heard he was here and wanted to chat with him.

You guys thought I was joking when I said he was worshipped by these people. I wasn't...It was ridiculous. He kept me by his side, but I was extremely uncomfortable being in the midst of so many Beautiful Ones. None of them was nice to me in school. I remember all of them laughing at me one time or another.

But since I was here with Tucker, they all pretended like none of it ever happened. Well... at least the men did. Layla, Laureen, and the rest of the hens laughed and talked about me behind their hands.

Goodness! You would think they were back in high school and not adults with careers and families.

Tucker was in his zone and seemed genuinely pleased to be around his friends again. So, I don't think he could tell I wasn't having a good time. I mean, for the record, I kept a smile on my face and pretended to be interested in whatever he and whoever had fought to be next to him were chatting about.

Meanwhile, Dillion stood off to the side of Laureen like the lump he was, giving me mean glances all evening. I know it's said that men are clueless, but Tucker had to know I wouldn't be comfortable at a party with my ex...right?

And not only that, an ex who left me for my sister, who was also at this party. It kind of felt like he was enjoying showing off the fact that he and I were together. His hand stayed on my lower back and every now and again he would lean over and kiss my shoulder. I'm not going to lie, all these things I would have loved if Dillion wasn't here watching it.

However, I reached my limit when Layla and her date, whatever his name is, made their way to our table to chat with Tucker. Before she could start her nice nasty act of picking on me and making jokes at my expense, I excused myself.

"I'm going to go to the restroom," I spoke close to Naphtali's ear so that he could hear me over the music.

He took my hand. "You alright? You want me to go with you?"

I smiled. "Yeah, I'm fine. And don't be silly...I'll be right back."

He wrapped his arm around my waist and pulled me in his lap before planting one of those kisses on me. Only it was hard for me to get into it because I felt the twins and Dillion's eyes and it was making my skin crawl.

As I headed to the restroom, the only thing I could think of was this wasn't good. Once this news got back to Angie, she was going to set out to destroy whatever it is me and Tucker thought we had. She didn't like for me to eat wealthy people's food, wear their clothes, go to the places wealthy people go, so you can imagine how she felt about me dating wealthy men. It was probably why she went out of her way to hook Dillion and Laureen up. Actually, I don't know if she was behind that...But I would bet money she was.

Anyway, she would really blow a blood vessel if she found out I was fooling around with Naphtali Pelletier, the heir of Aldshore. I can hear her now.

"You're way out of your league, little girl..."

"You're setting yourself up for a world of hurt..."

"He's just having a little fun with the poor black trash before he chooses a girl from his station and marries..."

"Do you honestly think his parents will allow him to marry someone like you? Really...honey? Awwww, that's so sad, she did..."

Damn it! I should have known when he said his friend was having a party that he was talking about one of the

Beautiful Ones. Of course, Layla and Laureen were going to be here.

When I was finished in the washroom, I looked back toward the ballroom and a strong sense of dread came over me. Layla, Laureen, and Dillon were waiting on me to sink their evil claws into my soul. My feet made up my mind for me and took me the other way. This house was so big it was like a museum. I looked for a quiet place so that I could call Rachel, needing to hear her voice. She always had the ability to shine a light on the shallowness of the folks we grew up around. I felt so alone here, I just wanted to talk to someone that was normal.

However, when I pulled my phone out of my purse, I saw that I didn't have a signal. The farther east I walked, the stronger it became. I hadn't realized I'd gone a good distance from the ballroom till it registered to me that the music now sounded muffled.

"So, are you trying to make me jealous, showing up here with Tucker? Tucker?! Really, Free?! How low can you go?"

With my back to him, I chuckled, shaking my head. Leave it to him to think I was here with Tucker to make *him* jealous. The fact that he thought he could hold a flame to Naphtali was laughable.

*Dear God, give me the strength.*

I was getting ready to tell him to get over himself, but when I turned to look at him, he had that crazy look in his eye. Once again, he was giving off those creepy vibes, like cut my body up into little pieces and hide them under the floorboards vibes.

I looked back toward the ballroom, now regretting

wandering away so far. On this end of this massive house, nobody could hear me scream.

"It's not what you think."

He took a step toward me and I took two back. "What? Are you going to tell me you're not sleeping with him? I saw him kiss you. He can't keep his hands off of you! For God's sake, Free, he bullied you all through high school!"

The fact that he was now raising his voice was a little scary. Oh, my goodness! When did Dillion become Norman Bates? Or has he always had the tendency and I'd been too blind to see, which makes me want to examine the motives behind me not seeing it—You know what?! Now was not the time, I'll revisit that later.

However, one thing was overwhelmingly clear, I made horrible choices when it came to men.

"I guess this explains why you haven't returned any of my calls."

"No, Dillion! The small fact that you left me for my sister is the reason I haven't returned any of your calls."

Like the lunatic he is, he shifted right in front of me and went from being a big angry man to a little pussy cat... Yep, definitely psychotic.

"But whyyyy? I told you nothing has to change between us. We can still comfort each other."

"What!? Do you hear yourself? Did you really think I was so desperate that I would be your side chick while you wife my sister?!"

His nostrils flared as he turned back into angry man. *Uh oh! Maybe I should have played it cool.*

"Is it because of him you don't have time for me, because you're giving it all to Tucker?!"

I laughed. "Please, you know better than that. Me and

the muscle brain have nothing in common. The only reason I agreed to come here is because he'd spoken to a group of children for me about the dangers of drugs, what with him working for the DEA and all."

Dillion thought on my words and nodded. "That makes sense." He chuckled. "For a minute, I thought you'd been abducted by aliens. The Free I knew fantasized about killing that douchebag."

I chugged his arm playfully. "I can't believe you thought I would actually have feelings for the guy that bullied me."

He laughed, relaxing his shoulders a bit. And I exhaled, so glad he was buying it. If I could just get within reach of another human being, I will be okay.

"So, what about us?"

I blinked, biting my tongue to keep from cursing him out. "What about us, Dillion?"

"You know we were meant to be together. Everyone knows that. It's always been us. I just need to stay married to Laureen for a year, and then I can divorce her and marry you."

*What-in-thee-hell?* I always thought Dillion was smarter than this. But in order to get away from him right now alive, I placed a smile on my face.

"Maybe…"

He smiled. "That's good. I can't really talk to you here, but I'll come by your office next week. We can do lunch… maybe we can go back to your place. I miss your honeypot."

*My honeypot??? Wow…*

I opened my mouth to respond to him, but something crashed loudly down the hall. The noise caused Dillion to slink into the shadows like the creepy man he's turning out to be. I took that as my cue to hightail it out of there.

Without looking back, I made my way back to the ball-room. As I walked down the hall, I found what the loud noise was. It looked like someone had crashed into one of the locked doors, completely shattering it. Probably some-body that had too much to drink or smoke. The smell of marijuana was so strong it was choking me.

Poor Tucker... he's going to have to stay sober while all his friends get high. If I wasn't so angry with Dillion, I would have found that funny. Can you guys believe that guy? When Rachel first said he was going to try and have both me and Laureen, I thought she was just being silly. Nooo...That idiot actually thought he was going to be able to have us both.

It reminded me of something Papa C always said, *Baby, pimping ain't easy, but somebody got to do it.* Chuckling, I shook my head; I tell you who can't do it... Dillion.

I weaved my way through the dancing bodies, heading toward the VIP area where Tucker now stood with a small group of his friends, that included Layla and Laureen. It was something about the way they all stood watching me approach that gave me an eerie feeling.

The smile left my face. There was something off with Naphtali, and he was smoking weed. The deadly eyes that stared at me through the smoke caused my steps to stall.

How could none of the people standing around him tell that he had changed? When he saw my response, he lifted one side of his mouth in an evil grin.

*Oh My God!* I couldn't tell for sure, but I think that is his other personality. He didn't seem as cold as when I'd saw him in high school, the day those guys came to the school to beat up Tucker. Yet, he felt different from the Naphtali I've been hanging out with for the last couple of weeks.

I turned to look back toward the door, thinking about making a run for it, but right then, Dillion walked through it and I quickly changed my mind.

DAMN IT! I was surrounded by predators.

"Stop being weird!" Layla yelled at me.

Of course, that caused the groupies surrounding Tucker, or who used to be Tucker to erupt in laughter. But I didn't care, my focus was on the killer staring back at me. He casually passed the blunt he was smoking to Layla's date.

I looked back toward the door and Dillion one more time before deciding against that direction. I hate to admit this, but I'd rather deal with the killer than the crazy mama's boy, Norman Bates fella. At least I was still attracted to the killer.

Is that bad?

Wow! It is something wrong with that line of thought, isn't it?

Balling up my fists, I slowly approached the Beautiful Ones and their deadly king.

"Hey," I squeaked, coming to a stop next to Layla.

Yeah, I was being a coward. I didn't care. No way was I standing next to that... that thing! And Layla and Laureen...the stupid fools that they are, were so focused on me, they had no idea they were no longer dealing with Tucker, at least not fully.

"Where have you been, little sister?" Layla asked with a smirk on her face that made me want to slap her. Just for that, if Tucker decided he wanted to go on a killing spree, I was going to escape and leave her dumb butt here to wonder what was happening.

His gaze felt like hot metal against my skin. It was so intense, I couldn't look at him. I didn't care that I was making a fool of myself. Everything about him felt deadly right now, I can't believe they couldn't feel it.

"I got a call from Rachel," I told her, trying to study the entity out the side of my eye. Goodness, my grandmother would have loved to have had him as a patient, she and her Dr. Baxter, who she completely sold her soul for.

"That's funny...Dillion disappeared too," Layla continued. I wanted to swat her like a fly for rambling in such dangerous times.

She looked at Laureen. "Have you seen Dillion?"

Tucker's fists balled up and the muscle started ticking like crazy in his cheek. *Oh my God!* He was trying to fight it. He was trying to fight whatever it was from taking over him. Something had happened to upset him.

"You're smoking..." I finally said, but I doubt if he heard me over the music, because I whispered it. This was scary. If he lost the battle and his other personality took over, what would it do? Stupidly, Layla and Laureen were cackling about something and didn't have enough sense to be afraid.

He took a pull of the blunt before exhaling a mouth full of smoke. "I am."

Oh man, guys, my heart was beating so fast. I don't even know why I was so afraid of this other personality, besides the fact that I was positive it killed people.

"Why?" I whispered.

His gaze fell to my lips before coming back to my eyes. A shiver went through me. Death looked back at me. I gasped when he moved suddenly, circling my waist with his arm, pulling me against his hard body. Before he lowered his head, blocking them from my view, I saw Layla's mouth pop open in appalled shock.

His lips brushed my neck and a shiver went through me so strong it took my breath. Oh my God! There was something wrong with me. No way I should be turned on by whatever it was going on with Tucker right now.

When his mouth came to my ear, my eyes drifted shut as I bit down on my bottom lip.

"You should run..."

THE BULLY/ Naphtali

WHENEVER I'M IN DANGER, the Bully takes over my body automatically. I can't stop it...and I can't control it. But then there are times when I'm not necessarily in danger but have been blinded by rage when I'm neither Naphtali nor The Bully...but an equal combination of both. Our thoughts, desires, and needs combine to form one entity. I hate these times...because I enjoy them the most. And I'm always tempted to stay this way.

It's the best of both worlds.

But I don't ever want to be like this around Free. It's not safe...she's not safe. I can't control the Bully any more than he can control me.

*Why the hell are we still concerned with her safety? Let's have her the way we've always wanted. Let's devour her. I want to taste her so bad. Safety be damned!*

I clutched my head, trying to shut that bastard up! Damn, Free! How could you do this to me?

*"Please, you know better than that. Me and the muscle brain have nothing in common. The only reason I agreed to come here is because he'd spoken to a group of children for me about the dangers of drugs, what with him working for the DEA and all."*

Her words were on repeat in my head, causing the bastard to laugh at me.

*Damn right I'm laughing. You been acting like a p\*ssy with this girl ever since we came back. That's why she just played yo' ass. You know what need to be done. Be yourself mutha f\*cka, and cripple her ass. Put some sh\*t on her that will make it impossible for her to ever doubt who the f\*ck she belong to. Stop holding back, buddy.*

"Hey, Nap, you alright man?" Koby asked. "You got a headache or something?"

I dug my palms in my eyes, trying to fight my impulses. I didn't want to hurt Free. I didn't want to hurt her because I love her. But she'd hurt me so deeply that there was no way the Bully was leaving until I got control of my emotions.

At first, I didn't want to believe her chicken head ass sisters... But they wore me down.

*"You're just going to let it go like that?"* one of them said. I don't know which one it was, Laureen or Layla, sh\*t they look just the f\*ck alike.

I frowned at her, irritated that she was standing so close to me, when she was clearly here with my boy, Koby. *"What you talking about?"*

*"Free... isn't she here with you? You going to let her just creep off like that and run to her ex?"*

*"Beat it..."* I went back to talking to Koby. But the

chicken head's words had struck a nerve. Hell yeah, I wanted to smash that bastard Dillion's face when I saw him step off the helicopter. I hated that mutha f*cka.

In school, she always had time for him, laughed at all his jokes, ate lunch with him, did everything with his p*ssy ass! When I found out she was dating him when I got back, I wanted to drive right to his house and make his b*tch ass disappear.

I can do it...I can do that sh*t, EASILY!

But then I found out that his dumb ass had left her for one of the chicken heads and I felt like I was on top of the world. But now her sister was making it seem like my girl still loved that punk.

And it didn't help when the other sister joined her and asked her had she seen Dillion.

*"He went to the washroom about ten minutes ago. Oh! And so did Free."*

*"Hey, man, I'll be right back. Imma grab another drink,"* I told Koby.

I ain't gon' lie. At that point, I had a bad feeling I was about to kill a mutha f*cka. My emotions were such a wreck that I could feel the Bully beating at my soul like a f*cking silverback gorilla.

*That's the only way yo' ass hear me...*

Shut up, man, Damn! I'm trying to tell the readers what the f*ck happened.

*Go 'head, sh*t. You gon' let Free escape. Look at her over there at the bar, checking her phone for a signal. She looking for a way out. And look at that b*tch ass bartender flirting with her! If he touches her, he's dead! She's so sweet, Nap. We need to make our move...I want to taste!*

Like I was saying, as soon as I walked out of the ballroom, I can see Free all the way down at the other end of the hall. And who do I see walking behind her? You got it! B*tch boy!

As I followed them, I tried my best to fight the rage that was flowing through my veins. I did...But by the time I got to the end of the hall, I was not alone.

*"Please, you know better than that. Me and the muscle brain have nothing in common. The only reason I agreed to come is because he'd spoken to a group of children for me about the dangers of drugs, what with him working for the DEA and all,"* she told him, touching the bastard's arm.

For a moment, I saw red. It took every bit of strength I possessed in my body to keep the Bully from snapping both of their necks. Naw...I take that back. I just now realized that I love Free. That is what kept the Bully from killing her. My love.

"That makes sense." The asshole chuckled. "For a minute, I thought you'd been abducted by aliens. The Free I knew fantasized about killing that douchebag."

At that point, even I wanted to kill him. The only thing that held me back is the fact that the Bully's bloodlust is unquenchable. What's to say he would stop at Dillion and not reach for Free?

She rubbed his arm. *"I can't believe you thought I would actually have feelings for the guy that bullied me."*

*"So, what about us?"* ass face asked.

*"What about us, Dillion?"*

*"You know we were meant to be together. Everyone knows that. It's always been us. I just need to stay married to Laureen for a year, and then I can divorce her and marry you."*

What-the-f*ck?! I was pissed for her. The f*ck he think he can step to her like that? Free the kind of girl that you snatch up. You don't let her slip through yo' fingers…Ass face!

Maybe if I had been kinder to her, she could love me back.

*Oh Damn! Would you shut the f\*ck up with all this whiny sh\*t? You killing me, man! This girl playing both of you goofy mutha f\*ckas! She need somebody to grab her ass and let her know who the f\*ck is in charge. She need somebody to f\*ck her right. You two p\*ssy ass niggas with all yo' making love sh\*t ain't doing it. Can't you see that? You need to lay it down on this girl! Make her scream yo' name, boy!*

I clutched my head, needing this nigga to shut up so I can think straight. Normally when I get like this, I just enjoy the ride. But I can't afford to do that with Free. One mistake can cost her life. And that was a price I was not willing to pay.

"Maybe…" Free said, agreeing with his bullsh\*t ass request. My heart turned cold. Her sister was right. Free was still in love with this b\*tch boy.

He smiled at her and I balled up my fists, wanting to smash his f\*cking face. *She's mine! How dare he smile at what's mine! For that he will die.* Now just wasn't the time.

"That's good. I can't really talk to you here, but I'll come by your office next week. We can do lunch…maybe we can go back to your place. I miss your honeypot."

*Honeypot!* The rage inside of me had reached a boiling point. The Bully's voice no longer sounded human, or maybe it was mine. At this point, I lost track as to who was who.

*That's my honeypot! Nigga!*

Not being able to take anymore, I turned away. Now

was not the time to deal with Dillion.... Nooo... I needed to deal with Free first.

After tonight, she'll never question who she belongs to! When I'm done with her, there will be no doubt.

The Bully was right... It was time to stop pretending!


FREE


AFTER A MARGARITA and three shots of tequila, I had worked up enough nerve to go and find a signal. And I think, I'd worked out a plan as well to get myself down off this mountain. Once I found a signal, I will Google my location, then I will find the nearest town and go from there.

Yes, I am a little tipsy, but whatever. I was ornery enough to make it all the way to the nearest town on foot.

"One more for the road..." I told the bartender, who had also been that really nice server that made sure my wineglass stayed full.

"Anything for the prettiest girl here," he said before he poured me another shot of tequila and slid me a lime on a beverage napkin.

"You are the best bartender in the whole world. Don't let anybody tell you different," I told him as I chugged my shot. I meant it...He'd sat here and listened to all of my problems while serving this rowdy bunch.

"Thank you, love. And if you don't remember me after tonight...remember my words. Your sisters are extremely jealous of you. There isn't a woman in here whose beauty can hold a candle to yours. When you stepped in here in that golden dress, every man, including myself was ready to lay it down for you. But then they saw who you came with and got scared. But baby…" He put his hand on his chest. "I don't know the mutha f*cka, so I ain't scared of him. I wish I wasn't working. I would whisk you away right now."

"Awww…That's the sweetest thing anybody has ever said to me." Yeah… I was tipsy. "But please…be afraid of him." I pointed to my head. "He's not right."

And then I gathered my stuff and headed toward the terrace on the east side of the ballroom. There was another on the west side, but for some reason, it seemed my phone favored the east.

I cried out in pleasure when I saw that this terrace overlooked that beautiful rose maze. Oh…I wish you guys could see it. It was so big it had to stretch out twenty acres or more. I know it took a team of workers to keep it looking so healthy and beautiful.

I was also pleased to see that the massive balcony was practically empty. There were only two couples out here, one at the far end and one smooching on the golden bench in a dark corner. Exhaling, I took out my phone.

"One bar… yes!"

I did a little victory dance because that was far better than I had inside. Holding my phone up, I walked toward the steps that led down into the yard area in front of the entrance to the maze.

*Two bars!*

Excited that I was getting closer to seeing that 4G symbol, I walked down the stairs.

*Three!*

Phone in hand, I took a few steps out into the yard, but

something shifted in the air. I looked back toward the ball-room and standing there looking like a dark angel was Tucker. He watched me with a gaze so deadly my pulse increased to the point that I could see it beating in my wrist. I couldn't believe this is the same guy that had looked at me as if I was his rarest jewel just hours ago.

What could I have done to garner so much animosity? Or did his other personality hate me? I'd been enjoying myself so much with him over the last few weeks, I barely thought of the fact that he suffered from an undiagnosed case of *Dissociative Identity* Disorder, and what it meant for me if something happened to trigger him while we were together. Because he was undiagnosed, there was no way of telling what kind of danger I was in.

The guy who followed Ryan around earlier, who I assumed was head of the estate waitstaff joined him. Without taking his intense gaze away from me, Tucker spoke quietly to him. The man nodded before walking and speaking to the other two couples on the balcony. I clutched my phone so hard my knuckles turned white when the couple and the server retreated into the ballroom, pulling the balcony doors closed behind them. The manager then signaled to another waiter to step in front of them and stay.

It was clear what just happened. Tucker told the server to clear the area and to make sure no one comes out here.

*My God! Was I in danger?* Did I risk standing here to try and reason with the *other* Tucker?

So, I think now is a good time to tell you guys some-thing that you may not know about me. Just so you'll understand my next action. It's true, I spent my four years of high school in a very rich neighborhood, but I was born and raised in the hood.

The moral to that story is, although reason told me I should be able to stand here and converse with the clearly aggressive man like two adults to see why he was so angry, my feet didn't give a flying frig about what I should be able to do in this moment. And while my brain was trying to figure it out, they very carefully slid out of the beautiful golden heels.

I felt like a deer that had just been spotted by a hungry lion. I could no more stop the step I took back than I could the gathering clouds in the sky. As if nature could sense the storm brewing inside of him, a loud rumble of thunder shook the earth before lightning flashed in the night sky, highlighting the deep darkness of Naphtali's eyes.

I took another step back and an evil grin appeared on his face as he rested his hands on the rails as if he dared me to take another step. The wind picked up just then, causing my dress to blow around my legs.

I took that step...

A cry ripped from my throat when displaying incredible strength and agility, Tucker leaped over the rail and landed on his feet like a feline.

*No way he should have been able to do that!*

That jump should have at the very least broken both of his legs. The railing was nearly two stories off the ground. However, I didn't wait around to see how he'd accomplished such a feat. He was coming for me.

Fast!

Heart pounding in my chest, I turned and ran toward the only way out...unfortunately, it was the entrance to the maze. Lightning ripped across the sky again as I flew around the beautiful hedges, trying to memorize the pattern.

Red roses on the straightaway…

Peach and white roses in the curves…

*Why was he chasing me? What had I done?*

Short turns, yellow roses…

Long, winding turns, pink…

The really scary part is, I couldn't hear him behind me, so I had no idea how close he was or if I'd lost him. My footsteps sounded loud to my own ears, but my prayer was that he got turned around in the maze and that his alternate personality's mind wasn't as brilliant as my own.

When after a while I still didn't hear anything, I slowed my steps. The maze was softly lit with lights that had been weaved into the hedges. They highlighted the roses beautifully. I wish I wasn't being chased by a crazy man; I think I would have enjoyed a nice stroll through them.

With hands that shook, I took my phone out of my purse. Tears burned the back of my eyes when I saw my bars had went back to zero. Thunder shook the earth again, scaring the heck out of me. But what did me in was when the lightning flashed, highlighting the shadow of a man as he jumped over the hedge, landing silently on the ground a couple of yards in front of me. Again, that was something he should not have been able to do, the hedges stood at least eight feet tall.

A scream escaped my lips as I turned around and ran the other way. The sound of his laughter followed me, taking me back to the days of me running from him in the library.

He was toying with me…

That had to be a good sign, right? He wouldn't toy with me only to hurt me…would he?

Yeah, still not a risk I was willing to take, I continued to run, weaving in and out of the lanes, but my steps skidded to a halt when he suddenly appeared over the hedge again, causing me to turn and run in a different direction.

I had no time to process the fact that he was leaping over the hedges like freaking Superman. Something was majorly wrong with that, but if I stopped and pondered on it, I would completely lose it, so instead, I kept running.

He and I played that little game of cat and mouse for another ten minutes. It became clear to me that he was directing me. If I ran the wrong way, he appeared in my path. My brain tried to tell my panicked feet to stop, that he was leading me into a trap, but I was freaking out.

I didn't have long to see where that trap was. I think I was in the center of the maze. My steps faltered as my breath was taken by the sheer beauty here. This place must be the in-between place because we could no longer be on earth.

The area was gently lit by the lights that had been weaved inside of the hedges. In the center was a wide stone bench that was covered in snow-white rose petals, because it sat under a beautiful arch that was laden down with a climbing vine. Spellbound by it, I took a step toward it, but right then, a twig snapped behind me. I whipped around to see Naphtali standing there watching me.

Lightning lit the sky for a moment, casting his handsome face in its glow. His dark gaze had changed. Yes, it was still hostile, but there was something else there. I know this is going to sound crazy, but it kind of felt like there were two men staring at me, my Tucker and somebody else.

I took a step back, holding up my hand as if I was warding off an angry beast.

"What did I do? Why are you chasing me?" My voice quivered as I fought off the tears that wanted to be freed.

He slowly began to stalk me. "I heard you talking to him."

Even his voice was different. Yeah, it sounded like him, but it didn't. It was so hard for me to explain this. It was not your classic case of Dissociative Identity Disorder.

I knew who the *him* was he'd heard me talking to. What are the odds?

"Wait, I can explain that."

He shook his head as he continued to stalk me. "Naw, Freebie, I don't need an explanation."

A squeak left my throat when the thick hedges stopped my retreating steps. My eyes rounded in fear as I watched him close the gap between us.

I reached out, putting my hand flat against his massive chest, stopping him. For a moment, he didn't speak, he just looked down at me with nostrils flared, taking angry breaths in and out. I was trying to remember all my training on how to deal with an angry patient, but for the life of me, I could bring nothing to mind.

I opened my mouth, but no words came out as tears that didn't fall filled my eyes.

"P-Please..." I whispered. I don't know what I was begging for. Maybe it was for him not to hurt me. Maybe for him not to be angry with me and just hear me out.

Slowly he went down to one knee in front of me. "Yes,

Free. I plan on it… I plan to please you… thoroughly. After tonight, you'll never question who you belong to."

I gasped when his hands came to the tie of my dress and violently ripped it open. A mixture of excitement, fear, and pleasure shot through me. My breathing became heavy as I tried to understand what was happening to me.

I was more turned on than I've ever been…and that was frightening. My purse slipped from my shoulder and my phone from my hands. Tucker smiled when he saw the need in my gaze.

"I've wanted to taste you for so long. Can I taste you, baby?"

I bit down on my bottom lip and nodded, completely under his spell. Resting my head back against the hedge, my eyes drifted closed when his hungry mouth touched my stomach, only to fly open when an angry growl left his throat at the same time thunder shook the earth. His hands came to the waistband of my panties and the sound of them ripping filled the night.

Gently he lifted my leg to rest on his shoulder. My world shattered sweetly, but as he came to his feet, there was a promise in his eyes. That would be the only sweetness I would be allowed tonight. Slowly he unbuttoned his shirt, revealing that smooth chocolate skin, needing my own taste, I leaned forward and ran my tongue over his muscled flesh.

He groaned, holding his head back, allowing me to serve him. But that only lasted a minute before his hungry mouth was taking mine in a drugging kiss. Wrapping my arms around his neck, I tried to get closer. But no matter how close I got, it didn't feel like it was enough.

He must have felt it too, because soon after, he lifted me in his arms, bringing my legs to straddle his waist.

*Mmmmm…he was so strong.* Had he always been this strong?

I had no time to ponder it before he was entering me.

Ohhh, guys, there is no way I can tastefully explain to you what took place over the next two hours because there was nothing tasteful about it.

It was raunchy, wet, hot…savage. He brutally brought me to peak three more times before finding his own release. After the second time, he laid me on the bench of rose petals and continued to ruthlessly drive into me. Lost in a storm of ecstasy, my nails scrapped across his back as I screamed out his name…over and over again.

"Who do you belong to?" he growled down at me, invading my soul, reconstructing it, combining us in a way that can never be broken.

"You…" I moaned.

"Say it again, Free! Who do you belong to?"

"You!" I screamed as my world shattered. "Oh God! I belong to you."

That didn't appease him. He had turned completely savage on me. What sounded like a roar left his throat as he flipped me on the bench before entering me again. I think that is when the rain started, or maybe it had started hours before, I couldn't tell. He had splintered my mind. I'd completely lost myself.

"Forever," he said in my ear before taking my lobe in his mouth. "Say you're mine forever."

I was going to die from the pleasure he was causing me to feel. The tears that flowed down my cheeks had nothing to do with the rain. It was too much! My body was on fire.

"Say it, Free! Say you're mine forever."

Squeezing my eyes shut to try not to go up in flames, I cried out what he wanted to hear just as my world shattered for the fourth time.

"Forever! I'm yours forever! I swear... Oh God, only yours. Forever, Tucker...only you." He wrapped me securely in his arms and moaned my name as his warm seed filled me.

And then, I think... I fainted or blacked out or something because when I came to and was once again able to recognize myself as an individual, he was carrying me out of the maze with my belongings tucked under his arm.

I wrapped my arms around his neck, burying my face in that spot just underneath his chin and whispered.

"I want to go home..."

# Chapter 12

HUNGRY EYES...

*If She's Amazing, She Won't Be Easy. If She's Easy, She Won't Be Amazing. If She's Worth It, You Won't Give Up. If You Give Up, You're Not Worthy...*

*Bob Marley*

## Free

EVER SINCE I was a little girl, I could remember handling trauma differently from those around me. When my mother died, I wondered if I was going to die with her. Instead, I stood at her funeral dry-eyed and evaluated my own feelings, breaking down the trauma and how it affected me. Five days later, after I had been deposited in Angie's basement, I sat on my bed and had a panic attack all by myself when it finally registered that my mom was gone.

The walls closed in on me and I couldn't breathe, the only thing I could do was ball up really tight and ride it out. That's when I realized I'd been holding onto my tears. Somehow, I felt that if I didn't cry, then it couldn't be real. It wasn't until I released the first tear that my attack began to subside. I lay in bed and cried that whole night and the next one after that.

You see, I have an aversion to tears. I know that sounds horrible, but it's true. I am terrified of the pain it takes to make me cry. So, after that day, after mourning my mother, I told myself I would never mourn again. And my whole life became about me avoiding having to mourn.

When my father died, I avoided mourning by reminding myself that he was never there for me and my mom. And afterward, he never stood up for me and allowed Angie to abuse me. Although there were times Tucker caused tears to burn the back of my eyes, I avoided shedding them by reminding myself that my time with him was only temporary. That thought became a lifeline to me, ingrained in the very fiber of my being.

Yes, I am aware that my aversion to mourning is unhealthy because tears are a part of life just like laughing and anger. And yet still, it's something that I struggle with. Seeing Dillion sitting on the couch with my sister as they announced their engagement was traumatizing and I told myself I needed to mourn; it was the healthy thing to do.

But I couldn't…

I couldn't shed one tear because he wasn't Tucker.

I've always known that I had to avoid loving Tucker because for some reason, he was the one person on earth that I knew had the power to break me. Even then, I didn't understand the bond between me and my bully, but it was there.

How cruel can irony be...

And now... now there was no running from my feelings. I love Tucker. I love him with my whole heart and soul. Up until the other night in the rose garden, I'd been able to lie to myself, to deny that he was a part of me and I of him.

But then he forced me to acknowledge our connection. Dear God! I cry every time the man makes love to me!

I guess if I'm honest with myself, I can admit that I've always loved him, since the very first time our eyes met in that classroom.

However, there was a very long list of problems that came with that admission, the main one being, I'm his doctor. There was no way around the fact that I was going to have to give him up as a patient. I could only imagine what Angie and the twins were doing with the information they have thus far. I'm sure I was soon to find out though.

And then, there was the small fact that he may freaking be Superman! Oh guys! My mind can't wrap around the things I saw him do. I know that he was a great athlete in high school. Folks all over Michigan still speak on his prowess. But what I saw goes beyond prowess. What I saw was supernatural.

As a psychiatrist, I was trained to believe in science, what I can touch, taste, hear, and see, but my mother always told me to search for God. She said God's will happens around us all the time and that it took more than the eyes to see it.

I've been doing Tucker a disservice by trying to use

science to define him. What was going on with him went beyond *Dissociative Identity* Disorder. Yes, there was some kind of multiple personality thing happening, but it was more like a dual personality, which is unheard of.

Two individuals can't occupy the same space at the same time... science. Yet, I witnessed two individuals occupying the same space at the same time. Not only that, he was faster, stronger... I-I can't wrap my head around it.

And unfortunately, because I'd played hooky and decided to go to the ball with prince charming instead of securing more employers for the job fair, I really didn't have time to look into it. My grandmother had medical journals that dated back to the late 1800s and more than anything, I wanted to curl up on my couch and search through them to see if something like this had ever happened before, but I just didn't have time.

There were a lot of people depending on this job fair to better themselves. And yeah, that was another reason I had to take a break from Tucker.

Hmmmm...

Oh! I didn't tell you guys I haven't seen him in three days and that it was killing me inside. Well, because I'd allowed him to talk me into abandoning my responsibility for a night of leisure, I was now playing make up in a huge way.

The really bad part about that is, I didn't even enjoy myself at the party... Well, except for the rose garden.

Mmmm...I can't think of the rose garden. Every time I do, a shiver starts in my core, shoots up my spine and into my throat, robbing me of my breath. Yesterday, I was having a meeting with Dr. Ross and a few of the food vendors that agreed to come out for the fair today and one of them mentioned a tea that they make with rose water.

*Roses...* A vision of him laying me on that bench covered in white rose petals flashed through my head along with the way his big powerful body loomed over me as he relentlessly drove into me and I gasped, clutching my stomach and my desk to steady myself at the same time.

Dr. Ross looked over at me with concern. "Dr. Robinson...are you alright?"

I held up my hand to stay him. "Yes, yes, I'm fine. Just a little tired from burning the midnight oil, that's all..."

WHAT THE WORLD?! Has that ever happened to any of you?

Anyway, luckily when Naphtali called Monday, I was honestly able to tell him that I was up to my elbows in work. Thank God he didn't push me and simply said that he understood and for me to give him a call when I can.

Well, it was Wednesday, and I was up at the crack of dawn running around Detroit like a chicken with my head cut off. I'd managed to secure a few more employers but honestly it was nowhere near enough. Over the last two months, I've had so many doors slammed in my face. As soon as I tell them the people and the community the job fair was for, I received a solid...*not interested.*

God! It was so frustrating it made me want to pull out my hair! There were so many good people in the Oakwood Heights community, and in most cases, they weren't given a chance because of mistakes they made when they were younger.

It vexed me beyond belief that young black youths are labeled criminals for doing things kids all over the world did. A group of boys get caught with a little weed, more than likely if they're a minority, they're going to get jail time... while the benefit of the doubt is given to other youths with a *boys will be boys* pat on the back.

You know what? Please don't get me started on the double standards this county runs on. I would never get anything done and I still had several runs to make before we opened the doors to the fair at nine.

————

"FREE, stop biting your nails. Everything is going to be fine... So what it's only nine companies here. The people are going to appreciate it, and those that are able, are going to take advantage of the opportunities you fought so that they can have."

"But that's just it. I should not have listened to Tucker and gone away for the weekend. I could have gotten at least two more companies. I was wearing Hale Aluminum down. If I had shown up at their place Saturday, maybe with a fruit basket or something-"

"Stop it!" Oaklee said, grabbing my shoulders giving them a good shake. "You did the best that you could do. I don't know anyone that deserved that magical weekend you had more. Look at you!" She stepped back and gestured at my body.

I frowned, looking down at my silk blouse and jeans. "What's wrong with me?"

"Haven't you noticed that since your supposed *bully*..." she held up air quotes when she said, bully. "Came back into your life, you've abandoned those old-prude-lady tweed suits and that ridiculous bun you're so fond of? You wear your beautiful hair down now and come to work in flip flops." She gestured toward my feet. I'd painted sunflowers on my toenails.

"That man has helped you find yourself, 'cause sista, you were lost. And whenever you stop being a scaredy-cat, you need to call him. As a matter of fact, when I see him again, I'm going to give him a kackle doodle for doing what he did for you. Spoiling you like that... How romantic."

I blinked at her... Kackle doodle??? Even I didn't know what the heck she was trying to say.

"Everything is going to be alright," she continued, rubbing her hands up and down my arm in a soothing pattern. "Listen, we still have an hour and a half before we open the gate to the parking lot. Why don't you go into your office and have a nice cup of coffee and a muffin... and then just breathe, girl."

I looked around the parking lot as the vendors and the companies continued to set up their areas. Maybe she was right... I'd barely gotten any sleep last night, and I could really use another cup of coffee.

Oaklee frowned at something over my shoulder. "Who is that?"

I turned to see a huge sleek black tour bus with the word Dyno Tech written on the side of it in gold pulling into the lot.

"Wow! You talked to Dyno Tech?!"

I shook my head completely confused. "No, I didn't... this must be a mistake." Oaklee and I walked to meet them, Dr. Ross joined us.

"Hey, is this 3265 Berker Lane?" A young man in a pair of khakis and a blue button-up shirt asked, stepping off the impressive vehicle. A cool breeze greeted us when the doors opened.

"It is..." I said. But before I could ask him how we could help him; he stuck his head back inside the bus.

"This is the place, let's set up." He turned back to face us. "Where do you want us? Sorry, we're late, my boss just told me about it last night. I had to pull a rabbit out of my ass to get everything prepared by morning. But hey, we're here." He was jotting something down on a clipboard as he spoke.

Because I didn't want to scare him away, I turned to face Oaklee as if we'd been expecting them the whole time.

"Oak, can you please show this gentleman where to set up their booth."

She nodded as if it was the plan all along. "Right this way, we have you guys next to Bobby's Sports Gear."

I smiled as they passed us, but as soon as he was out of sight, my surprised gaze went to Dr. Ross.

"Dyno Tech??" We both said at the same time.

"Do you think they got our address mixed up with Silicon Valley?"

I shrugged. "I don't know, but I'm not going to look a gift horse in the mouth. I know a few people in this neighborhood that would be an asset to their company. Ms. Geraldine was just telling me about her grandson that was in his second year down at the city college and was practically running the computer lab there."

Dr. Ross pointed toward the parking lot entrance. "Oh my God, Free, look!"

I turned to see what was going on and had to clutch his

arm. There was a van pulling into the lot with Prime Real Estate written on the side. Behind it was a truck with Amber's Furniture, behind it another truck... and another, and another.

"There are so many..." I cried, completely floored at what I was seeing.

"How is this happening?" Dr. Ross asked just as surprised as I was.

I turned to smile at him. "I don't know, but let's find out after we get everyone set up."

"Great idea..."

We spent the next hour trying to find a spot for everyone and to help those that needed electricity and Wi-Fi for the presentations get it. I had no time to stop and wonder how this miracle happened. We started out with nine companies...now we had twenty-nine.

But guys, that is not where the miracles ended. It wasn't just companies that showed up, there were also trucks and vans with portable carnival games. When I talked to the vendors, they said that all the games were free. And for prizes, the kids would win things like backpacks and other school supplies. And if that wasn't overwhelming enough, the food wagons showed up... Jerk Chicken, Burger Prince, and Chicago Beef Dogs.

Guys... it was all free. Of course, the vendors that I'd gotten to come out wasn't happy with that because the free food wagons pretty much guaranteed they will be making very little money today. But it was a tough break for them, no way was I turning away free food for my people.

All the activity was already drawing a crowd at the gate. This thing was going to be epic!

"Free... I know who did this!" Oaklee cried, sprinting toward me.

I smiled, knowing I'd put the right woman on the job. I haven't been able to get a clear answer as to who was behind this from anyone and didn't have time to really pry about it before someone was getting my attention for another matter. So, what did I do? You got it, put Oaklee on the case.

When she finally caught up, she had to hold onto the table as she fought to catch her breath.

"It was— it was—"

I wanted to tell her to spit it out already, but the poor child was struggling to breathe.

"Who was it, Oak?"

"Mayor Pelletier's office!"

"Mayor Pelletier?!"

She nodded, still fighting for breath. "I was talking to that guy over there and he said his boss said the mayor's son called in a favor. He's been instructed to hire at least fifteen people for the furniture making company."

*Tucker! This was all because of Tucker!*

"Girl, you alright? You look like you're getting ready to faint," Oaklee said, eyeballing me.

I shook my head... "No, I'm not alright." I really wasn't. I was in such a state of shock, for the first time in my life, my body was operating ahead of my mind.

"Why? Who is Mayor Pelletier?"

"He used to be the Mayor of Aldshore, and he's... he's Tucker's dad."

"Tucker?!"

I nodded... "This is all his doing. I don't know what to say to him. How can I ever repay him for this?"

"Well, you can start with a thank you. You're going to get your chance, he and a few others from your group will be showing up shortly to lend a hand. I put him and Papa C over the dunking booth."

It was my turn to grasp onto the table. "Oaklee! What?! When did you invite him?"

"Monday. Dr. Ross thought it would be a good idea if some of his clients come out and help. He asked me to call and see how many volunteers we could find." She shrugged. "So, I thought why not call some of your people too."

"Why didn't you tell me?" I screeched.

"You were busy! I was busy! It kind of slipped my mind till just now!"

"Oak-lee!!!!"

She grimaced. "Don't look now, but he's here. And oh, great! He has that bastard Asher with him!"

I turned just as Tucker with Asher in the passenger seat next to him, whipped his truck into the lot, parking it next to my car. Ladies, I don't know if my eyes were playing tricks on me or what, but when he stepped out of that truck, time seemed to slow down. Because he was dressed in a white tank top, the sun reflected off his beautiful brown muscled shoulders perfectly, causing his melanin to pop in a way that looked like art. He looked like a piece of art that can carry the world on his shoulders.

His gaze came to mine and I inhaled, suddenly remembering the last time I'd laid eyes on him. With that memory, came the quiver in my stomach. With that quiver…the scent of roses.

Something fell to the ground somewhere behind me, breaking the spell. I blinked, looking away from him.

"Dr. Robinson...we have a problem," the man that ran the Jerk Chicken truck said with a heavy Jamaican accent.

I glanced at Tucker one more time before turning away from him completely. "I'll be right there."

————

FOR THE NEXT hour or so, I walked around in something of a daze, although I was smiling, shaking hands, and talking to everyone, I did so on cloud nine. I couldn't have imagined this day would go so well. The people of the community were happy. Many of them were leaving with prospects of employment, some had even managed to score interviews.

The children were having the time of their lives, playing games, eating good food, gathering much needed school supplies for when classes start back in the fall. This was by far the best day of my life. And I owe it all to Tucker.

He really came through for me in a major way. Not only had he gotten his father's office to sponsor all of this, but he'd also gotten his father to make a guest appearance and with him the local news that ran a story about the event, helping to bring awareness to our cause.

Mayor Pelletier spoke to the people for a moment about the opportunities that were available for them and the opportunities he will personally make sure will be available for them in the near future. Apparently, the ex-mayor of Aldshore had his sights set on the White House.

This was going to sound silly to you guys, but can you believe I have yet to make my way to the dunking booth to thank Tucker for all of this? I'll admit I am a little nervous, I don't really know what to say to him now that I've admitted to myself that I love him. But that wasn't really the reason I haven't made my way over there.

Now, remember, I warned you it's going to sound silly, so please don't laugh at me. Okay...here we go. I hadn't made my way to him because I was enjoying his hungry eyes.

Mmmmhhhmmm, you guys heard me correctly. He stood dressed in a pair of name brand black sweatpants, brand new gym shoes, and that tank top looking good enough to lick.

Yeah, I wanted to lick him...really bad.

Anyway, he stood there manning the dunking booth. And of course, he had a dripping Papa C sitting over the vat of water while he handed the little ones the balls. But every time I should happen to glance his way, it was to find him watching me.

There was so much in his glance. He was sorry about scaring me the other night, he wondered if I was pleased with his gift, if I'd forgiven him... but mostly, he thought that I was beautiful. I was such an idiot. Do you guys know how many times I'd caught him watching me the same way in high school? But I was just too dumb to realize what the look meant.

Now I knew... it had me floating on cloud nine, and nothing could bring me down.

"Hey, Dr. Robinson...Isn't that your ex?" Dr. Ross asked from where he stood speaking with one of his patients not too far from me.

*Nothing can bring me down...Except that!*

Dillion stood by the entrance scanning the crowd looking for me. Not caring how it appeared in front of Dr. Ross, I ducked straight down.

"Is everything alright?" he asked, startled by my response.

"Shhh! Don't look at me! Is he looking at me?"

For just a second, poor Dr. Ross was confused and didn't know where to look. By the time his gaze came back to me, I was gone, weaving my way through the crowd toward our building and my office.

I know this was the coward way to handle this…But I just didn't want to deal with him right now.

Naphtali

I LAUGHED as Free's little friend threw the ball with all her might, aiming for the bullseye. Ever since Asher replaced Papa C over the tank of water, she's been trying to hit it nonstop. This was her third attempt. The little children waiting in line behind her were good and upset. But she didn't care, there was a fever in her eyes, she wanted to see Asher take a dive.

"Aw, come on, baby! You got to do better than that…" he teased her. "You throw like a whiny girl!"

His words only made her angrier. Because the games were free, she gave her dollars to the kids who waited in line behind her.

"I'll give you a dollar if I can have your turn."

"Deal!" The kid would say before snatching it and running away. She was on her fourth child and dollar.

"You going down this time!" she promised.

He opened his arms. "That's what you said the last three times."

I shook my head as my gaze sought out Free. She stood across the lot speaking with that other doctor that worked here, who couldn't seem to keep his f*cking eyes off my woman. Because I was in hot water, I will keep my cool, but I had my eyes on his ass.

Yeah, I was in hot water. I f*cked up! I allowed myself to be ruled by my lower nature and now she hadn't talked to me in three f*cking days. I wasn't too upset because I knew for a fact she'd been busy as hell planning for this event.

During my nightly watch, I haven't been able to stay away from her, so when she finally passed out from exhaustion, I let myself in her place and sat on the floor at the foot of her bed while she slept. By morning, I was always gone.

But Damn! Y'all don't know how bad I wanted to pull her in my arms and tell her to stop f*cking worrying about this event, that I would handle it.

My captain has been giving me daily reports on Rau. The mutha f*cka is determined to find his brother's killer. I was beginning to get a bad vibe about it. I would hate to have to pull Free away from her precious clinic, but if I even get a hint that Rau suspects me of the murder and is now looking for me, I was going to do it. I would stash her somewhere safe, go and take care of that bastard and any other loose ends, and then maybe she could return to her life.

I felt like sh*t. Because I couldn't stay away from her, I may have f*cked around and put a target on her head. It was cool though… there was no way I was letting her get hurt. I don't give a f*ck who I had to take out. All them mutha f*ckas can get it as far as I was concerned.

Speaking of mutha f*ckas that needed these hands, Free's lame-ass ex just walked in the lot. My gaze shot to her just as her eyes rounded in fear before she ducked down and hurried to her office.

I wasn't the only one that had noticed her action. Dillion had as well and wore that geeky ass peeved look on his face.

Grinning, I shook my head. Why the hell didn't I notice this the other night? I was so blinded by rage, I didn't see she was trying to shake this dude. But he obviously wasn't getting the picture that it was over and needed a little assistance.

"Aye yo, Asher!" I called to my boy, who was clearly in love with this chick, who was determined to knock him down a few pegs.

"Yeah!" He couldn't take his eyes away from her long enough to look at me.

"I'll be right back, I got to run in the clinic for a minute."

He waved me away. "Do yo' thang."

I smiled as I turned away… *I think I will, bro.*


FREE


"I GET IT! You obviously don't want to be with me!"

I closed my eyes… *So close! I was sooo close!*

I'd just made it to my office and almost had my door closed when he pushed it open behind me.

"Dillion, listen. I—" He continued to push inside, shutting the door behind him.

"No, *you* listen!" he hissed. My lips snapped shut. "I know Tucker is behind all of *this*!" He waved his hands in the air as if none of *this* mattered. Not the job opportunities for the people or the games and free food for the kids.

And you know what? That pissed me the hell off.

"All of this?" I snapped, waving my hand like he did. "I'll have you know that this day has changed the lives for a lot of people."

He laughed bitterly. "And look...you only had to whore yourself out to make it happen."

My mouth popped open as if he'd slapped me. I balled my fists up, preparing to swing at him. But before I could, my office door swung open, slamming into Dillion's back so hard it took him off his feet, causing him to smash face-first into the wall behind the door.

I grimaced at the sound of his nose cracking.

"Hey, Free, I was wondering..." Tucker began until he noticed what had happened. "Uh oh! Dillion...Buddy, are you okay?" he asked, reaching down to pull a screaming Dillion up off the ground by his collar.

My ex clutched at his nose that gushed blood. There was a bloodstain on my wall from where his face connected with it.

Angrily, he snatched away from Tucker and hurried out of the room.

"Buddy! I'm sorry! I didn't see you standing there!" Naphtali called after him. "Oh, and D man...I'm back, spread the word!" When he turned around to face me, I threw myself in his arms.

"What's the matter, baby? You're shaking."

"Nothing..." I moaned, pressing my face against his muscled chest as he tightened his strong arms around me, securing me in his embrace.

"Nothing, now that you're here..."

# Chapter 13

## WHEN THE TRUTH CATCHES YOU

*Letting Go Does Not Mean Giving Up, But Rather Accepting That There Are Some Things That Cannot Be...*

*Unknown*

## Free

I OFTEN WONDER IS THERE an unseen hand out there who determines who receives happiness, and if so, how do you make the list? There are very few times in my life where I can say that I was happy. Yeah sure, it came in spurts, like the time my mom took me to get two scoops of blueberry ice cream at the new ice cream parlor on the corner, or the time I got brand new roller skates for my seventh birthday. When I received my PHD, for truly I did it against all odds.

However, the thing about my happiness is, it doesn't last. And I know in general, nobody is happy all the time. For me, my painful days greatly outweigh my good ones. Still, I never let myself ponder on the possibilities that it wasn't fair. I've always thought that was prohibiting behavior. I was dealt my cards, so now I had a responsibility to play them. At least that's the way I've always looked at it.

But then something happened. The dealer of the card game called life, dealt me a new hand. Guys... for the last month and a half, I've been blissfully happy. No... I don't think you understand. I've been every day, blissfully happy.

And I had Tucker to thank for it. He is so amazing. Caring, loving, thoughtful...insightful. Goodness! The list can go on.

Do you guys know that since the job fair, he and I haven't spent one night apart? A few of those nights we spent at my place, but most of the time, we're at his. He even gave me a key. Of course, I gave him one in return, although my house was nowhere as near as nice as his.

Anyway, he always gets me there by calling me right before I close the clinic and telling me about some delicious dish he's whipped up especially for me. He's discovered my weakness, and the man can cook. He could take simple ingredients and string together masterpieces. I often joked that I was going to get him signed up for *Hell's Cafeteria*. Seeing him and the ill-tempered Jorden Ramblesby going toe to toe would make for good TV.

Anyway, as you guys know, I had to let him go as a patient. The next day after the job fair, I went to talk to Dr. Ross and he agreed to take Tucker on till Dr. Kimbell came back. Thank God Dr. Kimbell came back a week ago because for some strange reason, Tucker and Dr. Ross couldn't seem to get along.

I was in my office the other day with a client when I heard Dr. Ross's door slam across the hall. A split second later, an enraged Tucker opened my door, held a blunt up in front of him and lit it.

"My Doctor drove me to it!" he growled before putting it in his mouth and leaving, slamming my door behind him. My only thought was... *It's a good thing his captain still calls me for his weekly checkups and not Dr. Ross.*

Now, I believe I've figured out the secret to happiness...at least in my life. It's keeping Angie and the twins out of it. Of course, they tried to invade it anyway, but for the last month and a half, I can say I successfully thwarted all their attempts.

Because I was in her wedding, I had to communicate with Laureen from time to time, but outside of that, nothing. If Angie calls my phone, I send it straight to voicemail. One-time Tucker was over at my place and Layla showed up. I held my finger to my mouth, motioning for him to be quiet until she got the picture that I wasn't answering the door.

And guys, she was desperate. I guess word had spread that Tucker and I were dating, and it was driving her wild. Not only was she calling me more, but she'd even attempted to show up at the clinic a few times.

Okay, confession time. When we were younger, it was kind of a well-known fact in our house that Angie was pushing for Layla to snag Tucker. Somehow in her whacked out and extremely outdated mind, she felt that Layla and he were destined to be together.

In her vanity, she assumed that out of all the princesses in the town of Aldshore, that her Layla was the prettiest and surely would be the logical choice for his royal highness. Boy, it must really be rubbing her raw to know that his royal highness had chosen her unwanted stepdaughter, who had not come from the plush streets of the rich but had been born and bred in the ghetto.

Ohhh! Just the thought of it makes me chuckle. So, like I said, everything in my world is going beautiful, the winds have shifted for me and I was ready to soak it all up.

"Hey, baye, my parents are leaving for their European tour tomorrow. They want to have dinner with us at the Whitney," Tucker said when I arrived at his place after work.

He sat on his couch cleaning his guns. I found out this was something he did to clear his mind. Easing the grocery bags I carried down on the couch, I studied him for a moment.

"The Whitney? Wow! How long are they going to be gone?"

He shrugged, nonchalantly. "Six, seven months."

There were three subjects he and I barely spoke on, and it wasn't for lack of trying on my part. The fact that he may have *Dissociative Identity* Disorder, the fact that he may be a real-life Superman, and his parents.

As a kid, I thought he and his dad were close. The mayor showed up for most of his games and always seemed to be really proud of him. However, you should never judge a book from the outside. Tucker and I have officially been dating for a month and a half and this is the first time he's brought up his parents.

Of course, the doctor in me had to probe... just a little.

"Sure, sounds good. I would have to run home to find something to wear."

He nodded. "I told you, you need to bring more stuff over so that you don't have to run home every time something comes up."

I smiled; he had been pressuring me to practically move in with him. We nearly got into our first argument as a couple over whether or not I should have toiletries in his bathroom. He got upset that I used my things and then repacked them inside of my bag rather than leaving them at his place since I'm always here anyway.

Let me tell you...Mr. Man was still very much a bully. However, I'll go into detail about that later. I was not letting him off the hook before we can have a little discussion about his parents.

"So, they're going to be gone for a half a year, you're going to miss them. Huh?"

Without looking away from his gun he shrugged. "Not really."

"You guys close?"

"Nope."

I narrowed my eyes at him. So, he thought he was going to one-word answer me to death, did he? Well, he didn't know who he was dealing with.

"Why not?"

Chuckling, he finally turned to look at me. "Remember we agreed that just because my girlfriend's a shrink, she won't shrink me?"

I laughed, waving away his silliness. "Shrink you... Is that even a thing?"

"Yes, and we agreed that you weren't going to do it."

The smile left my face to be replaced with a pout. "*You*

agreed. I didn't agree to anything. Like normal people, I like to talk."

With that grin still on his handsome face, he shook his head. "You don't like to talk. You like to break everything down and find out the meaning and the reason behind it. That's not talking, and it ain't normal." He went back to cleaning his guns.

I snatched the grocery bags off the couch. "Fine, have your secrets."

———

"SO FREE, how long have you been working in the Oakwood Heights area? Fredrick and Naphtali tell me your clinic is a staple in that community. Great job, young lady."

I blushed, honored by Tucker's mom's compliment. "Wow! Thank you, Mrs. Pelletier-"

She waved away my words. "Please, call me Nadine."

*Wow! Tucker's mom wants me to call her by her first name!* Don't fangirl out, Free! As if he could hear my inner dialogue, Naphtali chuckled as he chewed his steak.

"Nadine," I said, testing it on my tongue. "I am extremely honored and grateful for all that your family did for the clinic. The community is still abuzz about it, waiting to see Mayor Pelletier's name on the ballot so that they can repay him for his generosity."

Oh yeah! I didn't make it this far not knowing how to snoosh. And don't stone me for wanting my boyfriend's parents to like me. You see how well my relationship was with Dillion's parents. Who wanted a repeat of that fiasco?

Tucker's dad puffed out his chest in a way that said he

approved my statement. Nadine patted her husband's hand. "Yes, Fredrick does have a big heart, and will do all we can for the community, sweetheart."

"I like her, son." The mayor told Tucker, who never looked up from his steak that he was cutting with his knife and fork.

"Thanks, Dad, you know how happy it makes me to have your approval," he said dryly.

There was definitely something going on with this group. Tucker barely hugged his mom when we walked into the restaurant. And when he did, she looked extremely uncomfortable. Every now and again, she shot him wary glances as if she feared he was going to snap and hit her or something. And his dad, goodness. For him, it was all about appearances.

He was the shifty-eyed type. His gaze had not stopped scanning the upscale restaurant to see who he could spot and who was spotting him. In a weird way, it appeared as if he was showing Tucker off. He'd motioned for several people to come to the table just so he could tell them that his son was home from Virginia for a little while.

Yeah…It was very weird.

But on the upswing, it seemed as if they liked me. For so long, Angie has been obsessed over traveling in this couple's circle, that I'd just assumed they were as evil as she was. Granted, I don't know how evil they are, but they were nice.

Well…nicer than Angie.

"Free, honey, is that you?"

My fork froze halfway to my mouth. That was a voice I'd successfully dodged for a month and a half.

"Angie!" *Great, Free! You've gone and spoke up the devil!*

And she wasn't alone. Layla, Laureen, and Dillion were with her.

"Mr. and Mrs. Mayor Pelletier, so good to see you again," she cooed, holding her hand out to shake theirs.

"Why yes, An..An-"

"Angelica," she said helping the mayor out.

I bit my bottom lip to keep myself from grinning. What is the irony? She'd obsessed over these people and they didn't even know her name.

"And how do you know our Free, Angelica," Nadine asked with a kind smile on her face.

"Why Mrs. Mayor, Free is my daughter," she spoke as if she was awed by the fact that she didn't know that, as if she didn't keep me hidden in the basement.

Nadine's surprised gaze came to mine. "Step," I said with a stiff smile on my face. "*Step*daughter."

"Well, it is so nice to see you again. We were just telling Free how proud we are of the work she's doing in the Oakwood Heights community. We need more people like her that's ready to pull up their sleeves and dive right in to help." Spoken like a true politician's wife.

"Thank you, Nadine," I told her, once again blushing from her compliment.

"Oh yes, Na—" Angie began, but Tucker's mother chuckled, cutting her off midsentence.

"Mrs. Mayor Pelletier is fine, dear."

*Oh God!*

*Help Me!*

*Take the wheel, Master... I wasn't going to make it.*

A giggle left my lips before I could catch. But I quickly recovered by picking up my napkin, pretending to cough in it.

"You alright, sweetheart?" Tucker asked with a grin on his face as he rubbed my back. It was that grin that made another giggle escape my lips. I had to look away from him. Instead I picked up my water and took a sip.

"Yes..." I said clearing my throat. "I'm fine, just swallowed my chicken the wrong way."

He still rubbed my back, but I could tell by the mischievous look on his face he was getting ready to try to tip me over. "Okay... be careful, we don't want you to choke like your stepmother here just did."

That was it, I was back to coughing viciously in my napkin. That Bastard!

"Well!" Angie hissed, good and insulted. "It was so nice seeing you again, Mr. and Mrs. Mayor." She actually bowed slightly.

What?! Who does that?!

Her gaze came to Tucker's. "A pleasure as always, young man. You and Layla will have to get together and hang out again, soon."

My eyes shot to his. Again! The muscle ticked guiltily in his chin. You bastard!

Knowing she'd nailed a deadly blow; Angie's piercing gaze came to me. "Free, we leave for Vegas next week, and you still have yet to tell me if you will be attending your sister's wedding alone or with someone."

Tucker's gaze shot to me... Damn it! I had intentionally not mentioned the wedding to him because I'd planned on going alone. No way was I going to take him so that he could witness our dysfunctional family dynamics.

In only the way true evil could, Angie's whole mood shifted when she sensed she'd successfully caused strife in his and my relationship. "Alone then…I'll let the wedding planner know. Chat with you later, dear."

Although she said that with a smile on her face, I knew it for the threat it was. She'd been embarrassed and insulted. Of course, she was blaming me and was going to try her damnedest to make me pay for it.

"So, when were you going to tell me you slept with my sister?" I asked him as soon as we got in his truck.

He exhaled, shaking his head. "Look…I was going to tell you. It happened before I met you, she was my first."

"Your first?!" I screeched. "Are you f*cking kidding me? My sister took your virginity and you didn't think to tell me this before I fell—" I caught myself.

No way was I going to admit that. Not now!

With his hands resting on his steering wheel, he angrily stared straight ahead out of the window. "So what? It's no big deal."

"No big deal? Really, Tuck? She took your virginity, that is a huge deal. You never forget the person who takes your virginity."

I'll never be able to forget you, bastard!

"You tripping, man, that sh*t only a big deal to women. We don't give a f*ck who we f*ck as long as we f*ck!"

Insulted, I sat back in the seat and folded my arms. I had to fold them or I was going to hit him. Now I had my answer about how it was he left me on the beach by myself the night he took my virginity.

Apparently, the only thing he cared about was f*cking!

"And you sitting yo' ass over there judging me for keeping secrets. When were you going to tell me about the wedding? How the f*ck you think you going to Vegas without saying anything?"

"Real easy...take me home."

"I ain't taking you nowhere until we work this sh*t out."

"Take-me-home!" I yelled, close to tears.

He growled something under his breath and threw the truck in gear, pulling off from the restaurant with his tires screeching. We didn't say a word to each other the whole way. When he pulled up out front, I slammed out of the car and watched appalled as he pulled off with the same loud screeching tires that he'd done back at the restaurant.

Damn it!

I stood there unsure of what to do. I didn't want to go in my lonely house. It never felt like home.

Layla and Tucker had slept together. She'd taken his virginity... Oh God! No wonder she's been acting as if I'd betrayed her. No wonder...

Turning, I made my way into my lonely book house. Because I didn't have the will to walk up the stairs, I collapsed on my couch. Tears were running down my eyes before my butt touched the cushion. This was the same feeling I'd felt that morning I woke up alone on the beach.

I was such a fool... I wasn't supposed to be feeling this way again, only it was worse, a hundred times worse. My heart hurt so badly I was finding it hard to breathe. I think that maybe I was going to have another panic attack.

Balling up on the couch, I gave into my tears and let them pour from me freely. The next morning when my alarm went off, signaling it was time for me to get ready for work, I lifted the lamp on my nightstand and smashed it.

I quit!

I was tired of caring for everybody and nobody caring for me. To hell with that clinic.

Rachel and Oaklee showed up that night. I didn't even get up to open the door for them, the heffas broke in.

"What the hell is going on here?" Rachel said, turning on my bedroom light.

"Turn it back off!" I yelled from the pile of covers I was under.

"Oh hell! She in here watching the Color Purple," Oaklee said, plopping her butt down on my bed. I started to kick her off but didn't want to be mean.

"Only one thing makes a girl curl up in her bed watching the Color Purple, eating—" Rachel picked up the empty container of ice cream from my nightstand so that she could read what kind it was.

"Chocolate obsession..." Her gaze came to mine.

"Chocolate obsession!" I cried as a fresh wave of tears came to my eyes. I missed my chocolate obsession...

She and Oaklee met eyes over my head. "Heartbreak," they said at the same time.

Rachel exhaled, climbing into bed next to me. "Go ahead, scooch over... and tell us what happened."

Oaklee climbed up the bed on my other side, sandwiching me between them. I didn't even have the will to lift my head from Rachel's shoulder as I told them what happened. And to give them both credit, neither of them said a thing until I was finished. But as soon as I finished, they let me have it.

"Girl, are you a f*cking fool?! If you don't get yo' ass up out of this bed, take a shower, and go get yo' man, I will kick you smack dab in the center of your forehead."

Both Oaklee and I looked at Rachel. "In the center of

her forehead, Rach? That's a little aggressive, don't you think?" Oaklee asked her.

Rach shrugged. "It may be, but it pisses me off every time she allows that witch to rob her happiness! I swear, one of these days, I'm going to take a bat and beat her brains out."

I put my hand on my friends arm. "You are very dark and angry. Has anybody ever told you that?"

She chuckled. "As a matter of fact, yes, the sheriff told me that just yesterday when he showed up at my house and I threatened to cut his balls off and feed them to him."

"Jackson came to your house?" I asked.

She shook her finger at me. "Naw, we not changing the subject. We talking about you and the fact that you ain't all that bright. Yeah, I know you got a PHD and whatever…" She waved her hand.

"But you ain't bright. You gon' sit here and get in yo' feelings 'cause he didn't tell you, yo' hood rat ass sister took his virginity. So the f*ck what, Free? She's a soul-sucker. I'm sure there ain't many boys in Aldshore who's virginity that viper hasn't snatched. Big deal…"

"That's the same thing Tucker said," I mumbled.

"And he was right."

"But now he's mad at me." Tears came to my eyes again. "He practically threw me out his truck and he hasn't even tried to call me today."

"I would be mad too!" Rachel began, but Oaklee signaled for her to let her talk.

"What Rachel is trying to say is, men show their affection differently from women. He loves you, Free… Just think about it. Have you ever seen him do anything like he's done for you for someone else?"

Dang it! Now that I think about it... Tucker can be a real big jerk. In high school, he barely acknowledged the girls he was with. He treated them so badly I often wondered why the hell they put up with it.

But he has been doing nothing but showering me with attention and affection, not to mention the fact that his generosity toward the clinic did not end that day of the job fair. He's gotten his father to use his pull to secure our lunch program. He and one of his buddies partnered up to sponsor our job grooming services. He'd even helped me get housing for a few patients that were trying to get their lives in order.

I put my hand to my mouth. "Oh my God! I made a huge mistake!"

Rachel nodded. "Yeah, you did. But it's one you can fix. Get up out of this bed and go to your man..."

I threw the covers back and bolted up from the bed.

"Thank you, guys so much! I love y'all!" I yelled as I ran into the bathroom, shutting the door behind me.

Rachel was right! I can fix this... I will just go to his place and talk to him. Let him know that I got a little scared. Although I didn't love Dillion like I did Tucker, it still hurt to see him with my sister. It would kill me to see Tucker with Layla. So quite naturally, I had a little case of Post-Traumatic Stress Syndrome and panicked.

That's understandable...right?

An hour and a half later, I looked at myself in the mirror and smiled. I'd like to see him resist me in this outfit. It was one of my racier pieces. The only reason I bought this little cocktail dress is because Rachel called me a prude when we were out shopping one day. And to prove that I wasn't, I purchased this little demo. Now I'm glad I did.

Grabbing my keys off the mail stand I opened the door, but came up short at the sight of Angie standing there with her hand raised as if she was getting ready to knock.

"Angie!" I cried, startled.

"Free…hey!" She was just as surprised to see me suddenly standing there, but then her eyes ran down my body, taking in my outfit and her judgment was clear as day on her face.

"Are you on your way to the stroll?"

"Wow! That was insulting."

"Well, dear, if you dress like a whore, don't be surprised if you're treated like one," she said as she glided past me into my house.

I clutched the doorknob, wanting so badly to tell her to get out. Instead, I exhaled and shut it behind her.

"Angie, can this visit wait?! I have to be somewhere."

She didn't answer me, she just took her time strolling around the living room looking at all the books on the bookshelves.

"You know…I remember when Dorothy bought this house. She'd been so sure of her little investment."

I didn't know my grandmother, so there was no love lost between us. However, I didn't like Angie talking about her like that, I don't care that she was her daughter-in-law.

"Outside of the house being a little old and in need of a few repairs, it's not a bad investment," I told her dryly.

Her gaze came to mine. "Oh! I wasn't talking about the house, dear."

I frowned. "What were you talking about?"

She smiled. "You."

"Me?"

She continued her perusal of the bookshelves. "She was so confident that she would pluck you down and you would be the perfect bait to capture the heart of the prince."

"Angie…what are you talking about?"

She laughed, confusing me more. "She was close… But I was quicker."

I exhaled. Her rambling was beginning to give me a headache. I wanted her out of here so that I could go back to my chocolate obsession.

"She was so sure, she convinced Gilbert to agree with her diabolical plan."

"What does my dad have to do with this?"

She threw her manicured hand in the air. "Free, keep up, will you? Gilbert is not your father."

"What?!" That is it! I've had enough of her sh*t!

"You've gone too far! You need to stop, Angie. My father is dead and gone, and you're standing here slandering him like this."

"Girl, Gilbert couldn't have children. His little swimmers didn't work."

"Liar!"

As casual as if she was flicking a piece of lint off her sleeve, she reached down in her purse and pulled out a folded piece of paper.

"This is the report from the last test we took. He and I had tried to get him treatment so that we could have a child."

With hands that shook, I snatched the paper from her. Tears that would never drop filled my eyes as I read.

"I take it being a doctor and all, you can comprehend what all those x's and o's mean on that paper?"

My gaze came back to hers. "I don't understand. How can this be?"

She laughed bitterly. "Your grandmother was a conniving snake, that's how. She would do anything it took to get where she wanted to go. She didn't care who she used or who she abused. She ruined many lives." Holding her hands up, she stepped back.

"But don't feel bad. She fooled me too. Her goal was to get her precious, sappy, half of a man son to marry into money. And it happened just as she planned it. She chose our town, she chose me..." her gaze hardened. "And evidently, she chose you too."

"But why?" My voice quivered so badly my words were barely recognizable.

She shook her head. "Honey, I can't get inside the head of a madwoman. I just thought it was time for you to know the truth." And then she headed for the door.

"Oh, here is your plane ticket. Our flight leaves Thursday at six. Make sure you get there at least an hour early. We all will have a day to get settled in and then the wedding will be Saturday evening." She handed me the ticket and opened the door.

"I have to go; I still need to run Tucker's ticket to his place."

"Wait!" I cried, grabbing her arm.

"Free?" She gasped, looking down where I clutched her in shock. Getting a hold of myself I let her go.

"Sorry about that," I muttered. "But did you say you had a ticket for Tucker?"

"Yes, he's Layla's date, dear."

# Volume Two

# Chapter 1

## Love Don't Live Here Anymore

*You abandoned me*
  *Love don't live here anymore*
  *Just emptiness and memories*
  *Of what we had before*
  *You went away*
  *Found another place to stay, another home...*

*Rose Royce*

January 9, 1973

*TODAY I ATTENDED the funeral of Daisy's mother, Mrs. Rose. I could not have wished for better luck. Daisy has become extremely dependent on LSD and quite a burden on her parents. I'm more than positive the stress of worrying about her daughter's mental state only escalated the complications Mrs. Rose was having in her battle with heart disease. This is a cruel stroke of fate, but what was even crueler was for such an amazing specimen to be born to two inferior parents. This was simply nature taking its course and putting Daisy into the hands of science, where abilities like hers could be more appreciated.*

*As I figured he would, her father approached me after the funeral and asked if I was interested in becoming Daisy's guardian, because he could no longer provide her with the care she needed. Of course I was careful to school my features and in the most solemn way that I could, I told him if he thought it was best, then I would adopt Daisy and provide her with the best care possible.*

*Fate is shining a light on me; my time is coming soon.*

## February 15, 1973

*"Good Morning, Daisy, how did you sleep last night?"*

*"Fine."*

*"Did you take your pills this morning?"*

*"Yes."*

*"And how do they make you feel?"*

*"They—they make me feel good. They make me forget all of my pain."*

*"That's good. I don't want you to be in pain."*

*"Thank you."*

*"I will always be here to give you your pills that chase away the pain."*

*"Thank you."*

*"Can you do something for me?"*

*"Yes."*

*"Can you tell me about the man with no shoes?"*

*"He's not a man…"*

*"What is he?"*

*"He's the most powerful angel in all of existence."*

*"How do you know that?"*

*"Because I saw him defeat the devil."*

## Free

"What are you doing?"

*What am I doing?*

The smirk on Tucker's face only fueled the rage I felt at this moment. *Keep your cool, Free! You are a professional! Don't let your enemies see you unraveled…*

"Can we help you? Go to your seat!" Layla sneered from where she sat next to *my man* in the first-class seats.

My gaze went to hers. "Yeah, you can help me. You can sit there and shut the hell up!" Her mouth popped open as if I'd slapped her.

And ohhhh! Believe me, it was taking every ounce of strength in my body not to slap her and pull those tracks out of her hair. The only thing saving her was that she'd wisely shut her flap. Maybe she could sense that I'd come unhinged. I'd never felt this way…Seeing Tucker with her was taking me down uncharted territory.

Dear God, my life was falling apart. Everything I thought I knew was false…everything is a lie, including the comfort and security I thought I had in this man sitting in front of me.

How can he do this to me? He made me feel loved… cherished. I felt as if he was the other half of me…Even now, although he sat here with another woman, his eyes took me in as if I was still his and he was still mine.

Lies!

And then there was my father... my dad. A shaky breath escaped my throat as I fought to hold on to my composure. If I exhaled too much, maybe I will exhale everything that made me...me.

Oh God!

My life is a lie! Everything I stood for and fought for... A lie!

I had no idea who I was, this feeling of loss was suffocating.

"Is there something you want to tell me? Is that why you're holding up the line?" Tucker asked, that infuriating smirk still on his face. How could I have forgotten how big of a bastard he was?

I brought this on myself. This is what I get for letting down my guard and letting my enemy in. Now he had me here on this plane contemplating acting way outside of my character.

I was aware of all the eyes on me, including Dillion's enraged ones. No doubt he was angry that I had not responded this way when I saw him sitting next to Laureen.

"You're really going to do this?" I hissed from between clenched teeth, my gaze focused solely on the liar. Everybody else faded to black. It was him that made me feel like he really cared! It was he that whispered sweet nothings in my ear and made me believe in love again! It was he that was the biggest bastard on this side of the heavens!

"Do what? Be nice enough to attend a wedding, after *someone* was nice enough to invite me?"

I narrowed my gaze at him. "You are such an asshole!" This only made him laugh. I balled up my fist, wanting to punch him so badly the anticipation was robbing me of breath.

"Excuse me, ma'am, can you please take your seat so that the other passengers can board the plane," one of the flight attendants asked as she quickly made her way to me, placing her hand gently on my arm.

Oh guys! I was losing it! I was trying to be brave, but my emotions were spiraling out of control. Angie's revelation about my father had split me down the middle, but seeing Tucker, *my love* with another woman was shattering me.

I nodded at the flight attendant, knowing she was watching me for any sign that I was an unruly passenger waiting to happen.

My gaze settled back on Tucker. "It's alright, this was my fault. You won't get a chance to hurt me like this again." That was a promise I will die to keep. It was all I had left...

The smirk left his face as something passed in his eyes. He opened his mouth to say something, but Layla put her hand up between us.

"Bye-bye!" she said in a whiny voice before she broke out in laughter. I turned away from them. I was done... so very done.

"I'm sorry for holding up the line," I told the flight attendant as I made my way towards the back of the plane. I had a first-class ticket but there was no way I can sit there and watch Layla play woman to *my* man and not lose my mind.

I walked down the aisle, scanning the economy seats

for someone who looks like they'd trade with me without making a scene and alerting the flight attendants. My eyes were drawn to a big dark-skinned man in a cowboy hat. He was reading what looked like the bible. It seemed small in his big hands. When he felt my stare, he lifted his eyes and took me in. I had to clutch the seat that was near me. The impact of the ancient gaze caused my knees to buckle.

His look had a different effect on me than Tucker's. When Naphtali looked at me, my belly felt like butterflies were dancing across it. This man's gaze was different. It felt… I don't know, familiar? But powerful…

My tortured soul needed to sit next to him. A bonus was the fact that he sat in that extra-wide aisle that was by the emergency exit, which meant extra leg room. My mind made up, I headed his way.

"Excuse me," I asked the young lady that sat by the window next to him. "Would you mind trading seats with me?"

She gave me a look that said, *yeah right, me give up my wide aisle seat…get lost.* However, her look did a complete about-face with my next words.

"My ticket is in the first-class section."

"First-class?" she asked as if she didn't believe me.

I nodded. "Yeah, I'm just not feeling the people I came with and don't want to sit with them."

She popped up out of her seat and snatched the ticket out of my hand. "No worries, I'll gladly switch with you." After she handed me her ticket, she high tailed it towards the front.

I smiled at the man in the cowboy hat as I went to lift my carry-on to put in the overhead compartment.

"Sorry about that," I told him, praying he didn't think bad of me for wanting to sit next to him.

"No need to apologize, baht. Here, let me help you." He stood to get my luggage and secured it for me. I was amazed by how big he was, and how easily he moved for one so big. He reminded me so much of Tucker.

*Grrr! Stop thinking about Tucker!!! Tucker is the enemy! Get that through your head!*

Ashamed of myself for thinking about the bastard, I took my seat. The cowboy returned to his and picked up his reading in his bible. I sat for a minute more than curious as to what he was reading. But because I refuse to be one of those annoying passengers that talked throughout the flight when all one wants to do is be left alone, I refrained from asking. It wasn't like I didn't have other stuff to do.

For the last two days, I've been pouring over my grand-mother's—no, through the woman I thought was my grandmother's notes, trying to find out who the hell was my real father and why they lied about something like that.

As soon as Angie left my place the other day, I got on the phone with a colleague of mine who works at the hospital where my father—no, the man I thought was my father and Angie had gone to try and get help conceiving.

Although it took quite a bit of coercing, I finally got him to look into the situation for me and sure enough, my fath —Gilbert's little swimmers were all duds. My world had been thrown into complete and utter disarray. I've been up for the last two days searching for anything that would give me a clue as to what was going on.

Why would Gilbert and his mother lie about something

like that? Why didn't my mother ever tell me he wasn't my father? And why had Angie sat on this secret for so long?

Past tired, I rubbed my eyes underneath my glasses. I don't know what I was doing anymore. Don't know why I was on this plane heading to the wedding of a girl I thought was my sister through marriage and my ex. I felt like a fool for staying loyal to them all this time. Stupidly, I clung to them because I thought they were the only family I had left.

What a fool I've been. The truth is, I was terrified of being alone... of being the girl with no family.

"Long Suffering..." The cowboy grumbled.

My startled gaze went to him. "Excuse me?"

He looked up. "Oh! Did I say that out loud?" Completely captivated by his ancient eyes, I nodded.

He pointed down at the scripture he was reading. "It's just that every time I read about the Master's words on longsuffering, it gives me a boost of renewed energy...you know?"

"Master?" I asked, my voice barely over a whisper. It felt like there was a fist in my throat. This man's presence, his voice, his ancient gaze were water to my troubled soul... and I just didn't know how to take it.

He nodded. "The MessiYah... Yahusha. Our Master..."

I'd studied some Hebrew in my second year at Grambling, so I recognized the tongue. I believe that Yahusha is the Hebrew name of Jesus.

"What did he say about longsuffering?" I asked, feeling like I was starving for his words. I'd been suffering my whole life.

"Have you ever read the Sermon on the Mount?" I shook my head.

"Here, I'll read it to you…"

I smiled and settled back in my seat as the plane took off…

"And seeing the multitudes, he went up into a mountain: and when he was set, his disciples came unto him: And he opened his mouth, and taught them, saying, Blessed *are* the poor in spirit: for theirs is the kingdom of heaven. Blessed *are* they that mourn: for they shall be comforted. Blessed *are* the meek: for they shall inherit the earth. Blessed *are* they which do hunger and thirst after righteousness: for they shall be filled. Blessed *are* the merciful: for they shall obtain mercy. Blessed *are* the pure in heart: for they shall see Alohim. Blessed *are* the peacemakers: for they shall be called the children of Alohim."

He turned to look at me then, drawing me into the abyss of his dark gaze. "Blessed *are* they which are persecuted for righteousness' sake: for theirs is the kingdom of heaven. Blessed are ye, when *men* shall revile you, and persecute *you,* and shall say all manner of evil against you falsely, for the Master's sake. Rejoice, and be exceeding glad: for great *is* your reward in heaven: for so persecuted they the prophets which were before you."

Although his words felt like food for my soul, they made me sad. Yes, it's true that I've often been called a fool for my actions, for the way that I handle situations…for the way I strive to keep the peace when others would strike out and try to hurt those that hurt them. But I don't know the Master this mystery man is speaking of…

I mean, of course I know about the bible. One of the things I remembered about my mother was her always telling me not to be weak like her, and to search for God.

I've seen her holding her bible many times, high, crying... She was so very torn.

But I'd lost my way. I didn't even own a bible... So that beautiful scripture the stranger just read did not apply to me. Angie, and the twins, my fake grandmother and father... Tucker, they'd not hurt me for the Master's sake...

I sat back in my seat and stared straight ahead... I didn't even belong to the Master. Suddenly my head felt too heavy for my neck and before I knew what happened, I rested it against the strong shoulder of this man that I didn't know from Adam.

Yet...He felt very familiar.

Oh God! I was such a wreck... My eyes filled with tears.

"I'm a doctor, but I'm the most broken person that I know... How come I can't fix myself?" I gasped, trying to swallow down my tears.

The flight attendant that had told me to take my seat spotted me and began to come my way. Panic filled my heart... She was going to make me go back to first-class and leave the comfort of the stranger.

"Excuse me, ma'am," she began, but the stranger lifted his hand and rested it gently against hers. At first, she looked down at his hand, appalled before her gaze met his... I don't know what she saw there, but a smile came to her face.

"Can I get you guys anything to drink?"

What the heck just happened??? My startled gaze went to the stranger, who smiled kindly at the woman.

"I'll have a cup of herbal tea if you have it."

She nodded. "Absolutely." Her suddenly kind gaze came to me. "And for you, ma'am."

Completely at a loss for words, I shook my head. "No--nothing, for me...th--thank you."

After giving us one more reassuring smile, she turned and headed back toward the front of the plane.

"What just happened?" I'd worked with patients for years and didn't get the kind of turn around he'd just gotten with the flight attendant with just a look.

He chuckled. "She was kind enough to inquire if we would like refreshments."

I shook my head pointing between him and the flight attendant. "No, there was something else there."

He turned then and gave me his complete attention. I inhaled... remember what I told you guys about his eyes.

"Yes, baht, there is always something else there. Although you can't touch it, taste it, see it, hear it...it's still there."

He gestured toward the front of the plane where my fake family and Tucker sat. "You think you are dealing with flesh and blood. People..." He shook his head. "You're not. You are dealing with controlling spirits; spirits that can see who you belong to, even if you can't see it yet."

He frowned at me. "You're extremely vain, child."

My mouth popped open. "Wow! I am not...you don't know. I'm the least vain person on this plane. Trust me."

He chuckled again, shaking his head. "That statement is very vain. You asked why you can't fix *yourself*. Vanity... If your patients could fix themselves, then why do they come to you?"

"How did—" Wait!

Oh, my goodness! I felt sick...

He continued to speak, words that felt like bullets. "Are you better than they? If so, what makes you better?"

He folded his big hands and waited for my answer. All the classic answers floated through my head. *I have a Ph.D. … I'm a doctor…I graduated with honors… I've studied under some of the best doctors in my field.*

But for some reason, I was afraid to tell him that, and his next words only proved me wise to had kept silent.

The flight attendant returned with his herbal tea and to my astonishment, let down the little table on the seat in front of him, placed his tea on it, opened two packets of honey and a packet of lemon juice, and stirred them both in his tea. When she was done, she gently tapped the little spoon on the side of the cup and smiled at him.

"Can I get you anything else, sir?"

He shook his head. "No…Thank you." I watched as she gathered all of her trash and then walked away.

*What…in…the…world?* Flight attendants don't pour honey in your tea. They give you the packet to do it yourself. He took a sip of his tea before he began to speak again.

"Were you there when the Ancient of Days laid the foundation for the earth? If you were, old wise one, please… tell me. Do you know who laid out its measurements?" Between each question, he paused to give me time to answer as he continued to sip his tea.

"The measurements of the earth?"

He nodded. "Yes."

"I don't think anyone knows that for sure."

"You would be wrong. The one who created it knows it well." He gave me the side-eye. "Let's try an easier question, doctor. *Who* laid the cornerstone?"

When I still had no answer for him, he continued.

"*Who* shut up the sea with doors, when it broke forth *as if* it had issued out of the womb?"

"*Who* said, here shall the sea come, but no farther: and here shall thy proud waves be stayed?"

"Was it *you*? Was it the big minds you studied under, doctor? Did you command the morning in your life span; *and* cause the dayspring to know his place?"

He tilted his head so that his piercing gaze could look directly into my soul. "Have the gates of death been opened unto you? Or have you seen the doors of the shadow of death?" He shook his head.

"When you went to school to receive your Ph.D. and graduate with honors to then study underneath the best doctors in the world to become a doctor yourself… did they teach you how to go to the grave and bring back the dead?"

"Did they teach you where the breath that circulates inside of your body comes from?"

I was floored for two reasons. One, I'm pretty sure he was somehow reading my mind. And two, these questions that he was asking, no man could possibly know. But who would even think to ask questions like these?

"So how are you any better than the next man?" His question was gentle but hit like a steel fist.

"What are you saying? I wasted my time becoming a doctor?"

"Absolutely not. You are exactly where the Ancient of Days wants you to be. Everything that you've experienced is exactly how it should have been. For even the hands of the physician the Master can use. But I am saying, that if you're going to *help yourself*, then your outlook on your status as a man must change."

"In the eyes of the Ancient of Days, there are no big U's and little them's. We are like ants to him. It's complete vanity for us to lord ourselves over each other. Vanity and pissing in the wind." His words tickled him because he had a good chuckle at that.

When I didn't join him in laughter, he sobered. "I don't know why nobody finds that funny," he muttered before he continued.

"The trick is, learning to look at the people in your care as human beings, just like you. They have fears and needs, desires...pain. Just like you. Instead of studying them as subjects, try and really see them the way you had hoped those that were supposed to love you had. For whom can appreciate that more than you, seeing how it was something you were deprived of. Surely you wouldn't deprive your fellow man."

*Why won't you see me, Free?* Tucker's question came to the forefront of my mind. *You never look at me.*

I've always thought myself to be very compassionate and caring. I was killing myself for that clinic. Not for me...but for the people. I thought I've always been able to see them.

He chuckled. "Tell me this; what is the difference between your patients' sickness and your own?"

"I'm not sick."

"Sure, you are. Your heart is heavy with grief. It's weighing you down. You suffer from panic attacks. In your own words, you say you are broken. What is all of this but sickness...the body is at dis-ease. Who determines the big dis-ease versus the little? I assure you, Yah does not put one above the other."

Wow, how many times have I said to Oaklee that I never really thought of my patients as anything but sick individuals who needed my help. I put my head in my hands… Oh my God! This stranger was right. I am vain! And yes, I do look at myself as better than my patients.

He stared off into the distance, seeing something that I could not. "In our vanity, we forget that we are all here on earth, fighting to live… Some of us in righteousness, and some of us in wickedness… but the thing we all have in common is the breath inside of us that belongs to the Ancient of Days. And it is He that you should seek if you want healing, child. But as for the scoffers and those that have persecuted you… You may not know it yet, but they do it for the Master's sake… The spirit on them can see the spirit that is guiding you, and it troubles them until they trouble you."

Right then, Tucker ducked under the curtain, carrying a soda in his hand. He scanned the seats until his gaze landed on me and the stranger.

"Oh boy," I sighed when he frowned at the man next to me. "I want to apologize now. The world's biggest jerk is headed our way."

The stranger chuckled. "No need to apologize, I've dealt with his type aplenty."

"I brought you a pop," Tucker said to me as he continued to frown at my neighbor. The fact that he was looking at him like that only angered me more. I snatched the bottle from him.

"Now go back to your seat!" I hissed.

My tone got his attention and his startled gaze came to me. "Why are you sitting back here instead of in your seat upfront?"

"That's none of your business!"

He exhaled, rubbing his hand back across his head. "Listen, Free, I—"

"No! *You* listen! I don't want to talk to you ever again! You think I want to hear your excuses? You lying, cheating, conniving bully! I shouldn't have talked to you in the first place!"

To say he was shocked to hear this kind of venom coming from me was an understatement. People's heads began to turn our way, but I didn't care. I saw red! He betrayed me... and then he gon' mosey himself back here with a funky soda pop! I felt like throwing this bottle at his head.

"Son," The stranger said, drawing Tucker's attention. "Why don't you let her calm down a bit. And then maybe trying again a little later."

I was sure Naphtali was going to show his behind and tell the man what he thought of his advice. But surprisingly, he didn't. He studied him for a moment before he nodded.

"Yeah..., okay." His gaze came to mine one more time before he grudgingly turned and headed back toward the front of the plane, back to the girl who took his virginity!

The bastard!

"He's so damn evil!" I sneered.

The man next to me chuckled as he shook his head. "Naw, he's just a jerk. A really big one."

I rested my head once again against the stranger's shoulder. Don't ask me how it was I felt comfortable enough to do this. Maybe I was losing my mind. But he felt... safe, like a warm blanket on a freezing cold day. He settled back in his chair and picked up his reading.

I'd been up for the last two days poring over my fake grandmother's notes, barely getting any sleep and now it was catching up to me. My eyes got heavy.

"I don't even know your name, Mr," I muttered as my eyes began to droop.

"Everyone calls me the Preacher." His words rumbled through his body, lulling me to sleep.

"Preacher?"

"Hmmm..."

"Can you read to me?"

"Sure, daughter..."

And so he did. I don't know when I fell completely under, but my last thoughts before I did was that there was no way the Preacher was a man. I'm convinced he's an angel. My mother told me she'd talked to an angel before. Yeah, he was an angel. He knew too much about me and had a way with people.

Tucker was an asshole to everyone. But the Preacher told him to go back and take his seat and he did it without question. Maybe like me, he could sense that there was something different about the cowboy. When I wake up, I'm going to ask him if he's an angel.

At least that was my plan. However, I was sleeping so well, I didn't feel the plane land or hear the captain give his spiel. I woke to the gentle nudging of the flight attendant.

"Sweetheart, we've reached our destination," she said quietly.

Blinking, I looked around for the stranger that comforted me in my time of need and was heartbroken when I didn't see him anywhere.

*This was the story of my life.*

Exhaling, I stood to gather my things, but something fell out of my lap hitting the floor. Looking down, I was amazed to see that it was the little bible he was reading. Quickly, I picked it up, clutching it to my chest.

*He'd left me his bible.*

I ran my hand softly over the top of it before opening it. And there on the inside of the front cover was written in bold lettering,

*"YOU'RE NEVER ALONE, Free...You belong to the Master. And although at times, you can't see him or touch him, He's always there. Be at ease, little one, you are loved." –The Preacher*

# Chapter 2

## Love Don't Live Here Anymore

*You abandoned me*
  *Love don't live here anymore*
  *Just emptiness and memories*
  *Of what we had before*
  *You went away*
  *Found another place to stay, another home...*

*Rose Royce*

### January 9, 1973

*TODAY I ATTENDED the funeral of Daisy's mother, Mrs. Rose. I could not have wished for better luck. Daisy has become extremely dependent on LSD and quite a burden on her parents. I'm more than positive the stress of worrying about her daughter's mental state only escalated the complications Mrs. Rose was having in her battle with heart disease. This is a cruel stroke of fate, but what was even crueler was for such an amazing specimen to be born to two inferior parents. This was simply nature taking its course and putting Daisy into the hands of science, where abilities like hers could be more appreciated.*

*As I figured he would, her father approached me after the funeral and asked if I was interested in becoming Daisy's guardian, because he could no longer provide her with the care she needed. Of course I was careful to school my features and in the most solemn way that I could, I told him if he thought it was best, then I would adopt Daisy and provide her with the best care possible.*

*Fate is shining a light on me; my time is coming soon.*

## February 15, 1973

*"Good Morning, Daisy, how did you sleep last night?"*

*"Fine."*

*"Did you take your pills this morning?"*

*"Yes."*

*"And how do they make you feel?"*

*"They—they make me feel good. They make me forget all of my pain."*

*"That's good. I don't want you to be in pain."*

*"Thank you."*

*"I will always be here to give you your pills that chase away the pain."*

*"Thank you."*

*"Can you do something for me?"*

*"Yes."*

*"Can you tell me about the man with no shoes?"*

*"He's not a man..."*

*"What is he?"*

*"He's the most powerful angel in all of existence."*

*"How do you know that?"*

*"Because I saw him defeat the devil."*

## Free

"What are you doing?"

*What am I doing?*

The smirk on Tucker's face only fueled the rage I felt at this moment. *Keep your cool, Free! You are a professional! Don't let your enemies see you unraveled...*

"Can we help you? Go to your seat!" Layla sneered from where she sat next to *my man* in the first-class seats.

My gaze went to hers. "Yeah, you can help me. You can sit there and shut the hell up!" Her mouth popped open as if I'd slapped her.

And ohhhh! Believe me, it was taking every ounce of strength in my body not to slap her and pull those tracks out of her hair. The only thing saving her was that she'd wisely shut her flap. Maybe she could sense that I'd come unhinged. I'd never felt this way...Seeing Tucker with her was taking me down uncharted territory.

Dear God, my life was falling apart. Everything I thought I knew was false...everything is a lie, including the comfort and security I thought I had in this man sitting in front of me.

How can he do this to me? He made me feel loved... cherished. I felt as if he was the other half of me...Even now, although he sat here with another woman, his eyes took me in as if I was still his and he was still mine.

Lies!

And then there was my father... my dad. A shaky breath escaped my throat as I fought to hold on to my composure. If I exhaled too much, maybe I will exhale everything that made me...me.

Oh God!

My life is a lie! Everything I stood for and fought for... A lie!

I had no idea who I was, this feeling of loss was suffocating.

"Is there something you want to tell me? Is that why you're holding up the line?" Tucker asked, that infuriating smirk still on his face. How could I have forgotten how big of a bastard he was?

I brought this on myself. This is what I get for letting down my guard and letting my enemy in. Now he had me here on this plane contemplating acting way outside of my character.

I was aware of all the eyes on me, including Dillion's enraged ones. No doubt he was angry that I had not responded this way when I saw him sitting next to Laureen.

"You're really going to do this?" I hissed from between clenched teeth, my gaze focused solely on the liar. Everybody else faded to black. It was him that made me feel like he really cared! It was he that whispered sweet nothings in my ear and made me believe in love again! It was he that was the biggest bastard on this side of the heavens!

"Do what? Be nice enough to attend a wedding, after *someone* was nice enough to invite me?"

I narrowed my gaze at him. "You are such an asshole!" This only made him laugh. I balled up my fist, wanting to punch him so badly the anticipation was robbing me of breath.

"Excuse me, ma'am, can you please take your seat so that the other passengers can board the plane," one of the flight attendants asked as she quickly made her way to me, placing her hand gently on my arm.

Oh guys! I was losing it! I was trying to be brave, but my emotions were spiraling out of control. Angie's revelation about my father had split me down the middle, but seeing Tucker, *my love* with another woman was shattering me.

I nodded at the flight attendant, knowing she was watching me for any sign that I was an unruly passenger waiting to happen.

My gaze settled back on Tucker. "It's alright, this was my fault. You won't get a chance to hurt me like this again." That was a promise I will die to keep. It was all I had left...

The smirk left his face as something passed in his eyes. He opened his mouth to say something, but Layla put her hand up between us.

"Bye-bye!" she said in a whiny voice before she broke out in laughter. I turned away from them. I was done... so very done.

"I'm sorry for holding up the line," I told the flight attendant as I made my way towards the back of the plane. I had a first-class ticket but there was no way I can sit there and watch Layla play woman to *my* man and not lose my mind.

I walked down the aisle, scanning the economy seats

for someone who looks like they'd trade with me without making a scene and alerting the flight attendants. My eyes were drawn to a big dark-skinned man in a cowboy hat. He was reading what looked like the bible. It seemed small in his big hands. When he felt my stare, he lifted his eyes and took me in. I had to clutch the seat that was near me. The impact of the ancient gaze caused my knees to buckle.

His look had a different effect on me than Tucker's. When Naphtali looked at me, my belly felt like butterflies were dancing across it. This man's gaze was different. It felt... I don't know, familiar? But powerful...

My tortured soul needed to sit next to him. A bonus was the fact that he sat in that extra-wide aisle that was by the emergency exit, which meant extra leg room. My mind made up, I headed his way.

"Excuse me," I asked the young lady that sat by the window next to him. "Would you mind trading seats with me?"

She gave me a look that said, *yeah right, me give up my wide aisle seat...get lost.* However, her look did a complete about-face with my next words.

"My ticket is in the first-class section."

"First-class?" she asked as if she didn't believe me.

I nodded. "Yeah, I'm just not feeling the people I came with and don't want to sit with them."

She popped up out of her seat and snatched the ticket out of my hand. "No worries, I'll gladly switch with you." After she handed me her ticket, she high tailed it towards the front.

I smiled at the man in the cowboy hat as I went to lift my carry-on to put in the overhead compartment.

"Sorry about that," I told him, praying he didn't think bad of me for wanting to sit next to him.

"No need to apologize, baht. Here, let me help you." He stood to get my luggage and secured it for me. I was amazed by how big he was, and how easily he moved for one so big. He reminded me so much of Tucker.

*Grrr! Stop thinking about Tucker!!! Tucker is the enemy! Get that through your head!*

Ashamed of myself for thinking about the bastard, I took my seat. The cowboy returned to his and picked up his reading in his bible. I sat for a minute more than curious as to what he was reading. But because I refuse to be one of those annoying passengers that talked throughout the flight when all one wants to do is be left alone, I refrained from asking. It wasn't like I didn't have other stuff to do.

For the last two days, I've been pouring over my grandmother's—no, through the woman I thought was my grandmother's notes, trying to find out who the hell was my real father and why they lied about something like that.

As soon as Angie left my place the other day, I got on the phone with a colleague of mine who works at the hospital where my father—no, the man I thought was my father and Angie had gone to try and get help conceiving.

Although it took quite a bit of coercing, I finally got him to look into the situation for me and sure enough, my fath —Gilbert's little swimmers were all duds. My world had been thrown into complete and utter disarray. I've been up for the last two days searching for anything that would give me a clue as to what was going on.

Why would Gilbert and his mother lie about something

like that? Why didn't my mother ever tell me he wasn't my father? And why had Angie sat on this secret for so long?

Past tired, I rubbed my eyes underneath my glasses. I don't know what I was doing anymore. Don't know why I was on this plane heading to the wedding of a girl I thought was my sister through marriage and my ex. I felt like a fool for staying loyal to them all this time. Stupidly, I clung to them because I thought they were the only family I had left.

What a fool I've been. The truth is, I was terrified of being alone... of being the girl with no family.

"Long Suffering..." The cowboy grumbled.

My startled gaze went to him. "Excuse me?"

He looked up. "Oh! Did I say that out loud?" Completely captivated by his ancient eyes, I nodded.

He pointed down at the scripture he was reading. "It's just that every time I read about the Master's words on longsuffering, it gives me a boost of renewed energy...you know?"

"Master?" I asked, my voice barely over a whisper. It felt like there was a fist in my throat. This man's presence, his voice, his ancient gaze were water to my troubled soul... and I just didn't know how to take it.

He nodded. "The MessiYah... Yahusha. Our Master..."

I'd studied some Hebrew in my second year at Grambling, so I recognized the tongue. I believe that Yahusha is the Hebrew name of Jesus.

"What did he say about longsuffering?" I asked, feeling like I was starving for his words. I'd been suffering my whole life.

"Have you ever read the Sermon on the Mount?" I shook my head.

"Here, I'll read it to you…"

I smiled and settled back in my seat as the plane took off…

"And seeing the multitudes, he went up into a mountain: and when he was set, his disciples came unto him: And he opened his mouth, and taught them, saying, Blessed *are* the poor in spirit: for theirs is the kingdom of heaven. Blessed *are* they that mourn: for they shall be comforted. Blessed *are* the meek: for they shall inherit the earth. Blessed *are* they which do hunger and thirst after righteousness: for they shall be filled. Blessed *are* the merciful: for they shall obtain mercy. Blessed *are* the pure in heart: for they shall see Alohim. Blessed *are* the peacemakers: for they shall be called the children of Alohim."

He turned to look at me then, drawing me into the abyss of his dark gaze. "Blessed *are* they which are persecuted for righteousness' sake: for theirs is the kingdom of heaven. Blessed are ye, when *men* shall revile you, and persecute *you*, and shall say all manner of evil against you falsely, for the Master's sake. Rejoice, and be exceeding glad: for great *is* your reward in heaven: for so persecuted they the prophets which were before you."

Although his words felt like food for my soul, they made me sad. Yes, it's true that I've often been called a fool for my actions, for the way that I handle situations…for the way I strive to keep the peace when others would strike out and try to hurt those that hurt them. But I don't know the Master this mystery man is speaking of…

I mean, of course I know about the bible. One of the things I remembered about my mother was her always telling me not to be weak like her, and to search for God.

I've seen her holding her bible many times, high, crying… She was so very torn.

But I'd lost my way. I didn't even own a bible… So that beautiful scripture the stranger just read did not apply to me. Angie, and the twins, my fake grandmother and father… Tucker, they'd not hurt me for the Master's sake…

I sat back in my seat and stared straight ahead… I didn't even belong to the Master. Suddenly my head felt too heavy for my neck and before I knew what happened, I rested it against the strong shoulder of this man that I didn't know from Adam.

Yet…He felt very familiar.

Oh God! I was such a wreck… My eyes filled with tears.

"I'm a doctor, but I'm the most broken person that I know… How come I can't fix myself?" I gasped, trying to swallow down my tears.

The flight attendant that had told me to take my seat spotted me and began to come my way. Panic filled my heart… She was going to make me go back to first-class and leave the comfort of the stranger.

"Excuse me, ma'am," she began, but the stranger lifted his hand and rested it gently against hers. At first, she looked down at his hand, appalled before her gaze met his… I don't know what she saw there, but a smile came to her face.

"Can I get you guys anything to drink?"

What the heck just happened??? My startled gaze went to the stranger, who smiled kindly at the woman.

"I'll have a cup of herbal tea if you have it."

She nodded. "Absolutely." Her suddenly kind gaze came to me. "And for you, ma'am."

Completely at a loss for words, I shook my head. "No--nothing, for me...th--thank you."

After giving us one more reassuring smile, she turned and headed back toward the front of the plane.

"What just happened?" I'd worked with patients for years and didn't get the kind of turn around he'd just gotten with the flight attendant with just a look.

He chuckled. "She was kind enough to inquire if we would like refreshments."

I shook my head pointing between him and the flight attendant. "No, there was something else there."

He turned then and gave me his complete attention. I inhaled... remember what I told you guys about his eyes.

"Yes, baht, there is always something else there. Although you can't touch it, taste it, see it, hear it...it's still there."

He gestured toward the front of the plane where my fake family and Tucker sat. "You think you are dealing with flesh and blood. People..." He shook his head. "You're not. You are dealing with controlling spirits; spirits that can see who you belong to, even if you can't see it yet."

He frowned at me. "You're extremely vain, child."

My mouth popped open. "Wow! I am not...you don't know. I'm the least vain person on this plane. Trust me."

He chuckled again, shaking his head. "That statement is very vain. You asked why you can't fix *yourself*. Vanity... If your patients could fix themselves, then why do they come to you?"

"How did—" Wait!

Oh, my goodness! I felt sick...

He continued to speak, words that felt like bullets. "Are you better than they? If so, what makes you better?"

He folded his big hands and waited for my answer. All the classic answers floated through my head. *I have a Ph.D. … I'm a doctor…I graduated with honors… I've studied under some of the best doctors in my field.*

But for some reason, I was afraid to tell him that, and his next words only proved me wise to had kept silent.

The flight attendant returned with his herbal tea and to my astonishment, let down the little table on the seat in front of him, placed his tea on it, opened two packets of honey and a packet of lemon juice, and stirred them both in his tea. When she was done, she gently tapped the little spoon on the side of the cup and smiled at him.

"Can I get you anything else, sir?"

He shook his head. "No…Thank you." I watched as she gathered all of her trash and then walked away.

*What…in…the…world?* Flight attendants don't pour honey in your tea. They give you the packet to do it yourself. He took a sip of his tea before he began to speak again.

"Were you there when the Ancient of Days laid the foundation for the earth? If you were, old wise one, please… tell me. Do you know who laid out its measurements?" Between each question, he paused to give me time to answer as he continued to sip his tea.

"The measurements of the earth?"

He nodded. "Yes."

"I don't think anyone knows that for sure."

"You would be wrong. The one who created it knows it well." He gave me the side-eye. "Let's try an easier question, doctor. *Who* laid the cornerstone?"

When I still had no answer for him, he continued.

"*Who* shut up the sea with doors, when it broke forth *as if* it had issued out of the womb?"

"*Who* said, here shall the sea come, but no farther: and here shall thy proud waves be stayed?"

"Was it *you*? Was it the big minds you studied under, doctor? Did you command the morning in your life span; *and* cause the dayspring to know his place?"

He tilted his head so that his piercing gaze could look directly into my soul. "Have the gates of death been opened unto you? Or have you seen the doors of the shadow of death?" He shook his head.

"When you went to school to receive your Ph.D. and graduate with honors to then study underneath the best doctors in the world to become a doctor yourself... did they teach you how to go to the grave and bring back the dead?"

"Did they teach you where the breath that circulates inside of your body comes from?"

I was floored for two reasons. One, I'm pretty sure he was somehow reading my mind. And two, these questions that he was asking, no man could possibly know. But who would even think to ask questions like these?

"So how are you any better than the next man?" His question was gentle but hit like a steel fist.

"What are you saying? I wasted my time becoming a doctor?"

"Absolutely not. You are exactly where the Ancient of Days wants you to be. Everything that you've experienced is exactly how it should have been. For even the hands of the physician the Master can use. But I am saying, that if you're going to *help yourself*, then your outlook on your status as a man must change."

"In the eyes of the Ancient of Days, there are no big U's and little them's. We are like ants to him. It's complete vanity for us to lord ourselves over each other. Vanity and pissing in the wind." His words tickled him because he had a good chuckle at that.

When I didn't join him in laughter, he sobered. "I don't know why nobody finds that funny," he muttered before he continued.

"The trick is, learning to look at the people in your care as human beings, just like you. They have fears and needs, desires...pain. Just like you. Instead of studying them as subjects, try and really see them the way you had hoped those that were supposed to love you had. For whom can appreciate that more than you, seeing how it was some-thing you were deprived of. Surely you wouldn't deprive your fellow man."

*Why won't you see me, Free?* Tucker's question came to the forefront of my mind. *You never look at me.*

I've always thought myself to be very compassionate and caring. I was killing myself for that clinic. Not for me...but for the people. I thought I've always been able to see them.

He chuckled. "Tell me this; what is the difference between your patients' sickness and your own?"

"I'm not sick."

"Sure, you are. Your heart is heavy with grief. It's weighing you down. You suffer from panic attacks. In your own words, you say you are broken. What is all of this but sickness...the body is at dis-ease. Who determines the big dis-ease versus the little? I assure you, Yah does not put one above the other."

Wow, how many times have I said to Oaklee that I never really thought of my patients as anything but sick individuals who needed my help. I put my head in my hands... Oh my God! This stranger was right. I am vain! And yes, I do look at myself as better than my patients.

He stared off into the distance, seeing something that I could not. "In our vanity, we forget that we are all here on earth, fighting to live... Some of us in righteousness, and some of us in wickedness... but the thing we all have in common is the breath inside of us that belongs to the Ancient of Days. And it is He that you should seek if you want healing, child. But as for the scoffers and those that have persecuted you... You may not know it yet, but they do it for the Master's sake... The spirit on them can see the spirit that is guiding you, and it troubles them until they trouble you."

Right then, Tucker ducked under the curtain, carrying a soda in his hand. He scanned the seats until his gaze landed on me and the stranger.

"Oh boy," I sighed when he frowned at the man next to me. "I want to apologize now. The world's biggest jerk is headed our way."

The stranger chuckled. "No need to apologize, I've dealt with his type aplenty."

"I brought you a pop," Tucker said to me as he continued to frown at my neighbor. The fact that he was looking at him like that only angered me more. I snatched the bottle from him.

"Now go back to your seat!" I hissed.

My tone got his attention and his startled gaze came to me. "Why are you sitting back here instead of in your seat upfront?"

"That's none of your business!"

He exhaled, rubbing his hand back across his head. "Listen, Free, I—"

"No! *You* listen! I don't want to talk to you ever again! You think I want to hear your excuses? You lying, cheating, conniving bully! I shouldn't have talked to you in the first place!"

To say he was shocked to hear this kind of venom coming from me was an understatement. People's heads began to turn our way, but I didn't care. I saw red! He betrayed me... and then he gon' mosey himself back here with a funky soda pop! I felt like throwing this bottle at his head.

"Son," The stranger said, drawing Tucker's attention. "Why don't you let her calm down a bit. And then maybe trying again a little later."

I was sure Naphtali was going to show his behind and tell the man what he thought of his advice. But surprisingly, he didn't. He studied him for a moment before he nodded.

"Yeah..., okay." His gaze came to mine one more time before he grudgingly turned and headed back toward the front of the plane, back to the girl who took his virginity!

The bastard!

"He's so damn evil!" I sneered.

The man next to me chuckled as he shook his head. "Naw, he's just a jerk. A really big one."

I rested my head once again against the stranger's shoulder. Don't ask me how it was I felt comfortable enough to do this. Maybe I was losing my mind. But he felt... safe, like a warm blanket on a freezing cold day. He settled back in his chair and picked up his reading.

I'd been up for the last two days poring over my fake grandmother's notes, barely getting any sleep and now it was catching up to me. My eyes got heavy.

"I don't even know your name, Mr," I muttered as my eyes began to droop.

"Everyone calls me the Preacher." His words rumbled through his body, lulling me to sleep.

"Preacher?"

"Hmmm…"

"Can you read to me?"

"Sure, daughter…"

And so he did. I don't know when I fell completely under, but my last thoughts before I did was that there was no way the Preacher was a man. I'm convinced he's an angel. My mother told me she'd talked to an angel before. Yeah, he was an angel. He knew too much about me and had a way with people.

Tucker was an asshole to everyone. But the Preacher told him to go back and take his seat and he did it without question. Maybe like me, he could sense that there was something different about the cowboy. When I wake up, I'm going to ask him if he's an angel.

At least that was my plan. However, I was sleeping so well, I didn't feel the plane land or hear the captain give his spiel. I woke to the gentle nudging of the flight attendant.

"Sweetheart, we've reached our destination," she said quietly.

Blinking, I looked around for the stranger that comforted me in my time of need and was heartbroken when I didn't see him anywhere.

*This was the story of my life.*

Exhaling, I stood to gather my things, but something fell out of my lap hitting the floor. Looking down, I was amazed to see that it was the little bible he was reading. Quickly, I picked it up, clutching it to my chest.

*He'd left me his bible.*

I ran my hand softly over the top of it before opening it. And there on the inside of the front cover was written in bold lettering,


*"YOU'RE NEVER ALONE, Free...You belong to the Master. And although at times, you can't see him or touch him, He's always there. Be at ease, little one, you are loved." –The Preacher*

# Chapter 3

I Do...Wait! What?!

Tucker

"PLEASE TUCKER, I'm on my knees," Layla purred from where she'd slid to the floor between my legs, rubbing her beautiful face against my d\*ck that hadn't stirred...not even a little bit. She caressed my belt buckle, but she knew better than to undo it without my permission.

"Tell me you're not going to come all this way with me and not let me taste it..." she moaned, licking her glossy red lips before making a sucking sound that left no doubt in our minds of what she wanted to taste.

Anthony, one of the best agents on my team who like me, looked more like a drug dealer than a cop, chuckled from where he sat on the leather bench next to me. Next to him, rubbing him in a very similar fashion was a sexy little number with a head full of flame-red dreads. No doubt she was making a killing here in Vegas. She was the type that caught the eye of the high rollers, but tonight, she had my boy Ant in her sights, which was good, because it meant he was secured in the character he was portraying.

He'd been undercover for the last year to bring down a drug ring that operated here in Vegas. I'd pulled him yesterday to help me keep an eye on Free. He was ecstatic; for him, it felt like a break from the constant stress that came with being clandestine in a crime organization.

To everyone on the outside, I was his boy from Detroit in town for a wedding and he was showing me a good time. But because a part of his image was getting high and drunk, something we've been doing since my plane landed yesterday, I'd also called in Will, another valuable team member. He sat at the empty bar under the guise of being here for business, wanting to blow off a little steam with an after-work cocktail.

Now, don't get me wrong, for us in the agency with the look that landed us in these types of undercover stings, we're trained to operate under the influence. You never know what you will have to do to make it out of a situation alive, snort a line, tut a rock, inject heroin. I've had agents who really had to enroll in rehab for things way stronger than marijuana. Hell, the night I took down Marcellus and twenty-two of his most loyal soldiers, I'd been drunk off my ass. It didn't take me being sober to initiate the Bully.

Still, I wasn't taking *any* chances with Free's life. She meant that much to me. I really wish her ass would have told me she was planning on coming here earlier, I would have talked her out of it. I don't give a f*ck who was getting married.

Vegas is a hotbed and if Rau knew about me, this would be the perfect place to strike, which is why I needed sober eyes watching her as well. And there was none as straitlaced as Will. He wasn't a big drinker, no smoking, no partying of any kind. He had a lovely wife and two children at home. Of course, all the fellas on our team envied him and poked fun at him a bit. But hey, maybe I'll have that one day too if my girl ever forgave me and stopped giving me the cold shoulder.

I rubbed my hands down my face. Sh*t, I really needed to go upstairs and try and get some sleep so I can sober up for the wedding tomorrow.

"Tuuucker!" Layla whined bringing my mind back to her. Using one of her painted nails, she grazed my d*ck again.

High as a f*cking kite, I grinned down at her. Damn, this was not a good look for her. She was begging me to f*ck her. "Girl, get yo' ass off the floor."

She pouted before her gaze went to Anthony. "Tell your friend to take me upstairs and f*ck me!"

Anthony held up his hands. "I can't do that, baby…"

"Come on, Tucker…" She was now whining like a little girl.

I chuckled, finding this sh*t hilarious. "Lay, you asked me to come to the wedding with you as a friend so that you didn't have to go alone. I was doing a favor for a buddy."

Yeah, I knew that was bullsh*t, but that's how she played it, so I was going to make her stick to her words. Truth was, I was coming to Vegas with or without an invitation to the wedding. Yes, the invite made things easier. Now I can keep an eye on Free from the inside rather than the shadows. *Thanks, Lay...* But now that my name was on the guest list, I really didn't have no use for her ass anymore, not that she was getting the memo.

When our plane first landed and everybody checked into the hotel, she had been at my door ten minutes later, begging to come in. I told her ass I was jetlagged and needed to take a nap. An hour later, Anthony was here, more than glad to see me and we've been at it ever since.

I didn't want to go too far from the hotel. Although I trusted Will, I still didn't want to take a chance not being here should something happen with Free. Lucky for me, she wasn't the partying type and had not left her room since checking in yesterday.

However, unlucky for me, Anthony and I decided to come back to the hotel and have a few cocktails before calling it an evening and were spotted by Layla.

The pout only grew on her mouth as she grazed my belt buckle one more time. "You know I didn't mean that. I was just saying that to get you to agree to come with me." She stood to her feet between my legs so that I could see how well the red dress she wore fit on her body.

"Tell me, you can resist all of this," she said, rubbing her hand up her thigh, dragging her dress up with it.

Both Anthony and I took in the matching lace panties she wore that she unabashedly gave us a view of.

I put my hand to my chest as my gaze slowly traveled up her body. "I—" I let my words trail off as our gazes met. A clever little grin spread on her face, so confident was she that she had me. She tossed her head back like she was the queen b*tch and we all were just peasants.

I bit my lip to keep from laughing in her face. "I can resist…" I gave her the sorry face and cooed, "Sorry."

Anthony began choking next to me as he tried to hide the fact that he was laughing. "Damn, Tuck!" he said, wiping at a little of his drink that wasted on his jeans as he still tried to muffle his laughter, but because the both of us were drunk off our asses, was failing miserably.

Layla's mouth opened, insulted. And sh*t, there went my attempt at trying to hold my amusement, my chuckle joined Anthony's. Damn, I needed to stop smoking…this sh*t was just mean. Good and embarrassed, she turned around and stomped away in a huff.

The girl that sat next to Anthony shook her head. "Damn, that didn't go how she expected it."

"Why you do her like that?" Anthony asked as he struggled to get a hold of his laughter.

Shaking my head, I drained my drink. "Man, that girl a viper. Yikes!" I shivered a bit for good measure.

"What you mean? She sexy… and promising you a damn good night. Since when you turn down the fo' sho' p*ssy?"

Leaning back on the bench, I put my hand on my chest. "Naw, buddy… Those days are all over for me. I'm in love."

He chuckled, shaking his head. "So it's true, huh? The Maverick said you was, but I didn't believe him."

Maverick was the code name we used for the captain when we were in the field.

"Damn, do you mutha f*ckas not have anything better to do than to gossip like women about me?"

"Hell naw, that sh*t made national news. Who this shawty that got you wide open like this?"

As if cued, the elevator doors opened and Free, looking sexy as hell, dressed in an oversized sweater that hung off her left shoulder, stopping just above her plump breast, and a pair of black yoga pants stepped off, heading toward the bar.

I groaned as the part of me Layla had been trying to get a response from stirred. It had been a week since I've tasted my girl. I was starved for her. I rubbed my hands down my face, fighting the urge to get up, throw her ass over my back, take her upstairs and make her come apart for me until she no longer remembered why the hell she was mad.

Damn! I didn't even know why the f*ck we were fighting. I would rather be making love...

Anthony frowned at my actions. "Nigga... what's wrong with you?"

I gestured her way just as she sat at the bar a few seats down from Will. "That's her..." I grinned. "That's my future wife."

His grin matched mine. "Oh! I have to meet her, come on, let's go holla at her."

I reached out grabbing his arm before he stood. "Naw, bruh." I nodded to the bartender sliding her a drink. "Let's let her ass warm up first. Last time I talked to her, she was cussing me out." My smile grew. "But after a few, she'll love me again."

———

Free

"Margarita with an extra shot of tequila, please," I told the bartender as I slid on the stool.

For the record, I was here against my will. I'd called to check on Grapefruit, who was staying with Oaklee while I was gone and Rachel, who'd happened to be over at Oak's house, grabbed the phone and berated me for being in Vegas and not enjoying myself.

I'd explained to her that I really didn't know what I was doing here anymore. After finding out my dad wasn't my dad, which meant my stepsisters weren't really my stepsisters, I no longer felt obligated to be in the wedding and sure the hell didn't feel obligated to join Laureen's bachelorette party expedition that was going on right now.

Of course, Rachel didn't spare my feelings at all...

"I don't give a damn about that heffa's bachelorette party. You're in Vegas, Free!!! Get yo' ass up out of the bed and go to a show or to a club...hell, go gamble! Get drunk! But don't wallow in your misery while everybody else is having a good time." And then she spoke in her DJ Khalid voice.

"They don't want you to have a good time...so what are you going to do?"

"I'm going to have a good time," I told her, just because I didn't feel like arguing about it. But after I got off of the phone with my friends, I lay there and considered ordering room services for the fifth time since check-in and continuing to read through my grandmother's journals that I'd brought with me, but right then, I heard a rowdy group of folks outside of my door heading toward the elevators, and yeah...it sounded like they were having a good time.

My gaze went to the journals and the tapes and

suddenly I couldn't stand to see them anymore. I felt like the answer to my question was in there somewhere, but I was tired of reading about the monster that had pretended to be my grandmother and poor Daisy, who had been her victim for so long. No, I wouldn't give up until I found what I needed to know, but…

*"I'm in Vegas!"*

Why the hell am I not enjoying myself? Throwing the covers back, I got up and got dressed. Remembering the nice bar downstairs, I figured I'd start there and see where the night led me.

Now glancing around the fairly empty space that was softly lit, I determined that this was in fact a safe place to map out my night. I just prayed I didn't bump into anyone I knew. The twins and their friends were out painting the town red. Laureen decided to have a bachelorette expedition instead of a party. They were going to spend the night drinking and club hopping. Shouldn't be too hard to avoid them, Vegas was a fairly big place. No doubt, Tucker had gone with them and was having the time of his life. I shrugged…to hell with them.

"Can I have another?" I asked the bartender as I pulled out my phone to look up some shows I may want to catch.

I don't know how long I scrolled through my phone, but after a while, the bartender placed a shot of tequila in front of me, when I gave him a questioning look, he gestured to a little old guy with glasses that sat at the end of the bar.

"From that gentleman over there." When my gaze landed on the old guy, he gave me a little wave. I thought about turning the drink down, the little guy had creep written all over him, but before I could, the bartender walked away. Giving the guy a look that said only this one and no more, I took the shot.

Whew! It was the good stuff. I mouthed thank you to the little fella and went back to scrolling through my phone. There was a lot to see and do in Vegas, but I think I had narrowed my options down to—

The bartender slid another shot in front of me. "From the same guy..." he muttered and began to walk away.

"Wait..." I told him, catching his hand. Oh yeah! I was starting to feel it. I'd just grabbed this guy to keep him from walking away from me.

I removed my hand from his wrist. "Sorry, about that."

Realizing I was a little tipsy, he smiled. "It's okay... what's up?"

"I don't want that guy to keep buying me drinks."

He nodded. "No worries, just keep this one because he already paid and tipped me, and I'll let him know that you're not interested...deal?"

I smiled. "Deal."

He stood for a minute, looking at me as if this was his first time. "You know, you have a beautiful smile."

And as you guys may have guessed, that only made it grow. "Thank you," I told him, taking the shot to cover up the fact that I was blushing. He wasn't a bad looking guy. No, he wasn't Tucker fine, which probably no mortal man could be, but he was nice.

"So, what brings you to Vegas?" he asked, studying me a little closer.

I opened my mouth to tell him but before I could, a man sat on the stool directly to my left. I frowned, the lounge was practically empty, he could have at least sat one stool over. Because he looked like he participated in the seedier matters in Vegas, I decided against giving him a piece of my mind. My gaze went back to the bartender, but he was looking at something to my right with wide eyes.

I turned to see what had spooked him and nearly jumped out of my seat. "Tucker!" I cried, bringing my hand to my chest to stop my heart from giving out. Naphtali sat on the stool directly to my right, he was turned toward me so that I sat between his opened legs.

"Why the hell are you sneaking up on me like that?!" I hissed, not appreciating the fact that he'd just scared the crap out of me and the poor bartender too, who had suddenly gotten busy at the other end of the bar. No telling what he'd done to him... knowing Tucker, he'd probably flashed his gun at him or something.

He grinned. "Maybe if you weren't so busy flirting with the barmaid you would have heard me."

I frowned. "Maybe if you weren't such an asshole I wouldn't have been flirting with the barmaid—" Stuttering a bit, I just realized what he'd called the poor man. "Bartender," I corrected.

The man next to me chuckled and my gaze shot to him. "Would you scoot over? Goodness, it's plenty of available seating."

"Hey! Don't be mean to my friend!" Tucker snapped, and for the first time, I saw that he was drunk and probably high too.

"Well, tell your friend to scoot over!"

With a little grin on his handsome face, he leaned closer. "Make me."

I narrowed my eyes at him. "Why are you bothering me? Can't a girl have a good time and enjoy her drink in peace?" I held up my glass, but it was empty. He chuckled, gesturing for the bartender just as a pretty young woman with beautiful fire engine red locs joined us, wrapping her arms around the man's who was obviously Tucker's friend neck.

"What can I get for you, sir?" the bartender asked, going out of his way to avoid looking at me.

Great! Somehow, this jackass next to me scared him away, I was just getting ready to ask him if he had any recommendations on shows.

"Twelve shots of tequila," Naphtali told him.

My gaze shot to his. "What are you doing? Are you trying to kill us?"

"You want to enjoy yourself? Well, I'm going to show you how it's done." The bartender slid three shots of tequila in front of each of us with a few wedges of lime on beverage napkins. Instantly, Fire Red and Too Close Sam began to down theirs. My stunned gaze went back to Naphtali.

He grinned, lifting his shot glass. "Oh come on, don't get scared now, Doc... Let me show you where the wild things go."

I chewed on my bottom lip as everything inside me warned against it. One of his cocky eyebrows lifted in a challenge as he took his shot.

"I don't think she's the type to go where the wild things go," the man muttered next to me, causing Red to erupted in laughter.

"Me either... not the type at all," she added in between chuckles.

Tucker shook his head. "Poor Doc, can't loosen up if she tried."

That was it! Everybody thought they knew me. But

none of them did…Honestly, at this point in my life, I didn't know myself. I downed all three of my shots one after the other and had to clutch the bar as a shudder ripped through me.

Tucker put his hand on my back with an amazed smile on his face. "You alright, Freebie?"

Fighting to keep those drinks down, I nodded. "Now… show me where the wild things go."

And oh boy…did he deliver. Guys, I'm not going to lie, most of the night I can't remember, just bits and pieces.

I remember going to a club getting the VIP treatment. The redhead whose name I found out was Juicy, got us into an exclusive party for some rapper. I can't remember his name, Little Trick Scooter or something like that. The drinks kept coming and I threw all caution completely to the wind. Tucker and I danced…it felt like I was floating on cloud nine. By some miracle, he only had eyes for me.

Granted, it may be due to Juicy. She told us about the invite she had for Little Shooters or Scooters party but said there was no way they were letting me in dressed like I was, so we ended up stopping by her place that was on the way to the club for me to borrow something of hers.

As soon as we walked through the door, Juicy's occupation was apparent. She had colorful clothes and costumes all over the place. She told me being a showgirl was very lucrative here in Vegas while she poured us all another round of shots.

I think this is when things started getting fuzzy for me. Juicy and Tucker's friend, Anthony disappeared in her bedroom while she left me to look through her many dresses and choose whatever I liked. Tucker plopped on the couch with his big arms rested on the back and said that he would help me choose.

Okay, sounds innocent enough, right? Well, let me tell you, it didn't stay innocent and it's really foggy on who actually crossed the line.

I held up several of the more modest dresses, but that wasn't saying much, they were more risqué than anything I owned. They made my little black dress look like a nun's frock.

"What do you think about this one?" My words slurred so badly, I don't know how he understood me.

He studied the sequin gown for a moment before shaking his head. "Too busy."

I agreed and reached for a little red dress. "What about this one?"

He didn't take any time thinking before shaking his head. "Naw, no red." His words were slurring pretty good at this point as well.

Farther to the back of the rack, I saw a yellow dress hanging. Grinning, I took it down, already knowing he was going to like it. For some reason, this man had a thing about yellow dresses. Turning, I held it in front of me.

As I figured, he was nodding before I could say anything. "Yep! That's the one…"

I went into the small bathroom to change, but the dress had a zipper on the back that I couldn't reach. I peeped my head out the door and made eye contact with Tucker where he still sat on the couch.

"I need you…" I told him.

One of his eyebrows went up and a devious grin spread across his face as he rose from the couch with the grace of a leopard, which was amazing, considering all the alcohol he'd consumed.

"How can I be of service, Freebie?" he cooed, coming to stand in front of the bathroom door.

And I don't know… something about that question combined with the rumble of his deep voice went straight through my body, causing a quiver to shoot through my core.

I licked my lips. "Mmmmm…I umm…" I had to focus to remember what I needed. "I can't zip my dress."

He stood studying me with that gaze of his that missed nothing. There was no doubt in my mind he knew what was going on with my body.

"Can I come in?"

I stared at him for a moment, both of us knowing what his question meant. Slowly I nodded, stepping back so that he could come into the small space. The hunger in his gaze as he shut the door behind him was my undoing. My hand held the dress to my front. It was one of those pieces that had a bra built in, so my bra lay on the floor at our feet.

His gaze lowered to it before it slowly rose up my body. I took another step back until the wall prevented me from going farther.

"I missed you, Free," he whispered.

Swallowing, I nodded. "I missed you too."

"Here, let me help you with your dress." Lifting his hand, he grabbed it where I clutched it in the front and lowered it until my breasts sprang free.

The pained look in his eyes before he groaned was all I needed to reach for him. When our lips touched, my world nearly shattered right then. His mouth devoured mine, showing me how much he'd missed me. The kiss was intoxicating. When his greedy mouth lowered to my neck and then to my aching breasts, I was lost.

By the time he lifted me, wrapping my legs around his waist, I was wild with need. His strength felt so right and he smelled so good. I needed to feel him inside of me.

"Please, Tucker..." I moaned against his lips.

"What do you want, baby?"

"I want to feel you inside of me!"

"Damn, girl! F*ck!" he hissed as he wrestled with his belt buckle. "Can't get enough of you... You in my blood, Free!" And then he was filling me.

My head fell back against the wall as he drove into me, I wasn't sober enough to try and muffle my cries of pleasure. At this moment, it was just him and me. Nothing and nobody else existed. I've denied my body this pleasure for too long and could not deny it any longer.

He hit the wall with his hand as for a moment he lost control. His grunts mingled with my cries left little to the imagination on what was going on in here. But still, I didn't care, and when my world shattered and a million stars burst before my eyes, a scream tore from my lips. Moments later, he cried out as his warm seed flooded my soft tunnel.

Together, we stayed in that position, connected until our breathing had evened out. Reaching over, he turned on the shower. I giggled as I slid in and watched him struggle to maneuver his big body in it around me.

Taking pity on him, I used the soap and my hands to wash him. He was so big and the shower was so small, he looked like a sardine in a can. And well, you know, one thing led to another, and well...we got a little sidetracked again. But eventually, we helped each other get dressed.

"Well, okay…" Juicy said with a huge knowing grin on her face, holding another round of shots in her hand when we exited the bathroom. "I guess we're all ready now."

Because Juicy and I wore a different sized shoe, I wasn't able to borrow a pair of hers and had to make a go at it in my tennis shoes. She was afraid that the bouncer would not let me in, but Tucker ended up pulling him to the side, saying something to him before sliding something in his hand, which caused the bouncer to smile at me and hold the red rope to the side.

"Welcome to the Ice Bar."

Ohhhh, guys! We danced and laughed… And yes, he had eyes only for me. I drank so much until the club started spinning. At one point, I didn't know if I was dancing or standing still. Somehow, we lost Anthony and Juicy. I think Tucker and I agreed that we were hungry and was going to go and find food… I think.

But we were walking down the street, or more like he was walking and I was clinging to his arm like a monkey, letting him guide me, because yeah, everything was spinning. My shoe came untied and he walked to a bench.

"Here, baby, sit, let me tie your shoe."

I sat or more like lay. But as I watched him go down on one knee in front of me, I thought, how pathetic am I. Here this fine man took a knee in front of me, but not to ask me to marry him… he did it to tie my shoe.

What was wrong with me? Why am I thirty-four and no man has asked me to marry him? Laureen was getting married and she was a nasty, hateful human being… what was wrong with me? Tears came to my eyes.

"What's the matter, baby?" Tucker asked when he saw

that I was crying. Still kneeling, he wiped away my tears. His action only made me cry harder.

"I'm thirty-four," I wailed, wrapping my arms around his neck, burying my face in that spot just under his throat. He encased me in his strong arms, rubbing my hair that was all over my head. After all the dancing and sweating, forget about it...

"Yeah...so. That's a good thing, right?"

I lifted my head to look at him. "No, it's not a good thing! I'm an old maid. All of my prime years are gone. Now I'll never find a man that want to marry me."

He frowned. "What about me? I'm a man..."

I grinned, using my finger to tap the tip of his nose. "Yes, you are a man." I tried to shift my eyebrows cleverly, but I'm sure I failed big time. "A sexy man, you are."

His frown grew as he studied me. Something I'd said upset him. "What about the marrying kind?"

It was my turn to frown. "I don't know...I've never taken you for the marrying kind."

He drew back, taking away his body heat. That made me pout and reach for him, but he tapped my hands away.

"Why not?"

I grinned, trying to pull him back to me. "Why not what?"

"Why ain't I the marrying kind?"

"Cause you very good at being the sexy kind," I told him, wrapping my arms around his neck.

He took them back from around his neck. "So you're saying I'm good enough for sex, but not good enough to marry?"

I sat back and blinked at him, trying to bring him into focus. I couldn't understand why he was being so grumpy.

"Do you want to get married?"

"Hell yeah, if it's you." He growled.

Surprised, I put my hand to my chest. "You would marry me?"

"In a heartbeat."

I smiled. "Awww! Tucker, that is so sweet." I reached for him to pull him into another hug, but he took my hands, bringing them back into my lap.

"So then let's do it!"

"Do what, silly?"

"Get married. Let's get married right now!"

I shook my head. "I don't think so… I'm still mad at you," I told him, pointing at him. At least I think it was at him, I was seeing three.

"Don't you want to get married before your sister?"

That hit a nerve. "Yeah!" I roared.

It was his turn to grin. "So, let's do it!"

"Okay!" I cried, standing. This was a great idea. But he had to hurry to catch me because I damn near went right back over the bench.

In one swoop, he lifted me in his arms. "Are you going to carry me over the threshold?"

He chuckled. "Got to carry you to the chapel first." And so, he did. He carried me all the way to the chapel, Blue Suede Shoes Chapel to be more precise. And by some miracle, Juicy and Anthony met us there.

I found myself looking down at wedding rings, but I couldn't get them to be still long enough so that I could pick one.

"What kind of ring would the lovely couple like?" Elvis asked us.

Oh, did I forget to tell you guys? Elvis was nice enough

to take the time out of his busy schedule to marry us. Can you guys believe that? I didn't know he was ordained, what with being a big star and all. Apparently, the rumors were true...he's not dead. He runs the Blue Suede Shoes Chapel in Vegas.

"Ummm..." I looked up at Naphtali, who stared down at the rings as if he too was having trouble bringing them into focus. "What do you think?"

He shook his head. "Pick any one of them you want."

"Is there a certain price we're looking for?" Elvis asked, smiling at us both.

I begin to nod, but Tucker cut me off. "Price doesn't matter..." he declared. "For my Freebie, I'll pay anything."

"Well, why didn't you lead with that, my good friend?" Elvis said, closing the box of rings we were looking at. "Follow me, I'll show you the forever rings. Don't you guys want to be together forever?"

We both nodded vigorously, he smiled. "Sure you do, right this way."

He led us to a room that wasn't a room, but a vault. When he hit the light, a very impressive display of diamond rings sparkled to life.

My eyes were drawn to a beautiful ring that glistened blue. "Aww, the Blue Nile has caught the lady's eye." He lifted it from under the display glass. "It is said that Nefertiti herself once owned this diamond."

"Wow!" I cried. "Really?" He nodded, handing the ring to Tucker.

"You like this one, baby?" Naphtali asked, staring into my eyes with a gaze that held me hypnotized.

"Yes."

Slowly he went down to one knee in front of me, taking

my hand in his. "Will you make me a man deserving of you and marry me?"

Tears came to my eyes as I nodded. "Yes."

He slid the ring on my finger, amazingly it fit perfectly. I felt like Cinderella. Then he stood and pulled me into his arms.

"Thank you, Freebie! For finally seeing me."

# Chapter 4

Bloody Nuptials

*You're Always One Decision Away From A Totally Different Life...*

*Unknown*

## Free

ONE OF THE things that have always amazed me is how quickly life can shift and throw you in a whole different direction than you were heading. The first time it happened to me, my beautiful mother looked at me and told me she loved me for the last time. I wonder if somehow, she knew that time when she partook of her drug of choice, it would be her last.

Is that possible?

Do people get a premonition or a feeling of death? If so, I wasn't one of those people. You ask how I know?

Well…today is the day I died.

I had no warning, no feelings of impending doom, nothing. One minute I was here living my life and the next, I wasn't. Yeah, I know… That sounds bazaar, but it's true.

This is the day that I died...

Oh… and also the day I got married. LOL! What's the irony? This should have been the happiest day of a new bride's life… But it would turn out to be a nightmare for all brides present.

A bloody nightmare…

I don't know what woke me that morning, but upon coming awake, my first feeling was comfort. After days of not being able to sleep because this warm body was not next to me, I was now back in his arms and my world once again felt right. My head rested against his chest and my leg was draped over his. Still more than half asleep, I let my hand rub up his muscled stomach to rest against his hard peck. When he felt me move, his arms tightened around me, pulling me closer. Inhaling a satisfied breath, I began to drift back to sleep.

However, an irritating screech pierced the air before someone began to rip at the covers and my hair.

"Owwww!" I yelled, coming awake, but the body under me reacted instantly. In the blink of an eye, I was under him, and in what seemed like one fluid motion, he snatched his gun from somewhere on the side of the bed and was pointing it at whoever it was that had tried to attack me.

"Wait! Don't shoot!" Angie and Layla cried, throwing their hands up while cowering back against the wall.

"Please don't shoot!"

*What was going on?!*

My brain felt like a giant cotton ball, it was taking it a while to process what I was seeing. Tucker scowled down at the two women from his position on his knees in the center of the bed, his gun aimed directly at them.

"What the f*ck are you doing in my room!" he roared. Yep, that did it! That caused my brain to click on.

Angie and Layla were practically hugging each other, trying to escape his wrath. Layla's eyes were squeezed shut. Even I backed up a bit from him as I blinked, looking around, trying to get my bearings about me. Okay, so we weren't in his room, we were in mine, which would explain how they got in. No doubt Angie got the front desk to let her in after giving them the, *my daughter isn't answering her phone and I'm so worried* spiel. Yeah, she does stuff like that.

However, when my eyes landed back on Tucker, they widened. He was completely naked. Every inch of that perfect chocolate body of his was on display. Poor Angie, who had a front view of him didn't know what to look at, the gun, his very impressive manhood, or his rage-filled eyes.

"Answer me! What the f*ck are you doing in my room?!" His fury was a horrible thing. He was so angry he still hadn't tried to cover himself or lower the gun.

"Th—this isn't your room, it's Free's!" Layla cried, her

voice quivered so badly her words were barely recognizable.

Frowning, Tucker looked around until his bloodshot gaze landed on me. "Are you alright?" I nodded, pulling the sheet to my chin.

*What do you know? I'm completely naked as well.* And judging by the slight soreness I was experiencing and the stickiness between my thighs, we'd had a very interesting night indeed.

Right then, images of me lying face down on the bed with both of my hands being imprisoned over my head by one of Tucker's big ones as he drove into me from behind flashed through my mind and I gasped as the answering spasm shot through my center.

I had to clear my throat to get myself together. When he saw that I was okay, he lowered his gun before angrily jerking the other sheet and wrapping it around his middle as he stood from the bed.

Only then did Angie and Layla exhale, but they continued to watch him with startled eyes. Grumbling under his breath about *'worrisome ass women,'* he made his way to the little kitchen area before placing the gun on the sink and jerking open the little fridge. He must have been looking for water, when he didn't find any, he grabbed the ice bucket, ripped the top off, and proceeded to drink the water from the melted ice.

For a moment, all the three of us could do was stare at him. He made quite a sight, all chocolate muscled Adonis with only a sheet wrapped loosely around his waist, drinking water from the ice bucket like a complete savage. Unconsciously, Angie's hand lifted to her chest as she continued to take him in, helpless to look away. The man's body was a true work of art.

It was me that found the strength to look away first, and that's simply because my stomach was doing some odd things. Angie and Layla were both dressed in their wedding outfits and I started to get a bad feeling as I reached over and grabbed Tucker's watch off the side table.

"Oh my God! It's twelve o'clock!" I jumped out of the bed, clutching the sheet around my naked body. The wedding started in an hour! But I shouldn't have moved so suddenly. It was at that point that everything went south. Not only was the room spinning, my head had begun to pound something viscously and my stomach revolted brutally.

My voice must have snapped Layla and Angie out of the Tucker stupor because they both turned on at the same time.

"What the hell is going on here?!" Angie yelled.

I clutched my head as a pain shot through it. Judging by the groan I heard coming from the kitchen area, her yell had the same effect on Naphtali.

I held up my hand. "Angie, please. Let's use our inside voi—"

Layla pointed at my hand. "What the hell is that on your finger?!"

God! Did they know how to speak without yelling?

"Lay—" I began to reprimand her, but just then, the huge diamond on my finger winked at me, flashing blue in the sunlight that spilled through the window...

Unnecessarily I brought my hand closer as if I couldn't see the huge rock on it from a mile away. There were a beautiful engagement ring and the matching wedding band on my finger.

"Oh my God!" My gaze shot to Tucker.

Still standing in the little kitchen area, he frowned at my ring before lifting his hand to see the matching wedding band on it.

A startled grin appeared on his face. "Oh sh*t! That happened..." When he said that, all hell broke loose.

"You man-stealing whore!" Layla screeched, trying to come at me, but Angie's arm shot out, stopping her.

The inside of my stomach wanted out right now! I put my hand on my mouth and made a dash for the bathroom, only managing to get the door locked before I threw myself at the toilet and began to throw up everything I had inside of me.

Oh God!!! I felt like death! My head was pounding really bad and each time I retched, it only made it worse. And it didn't help that both Layla and Angie were now yelling at Tucker and me for going behind Layla's back and getting married last night.

Blessedly, only bits and pieces of the chaos that was going on outside of the bathroom door bled through to the other side. Poor Tucker, they were laying into him.

"Woman, are you f*cking nuts? I was never going to marry Layla!" I heard him growl as he put his clothes on.

At some point, he knocked on the door. "Free, you okay?"

"Just go, Tuck!" *Save yourself.* "Get ready for the wedding...I'll meet you downstairs!" I managed to get out before I was vomiting again.

"Do you need anything-" he began, but Angie cut him off.

"Free, how can you do this to your sisters?! The wedding starts in forty minutes and you're not even dressed!"

"She's a backstabbing bit—" Layla began, but Tucker's growl cut her off.

"Can you two please shut the f*ck up! I'm trying to see if she needs anything!"

Angie gasped. "You can't talk to me like that, young man!"

"I just did."

Although I was vomiting and my head felt like someone was hitting me with a sledgehammer, I couldn't help the smile that came to my face from hearing their banter.

Their argument left from in front of the door, so it was hard for me to hear what was being said. But Tucker, bless his heart, said something that got them to leave me in peace.

However, Angie, not to be defeated, left me with a parting threat. "You better be downstairs in thirty minutes or so help me God, I will singlehandedly destroy your precious clinic, brick by brick. You know me, Free, and you know that I am not lying. You will not embarrass the family this way." I heard the front door slam behind her.

Layla must have stayed behind and tried to talk to Tucker because I heard what sounded like a little scuffle before the hotel door opened and Layla whining, asking him why he was doing her like this, and then the door slamming before someone's angry hand hit it.

Oh God! What a mess...

"Free..." Tucker's gentle voice came from the other side of the bathroom door.

"Yeah…" I groaned, really wishing he would leave so that I could die in peace.

"Are you going to be alright?"

"Mmmhhhmmm…" I managed to get out before my stomach rolled over and I retched violently again.

"Baye, open the door so I can help you."

"Just go, Tucker!" I cried. "Please! Just go! You have to get dressed."

He stood there for a moment, knowing him, he was probably debating whether or not he should break down the door.

"Okay," he finally spoke. "I'm going to go downstairs and get you some aspirin, then I'll get dressed."

"Okay, thank you!" I was willing to say anything to get him to leave. When I heard the door close, I exhaled, but my body exploded in another fit of dry retching.

Minutes later, Tucker returned. "Free, I have aspirin and water here for you."

Thank God I'd stopped retching, but I still sat on the floor with my head resting on my hand and my elbow on the toilet seat just in case.

"Thank you… can you set it on the table for me?"

He paused for a minute. I could tell he still stood by the door. "Bae…don't you think we should talk about the fact that we're married?"

Holding up my hand, I took in my beautiful rings. He was probably freaking out right now, wondering if I'll give him a hard time about correcting the mistake we made last night. I shook my head, just like a man. Still, that thought made me sad. I didn't want to correct the mistake we made last night, because I don't quite feel that we made one.

Closing my fist, I brought my hand to my chest. I didn't

want to take my rings off just yet, I wanted to bask in the fact that I was married… If just for the day.

"Free?" he called.

"The wedding starts in thirty minutes. Why don't we get through it and then we can clear up this mess."

I heard his head come to rest against the door. "Free…" he groaned.

Tears came to my eyes as my heart broke. "We were both wasted last night, I get it! No worries, okay?! Mistakes happen…just go get dressed, I'll meet you downstairs."

———

Tucker

With my head still leaning against the bathroom door, I balled up my fist and brought it to rest against it, stopping myself from punching a hole through the mutha f*cka and forcing her to talk to me.

*Mistakes happen?*

*What the f*ck?!*

I know we were drunk, but there had to be a part of her that wanted to marry me too, or else she wouldn't have done it. The thought of being married to me had caused her to throw up.

*What the f*ck?!*

I felt that restless energy begin to pace inside of me. Taking several deep breaths, I tried to control my anger. The last thing I needed right now was input from the Bully.

*Mistakes happen…*

She wanted to undo what we did last night. Yeah, I was

drunk, but I knew exactly what I was doing and I wouldn't change it for nothing in this world.

*Mistakes happen…*

F*ck, I was losing the battle; the Bully was now violently banging on the walls of my resistance. He wanted to be let loose, and I wanted to let him loose.

*Let me free, boy!*

I shook my head. No! I needed to be able to think with a straight head. God! I wish I had the strength to let her go.

*You sound like a b*tch! You been wishing you was her nigga since the first time you laid eyes on her! Now you have her! She's ours! Legally!*

This is true, by law, she belonged to me. She had my ring on her finger…she was mine.

*Hell yeah, she is! I don't give a f*ck about her saying ya'll will figure this thing out later… there will be no divorce!*

I straightened as me and my alter ego became one, lifting my head from the door, rotating my shoulders.

Hell yeah! There will be no divorce…What the f*ck was I worried about?

"Okay baby, I'm going to leave the aspirin on the table for you," we told her.

"Thank you! I'll see you downstairs in a minute."

As we headed out the door, I shot a text to Will and told him I was going back to my room and he needed to keep an ear out for Free. Luckily, we were able to get him a room right next door to hers.

*Now… let's go get dressed for this wedding. Got a feeling sh*t finna hit the fan!*

I grinned… The Bully always had a feeling shit was getting ready to hit the fan…

---

## Free

Oh my God! I really felt like death! No, I take that back. The dead was dead, so even they didn't feel this suffering.

I don't know where I got the strength to pull myself up from the bathroom floor and stumble in the shower, but by the time I made it out, I felt a little better. The aspirin Tucker left for me helped a lot.

By some miracle, I got myself together and down to the hotel terrace where the wedding was taking place in time to march in with the groomsmen I'd been partnered with. However, before we walked down the aisle, Angie threatened both Layla and I with murder if we made a scene in front of all her snobby guests.

"Tell her to take off that ring!" Layla whined. And I couldn't help the dry chuckle that left my lips. Yeah right! As if she could... For good measure, I used the hand with the huge blue diamond on it to adjust the ugly flower arrangement Laureen had chosen for us on my head.

Mmmhhhmm... I know it was petty, but I couldn't resist. Layla's mouth popped open, but Angie gave her a murderous look that said *get it together or die* right before she half shoved her through the door that led out to the terrace.

As I walked down the aisle, I found myself searching for Tucker. My husband... Wow! My husband. At least for now. From the sound of his strained voice at the bathroom door, he was freaking out to find himself saddled with a wife upon waking up. No doubt, the first thing he did when he went back to his room was call one of his family's fancy attorney's to see what was the quickest way to undo what he mistakenly did last night due to too much liquor consumption.

I sucked up the pain that thought brought. I can't remember much about our little impromptu wedding, but the little I can remember was very sweet and I wouldn't trade it for the world.

Sighing, I shook away those thoughts. No need to dwell on something that can't be. I had to get myself together. My life was a complete mess right now and this thing with Tucker was only making it more so.

When I didn't see him sitting in any of the chairs, my heart dropped. *So much for getting my life together.* What made me think he was going to be here after making the biggest mistake of his life last night? He was probably already on a plane back to Detroit.

My gaze went back toward the front, Dillion stood there watching me come down the aisle with a look on his face that I couldn't quite read. Poor bastard, I think I felt sorry for him; he was tying himself to Laureen. A more shallow creature had never existed. How the wor--

My thoughts came to a halt as a chill suddenly washed over me. It was the same feeling I got the night of the party. Once again, I let my eyes scan the crowd, looking for the source. Standing to the side, casually leaning against one of the big white pillars was Tucker, only… he wasn't alone.

When he, or…they saw that I was looking that direction, he winked. I nearly stumbled. If not for the arm of the man escorting me down the aisle I would have.

What was going on?

Why has Tucker's alternate personality resurfaced?

Did he suffer something traumatic from the time he left

my room to go back to his? If so, what could it possibly have been in such a short time?

Now that it was here, were we in danger?

These were all questions that raced through my mind as the wedding proceeded. So consumed was I in my thoughts that I barely noticed when everyone stood as Laureen walked down the aisle. My troubled gaze kept going to Tucker, waiting for him to do something drastic.

I really wish I had more time to study his alternate personality, maybe even spoken with it. I've been trying to pry into his head a little bit without alerting him to what I was doing, just to see what could have happened to him so traumatic that it would bring on such a severe case of Dissociative Identity Disorder. But of course, every time I did, he would freeze up and accuse me of trying to be his doctor rather than his girlfriend.

The hairs on the back of my neck stood as that uneasy feeling grew. I don't know if it was because the deadly eyes that watched me from Tucker's body felt demoni---

No, Free... Logic and hours of study tell you those thoughts can't be true. There are case studies of patients with Dissociative Identity Disorder who have done astonishingly horrible things only to come back to themselves appalled and ashamed of what they've done. Mothers have murdered their babies, husbands their wives, children their parents. There's no hocus pocus to this, just simple psychosis. That's all this is… nothing more.

Except that uneasy feeling kept growing inside of me, so much so, Angie gave me the evil eye from where she sat motioning for me to pay attention to the pastor. She was a fool and had no idea what was taking place around her.

As if to prove my point, Anthony, Tucker's friend from

last night suddenly came through the door on the other side of the terrace that the wait staff used. The look on his face said something was going on. He made eye contact with Tucker, giving him a slight nod.

Tucker inhaled before he stood up straight from leaning against the pillar. When his gaze came to mine, I knew... I can't tell you how I knew, but just like that day on the football field when he got into a fight with those guys, Tucker was gone, and standing in his place was a destructive force. There were no other words that can describe him accurately.

The pastor had begun the part of the sermon where he had the couple repeat after him, but before Laureen could say I do, the terrace doors were violently thrown open and a group of masked men came through them carrying big guns pointing them at us, demanding for us to remain sitting.

A few women screamed, but one of the masked men held his gun in the air, letting off a couple of shots, bringing the cries of alarm to a halt.

"Please excuse the interruption," a very handsome Hispanic man dressed in an expensive suit said coming through the door. "What I have to say won't take long. However, if you value your lives, I'm going to need you to remain sitting."

Judging by how crude his English was, I don't think he spoke the language much at all. My gaze flew to Tucker, only to surprisingly see the spot where he stood empty, and he nowhere in sight.

"Now wait just a minute, young man!" Angie cried coming to her feet. "I think you have made a terrible mistake! This is the—"

The guy moved so fast I barely saw him reach behind his back and pull out a handgun. However, the next few seconds will always be seared in my memory because they seemed like hours. With a deadly grin on his face, he pointed the gun at Angie and without an ounce of hesitation, pulled the trigger.

I blinked when something warm splattered on my face and dress. There was a sharp ringing in my ear as my mind calculated what happened. Angie's brains had been blown all over the bridal party. That ringing in my ear wasn't ringing at all, but Laureen screaming.

Oh my God!

Angie was dead!

The man in the suit had killed Angie. I don't know if it was the sound of my heart or my blinking, but it sounded like a drumbeat in my ears. For a collective second, everyone stared down at Angie's body in complete and utter shock!

Angie was dead!

A loud crash came from the back as the body of one of the masked men came flying through the doors, taking down three of the men with guns. And that's when complete chaos erupted. Everybody stood from their seats and ran for the nearest exit.

"Get the girl!" the man in the suit cried over the panic sounds of the guests. "I need her alive!"

It didn't take me long to realize I was the girl because four big burly men broke away from the group and rushed toward me. There was more commotion going on toward the terrace door that the man had just been thrown through, but I didn't stick around to see what. Kicking off those ugly shoes, I ran for the door nearest me. I felt some people following me, but I didn't look back to see whether they were friend or foe.

Word must have gotten around the hotel that there were active shooters on the premises because people were running every which way. I quickly made my way down the service hall to what looked like the kitchen. I could see an exit sign on the other side, but before I took a step in that direction, more masked men came through it.

Quietly, I made my way between two tall racks that held pots, pans, and other kitchen utensils. With hands that shook, I eased one of the butcher knives out of the tray before squatting down so they couldn't see me.

They spoke to each other in Spanish as they continued to look through the kitchen.

Oh God! They knew I was here.

"Free! What's going on? Who are these people?!" My startled gaze went to Dillion, who was trying to squeeze in between the racks with me.

I shook my head, motioning for him to be quiet. "Go, you can't fit through there..." I whispered, but his eyes were in a panic.

"They killed Laureen! She's dead...they're all dead!" he said, still trying to force his way between the slit that was barely big enough for me. I tried to shoosh him and get him to calm down, but in his haste, he bumped into the rack, causing the pots and pans to knock together, alerting the masked men to our location.

When they saw Dillion, they opened fire. I stepped back against the wall, holding my hand over my mouth to keep from screaming as they riddled his body with bullets.

Tears filled my eyes...

They were coming...they were coming for me.

The first man stepped into my line of view, pointing his gun at me. "You…Come!"

I shook my head, but he shot at the wall behind me, causing me to cry out as I hurried out from my hiding space. My heart was beating so fast it felt like it was going to beat out of my chest. I clutched the butcher knife in my sweaty hand, keeping it hidden in the fluffy material of my dress.

Stepping over Dillion's body, I inhaled when I felt his warm blood under my feet. It was then that something settled over me. I was not going to willingly walk to my death, if I was going to die, I was going to go down fighting.

Waiting till I was only feet away from the man that beckoned me forward with his gun, I pretended to slip and when he reached out for me, imbedded the sharp knife in his chest. His eyes widened as his gaze went down to the handle of the knife before they rolled to the back of his head.

*Move! Now!*

I didn't wait to see his body hit the ground before taking off toward the exit sign. However, I didn't make it far before someone roughly grabbed my hair and threw me into the rack. Pain shot through my body but I didn't pay it any mind. I grabbed the nearest thing to me that just so happened to be a metal pot and swung it with all my might, clipping the asshole on the face.

Not waiting around to see what damage was done, I made a run for the door again, but he grabbed me and delivered a blow that really did cause ringing in my ears. As I fell to the floor, it felt like I was falling in the sea. I lay there fighting to remain conscious.

He reached down for me, but something violently snatched him up...Way up in the air before slamming him face-first to the ground. My eyes widened as his face splattered on the floor in front of me.

Dear God!

Tucker came down to one knee next to the man's body, ripping off his gun that was still connected to his arm and fired at the three men that spilled in the kitchen behind him, killing them. Someone charged him from our left, without looking away from the door, he brought the gun back over his shoulder, smashing the guy in the face before turning and firing the gun, killing him.

By this time, I had all but balled up into a fetal position because the loud gunshots right above my head were an overload to my system.

Several more men spilled into the kitchen and I lay there and watched Tucker flawlessly take them out in complete awe. He moved like a machine. No mortal man can move that fast, not even one that suffered from Dissociative Identity Disorder. In some case studies, a person may show signs of heightened aggression or like I said earlier, violent tendencies, but a person does not suddenly become superman.

No, I don't think you guys understand what I'm saying! He wasn't just fast; he was super freaking strong. He broke arms and legs as easily as one would a pencil. And those men must have had orders to take him alive as well because they all foolishly continued to try and fight him rather than shoot him.

They kept coming and he kept killing them. The bodies were piled up around him. He used anything and everything he could get his hands on…guns, his fists, his kicks… a wine glass.

Yeah! He killed a man with a wine glass. I sat here on this floor and witnessed it with my very own eyes. Tucker picked up the glass and in the scuffle, the bottom of it broke off. He then proceeded to jam the stem of the glass in the man's eye before swiftly kicking the glass to make sure it went in all the way.

That sounds terrible, but I wish I can say that was the worst thing I saw him do. IT WAS NOT! There is a guy whose head was stuck in the brick wall. How did it get there you ask? Well, Tucker kicked it through there, that's how.

"Walk gently through the field of lilies," the Hispanic man that had killed Angie said coming through the kitchen door. When Tucker saw him, he did quick work at killing the last few remaining men he fought before he went after the man.

"Walk gently through the field of lilies!" the guy cried, stumbling back out of the kitchen. Tucker never slowed his pace.

"Why isn't it working?!" The guy was so afraid at this point, his English was barely legible.

"Because," a very calm voice with an accent I didn't quite recognize filled the kitchen. "He's in love and you are threatening his love."

Right then, a very handsome dark-skinned man dressed in a cream linen suit stepped over a body and casually strolled into the kitchen. Tucker's steps came to a halt as he took in the stranger. Realizing he was saved, for now, the Hispanic man exhaled, putting his hand on his chest.

"Gotdamn, bro! What took you so long to get here? That big bastard almost did to me what he did them…" He nodded toward the pile of bodies on the floor.

With his hands folded behind his back, the dark-skinned stranger slowly circled Tucker, who stood as if he was frozen.

*What was wrong with him?*

"So beautiful…" The man muttered as his gaze raked Tucker's body.

African… This man's accent was from Africa.

"You see, Rau? Didn't I tell you? These sons of King Dawid make for the perfect weapons."

Rau didn't seem impressed. "Yeah well, that mutha f*cka almost killed me," he said, dusting something off the sleeve of his expensive suit.

"Who are you?" the African guy asked Tucker.

"I am The Bully 373492."

"Do you know who I am?"

Still in some kind of daze, the Bully nodded.

The man smiled. "Who am I, child?"

Tucker lifted his head to look the man in the eye for the first time. "Baalam, my master."

# Chapter 5

The Devil's Den

Free

"TAKE DEEP BREATHS WITH ME," I told Megan, the beautiful frightened blond teen, who'd been kidnapped two days ago or what I think was two days ago.

"Close your eyes, sweetheart, and hear the breath flowing through your lungs and out your mouth." Her hand shook so badly inside mine I feared she was close to having a full-blown anxiety attack.

"Can you hear it?"

She nodded. I knew this because I felt her body move, not because I could see. It was pitch black inside the freight truck we were being carried in. The only light was coming from the little slits of the two metal doors toward the very back of the truck. I'd lost count of the number of women jammed inside.

"Doc! I can't breathe!" the teen cried out, clutching my hand to the point of pain.

"Yes, you can, Megan. You can do this. You've survived worse things. Remember you told me how it was *you* that went and got help after your father's car flipped into a ditch? You crawled through the window, although you were hurt, and you went and got help for your father. If not for you, he wouldn't have made it." I'd found this information out due to the impromptu counseling session we'd had when she was first kidnapped, something I'd had to do with nearly every woman in back of this truck.

"You are so brave and strong, Megan." Also something I had to constantly remind every woman in back of this truck. "This is nothing. Listen to my voice…can you hear my voice?" With jerky movements, she nodded her head.

"Breathe with me. In and out…in and out."

Although she was terribly afraid of cramped dark spaces, she was finally taking steady breaths. I gently fingered her wrist under the guise of getting a better hold on her but was actually checking her pulse.

"Anxiety is a state of mind. You have the power to change your mind." I kept my voice calm, careful not to let any of my own fear bleed through.

This had been the twelfth or thirteenth time I'd had to talk one of the women that had been kidnapped like myself, down from the ledge. If one of them panicked in this tight dark space, they could harm someone else.

I've tried to keep track of the days since we were taken from the casino and if my calculation is correct, it's been six. I was able to tell this not only by how many times the light that bled through the cracks darkened and then became light again, but because every time we stopped to pick up another batch of kidnapped women, they allow us to come off the truck and relieve ourselves in whatever stranded area they'd found.

If we're lucky, it's at an old rundown gas station that was one step from being abandoned. However, we're not always lucky, and sometimes it's out in the middle of the desert or once on the side of an abandoned road, where we had to handle our business under the watchful eye of the men who escorted us.

I've also tried to memorize things in whatever area we're in to do my best to plot our journey so that as soon as I find a way free, I can find my way back home. I was positive I'd been kidnapped by some kind of sex slave ring and from the number of girls and women they'd managed to cram in the back of this truck, a very big one. We'd crossed the border into Mexico and was heading south, but outside of that, I had very little information.

However, although it was possible I was on my way to becoming a sex slave, I was more worried about Tucker. Guys...

Oh God! I can't believe I'm saying this. It goes against all that I've been taught. All that I could cognitively reason away. I should have listened to the Preacher's warning.

The man that Tucker called Balaam was a...a witch, or whatever male witches are called. He did magic.

And yes, I know that sounds completely crazy. But guys... I saw it. I saw it with my own eyes. His voice alone had power over Tucker.

No, not Tucker...The Bully. The Bully called him master. He did everything Balaam told him to do, including sticking himself with a needle filled with a drug that knocked him out cold.

But I know my Tucker was at war with his alter. Before his eyes rolled to the back of his head and his big body collapsed, his tortured gaze came to mine. And it was Tucker looking at me. But it was too late, the Bully had already drugged them.

I got to my feet, ready to attack Balaam for hurting him. But he just looked at me and my whole body felt frozen in place, my eyes opened wide when an unseen force lifted me off the ground and held me suspended in the air. I couldn't move, talk… or anything.

With a grin on his face, Balaam walked toward me, coming to a stop where I was being held in the air.

"Oh, doctor." He shook his head. "How will you ever convince your practical mind all this really happened?" He held his hand in the air and the men that Tucker had killed and the one that I'd killed, stood straight up from the floor. Even the one whose head Tucker had kicked through the wall pulled himself out of the cement and stood to his feet, dusting the debris off his shoulders.

My eyes widened even more…but this time in horror. No way this was possible. Those men were dead.

"You'll probably need hours of therapy to convince yourself you're not crazy and this was all a figment of your imagination brought on by too much stress from the work-place and lack of sleep." He chuckled. "Just think, all this because you have attractive genes." His gaze went to Tuck-er's body.

"Poor fool was doomed before he knew what hit him. Love… the only thing my spells cannot control." He shrugged. "Well…that and death."

Dismissing me, he turned and spoke with the Hispanic man in the suit. "I will take him; you can have the girl.

These smart types should fetch a high price in your line of work."

Rau frowned. "Hey man, that wasn't the deal. I sacrificed my old lady for your assistance. You're supposed to help me get revenge for Marcellus."

Balaam's gaze rose to his and Rau wisely took a few steps back, removing some of the bass from his voice. "He needs to die for what he did to my brother."

With hands clasped behind his back, Balaam slowly made his way to stand next to Rau, who was now visibly nervous. "Do you think it was a coincidence that you happened upon my conjuring spell?"

Rau swallowed but wisely remained silent. "Did you think *yo' mama's* Santeria was powerful enough to summon me?"

He laughed. "You foolish boy! I'm here because of him. I can give a damn about the life of your silly girlfriend or your brother, you... peon! You have no idea what's at stake." Rau balled his hands into fists at his side, the little muscle ticking furiously in his chin.

Balaam gaze hardened as he growled through clenched teeth. "You have no idea."

Releasing Rau from the intensity of his gaze, he headed toward the door. "Bring him," he hissed at the guards on the way out.

"Worry not, Rau," The sorcerer's voice somehow filled the room, although he was gone. "When my gladiators are done with him, there will be no meat left on his bones. Those boys really have a taste for human flesh. You didn't kill your woman in vain. Your brother will be avenged."

Rau's gaze came to me where I was still suspended in the air. "Hey, bro, what about her?" he called after Balaam.

A squeak left my throat when I was suddenly released from the air to be caught in the arms of another one of the goons that instantly gagged me and tied my hands.

Helplessly, I watched as Tucker was carried away to be eaten by gladiator cannibals. I felt sick with worry, my mind raced with ways to save myself so that I could try and save him. Where the heck had they taken him where there were gladiators? Did Balaam really mean gladiators or was he just saying that?

God! I have never felt as helpless as I do right now. Over the last six days, I've tried to reason with the men who transported us to whatever hell awaited us. If I could just get to a phone, I could call Rachel and tell her to get in contact with Jackson, telling him that both Tucker and I had been kidnapped. There was no doubt in my mind that Jackson and Asher would find us. They wouldn't rest till they did.

I tried to bribe the men with money if they would just let me call my sister and let her know I was alright, promising I won't report them to the police. But it was a completely useless effort, they didn't know a lick of English, and the little bit of Spanish I knew only made them laugh when I attempted to talk to them.

And then there was the little matter of Layla.

Oh, did I forget to mention that I wasn't the only one to be taken from the casino? Yeah, they got Layla too. She said she'd lain between Angie and Laureen's bodies pretending to be dead. Thinking that all the men were gone, she sat up only to find a few still lingered. She thought they were going to shoot her too and begged for her life, and well, here she is.

She was the first person I had to talk down off the

ledge, panicking as soon as they threw us in the back of the truck, she began to claw at the metal doors, ripping her nails from their socket. Now, in her fear, she'd become almost infantile, sticking so close to my side, I often had to pry her arms from around my waist to help one of the other ladies.

As it was, I didn't have much time to feel sorry for myself. Everybody was terrified and had no idea what lay in wait for them. So, I did what I've been trained to do… convince them that everything was going to be alright, even though I knew it was a lie.

However, after day ten of being in the back of the dark, hot, smelly truck…even I had lost hope. Wherever we were, we were a long way from home. The driver stopped to rest each night. In that time, they allowed us to relieve ourselves and tossed bags of fast food in the back for us. But not many had appetites, and then there were those that didn't want to risk eating too much because the stops to relieve ourselves were too few and far between.

When finally I thought I was getting ready to lose my composure because I didn't have the strength to be brave for the ladies any longer, our journey came to an end. They hustled us all off the truck and I saw that we stood in the middle of some kind of crime compound that was surrounded by a tall metal wall. There were men with guns everywhere.

From what I could see, there were several buildings inside the compound, one of which was a beautiful villa that had a fountain of a man on a horse in front of it. They ushered us to a building that had bars on the doors and windows.

"What is this place?" Layla whispered, clinging to my

side. I wrapped my arm around her, holding her close. Funny how certain tragedies can change one's disposition.

"I don't know, Lay. Just hold on, I'm going to find us a way out of here."

Three men ushered us into a room and then told us to strip. When nobody moved to do what they said, several more men came in with guns pointing them at us.

"Strip!" the man that spoke the best English said. "Put all of your valuables in this pile." He continued pointing to a spot right in front of him.

Layla fingered the diamond necklace around her throat. "Oh no," she whispered.

Careful not to draw the attention of the men, I eased my wedding rings off my finger and stuffed them in the bun of my hair. They were all I had left of Tucker. I don't know what's going to happen to me or him for that matter, but I wasn't losing the last good memory I had of him.

I lowered my hand just in time, one of the ugly goons pointed his gun at me and Lay and gestured to the growing pile on the floor. There were no cellphones or anything like that. All the ladies said that was the first thing they took from them.

With hands that shook, I took the gold bracelet that Rachel and Oaklee had gotten me for my birthday off and added it to the pile before taking the fake pearls I'd worn for the wedding from around my neck, adding them.

"No!" I heard Layla cry out. She'd just snatched her arm away from one of the guards who was trying to take the diamond bracelet from around her wrist.

*Damn it, Lay! Don't pick now to be brave… Just give them what they want!*

"Get your hands off of me! You're not getting my diamonds!"

"Hey!" the English speaker said, pointing at her. "Take that shit off and add it to the pile!"

With a crazed look in her eyes, Layla's gaze connected with mine as she backed away, shaking her head. I silently pleaded with her to give them what they wanted. They'd found her Achilles heel. I'd never understood that about her. She would die for material gain. No doubt during this whole harried event, just knowing she still bore the symbols of wealth is what carried her through it. And now they were trying to take that away from her. Sadly, there were those that would rather be dead than poor.

"We're not going to get away from here," Layla cried.

Tears came to my eyes as I put my hands together, begging her to just give them what they want.

She shook her head. "I can't be that girl, Free..."

The guard lost patience with her and slammed his gun into her stomach. I cried out and went for her, but another guard shoved his gun in my face, shaking his head.

The English speaker walked to Layla and roughly pulled her up from the floor by her hair. He said something to one of the other guards in Spanish before the man nodded and quickly left the room.

"You stupid b*tch!" he hissed. "You should have just given up the jewelry." He snatched the necklace from around her neck, the bracelet from her wrist, and brutally snatched the earrings out of her ear, causing them to bleed.

I was about to beg the man to stop when one of the other women that I'd helped grabbed my hand, pulling me back.

"No, Doc, she made her choice," she whispered in my

ear, wrapping her arm around my neck, preventing me from stepping forward. "We all need you to make it through this."

I watched horrified as the guard came back in with a syringe full of clear liquid. Layla went wild, hissing and cussing at them, calling them Mexican dogs. I cringed. We were so far from Mexico; I believe we are somewhere in South America. They stuck her and whatever it was that was in the syringe caused her eyes to glaze over. I squeezed the girl's arm who held me to stop myself from calling out as they roughly dragged her out of the room.

I think that was the point the hopelessness settled in on me and I realized Layla was right; we weren't going to get away from this.

With urging from the guards, we continued to remove our clothing. The bridesmaid dress I wore was little more than a rag. My heart hurt too badly for me to feel embarrassment at so many of them seeing my body. What did it matter? There was a good chance I will end up dead like everybody else anyway.

Angie, Laureen, Dillion, Tucker, and now maybe even Layla...they were all gone. The feeling of bleakness that settled in my soul left me numb. The other women looked at me for encouragement, but I had nothing left.

After we removed all our clothes, they came into the room with a water hose and several bars of soap. We were instructed to scrub while they used the hose on us. When we were finished, they gave us all a pink jumpsuit and a pair of flipflops to put on. Once dressed, they led us to another room that was bigger than the first and had floormats neatly lined against the wall, there were already several women who all looked heavily drugged inside.

After throwing more bags of fast food on the floor, they locked us in.

We all settled on a mat, eyeballing the women, who had clearly been abused. They were so drugged and worn out they barely acknowledged our presence. That feeling of doom settled in deeper. They were going to drug us and then rape us. They'd already drugged Layla...only God knows what they were doing to her now.

We all sat lost in our thoughts. No doubt like me, each was thinking about their loved ones and how it was very possible they would never see them again. The lump in my throat was suffocating. There was no hope. I remember reading about the problems the government in this part of the world was having with the drug cartel. They held supreme rulership. No one will be crazy enough to challenge them. There was no one coming to save us. We were good and doomed.

At least...that's what I thought.

Little did I know that trouble with a capital T was going to show up the next day. It all started with a commotion outside of the metal door of the room we were being held in. The guards had just come and dumped several brown paper bags of greasy food on the floor.

When the door opened again, we sat surprised as they shoved a beautiful woman dressed in the pink jumpsuit in. She fell to the floor and the guards hurried to shut the door before she could get back to her feet. And got back to her feet she did, running to the door cursing and banging on it.

"Open this door, you cowards!" she said a slew of words in Spanish that I was more than positive weren't compliments.

"You assholes!" she yelled, once again speaking English

before giving the door one more hit. And then I kid you guys not, she just turned off her anger.

"Nossa...what smells so good?" When she finally turned around to face us, I was taken aback at how beautifully innocent she appeared. She definitely didn't have the kind of face that fit the words I just heard come out of her mouth.

Her gaze carefully took in the room before settling on me. "Found her."

I frowned, who was she talking to?

"Yes, she's right here!" she suddenly snapped, causing us all to jump. "Would I say I found her if I didn't have eyes on her?"

She put her hand on her hip. "I swear, I'm going to stuff that damned smoothie down your arrogant throat when I get out of here."

*What the world?* Poor thing was talking to herself. She'd been drugged and abused for so long she'd lost touch with reality.

The women who knew I was a doctor looked at me in a way that said, *how are you going to help this very special case?*

The beautiful woman's gaze landed on the greasy brown paper bags that have yet to be touched and her eyes lit up.

"Oh yes, this looks promising," she muttered, squatting on the floor and snatching up one of the bags before shamelessly digging in.

"Empanadas!" Her level of excitement took us all aback. There was no way empanadas should have been able to make one this happy with the fate that awaited us.

We all sat dumbfounded as she unwrapped the foil as if she held a delicacy in her hand before taking a massive bite out of the beef-filled patties. As she chewed, she closed her eyes, doing a little dance like she's never tasted anything as good as that empanada.

"Mmmmm!" she moaned. "It's been a long time since anything this good has been in my mouth."

Something made her laugh. "You are such a peacock. Get over yourself."

Oh dear…this was getting out of hand. The doctor in me couldn't continue to sit here as this poor woman held a conversation with herself.

I cleared my throat. "Are you alright, ma'am?"

Her gaze came to me and she nodded with a huge smile on her face. "Right as rain, now." This she said before stuffing the last of the empanada she was eating in her mouth, reaching for another.

"Oh… shut up!" she snapped.

"Excuse me?" I asked, completely confused. Why was she telling me to shut up?

She grinned as she chewed. "Not you. I'm talking to my husband. He's upset that I'm eating something that actually taste good."

Wow! This was worse than I thought. "Do you and your husband argue often about food?" I needed to feel her out and see just what I was dealing with. More than likely due to the trauma that came from being a sex slave, she'd developed a slight case of schizophrenia.

"Girl, yes…he's a food Nazi. Shut up!" she snapped.

Oh, Dear God!

"You can't make me. I'll eat every one of them, watch me." She pointed at the other bags. "You ladies aren't going to have any?"

A little afraid of her now, we all shook our heads.

She shrugged. "More for me."

Amazingly, she took out three more empanadas before she went on another tangent.

"Fine! I was full anyway!" she snapped, coming to her feet. "You're just mad 'cause I had something good to eat and you had a carrot stick. Alright, ladies…" She clapped her hands together and turned to face us. "Are you guys ready to get the hell out of here?"

Okay, I take that back… She had a *severe* case of schizophrenia.

"Are you going to help us get out of here?" I asked nice and easy.

With schizophrenic patients, one must be careful at how they dissolve their delusions. If done improperly, it could send the patient off into a fit.

"Yeppers…" she said while wiping the grease from the empanadas from her mouth and hands with a napkin. "They didn't bring you guys anything to drink. Sprite, coke…anything?" We all shook our heads.

"Bastards! How in the hell do they expect you guys to eat those spicy ass empanadas with nothing to wash them down with? I'm coming!" she snapped. Once again causing us all to jump, startled at her sudden outburst.

"Are you speaking with your husband again?" I asked nice and easy.

She rolled her eyes. "Yeah, he's being a dick."

I inhaled. "Okay…and does your husband have a name?"

She grinned. "Yeah, Asshole…"

Wow! Ohhhkay…

"And…do you have a name?"

The grin left her face. "Why are you talking to me like that?"

I smiled then. "Like what, sweetheart?"

Her eyes narrowed. "Like you think I'm bat sh*t crazy."

I shook my head. "I don't think anything of the sort."

"What the hell are you laughing at?" she hissed to no one in particular.

The other women were now good and afraid. I slowly came to my feet, holding my hands out in front of me to show her that I was no threat.

"No one is laughing at you." Again, my words were nice and easy. She seemed pretty upset now.

"Not you! My husband."

"Your husband is laughing at you?"

"He thinks it's funny that you think I'm crazy. He knows how I feel about people calling me crazy!"

I shook my head. "But I don't think you're crazy."

As she studied me, a little devious grin settled on her face. "So, you believe me when I say I'm going to get us all out of here, right?"

I pressed my lips together as I tried to think of the best way to deescalate this situation. "Do you have a name?" I asked instead.

She nodded. "Yeah, the idiot that married the asshole."

"Hmmm… I don't think your name is idiot."

"How about this? I'll tell you my name once I get us out of here. Deal?"

Before I could say anything, she turned and banged on the door. "Oh My God!! Help me!!! I'm bleeding…this b*tch stabbed me!!! Come quick!!!"

Turning around, she winked at me as the sound of running feet approached the door. Stepping back a bit, she clutched her stomach, bending over just as the door was thrown open and one of the guards hurried into the room

He said something in Spanish as he approached her. What happened next completely blew my mind. Without standing up straight, she clutched her stomach with one hand while waving him over with the other. When he was within arm's reach, she struck, hitting him in the throat with a blow that crushed his Adam's apple. Unable to yell out, he grabbed his aching throat and she climbed him like a tree before using her legs to snap his neck. We all watched in awe as his body fell dead at her feet. She grinned as she reached down and grabbed the high-powered assault weapon he carried on his arm.

"Still think I'm crazy?" In awe, the only thing I could do was shake my head.

"Good, sit tight. I'll be back to get you in a sec. Go ahead and eat one of those empanadas, they were a little dry, could have used a little hot sauce, but they were still good."

She ran out of the room and a few seconds later, we heard what sounded like WW3 taking place. We all huddled together, expecting a brigade of men with guns to rush the room. When that didn't happen, I eased away from the group towards the door.

"Doc, she told us to wait here," Megan said, reaching for me.

I gestured for her to be quiet. "Yeah well, the door is open now. This could be our only chance at escaping."

Very carefully I peeked around the corner before quickly dipping back into the room again. I nearly ran over all the girls who had gathered in a cluster right on my heel.

"What is it?!" Megan asked, her big green eyes opened wide in fear.

"There's a bunch of dead bodies out there. Let's go…"

The gunshots were at a distance. There was nothing or no one moving in this building. We carefully made our way to the door, stepping over dead bodies. Could it be possible that innocent-faced young lady had wreaked this much havoc?

*Surely she had help.*

I motioned for the ladies to stand still while I took a little peep outside. What I saw caused my mouth to drop.

The lights in the villa were all out, the only thing that could be seen was the flashes from the many guns going off at once. The courtyard was littered with bodies. The few remaining men that were left ran towards the villa with their guns drawn.

The ladies surrounded me as we strained to see what was going on. The gunshots had gone quiet in the house. Carefully, the six or seven men who seemed to be the last ones standing approached the door. It was almost as if they were afraid to see what was on the other side. Right when the first one reached for the knob it flew off the hinges.

*Oh, my God!*

That empanada eating beauty had just kicked it. She had one arm wrapped around Rau's neck with a gun to his head.

"Get the f*ck back! Or I will blow this b*tch's brains out!" she yelled, pressing her gun into the frightened man's temple.

Rau was speaking rapid Spanish. His last remaining guards took several steps back.

"Toss your weapons!" she continued as she and Rau carefully stepped out into the courtyard.

When neither of the men moved to toss their weapons, she cocked the pistol she held to their boss's head. Rau cried out before he spoke to his men again. One at a time they tossed their guns away.

It was at this point, every woman that had been hiding began to step forth from the shadows. Some were half-dressed from where they were being abused when the showdown started, some were beat up pretty badly. I couldn't believe how many there were. There had to be well over a hundred. I looked for Layla but didn't see her amongst the crowd.

The woman tossed Rau away from her, keeping her gun trained at his head. He fell at her feet and instantly began to beg for his life.

"Who are you? Why are you doing this?" he cried.

She tossed the gun in her hand away before reaching toward her back and pulling a... *gold bat* from a silken sheath.

"I am the vengeance of God, Rau," she told him as she rotated the bat in her hands until she found the grip she was looking for. "And I'm doing this because you are a bad man. A cancer to the planet Earth. Your time has come to an end." She gazed up at one of the cameras.

"Give me some background music, babe, so I can teach this old boy here a lesson about f*cking with me."

*I'm so Hoooood!!!*

Suddenly began to blast from the overhead speakers.

*Yeah, I wear my pants below my waist,*
*and I never dance when I'm in this place,*
*Because you and yo' man is planning to hate.*
*I'm so hoooood*
*And I got these gold up in my mouth.*
*If you get closer to my house*
*Then you'll know what I'm talking 'bout*
*Hood*
*And if you feel me put your hands up, hood*
*My hood niggas can you feel me*
*If you not from here you can walk it out*
*And you not hood if you don't know what I'm talking about...*

SHE MUST HAVE APPROVED of the choice of music because a huge animated grin transformed her beautiful face to angelic.

When Rau saw that she only carried a bat, some of his bravado returned. "Kill this b*tch!" he cried.

His last remaining men rushed her. And... Oh My Goodness! I thought she was amazing with a gun, however, what she was doing with this golden bat was pure art.

"She is bad-ass!" Megan cried as her eyes brightened at the sight of the men who'd kidnapped her being beaten horribly.

"Yeah she is!" I agreed. I had a new hero! Watching her beat the men that had hurt so many women was almost as good as sex with Tucker.

Almost!

When she was done, she turned her rage-filled eyes on

Rau, who still sat on the ground, but was trying his best to back away from her.

"Wait! I can make you a very rich woman!" he said, holding up one hand as he used his other to try and scoot away.

She smiled down at him, slowly stalking him. "I'm already a very rich woman!"

He opened his mouth to say something else, but never got a chance. Her eyes glazed over with amused rage as she cocked the bat back and then swung forward with all of her might, hitting him in the mouth. Teeth and blood splattered everywhere and the women began to cheer. Several of them that had been here for a while, in their fervor to see this man pay for all the pain that he caused was now standing right alongside the woman and watched anxiously as she continued to whale on him with the bat.

One of the women picked up a gun from the ground and slowly approached the man that was already half dead. She looked at the woman with the golden bat, and whatever it was in her eyes caused our rescuer to stop swinging and step back. With a grin on her face, she nodded. The woman with the gun didn't hesitate, she pointed it at Rau's head and pulled the trigger.

A collective gasp went around the compound.

*We were free!*

*The devil was dead...*

The big metal wall began to open, and a fresh wave of fear hit me. *Oh no! More of Rau's men were here.*

However, when the wall finally opened, there was only one man standing there. A very handsome man. The woman who had rescued us eyes brightened as she slid her bat back into its silken sheath.

She held her head back and let out a war cry before taking off at a sprint and jumping into his waiting arms. After wrapping her powerful thighs around his waist, she palmed his face and kissed him as if her life depended on it.

I grinned. Well…will you look at that. That must be the wild woman's husband.

*She's not so crazy after all…*

# Chapter 6

Brother's Keeper

---

*Don't Ever Think That the Reason I'm Peaceful, Is Because I Don't Know How to Be Violent...*

*Unknown*

---

## Naphtali

"SO, WHAT DO YOU THINK?"

"I think Rome is right. Your boy is definitely hiding something."

"My boy? You mean yo' brother?"

"Yeah well, I just met him, so that really doesn't count."

I frowned at the voices that woke me. My body felt

385

funny, but my mind wasn't awake enough to figure out why. Slowly I opened my eyes to see that I was back in Free's hotel room. The covers ruffled next to me as she turned in my arms and smiled sleepily at me.

*"Good morning, beautiful."*

"Good morning," she whispered, nuzzling her face against my chest. I loved it when she did that.

"Who's he talking to?" one of the male voices that woke me said.

"I don't know. Maybe he's dreaming or something."

*What the hell?*

Looking around the hotel room, my frown grew when I saw no one was there but Free and I. The sunlight that drifted in the window was more beautiful than I'd ever seen it. It cast a warm glow around my lady, making it appear as if she glowed from within. She was simply gorgeous. I am the luckiest man in the world because she loved me.

Her little nose tilted up slightly. *"What's wrong, baby?"* she asked, concerned about the frown on my face.

I listened for the voices. *"Do you hear that?"*

Her gaze went toward the kitchen area of the room. *"Hear what?"*

*"Two men… talking."*

She shook her head. *"No, I don't hear anything."*

"Do you think Judah used us as bait? The way he just sent us in here is a bit strange, isn't it?" the voice came again. Whoever was talking was standing right by me.

"Yeah, it is. But what worries me is how easy it was to get to this point. I thought these nests were supposed to be protected by some kind of invisible spells or something.

We practically walked right in. No guards, nothing. Let's just grab this guy and get the hell out of here."

Shaking my head, I tried to clear the fog from my brain. Free scooted up my body until her lips were only inches from mine.

*"I have a surprise for you,"* she whispered before gently kissing me.

*"Oh yeah, what is it?"*

She reached for the table on the side of the bed and grabbed a little white stick, handing it to me. It was one of those pregnancy tests, the kind you have to pee on. I took it, looking at the two little plus signs.

*"What is this, bae?"*

She grinned. *"What does it look like, silly? We're having a baby."*

I was speechless! My heart felt as full as it ever had. Free was having my baby! I couldn't believe it!

*"Are you serious?!"* The grin on my face now matched hers.

She nodded. *"Yep! We're having a baby!"*

Overrun with joy, I reached up and palmed her face with both hands, bringing it down so that I could take her lips in a real kiss, none of that little teasing pecking stuff.

"Hey!" the irate male voice came again. "Let me go, mutha f*cka! What you doing?!" Free began to buck in my arms, fighting to get away from me.

Damn! When she get so strong?!

Male laughter came from somewhere in the room before Free held her little fist back and decked me right in the cheek.

*"Hey, man what the hell is wrong with you?!"* Free said with a male voice to match the blow she just gave me.

I came awake with a start and for a moment, my whole system was in shock. I was staring at... *myself.*

No, I mean, myself was staring at me, angrily wiping the back of his hand across his mouth.

"What's going on?" I whispered, trying to process what I was seeing.

"You tried to kiss me! That's what's going on," myself angrily hissed.

Wondering if I was somehow staring into a freaky mirror or something, I reached up and tried to touch my face, but my doppelganger slapped my hand away...hard.

"Ouch! Why did you do that?"

He pointed at me. "Look, man! I ain't with that funny sh*t!"

Standing next to him, laughing at us was an older man that looked like Billy Dee Williams. What was going on? Where was I? Sitting up a bit, I took in my surroundings. It looked and smelled like I was in a cave. A small fire burned in the center of it. I'd been resting against a rock; I knew this because my back was hurting like a son of a b*tch.

My gaze came back to my reflection...at least, I think it was my reflection. My mind felt hazy like I'd been drugged or some sh*t. The last thing I remembered was stepping back, letting the Bully take control to keep Free safe at the hotel.

"Where am I? Is this a dre—" My words came to a complete halt as a thought suddenly came to me.

"Oh, sh*t! Am I dead? Is this heaven?"

My doppelganger looked at me as if I was the dumbest mutha f*cka on the block, before slowly shaking his head.

"Do this look like heaven to you?" he asked, opening his arms, gesturing around the dark dank cave.

I shrugged. I don't know what heaven looks like. I mean...it could be. But then another thought hit me.

"Is it...*hell*?" I whispered, now very afraid of his answer. I know I ain't been living my life right, but I always thought I had time to get my sh*t together.

He looked around. "Maybe."

"What you mean, maybe? You don't know?" This must be hell, I ain't impressed with the service thus far. If he was supposed to be me to guide me through the afterlife, I was in trouble. This guy ain't nothing to write home about.

He shook his head. "Naw, we just got here."

I blinked at my look-alike. "What the hell kind of half-ass spiritual guide are you? How you gon' show me around the afterlife if you don't even know your way?"

It was my turn to shake my head. "Whatever this place is, I see I'm not too bright here."

My other self pointed at me. "First of all, smart-ass, I'm not you. And you for damn sure ain't me. I'm Jo, your brother."

"So, I'm not dead? Wait—my what?"

The older man squatted down next to Jo. "Hey, kid, I know this all is a bit confusing, but this place is really giving me the creeps. Why don't we get out of here and then we can tell you all about it?"

Confusion doesn't touch the surface of what I'm feeling right now. I palmed my sore cheek as I stared at Jo. I was freaking the f*ck out on the inside. This dude looked exactly like me. How in the hell was that possible? I'd always thought I was the only child, but the truth is, how could I know? I've never seen any family records or anything like that with my adoption papers. I have no idea who my real parents are. The few times I'd asked as a kid, my adopted parents said they didn't know. They said the agency they'd worked with to get me had nothing about my real parents on file. I always felt like they were lying about that though; just one more thing that stood in the way of me feeling like they ever really cared about me.

As I rubbed my cheek that was throbbing, something else became clear.

My gaze shot back to Jo's punk-ass. "Did you hit me, man?"

This real arrogant ass look came over his face, the kind of look that made you want to knock him out.

"You tried to kiss me, so, I socked you."

This mutha—I charged his ass, but the Old Man threw himself between us, holding me back.

"What the f*ck is wrong with you? Hitting a man while he asleep!"

He shrugged. "I told you, I ain't with that funny sh*t, bro! You were real aggressive with it too. I had to protect myself, you were trying to take my innocence."

"Yeah, I got yo' innocence mutha—" I began but my words were cut off by a gruff voice.

"I see you two have managed to pick up exactly where y'all left off."

*What the uncivilized sh*t is this???*

The guy that walked through the mouth of the cave carrying a black duffle bag didn't look real. He had long full locs that fell down his back and a face covered in a beard. He looked like some kind of crazy-ass mountain man or some sh*t. I shook my head, I didn't think brothas did sh*t like this.

"When you were kids, you two fought all the time," he continued to speak as he began to hurriedly place small black boxes around the cave walls. "Only one that could get you two to stop fighting was Levi."

The Old Man looked at the dread. "There you are. I thought you had sent us in here as bait."

The chuckle that came out the dread's mouth was so rusty it sounded like grunts. It was obvious he didn't do it often.

"Yeah, I know. I heard you over the earpiece."

"Who is Levi?" I asked, keeping a wary eye on the dread. This cat was bad news. Everything about him screamed violence. I knew a killer when I saw one. What was surprising was the fact that the Bully was quiet in his presence.

"Levi is another one of your brothers. In fact, you, he, and Jo here are triplets." The Old Man said.

*Triplets!*

I opened my mouth, but the only thing that came out was "Wha—" before the cave began to tilt.

"Catch him, Jo, he's going down," the Old Man called out just as the cave floor came up toward my face. Jo moved fast, catching me before I hit it.

The only thing I could do was stare at him. He was my brother? Triplets? *What the f*ck?!*

"Is this real?" I whispered, clinging to him for dear life. I don't know if I clutched him like this to keep from falling to the floor or because for the first time in my life, I had something in my hands that felt familiar. I could feel the connection between the two of us.

He felt like me...like he was my own.

As if he understood the feeling completely, he kept his

arm wrapped around my waist even after he helped me back to my feet.

He chuckled. "I'm afraid so, bro."

"How?" I asked, but before he could answer, the dread spoke.

"Rome..." he called out, stepping to the middle of the cave. "Can you see the spell over this room?

I frowned at Jo. "Who is he talking to?"

He shook his head. "Rome is the tech guy. Don't worry, you'll meet him. I'm warning you now, he's a punk-ass kid, who you're going to want to punch in the face half the time."

"Kind of like how I want to punch you in the face, huh?"

He grinned. "Yeah, kind of like that."

The dread walked to one of the boxes and began to adjust it. "What about now? Can you see it?"

I nodded toward him. "Who's that?"

Jo's grin grew. "That's our big brother, Judah... A real mean son-of-b*tch. Don't worry, you'll get to know him too."

After Judah adjusted another box, he programmed something in his watch. "Okay, show it to me."

Soft blue lights came from the boxes and lit the cave just enough to highlight some strange writing that was all around it. Judah walked toward one of the cave walls and began to study it.

"Can you override the program?" he spoke to Rome, who was apparently on a device in his ear. I looked at Jo and the Old Man and saw that they too had a device in their ears. They were all dressed in military-issued cargo pants and black T's.

"Can I override the program..." This came from a face that suddenly appeared in the blue lights, it almost looked like a hologram image but not quite.

"Well now, will you look at that... It's two of 'em. Man, I sure hope you're not an asshole like yo' brotha," the guy said as his hands flew across the keyboard. It looked like he was in a surveillance vehicle. We used similar ones at the agency.

"Let me guess... Rome?"

The younger man nodded. "Yours truly."

Jo, who had let me go to stand on my own feet, chuckled as he walked toward the image. "Yeah, this here is Romeo, our tech guy. And just to tell you a little bit about him, in his spare time, he likes to take long walks in the park, observe penguins in their natural habitat, especially during mating season." He did something silly with his eyebrows before he continued. "And when he's feeling really sexy on the inside, he likes to act out movie scenes. As a matter of fact, he and his wife just recently did an outstanding performance of the, *Nobody Puts Baby in the Corner*, scene from the movie, Dirty Dancing. It truly was a touching rendition; his movements were as fluently graceful as the actor himself."

I, Judah, and the Old Man had a good chuckle at that. Rome didn't come across as a dancer, I couldn't see all of him, but what was revealed came across as a little street. Can't really see this guy doing what Jo just said. But the way Judah and the Old Man shook their heads chuckling, made me wonder if it was true. One thing was clear though, Jo is definitely an asshole.

"You need some new material, grandpa," Rome muttered as his hands continued to fly across the keyboard. I could see the strange letters that were around the cave changing.

"Did you guys find Free?" Judah asked.

"Free!" I walked towards the image. "My Free? Where is she? Is she okay?!"

Rome held up his hand. "Calm down, big guy. She's safe. My girl, Nak in there with her right now. They should be coming out any minute." He pressed a button and spoke into a microphone that was off to the side of him. "If somebody could stop stuffing her face with those poison-ass empanadas."

He let go of the button before muttering under his breath, "I swear, that damn girl eat more than a man."

"Fine! I was full anyway!" A female voice snapped back at him. "You're just mad 'cause I had something good to eat and you had a carrot stick."

"Hold the f*ck on!" I'd had enough. I needed to know what the hell was going on with Free. "Where is my wife? Why wouldn't she be safe?" I don't remember how I got here from the hotel, but I do remember ghosting all the mutha f*ckas that had come in there on us. Free should have been safe.

"Your wife was kidnapped from the hotel in Vegas." It was Judah who now spoke. "When I found out, I sent Rome and Nak after her while we came after you."

I shook my head, even more confused. "Can you start at the beginning?"

Judah's gaze went to Rome. "How much time do we have?"

"I'll need at least three minutes," the man responded as his hands flew over the keyboard. The strange lettering that surrounded us continued to change.

Judah nodded as he went down to one knee in front of the duffel bag and began to pull clothes out of it. "I'll have to give you the quick version, but as I talk, you change."

He threw me a pair of cargo pants and a t-shirt. For the most part, I still wore what I'd put on for the wedding, minus the suit jacket. I wonder how long I've been out.

"The little brother of the guy you killed last year made a deal with a demon named Balaam to find you," he began as I quickly changed into the clothes he'd given me. However, when he mentioned the word demon, I paused for a moment.

"Yeah, I know that sh*t sounds crazy, but it's true. I'll fill you in on the details later." He tossed me a pair of boots. "Any time you go to one of the demons or the fallen for help, they require a blood sacrifice. Rau sacrificed his long-time girlfriend. Balaam led him to you in Vegas. But instead of holding up his end of the bargain and letting Rau kill you, he took you for himself and gave him Free."

"Rau then took Free back to Argentina to try and add her to his famous whorehouse. But the geek found her before any harm could come to her. You don't have to worry…she's safe now," Jo said, somehow understanding what I needed to hear. Judah should have led with that sh*t. I needed to know that Free was safe, everything else I can figure out as I go.

"By geek, I'm guessing you mean him." I pointed at the computer image. "So, who is Nak?"

"Rome's wife and my best soldier. She will get your wife out safe."

Jo's stunned gaze went to him. "Nak's your best soldier? I resent that."

Judah shrugged. "I don't care…it's true."

"Yeah, it is…" Rome agreed as he continued to type away.

"But it's not. I've saved Nak's ass more times than I can count."

"The Politician saved Nak's ass…You ain't did sh*t," Judah responded very matter of factly.

"Who is the Politician?" I asked, struggling to keep up with the conversation.

"Jo's alter…" The Old Man responded.

My surprised gaze went to Jo. "You have an alter too?"

He nodded. "We all do."

"All?"

The Old Man chuckled. "Yeah, kid. It's five of you all together. Judah is the oldest of you, then it's the triplets, you, Jo, and Levi, who we still have yet to meet. And then you guys have a baby sister named Debra."

I opened my mouth to ask more questions but Judah, who was now studying the letters on the cave wall, spoke first.

"Listen to me, we've run out of time. We are on Balaam's territory, which means your alters are not going to do you any good here. Balaam is their creator; they will never turn against them." He held up his index finger. "This is why they cannot be trusted."

"Our alters?" I asked, confused. I mean, don't get me wrong, I hated the Bully just as much as I loved him. But he'd never not stepped in to keep us safe. He could be trusted to at least do that.

Judah's hard gaze came to me. "Your alters are your biggest enemy… and now, you're getting ready to see why. Rome…show us the way out of here."

I looked back toward the mouth of the cave. "Why can't we just go that way?"

No sooner had I asked, the strange lettering around us began to disappear, and with it, the nice cozy cave.

"What the f*ck?!" I cried out, feeling like I was stuck in a dream. This couldn't be real. We were now standing in what looked like an old, abandoned train. But this mutha f*cka was straight out a horror movie. There were human bones everywhere; the smell of rotting flesh was strong in the air.

I didn't want to look like a pu**y, so I bit my tongue. But I wanted to yell out for somebody to tell me what the f*ck was going on.

"Okay, it looks like you guys are in a labyrinth." A map appeared where one of the cave walls once were.

"This is you," Rome continued, lifting his hand to touch the red X. "You're fifty-three levels below ground."

A surprised noise came from the Old Man. "I swear, I will never get used to this sh*t. How in the hell are we fifty-three levels underground when we just simply walked through the mouth of a cave on the beach?"

Rome chuckled. "Come on, old Al... you didn't think it was going to be that easy, did you?"

"As soon as our chopper landed in this jungle, we were under Balaam's spell. He has several areas in the world that he calls his playground. This one is where he keeps the gladiators," Judah told him dryly. "He's playing a game with us, showing us only what he wants us to see. Trust nothing you see with your eyes."

"You're going to need to get here," Rome continued, dragging his finger across the virtual map, causing a red line to follow in its wake. "If you can, avoid these areas."

He began to circle several spots. "They're covered in a strong spell and I don't have time to cipher them right now; sounds like Nak is wrapping things up. I'll send you these coordinates to your watches."

Reaching in the duffel bag, Judah pulled out a shoulder holster that was like the one I normally wore and tossed it to me. Once I secured it in place, he handed me two government-issued 1911s. Now, there was nothing special about your everyday average 1911s. However, the two chrome beauties he'd just handed me I'd only heard rumors about to this point. Word is, only about a hundred of them were ever made. We called them phantom pistols at the agency. Yeah, a few people say they'd seen one with their own eyes, but nobody really believed them. You needed top clearance to get yo' hands on some sh*t like this.

My gaze came back to Judah. And here he had two of 'em. "How in the hell you get a hold of these? You CIA?"

He chuckled. "I'm whoever I need to be in order to get the job done. Your marksman record has yet to be beat at the academy in Virginia." He handed me several more clips. "I'm assuming you still know your way around artillery like this."

It was my turn to chuckle. "Well, you know...some things a boy never forget."

"Good. Aim for the head or the heart. Body shots won't stop what's on the other side of these doors." He reached behind him and came from under his jacket with a bad-ass short sword. "Taking their heads off is even better. You'll start your sword training later...for now, make every one of those bullets count."

I nodded, but my mind raced with questions. What

kind of mutha f*cka could take a hit to the body from a 1911 40 cal and it not put them on their ass? I was getting a bad feeling about this.

"Now, my great leader," Rome spoke from his surveillance vehicle in Argentina. "Allow me to put on a little background music while you prepare the troops." And I'll be damned if 8Ball & MJG, *You Don't Want Drama* didn't fill the space. My stunned gaze went to Jo, he shook his head.

"The kid needs a theme song to do everything."

I grinned. Sh*t...I liked it! Made me feel grounded.

"You grew up believing you needed yo' alters to tear sh*t up," Judah began, his deadly gaze pinning each of us to the spot as he skillfully rotated the sword in his palm.

"That's a lie. The very blood that run through your veins is an ancient one." He took the hair tie that held his locs together loose, shaking his hair out till it surrounded his head like a lion's mane.

"You are the descendants of one of the greatest warriors to ever live and they all know it. It's his blood that runs through your veins." As he spoke, we could see the last layer of civilization fall away from him. He was violence personified. The bloodlust in his eyes was fuel for my soul. A deadly grin came to his face. He'd allowed the rage that simmered underneath the surfaces of his flesh to come forth.

"You know that feeling you get, the one that urges you to f*ck some sh*t up?! To destroy some sh*t?! The one yo' fancy handlers paid a lot of money for some doctor or teacher to train you how to control and rein it in?" This he sneered, as if the very thought of controlling the urge to kill disgusted him

Hell yeah! I know exactly the feeling he talking about. Jo nodded; I could see in his eyes that he too knew and understood.

"Listen to yo' big brother today! F*ck everything they taught you! It's a reason you have that feeling. We not meant to be like everybody else! Embrace it and you'll never need yo' alters again." He rotated his neck as if he could barely contain his need to damage something. "There was a time, boys, when the very thought of us put fear in the heart of men. Let's remind these mutha f*ckas why. Rome, open the doors."

The train doors opened. Judah walked toward it but before he walked out, his gaze came back to the three of us. "I wouldn't have you here with me if I thought you couldn't keep up. So…Keep the f*ck up!" he growled.

Sh*t, I don't know what we were getting ready to face, but I was ready to crush some sh*t. Judah…I see his power.

"I'll see you boys on the other side," Rome said as we followed Judah off the train. "Hey…Nap."

I turned to look back at him. "Yo' wife will be waiting for you, man."

I nodded. "Thanks."

# Chapter 7

## The Gladiator

### Naphtali

"HEY, wait, bro, this is one of those areas Rome said we should try and avoid. The way out is that way," Jo said, pointing in the opposite direction from where we were going. But he might as well have saved his breath. Judah was clearly on a mission that did not involve us leaving. He didn't even bother responding to his little brother. Jo and the Old Man, who I found out name is Al, but they actually call the Old Man, shared a look. There was some other sh*t going on but neither of us had time to ponder it because up ahead appeared two black doors.

Frowning, I turned around to make sure the dark, slimy, stinky tunnel of the abandoned subway was still behind us. It was...

*What the f*ck?!*

This was some wild sh*t! Besides the fact that there was an abandoned subway system underneath the jungle, we found more human bones along the way. But that wasn't the wildest sh*t. The bones we passed looked like they'd been chewed on. Every now and again, a piercing scream could be heard in the distance followed by the sound of bones crunching under teeth. The whole time, I'm waiting to feel something, anything from the Bully. Nothing...the nigga was ghost.

I ain't no punk or nothing, but I was with Jo, I was ready to get the f*ck out of here. But our boy Judah had different plans, 'cause this mutha f*cka was walking straight for the two spooky ass doors that appeared out of nowhere, again, some sh*t I didn't think brothas did.

"Jud—" Jo began but that was all he managed to get out before his brother turned and nailed him to the floor with a look that dared him to say something else. I'm telling y'all...this nigga was like a wild ass animal.

"I'm tired of hearing yo' b*tching," Judah growled.

I shook my head. If I was Jo, I wouldn't stand for that sh*t. As if he could hear my thoughts, the crazy mutha f*cka's gaze came to me. I got busy studying the door. I'd never seen wood like this. Y'all can laugh at me if y'all want, but I'm telling you, it's something off about Judah's ass.

"Rome don't run sh*t here. Understood?" he growled.

Jo sized him up for a minute. Amazingly, I think I know what he was thinking. He was wondering if he could take him. He was tired of putting up with his bullsh*t. He didn't take this kind of lip off no man, so why the hell should he take it off a crazy man? His gaze came to me and then the Old Man before he reluctantly nodded because he seriously doubted his brother would hesitate to kill him. Damn...that's messed up. But I think he made a wise choice.

Judah looked at Al next. "Do you understand?" The Old Man didn't need to think about it before he nodded.

"Yeah, completely."

Then Judah's gaze fell on me.

I held up my hands. "Hey, I don't even know the nigga." Sh*t...it's the truth.

So, although none of us but Judah wanted to, we ended up walking through those doors. Now, this is where sh*t got real strange. We stepped into what looked like an abandoned mansion, spider webs and all. The only thing missing was the creepy music. We were on the second or third floor. Judah walked toward the stairs like he knew where he was going.

"Hey, man, if I was you, I wouldn't have let that dude talk to me like that," I told Jo on the low, falling into step next to him as we carefully made our way downstairs. Judah and the Old Man were ahead of us a good ways.

Jo smacked his lips. "Oh yeah? I sure didn't see you stepping forward to help a brotha."

I chuckled. "I just met you, bro. The bond ain't that strong yet."

"I bet."

"Is he always like that?"

"Yep. That guy needs some professional help. He don't know how to be around other human beings. The other day, my mother-in-law tried to invite him over for dinner, she felt bad that he was always alone. Even though we tried to warn her that he prefers to be that way, but she's one of those soft-hearted people and thought all he needed was some of her good old fashioned home cooking. So, off she goes to talk to the big bad wolf. Do you know this guy just stared at her for a minute and then sneered until she squeaked out a, *never mind,* and practically ran away from him? Now, nobody tries to invite him over anymore."

I chuckled, shaking my head. I could actually see him doing that. I went to ask Jo another question as we reached the bottom of the stairs, but the sound of ice hitting a glass stopped me.

"So, you decided to come after me?" A heavily accented voice filled the air.

We all came to a stop, looking around to see where it came from. Another ice cube hit the glass.

"I cleared the way for you, gave you a straight shot to the door. And yet, you still decided to come for me. Why?"

Right then, a light came on over a fully stocked bar to reveal a slenderly built African man dressed in a linen suit. He was making himself a drink. The bar did not fit the rest of the house, it was state-of-the-art nice while the rest of the house was covered in spider webs and dust.

In fact, I wasn't just imagining it; the rest of the house was gray, everything from the furniture that was half-covered in sheets to the peeling wallpaper. It was all gray as if it had somehow lost its color. But the bar where the African man stood was full of color, rich browns and ambers, golds, greens, and reds.

What the f*ck?! This is some Twilight Zone kind of sh*t.

When Judah saw the man, his hand squeezed the handle of the blade he carried so hard his knuckles turned white.

"Balaam!" he growled. The rage he felt at the sight of this man nearly made his voice unrecognizable.

"Young Judah…" the man responded before lifting his drink to his lips. "So…you think you can kill me, huh?"

Judah clutched the blade handle tighter. "Fight me!"

The man chuckled before shaking his head. "Why would I do that? I don't want you dead. In fact, I don't want any of you dead. It's why I saved your brother. Now take him and go." He waved Judah away as if he was a pissant.

"You had my father killed!"

Balaam laughed. "What are you talking about? Baxter killed your father when he had no more use for him."

"Liar!" Judah growled. He was barely holding on to his rage. He wanted this man dead so badly he was shaking with anticipation. "Baxter was your puppet. They are all your puppets! You told Baxter to kill my father and then you told him to kill me. You're the reason my brothers and my little sister got sold away. You're the reason my people got sold away. You're the reason we fell. It was *you*, you bastard!"

As he spoke, Balaam smiled down at the glass he held in his hand. "So, what now? You think you're strong enough to take me on?"

Judah held his blade with both of his hands. "Hell yeah!"

"Fool!" Balaam hissed, throwing the glass against the wall, causing it to shatter. He didn't sound human. This sh*t sounded like it came straight from the devil. It no longer had the accent. I drew my weapon. Unsurprisingly, so did Jo and the Old Man.

"You are nothing without your power!" the devil voice continued. "You come to me, just a man! You've brought your brothers to me, just men. You are a fool!" As he spoke, his eyes turned bright ass devil red. But it seemed as if he got control of his temper because his eyes slowly faded back to their original color as he smoothed down his suit.

"I tell you what, young Judah." His voice had gone back to normal, accent and all. "You want your shot at me?"

Judah grunted. "I do."

"Fight and defeat my champion and you'll have it. If you lose, you and your brothers will feed my children."

Judah's gaze came back to us. I don't know what the African guy meant by feed his children, but there was hesitation in Judah's eyes. It didn't last though, he must have remembered his hate for this man because his eyes grew cold. I now know what made Jo doubt his brother would not kill him.

Judah didn't care if we died...all he wanted was revenge.

"Deal!" he growled.

Jo's gaze came to mine before it connected with the Old Man's. He felt the same thing too. The smile that appeared on Balaam's face made my skin crawl. He nodded just a bit. "Your hate rules you. You are so careless with the lives of your brothers. But at last, a deal is a deal." He held up his hand, gesturing toward two hooded figures that seemed to appear out of nowhere.

"Please be so kind as to follow my servants to the arena to prepare for the games."

For a moment, neither of us spoke. No doubt like me, Jo and the Old Man was wondering what Judah had gotten us into and if we had been foolish to follow him.

"You all must learn to trust me," Judah muttered as we followed the hooded figures down a hall that was too long to be in a house. It was damn near two blocks long.

"I don't know, bruh. Some things ain't adding up," Jo told him.

"Yeah, kid, I got a bad feeling about this. What did he mean we will feed his children?" the Old Man asked.

"He means, if we lose, his children will eat us."

"Damn! Are they cannibals?" I asked.

"They're monsters..." was Judah's only answer. Before I could ask him what the hell he meant by that, we walked through a door that let us out in-- *Ancient Rome???*

"What the hell?! Is this Rome?" I asked, looking around at the people that walked along the busy cobbled streets, going about their business as if there was nothing abnormal about them still existing.

"Remember, trust nothing you see with your eyes in this place. We're still in the jungle. Balaam can program things to look however he wants," Judah said as we followed the hooded beings into an arch entrance of the Coliseum.

They led us to an area where other men and boys waited to fight. Some of them were dressed like gladiators and some of them were dressed like us.

I gestured at a group of boys that looked like your everyday average teenagers. "Are they real?"

Judah nodded. "They are."

"Wait! So, we're not the only ones stuck in this f*cked up place?" Jo hissed.

Judah shrugged out of his jacket. "People come up missing all the time. The lucky ones end up falling prey to a psychotic serial killer. The unlucky ones end up in places like this or in a nest."

"This isn't a nest?" Al asked.

Judah shook his head. "This a neutral area, a place where beings from all over will come to see Balaam's gladiators. The demons are more protective of their nest. They don't like any that aren't of their bloodline in their territory. Plus, he would have never taken a slayer back to his home, even an inexperienced one. The risk is too high."

I had several questions. What the hell is a slayer? And was he talking about me? But most importantly, what the hell was a…

"Nest?" I asked.

"Hideouts for fallen angels and their demonic children," the Old Man said, checking his gun to make sure it was ready to fire.

"Like…angel, angels?" I hated to sound slow, but all this sh*t was blowing my mind.

"Yeah, angel, angels," Jo answered, as he too prepared himself to fight.

"Angels can't have children."

All three of them turned to look at me then, but it was Judah that responded.

"And one man shouldn't be able to move like you or be as strong. You ever wonder if what was going on with you was supernatural? Or did you think The Bully was normal?"

Grinning, I put my hand on my chest. "Oh sh*t! Is our daddy an angel?!"

Judah gave me a look that said he clearly thought I was a dumb ass before he walked to the wall of weapons. "What?" I asked.

"Naw, he wasn't an angel, just a man, but a man with extraordinary abilities. If we survive this, I'll tell you all about it," Jo said, clapping down on my shoulder. "Let's go see what we're up against."

We walked toward the twenty-foot gate to look out into the arena. The place was packed. But I was surprised to see that it wasn't Romans sitting in the stands, but fancy, modern-dressed people with masks on.

"Are they real?" I asked Judah when he came to stand next to us.

He nodded. "They are the very rich and powerful of the world. Most of them are servants to the fallen and their demon seed, Gods of men. Bankers, Judges, Kings, Queens, Politicians, Movie Stars... They come here to feed their need for evil. They like to watch these gladiators kill and butcher humans."

"What the hell kind of gladiators are these?" I asked, not believing what I was hearing. In my line of work, I thought I'd seen the most vile and evil, but apparently, it had been only the tip of the iceberg.

Judah nodded toward a fifty-foot gate on the other side of the arena, just as it began to open.

"What the f*ck?!" A giant of a man walked out. The ugly mutha f*cka had to be at least 10 feet tall. He held up his hands as the people in the stands cheered for him. Two hooded figures, I don't know if it's the same two that led us here, came for a man that wore a postman uniform.

"No! I don't want to go!" he cried. "I have a wife and two daughters. They need me!" But the beings didn't much care. One of them snatched a sword off the wall and shoved it in his arms before dragging him out of the gate and into the arena. When the giant saw him, he began to salivate as he beat his chest.

Balaam, who was now dressed like Julius f*cking Caesar, stood from where he sat in the main spectator box. When he held his hand in the air, the crowd quieted instantly.

"I have a special treat for you, my lovelies. Tonight's main event will be one you will not soon forget. It will be one talked about for many decades to come. Settle back and enjoy the carnage!"

The crowd stood to their feet and cheered, just as the giant charged the mailman. I commend him. Although he knew he faced death, he raised his sword that shook in his hands. But Balaam was right. It was carnage. The giant drew his own sword that was the biggest damn blade I'd ever seen, one blow from it sent the mailman's sword flying across the arena. Only then did the poor fella turn to run.

With a wicked grin on his ugly face, the giant pulled out a lance and swung it with all his might before sending it plowing in the postman's back, causing his body to explode. I clutched the gate at the gruesome scene it made. The crowd cheered as the monster ripped the arm off the twitching body and bit a huge chunk of meat out of it.

My stunned gaze went to Jo's. If he was like me, he was wondering where the hell was his alter. Grisly scene after grisly scene went by. Men and boys alike became food for the giants. They were butchered as the crowd cheered till at last, we were the only ones left.

"Listen to me," Judah said as he pulled his shirt over his head. "They may be big, but these mutha f*ckas die like men. Jo, you and Nap, put a bullet in his head. It will slow him down enough for me to chop the mutha f*cka off his shoulder."

*What?!*

*What the f*ck did this nigga just say?!*

He tossed Al a sword. "Al, you go after his ankles. Chop the mutha f*cka down."

The Old Man looked at him as if he'd lost his damn mind. "I don't know how to work one of these things…" he began but Judah didn't let him get out another word before he charged him with his own sword, swinging with deadly blows.

Do y'all know the Old Man blocked each one and paired with some impressive ones of his own? When Judah ended his assault on him, Al stood staring down at his blade in shock.

"H-how is this possible?"

"You have a lot of skills that you were programmed to forget once they assigned you Jo's detail. Adrenaline and muscle memory can bring them back to the surface."

I shrugged out the jacket Judah had given me. Well, alright! I guess we were getting ready to do this sh*t. I'm going to admit, I was a little worried about the Old Man, but after seeing him move with the sword, I think he can handle himself.

The gate that up until now remained closed began to

rise as all the lights in the arena turned off and a spotlight shined in on us.

Balaam stood from his chair and his voice rang out over the vast space. "Many of you remembered when the great King Dawid walked the earth. We all witnessed thousands fall at the hands of one man. Malakim and demons alike trembled in fear of him. How unfortunate it was to see such a specimen fall prey to age and then death. But, we have a special treat…tonight, we have three of King Dawid's descendants here to challenge our champion!"

The crowd went wild as we stepped out into the arena. Jo smiled and waved at them like he was the f*cken president.

"However!" Balaam's voice boomed, hushing the crowd, his eyes locked with Judah's. "We all know King Dawid's throne fell from grace."

A growl came from our brother's throat as his knuckles once again turned white around the handle of the sword.

"Long gone are the days where the mere mention of the Tribe of Judah strikes fear in anybody," Balaam continued, "they've been reduced to a mindless mass of drug dealers and baby mamas." He sighed. "If only the great king could see his lineage now. Oh, how I would love to see his face. To know that he was forgotten. Moses! Forgotten! Your God! Forgotten…" His gaze came back to Judah. "This is our world now. No longer will we be bowed under the likes of men. May I present my champion, Goliath!" He held his hand toward the fifty-foot gate just as it began to open.

When the spotlight landed on it, my mouth nearly dropped. I was expecting to see another 10-foot bastard standing there. Up until this point, they'd all been around that height. That was not what greeted us. The muthaf*cka's kneecaps were about at the 10-foot point. The spotlight continued to rise up a very muscled, very f*cking tall body.

"Got damn!" the Old Man hissed as the spotlight finally came to rest on the ugliest face on this side of heaven. But the f*cka sat on his shoulders at least 25 feet in the air.

"Goliath! Goliath! Goliath!" the crowd cheered as he stepped out.

"Is that the ground rumbling?" Jo asked out the side of his mouth.

I nodded. "Yeah, I think so."

"Now, I know you boys are thinking this is a bit unfair," Balaam said, causing the crowd to once again fall quiet. "You're saying to yourself, how is it possible we would even stand a chance against one such as this..."

I mean...yeah! That's exactly what the f*ck I was thinking.

Balaam's mouth opened in feigned surprise. "Oh wow! So, you boys don't know..." His gaze fell on Judah. "Tsk! Tsk! Tsk! You haven't been honest with your brothers. After all these years, you're still ashamed of who you are. How can you carry such a secret? Goliath, show them."

The giant wasn't just big, he was fast. He moved so quickly, neither of us had time to prepare...in one swoop, he picked up a big metal ball that had to weigh a couple of tons and sent it sailing at us. It came so fast we had no time to dive out of the way. I flinched, trying my best to prepare for the impact, but it never happened. Hell, I must have had my eyes closed too, 'cause when I opened them, Judah stood in front of us, holding the damn ball.

*What—The—F*ck?!*

But wait! That ain't it. The mutha f*cka then sent the b*tch sailing back at Goliath, who had to duck or it would have taken his big ass head off his shoulders. All three of our stunned gazes came to Judah...but he had eyes only for Balaam. If we thought he was pissed before, it was nothing compared to the rage that was coming for him now.

"Oopps!" Balaam brought his hand to his lips. "Did I spill your little secret? I can't believe you never told your brothers why your hair is so long. I wonder if the Patriot knows." He shrugged. "Well, he does now."

"Enough!" Judah's roar filled the arena. It was so loud it shook the stands. The smile even left Balaam's face.

Me, Jo, and the Old Man's eyes met. The fear that we felt earlier was no more. Neither of us knew what the f*ck Judah was, but I can tell you what he ain't... A mutha f*cka to be f*cked with.

"Let the games begin!" Balaam cried.

Judah could contain himself no more; with his blade in hand, he took off at a speed that even the Bully could not match. He let out another loud roar before he half-ran up the nearest wall and propelled himself through the air toward the giant's neck, sword raised.

For a moment, it looked like Goliath was not ready for him, but at the last minute, he raised his mighty hand, backhanding Judah, sending him flying back to crash into the wall.

Both mine and Jo's guns were out in the blink of an eye, sending shots toward the giant's head. You would think something this big would be slow as sh*t, but he wasn't. This mutha f*cka dodged bullets like Neo from The f*cken Matrix.

"Run!" I yelled when he charged us. He kicked Jo like a football and punched me, sending my body crashing into the wall.

Oh sh*t! That hurt! Real bad…

"Come on, you big, ugly son-of-a-b*tch! I ain't scared of you!" the Old Man taunted as he took several steps back. Seeing him as no threat at all, the giant actually laughed at him as he stalked him. Still lying on the ground, I eased into a better position, careful not to move too much to catch the giant's attention.

"Laugh at this, mutha f*cka.." I whispered before I shot.

Goliath's hand flew to his eye. *Bullseye!*

He whipped to face me, mad as sh*t now, but Jo, who was also crouched down like me a few meters down, shot and took out his other eye. Now clutching both eyes, he yelled. The Old Man moved then, spinning his sword around his hand much like Judah did before bringing it down in an arch, slicing across both of the giant's Achilles Heels. He let out a loud roar, swinging wildly as he fell to his knees. The Old Man jumped out of the way just in time to avoid a deadly blow.

Judah sped past us before sailing through the air, dreads flying in back of him, sword raised. He let out a rage-filled bellow that once again shook the arena before bringing his sword down across the giant's neck with such force it sent the big head flying through the air to crash into Balaam's spectator box. Cursing, the African man jumped out of the way to avoid being hit by it.

For a moment, all the audience and Balaam could do was stare at the head in shock. Several of the other smaller giants came from the back to see for themselves that

Goliath was dead. Like Balaam, they wore looks of surprise on their faces.

Judah chuckled. "Something happened that night with my father in that Vietnamese jungle. Something happened to reverse everything that you've done. Long gone are the days where the mention of the Tribe of Judah strikes fear in the heart of demons you say. Well, I say that at long last, the Tribe of Judah is being restored to its rightful place, and there ain't nothing you or your legions of demons can do to stop it!"

Now good and angry, Balaam leaped out of the box and onto the arena floor. "That's funny! That's the same thing your kinsman Moses said to me the day he took away my body. But unlike him, I am more than just this flesh. What I am, you alone cannot defeat." His eyes flashed red as his flesh began to fall away from him.

"What the—" The Old Man began stepping back, as where Balaam once stood, a big ass fire-breathing dragon now stood. The smell of sulfur was so thick in the air it was suffocating.

"You see, you foolish boy?! You are nothing without your power!" His voice had once again changed into that of the devil.

Not frighten in the least, Judah smiled, lifting his sword that still dripped with Goliath's blood. The dragon's gaze went to something behind us before it hissed, taking a startled step back. The people in the stands began to flee as if their very lives depended on it. They were so scared they were stepping on each other to get out.

Frowning, I turned to see what the hell had scared the living sh*t out of everyone and was surprised to see a huge man with long locs much like Judah's, standing in the entrance we had come out. It looked as if his eyes were closed. Next to him was the biggest damn lion I'd ever seen.

"F*ck," Judah said underneath his breath as he lowered his sword.

When the man's eyes opened, it flooded the arena with a light so bright and pure, it took my breath. The dragon let out a loud screech, disappearing into a puff of red smoke that seeped out of the walls of the arena. The people in the stands were now yelling and screaming as they continued to flee. The ground began to shake as three huge giants that were around the size of Goliath ran from the back, barreling toward the man.

What happened next was the single most amazing thing I'd ever seen. The man took off at a sprint, the lion next to him. As he ran, he snatched up a huge spear that one of the giants had used on its victim earlier and sent it sailing through the air like a f*cking missile. It hit the first monster with such force it took him off his feet, but the spear didn't stop there. It burst from his back and went into the chest of the next giant and then the third, taking all three of the 25-feet beasts off their feet and sending them flying back into the area from which they'd come.

The man looked around with those eyes that saw but didn't, looking at each of us. All four of us fell to our knees when that light shined on us. It brought all of my filth to the surface, causing me to choke on the shame I felt. His gaze went into the stands where the people were still fleeing and then he let out a roar that made Judah's sound like the bark of a puppy. That big ass lion next to him followed, causing the ground to shake.

The people began to drop, probably from f*cking heart

failure. I was damn near balled into a fetal position myself. I didn't give a f*ck that I looked like a b*tch doing it either. My eyes were squeezed tight; I couldn't bear the light anymore. I was too unclean; it was going to kill me.

After a while, when things seemed to quiet, I opened my eyes to see that the arena was gone. Jo, Judah, the Old Man, and I were all on the ground. Standing in the middle of the cave was the man with the lion. The light began to fade from his eyes. I didn't breathe easily until it had faded completely. When the man's gaze was back to normal, it came to Judah but seconds later, his eyes rolled into the back of his head and his big body began to crash to the ground. Judah moved then, catching him before he fell.

"I got you, ach!" Judah cried, staggering a bit under his weight. He was still unsteady himself from his encounter with the light.

A loud explosion rocked the cave just as several men sprinted from the back towards us. I don't know how I knew it, but they weren't Balaam's. A dark-skinned man with long braids followed by a big black wolf, frowned at Judah before taking the big man out of his arms and throwing him over his shoulder as if he weighed nothing. Afterward, he took off as another explosion rocked the cave, the lion, and the wolf right behind him. The explosions sounded like they were getting closer.

"Come on, we have to get out of here! They're destroying the compound!" Judah yelled before taking off after the men. We had to run nearly a mile to the opening. I felt like sh*t. After only running for about eight minutes I got winded.

*F*cking weed!*

The only thing that kept me going was the fact that I

was with a group of spectacular mutha f*ckas and I'll be damned if I'm the weakest link. The man that carried the lion-man on his back never slowed. He leaped over rocks and jumped across open spaces as if it was a simple bag of flour slung over his back and not a huge brotha.

You already know what Judah is capable of and there was no doubt in my mind my twin was the sh*t. Even the Old Man had no problem keeping up, leaping over rocks and jumping over the open spaces, making the sh*t look easy. I don't know who these men are, but I wanted in. I wanted to be one of them.

As we all raced out of the cave, explosives continued to ignite. These men who came later had completely laid waste to this joint. Good riddance. The horrors I seen happened here will haunt me for a long time. Who knew this type of sh*t was going on behind the scenes? F*cking spells, cannibalistic giants, African men who turned into dragons, rich people who wore masks to watch people get killed in the most brutal ways.

*What the f*ck?!*

I needed my Free. I needed to just hold her in my arms so that she could center my world again. I felt unbalanced like I didn't know who the f*ck I was. I had brothers and a sister...My whole life has been one big f*cking lie.

To my chagrin, we didn't stop running once we exited the cave. These brothers kept pushing it. I could feel the ground rumbling under us from the explosions that continued to go off, but my lungs were on fire and I didn't know how much longer I could go.

Right when I thought I was getting ready to embarrass the sh*t out of myself and just collapse, we broke through the trees to see two choppers waiting in the clearance, only then did the squad slow down. The wolf-man lay the lion-man down on the ground, resting his back against a tree, then he slapped him a few times, none too gently till the man jerked awake. When he did, he grabbed the man's hand before he could hit him again with a deadly look in his eyes, but when he saw it was his boy, he grinned.

"You wake, senior citizen?" the man asked him.

"Yeah, I got yo' senior citizen..." the lion man grumbled, making his way slowly to his feet. When his gaze landed on Judah, who believe it or not, stood off behind the other men like a little brother that was in trouble with his older brother, a frown creased his brow.

I haven't known Judah long, but I've known him long enough to know this mutha f*cka was a force to be reckoned with. So, you can imagine the shock to my system at seeing him subdued like this in the presence of the wolf-man and the lion-man, who were both some next-level kind of sh*t.

"What's wrong with you, man?" The lion-man growled, taking angry steps to Judah. The other men cleared out his path like smoke.

Judah shook his head. "Listen, Lyon, I had it. I didn't need your help."

Oh! Okay, so his name was Lyon... fitting.

The anger that came on Lyon's face at my big brother's words was intimidating as hell. "You had it? You had it?" He turned to face his men.

"You hear this? He had it?" Lyon whipped back to face him. "Had *what*, nigga?"

The muscle ticked in Judah's jaw as he fought his own anger. "It..." he hissed.

Lyon poked him in the chest hard. "You had nothing!

You showed up to a gunfight with a hula hoop. Balaam was getting ready to chew you up and spit you out!"

The muscle was now going crazy in Judah's jaw... I don't know, y'all. I think my big bro was going to try and take this dude.

"You need to give up your obsession with hunting this dude. Look how low you've stooped. Dear Yah, you working with demons and the Fallen just to get at him! How long did you think you were going to be able to do that? Let it go, bruh... You need to come to the Lyon's Den so you can be properly trained. That way, you can properly train those in your care."

Judah shoved his hands away from him. "I told you, man! That ain't for me! I'm good! I take care of mine and I know how to fight!"

Lyon got angrier. "Fighting with these ain't the only way, boy!" he hissed, holding up them haymakers he had for fists. "You need to learn how to fight spiritually."

Judah shook his head. "Like I said, I'm all good. I made it this far on my own. Wasn't no spirits there to see me through. I'll make it the rest of the way...On my own!" he hissed.

The frown on Lyon's face increased. "You think you was the only one with a rough life man?!" He took a step closer. "You think you special, nigga?! I ain't going to be able to keep saving yo' ass! And now you dragging yo' little brothers into yo' BS! You not showing them the right way!"

Judah lost it and shoved him. Had that been anybody else, they would have gone flying across the clearing, but Lyon barely budged. In fact, he laid hands on my big bro and I kid y'all not, tossed this dude clean out of the clearing to crash hard against a tree where his body dropped like a log.

*Damn! That's messed up...*

The only thing Jo, the Old Man, and I could do was stare completely stunned in that direction.

"Y'all need to holla at yo' brother. That nigga's neck is stiff!" Lyon hissed. "Let's roll." He told his crew.

We watched as he, his men, the lion, and the wolf all loaded into one of the choppers and took off. Neither of us said a thing until they were completely out of sight. Jo was the first to break the silence.

"Wooow! I can't wait to tell Rome this sh*t!"

The Old Man chuckled. "What a night."

We looked up just as Judah came limping out of the trees, holding his side. He was not happy with us.

"What the f*ck?!" he growled. "Y'all just stand there and watch me get manhandled, no f*cking assistance?! What the f*ck I even bring y'all for?!"

Jo looked at him like he was strange. "Bro, do you hear yourself? We just watched this man toss you like a pebble. Not even a rock...a pebble, bro! What the hell was we supposed to do?"

"Shut up! Get on the f*cking chopper!" Judah hissed, angrily shoving past us.

I grinned. Oh yeah! After all these years, I'd finally found where I belong...

# Chapter 8

Uncertainty

Naphtali

"MY PARENTS ARE DEAD?"

Jo and the Old Man both stared at me dumbfounded before their gazes shot to Judah, who stood by the window of the loft-style office we now sat in. After leaving that freaky-ass cave of smoke and mirrors, the chopper touched down on top of an unmarked building in Virginia, where we were met by a man named Ryan, a clean-cut, ex-military type. Judah's boy...seem like they went way back and had genuine comradery between each other. When I asked why the hell we were stopping here instead of in Detroit, where Free was waiting for me, Judah's only reply was 'briefing and fuel.'

I was allowed to shower and freshen up a bit while we

all swallowed a few sandwiches. Judah disappeared with Ryan for nearly two hours, in which time, Jo and Al kept their promise and told me what they knew about all of this. They told me about James Law, our real father and the doctor who did this to us. They also told me about the torture sessions that were used to splinter our minds and about the experiments. By the time they were finished, I was ready to kill. The cherry on top being that all this sh*t had been government funded in their never-ending quest to achieve the super soldier.

Shortly after that, Judah walked in and tossed me a newspaper. Frowning I looked down at it, seeing that the paper was printed ten days ago. *'Massacre in Vegas'* was written in big bold print on the front page.

"Naw—" I said, floored at what I was reading. Apparently, both Free and I, along with a few more members of the wedding party including the bride and the groom, had gotten caught in the crossfire of two rival Vegas mobs and were shot dead.

My gaze rose to Judah. "What the f*ck is this?"

"We have many powerful enemies. One you met... Balaam. There are others. Others who profit greatly from our ignorance. But awake, we become a threat to them. You boys were safe as long as you were a part of the program, using your particular set of skills for the powers that be. Now that you know who your father is...and what happened to us, you not only threaten your enemies but the very system they built off your sleeping bodies." He paused for just a moment, gazing out the frosted window. Winter had come to Virginia.

"If they think you're dead, your remaining family and friends will be safe," he continued quietly.

"Who the f*ck is they? Point them out and let me take care of them. I can't let this sh*t ruin Free's life. If she can't go to her clinic and tend to her patients, she'll be miserable. She's going to f*cking hate me! Just show me who they are, and I will handle the mutha f*ckas. But I can't drag Free into this sh*t!"

Judah's eyes glazed over in anger. "Do you think this is a joke? How are you going to handle them? Like you handled Balaam when he put yo' ass on pause for ten days? These mutha f*ckas ain't playing with you. They are fighting for their lives. They will take Free out just like they took out your handlers."

My gaze went to Jo for clarification. "Handlers?" I asked him.

"Parents," he muttered.

"My parents are dead?!"

"We-we thought you knew," my lookalike continued, clearly unsure of what to say at this point.

"When? How?"

"The morning all that sh*t went down in Vegas." This came from Judah. "The police report said there was a malfunction in the boat's bilge area. We were sure your sheriff friend contacted you about it; your little town is abuzz with the deaths of so many of its prominent residents and all on the same day." He gestured toward the paper. "Last paragraph."

The article continued by saying the recent deaths come as a shock to the small Michigan town that just this morning, learned of the deaths of its beloved mayor, who held the position for nearly twenty years before retiring last fall, and his lovely wife from a boating accident in the south of France.

My gaze lifted to Jo's. "Did they kill your handlers too?"

He shook his head. "Naw, I killed mine myself. They called a hit on my wife, child, and Al."

Judah grunted. "His handlers weren't as loving as yours."

"I wouldn't call them loving."

He shrugged. "Then why the hell are we still talking about them? Come on, let's go home. I need a beer." After snatching his bag off the table, he exited the room.

Jo looked toward the door Judah had just exited, shaking his head. "That guy needs a hug or something."

I chuckled. "Naw, bruh...he need a little more than that."

During the chopper ride to my new life, I evaluated my feelings. Hearing that my paren—handlers were dead was a blow. Although they never felt like genuine, loving guardians, they weren't cruel to me. In fact, they gifted me with anything I wanted, all except for love. But who can blame them? I had no idea what was going on with me, but maybe they did. How can you love an experiment? Regardless, it wasn't their love that I needed. The only person's love I ever needed probably hated me right now. Not only did I trick her into marrying me, the price she had to pay for it was the loss of her life as she knew it. Her friends, her little house, her clinic...

F*ck!

"I need to talk to Free." At that point, nothing else mattered...Because it was her love I couldn't live without.

———

"WAIT!" I told Jo and the Old Man as we headed up the walkway to my new home. "Free's in there right now?"

Jo nodded. "Yep, Rome said Journey and Nak helped her get settled in yesterday."

"Okay, come here. I need you guys to do me a favor." I gestured for both him and Al to take one of my arms each.

"Ummmm, is there a reason for this?" Jo muttered as he hesitantly walked my way. "You keep wanting to embrace me, and I'm not going to lie. It's starting to worry me, bro."

I wrapped my arm around his neck and jerked him toward me. *Pompous asshole.*

"The last time I talked to my girl, she wasn't too happy with me."

One side of Jo's mouth lifted in a grin. "What did you do?"

"How do you know it was me that did something? It could have been her." He gave me a look that clearly said he wasn't buying my bullsh*t.

"What did you do?"

I exhaled. Sh*t, he had me. "I tricked her into marrying me."

The Old Man chuckled, eyeballing Jo. "Why am I not surprised? Where have I heard this story before?"

Jo held up a finger. "First of all, you old bastard, I didn't trick Journey into marrying me. I did it the old-fashioned way. Got down on my knees and proposed like a man."

"I proposed like a man!" I hissed. *What the f*ck?! Do he think I'm some kind of animal?* "I just got her sh*t-faced drunk first. The next morning, she took one look at her wedding rings and went running for the bathroom, where she threw up everything in her stomach."

Both Jo and Al flinched. "Yikes!" The Old Man muttered shaking his head. "That doesn't look too good, kid."

"Naw, it doesn't," I agreed.

Jo put his hand on my shoulder. "We are at your disposal. What's the plan, bro?"

I grinned. "Okay, Free is one of those softhearted people, plus, she's a doctor. Her kryptonite is the sick and wounded. I need you guys to carry me in there like I'm half dead. Drop me off on the bed, then get the hell out."

My gaze centered on Jo. I have only known him for about two days, but it was long enough to know this mutha f*cka loved the sound of his own voice.

"Don't be in there trying to hold a long-ass conversation, man. Just drop me off in the bed, and then get the hell out. I need to have some alone time with my woman."

Understanding washed over his face as he nodded. "Yeah, that's a good plan. And don't worry, I'm not going to mess it up."

The Old Man chuckled. "If I doubted you two were brothers before today, this would definitely squash all doubt. How about you just go in there and tell her the truth. Tell her how you really feel about her."

I frowned, but it was Jo who spoke. "That's the dumbest idea I've heard today."

I nodded in agreement. "Yeah, it is. This ain't the '20s no more, man. These modern-day women don't think like their great-grandmothers."

Jo laughed at my dig at Al, who narrowed his eyes at me. "I was born in '54, you asshole. And I'll have you know, it ain't many as good with the ladies as ol' Al." He looked at Jo. "Ask yo' brother. He and I had a joint wedding just the other day. Ol' Al married his mother-in-law. And I guarantee you, my wife will run circles around both of your wives. And who got her?" He pointed to himself. "Mack daddy Al got her. I can teach you young whippersnappers a thing or two. But that's just like yo' generation, young, dumb, and can't be told nothing. I'm a OG—"

"Damn, Al...we get it!" Jo said interrupting the old player. I chuckled; my man was getting ready to recite pimp poetry if Jo hadn't stopped him.

"Shut up, both of you!" he grumbled, grabbing my arm and roughly placing it around his neck. "Now I have to deal with two of you. I think it is time for me to retire," he continued as they half carried me up the stairs. I hung my head and grimaced with every step they took.

And for the record, I wasn't lying, well, at least not that much. Getting hit with that f*cking giant's fist felt like getting hit with a wrecking ball. It just so happened my body healed a little quicker than most, and I can barely feel my injuries anymore. But I remembered them, and I drew on that to channel each flinch I made in pretense.

No sooner had they rang the bell, the door was thrown open and a freaked-out Free appeared. I knew that look in her eyes, she'd had the same look the year she'd lost an important part to her science project, and she thought she would get a failing grade because of it. Or the time I put her in my truck on prom night, and she didn't know what to expect of me. She had the same wild look in her beautiful eyes. Damn... I've missed her so much. My life was in complete shambles, but I'd be lying if I said it didn't feel bearable because she was here.

I almost blew my own plan by grabbing her and taking

her plush lips in a kiss I was hungry for. I needed her in the worst way. I needed to hold her in my arms so that the feel of her can re-center my world.

I can live without my handlers; I can live with everybody back home and at work thinking I'm dead. What I can't live without is Free.

"Oh my God! What happened to him?!" she cried trying to take me out of their arms. I pretended to flinch as she hugged me tightly. My gaze went to Al's over her head and I gave him a little wink. Ol' Mack daddy Al trying to tell me how to deal with *my* woman.

Ha! I don't think so.

"I'm okay, ba—" I began, but that asshole brother of mine interrupted.

"You must be Free." He shrugged my arm from around his shoulders as he held his hand out for her to shake. The sudden loss of his support caught both Al and me off guard and I hit the floor...hard.

*This mutha f\*cka!* I mean mugged his ass as I stared up at him. *Hardheaded!* I told him to drop me in the bed, not the floor.

"Oh no! Are you okay?" Free cried trying to pick me up.

"Joseph at your service, ma'am. I believe you met my beautiful wife, Journey. The older guy over there name is Albert." The idiot continued, holding his hand out for her to shake like I wasn't lying on the floor. The Old Man chuckled shaking his head.

Frowning, Free stared at his hand before her confused gaze went to his face. She looked back toward me, probably not understanding why the hell he was trying to shake her hand after dropping me on the floor. But then her startled gaze shot back to his face.

"Ohhh—" she gasped, putting her hand to her lips. She looked back at me... "Ohhh!"

———

## Free

Twins! They're twins... Journey told me she was married to Tucker's brother, but I didn't know they were twins. This is amazing!

In a state of shock, I reached up and pinched the other one's cheek just above his beard, pulling it a bit to see if he was real. Who knew there could be two chocolate Adonises walking the earth? I thought for sure Tucker was one of a kind.

And then he grinned. I sucked in my breath. It was Naphtali's grin. An angry throat cleared from the floor.

"Can you stop touching my brother and maybe help me up? I'm injured here..."

"Oh! Yes!" I cried jumping back into action. As Albert and I helped Tucker, his lookalike strolled leisurely around the house.

"Wow! This is nice! We hadn't gotten a chance to take a peek in here, but I could tell it was going to be nice from the outside. How are you enjoying it so far?" he asked as we struggled without his help to get Naphtali up the stairs and into bed.

"Ummm...fine, I guess. Everything is a bit confusing."

"Yes, I'm sure it is."

"What happened?" I asked Tucker as I positioned the

pillows behind his head. He clutched my hand, bringing it to his lips.

"I—" he began.

"He got beat up," Joseph interrupted, plopping on the bed next to him.

I was so taken by the fact that it was two Tuckers, I barely noticed the angry gaze Naphtali shot to his brother.

"Who beat you up? Are you alright?"

"He barely made it, sweetheart. You should have seen the size of the guy that violated him."

My gaze flew back to Tucker's. "Oh my God! You were…violated?"

If looks could kill, Joseph would be dead. Tucker shook his head. "No, Doc…nothing like that."

I placed a reassuring hand on his arm. "You don't have to be ashamed. You didn't choose to be violated."

Fighting to hold back a grin, Joseph blinked innocently. "Yeah, bro, you don't have to be ashamed. He was stronger than you and way bigger. It's not your fault he snatched your manhood away in such a vile manner."

"He didn't snatch my manhood…mutha f*cka!" Tucker growled between clenched teeth. His gaze came to me and he managed a smile. "Freebie, do you mind getting me a glass of water?"

"Sure, I'll be right back." I hurried into the beautiful, conjoined bathroom to get his water. I thought I heard a growl before a thump and then a loud crash. My heart dropped as I rushed from the bathroom just in time to see Joseph pulling himself up from the floor, holding his head; he was shooting murderous eyes at his brother. Albert stood chuckling, and Tucker still rested back against the pillows I'd set up for him as if nothing at all had happened.

"What's going on?" I asked frowning at the three. There was something afoot, but I couldn't quite put my finger on what.

"I must have had a muscle spasm in my leg or something. Sorry, bro..."

"Your leg spasm caused you to kick me in the head?" Joseph growled.

Tucker shrugged. "It's hard to tell what a violated leg will do. Again, so sorry."

Joseph balled up his fists. It looked as if he was going to leap on his brother. He opened his mouth to say something else, but Albert put his arm around his shoulders, guiding him toward the door.

"Let's leave these two to comfort each other. I'm sure they have a lot to talk about. And you owe a certain young lady a honeymoon."

Joseph's angry gaze came back to Tucker as he exited. "Holla at you later, bro!" That sounded like a threat.

With his eyes now closed, Naphtali lifted his hand and muttered. "Enjoy your honeymoon..."

After the bedroom door shut, our gazes met and for a moment, I was paralyzed. Over the last couple of weeks, I'd been so worried about him. I thought I would never see him again. I thoug—I thought he was dead.

"I was so worried about you." He spoke the words that fluttered in my heart. Tears came to my eyes as I nodded.

"I was worried about you too."

He opened his arms. "Come here, baby."

I didn't need to be asked twice. Running across the

room, I had to force myself to be careful of his injuries as I threw myself into his arms.

"I thought you were dead?!" I cried, not able to hold back any longer.

"I know. I'm so sorry you had to go through that. Are you alright? Did Rau hurt you?"

I shook my head. "No… Nak and Rome saved me. But —" My words died as I thought of Layla.

"But what?"

"They didn't make it in time to save Layla."

"Layla survived Vegas?"

I nodded. "Yeah, she did. When we got to the compound in Argentina, they told us to take off all our jewelry, and she lost it. They injected her with something and dragged her kicking and screaming out of the room. After Nak did her thing and destroyed the place, I didn't want to leave until I found Lay. But Rome told me I didn't want to see her. He said that he'd seen a few men dispose of her body earlier that day."

I buried my face in his neck; I didn't have to coax my tears out of their ducts; they flowed freely. Angie, Laureen, Layla, and Dillion had been royal pains in my butt for a long time, but they didn't deserve to die the way that they had.

Up until this point, during this whole ordeal, I'd felt numb. Life as I'd known it had come to a violent halt. Not only had I seen the only people I knew as family since I was twelve years old murdered, I'd been kidnapped by the cartel and nearly became a sex slave. But the most traumatic blow of it all was when Rome and Nak showed me the newspaper that announced Tucker's and my death, explaining that it was necessary to keep us and our friends and family safe.

"Tucker, I'm so confused. What's going on? The whole world thinks we're dead. My friends, my patients…they all think I'm dead."

Exhaling, he gently rubbed my hair. "Yeah, baby. I know it all sounds crazy, and I'm so very sorry that I brought all this chaos into your life. I know you regret the day you ever laid eyes on me, huh?"

"What?!" I sat up in the bed facing him with my legs folded Indian style. I wanted to see his eyes as we talked.

"That's not true…I lov—" I caught myself before I could utter those words. Was I ready to cross this line? I still didn't know how he felt about me. Last time I saw him, he was regretting our marriage. If I—

He grabbed my hand, bringing my thoughts to a halt. There was genuine desperation in his eyes. "Please, bae…say it. I need to hear it. I've waited my whole life to hear it." His gaze dropped to my wedding rings. "It's the one thing that would have made the two best nights of my life complete."

"What two nights are those?" My voice was barely over a whisper.

He kissed the palm of my hand, causing a quiver to shoot through my body. "The night you gave me your virginity, and the night you gave me your hand in marriage."

I exhaled a breath I wasn't aware of holding. You guys may think I'm lying, but those few words he'd just uttered seemed to right all the wrongs that have happened to me over the last two weeks. Is that possible?

But wait…

"If that night was so special, why did you leave me alone on the beach?" I flinched at how bitter that sounded.

He frowned. "I didn't leave you alone. I was there, watching you from my boat." He paused for just a moment. "I was scared that when you woke up sober, you were going to take one look at me and freak the f*ck out, kind of like you did the other morning. When I saw you starting to stir, I got up, ran to my boat, and like a big-ass coward, watched you from there."

*WHAT?!*

*He was there?*

"You were so beautiful sitting on the beach that morning in that yellow dress. I took a picture of you with my phone and looked at it every night during my time at the academy." He chuckled. "Do you know, although I don't use it anymore, I still have that phone packed away in my boxes just because of that picture?"

I put my hand over my mouth to hide the fact that my lips quivered.

*He was there!*

He was there the whole time! For so many years, I've carried that burden with me. And he was there!

Oh God! I was going to start crying again.

"Noooo! Bae, what's the matter? Why are you crying?" he asked, taking me back into his arms.

"I thought you left me. I felt cheap and neglected for so long because I thought you left."

"Free, I've loved you since the first day you walked into my geometry class. All four years of high school you drove me crazy 'cause I wanted you so bad. Prom night, you made me the happiest brotha in the world. I just didn't want you waking up regretting what we did. That sh*t would have broke my heart... for real."

*Did he just say he's loved me since geometry class freshman year?!*

How could I have been so blind? Now so much of his behavior makes sense. For so long, I thought he tortured me because I was one of the poor kids from the wrong side of the tracks. He tortured me because he was trying to get my attention and like the big jerk he is, just didn't know how to go about doing that the right way.

In my mind, I was doing the silliest happy dance, the-Tucker-loves-me dance. If I didn't think it would hurt him, I would squeeze him and plant kisses all over his face. Instead, he squeezed me, causing me to giggle a bit.

"Sh*t, girl...You know I'm sensitive." That lie caused me to laugh right out. But then my laughter died when I thought of something else he said.

Lifting my head, I rested my chin on his chest. "What did you mean, like the other morning?"

He frowned confused, so I clarified. "You said you were scared that when I woke up sober, I was going to take one look at you, kind of like I did the other morning."

Understanding washed over his face. "Ohhh yeah. Like you did when you saw my rings on your finger and learned that we were married. You took one look at the f*cking rings and ran to the bathroom throwing up everything in your stomach."

"What!? You jerk!" Before I could catch myself, I punched him in *his* stomach.

"Ooof!" he gasped, flinching from my blow.

"Oh my God! I'm so sorry!" I cried sitting up so that I could cradle his head. I forgot all about his injuries.

"Brotha can't get a break. Now my woman beating me

up too." His muffled voice came from where I was practically smothering him in my boobs.

I chuckled. "What is wrong with you? How can you think I was disgusted by your rings? Do you know what I went through to keep those horrible men from taking them from me?"

The smile left his face as a frown quickly took its place. "What did you go through?"

I gently punched him again. Leave it to his dirty mind to go there. "Not what you're thinking. That same bun that you hate is how I hid them. That first day, I only had time to stuff them in the bun before the guards saw me. But after they left, I took my hair down and braided the rings in the bun to make sure they would not fall out. Now... does that sound like the action of someone that's disgusted with your rings?"

He grinned. "What was I supposed to think when you ran away throwing up and sh*t?"

"I threw up because some asshole got me stupid drunk the night before and all that liquor needed to come out, not because we got married."

For a moment, I was held captive by his intense gaze. He was studying me in that way he does, that way that makes me feel as if he can see within my soul and know my deepest secrets.

"So, you're not disgusted with the idea of being married to me?" Now it was his words that were barely over a whisper, as if he was afraid of my response. Although this man has always oozed confidence and charm, I could see that this was a big deal to him.

I shook my head. "No, not at all."

His grin grew. "Would you say that the idea of being married to me makes you happy?"

Instead of answering him, I lowered my head and gently kissed his lips.

"How hurt are you?" I whispered before kissing his lips again, but this time making it clear what was on my mind.

He moaned, deepening the kiss, but I could feel the battle he fought within himself. He wanted an answer to his question, but his lust was overruling him. However, it was his need for that answer that won, because although it seemed like the most painful thing he's had to do in a while, he pulled his lips away from mine.

"Why aren't you answering my question?"

I went for his lips again, but he turned his head. "Free..." he growled.

"How hurt are you?" I repeated, letting my hand slip under his t-shirt to caress his beautifully sculpted abs. The muscles tensed under my touch.

"Free...bae. Answer me." He was pleading with me now, that cocky confidence slipping by the wayside. Damn! That was so hot...

I gently straddled his lap, grasping his t-shirt and pulling it up his body until he was forced to sit up a bit so that I could pull it over his head.

"Tuuucker...answer me. How hurt are you?"

He was losing the battle with his lust, but I was going in for the kill. I lowered my head and tasted that chocolate chest of his while letting my hands move lower. My goodness! This man's body was simply amazing.

He moaned. "Damn it, Free! You're trying to distract me."

I grinned up at him as my kisses made their way down

that deep crevice between his muscled abs. "Is it working?"

"I mean… yeah, it is. But why won't you answer my question? Are you happy that I'm your husband?"

"I'm not answering you…" I muttered as slowly undid the button on his jeans. "Because I prefer to show you."

It was his turn to grin. "Oh, hell yea! I support that!"

"But first…" I let my tongue run teasingly inside of his belly button. "You have to tell me just how hurt you are."

He shrugged. "If you promise to be gentle with me, I think that I can handle it—" The last of his statement was a moan as I began to show him just how happy I was with the fact that he is my husband.

Although our lovemaking was gentle that night, there was an undertone of desperation. We touched each other in a way that said we were all we had left. He and I felt like the only two human beings in the world. Well…at least *our* world. We lay in a strange new house, in a strange new town amongst strange new family. And yet, we felt as if it was only him and me left alive.

We made love on and off throughout the night. Between the loving, we talked about his siblings, his parents who he just learned died in a boating accident that wasn't an accident. We talked about our friends and how the only thing keeping them safe is our supposed deaths. We even talked a little bit about his other personality. Of course, I was thrilled because he'd never said even this much to me before, which only cemented the fact that we now felt as if we were all we had left.

Morning came; we slept a little, but neither of us could remain so for long. I helped him out of bed, and we took our time looking around our new home. It looked as if it had just been freshly built.

"Nak told me the house comes with your new job," I told him as we made our way to the empty kitchen. He grunted but didn't say anything.

"What does that mean?"

"I don't know if this is a job I want to take."

I wondered about that. Although he opened up to me a bit more about his split personality that he called the Bully, he still had yet to go into detail about what happened to him after Balaam took him from Vegas.

The only thing he told me was that he was in some kind of coma for ten days, and when he woke, Joseph was standing over him f*cking up his mind… his words. But that after he realized he wasn't looking in a mirror, he met his older brother, who he says has serious mental issues, and Al, the very nice older fella that helped me get him into bed yesterday.

*"Freebie, I don't want to relive what I saw. I just want to forget it, bae. The sh\*t was that horrible. And I definitely don't want to pollute your mind with some sh\*t that you can never unsee once you see it."*

And well, that was that. I let the subject drop for the moment. One of the things a good psychiatrist learns is to know just how far to push the patient before stepping back. Whatever happened to him had traumatized him. I could see it in his eyes.

In fact, over the next three days, he didn't want to leave the house. He didn't even want to talk to Joseph or Rome. Whenever they came to the door, he told me to tell them he was still in bed and wasn't feeling well. And because I didn't want to upset him or leave him alone for any length of time, I stood on the porch and talked whenever Journey and Nak came by to visit and bring us supplies.

"I made you guys meatloaf and mashed potatoes today," Journey said, handing me the dishes she'd prepared. "And I raided Joseph's closet and got a few things that I think your husband would like."

"Thank you so much!" I told her, taking everything from her and Nak's hands and stacking them just inside the door. She was really a godsend. Although Tucker was being super antisocial, she and her lovely mother continued to prepare meals for us.

"How is he doing?" Nak asked, taking a seat on the porch.

I exhaled. "He still doesn't want to leave the house. I tried to get him to take a trip into town so that we could shop for a few pieces of furniture, but he claims his ribs are still hurting him pretty badly."

Nak nodded. "He'll come around. All this just takes getting used to. Luckily for me, nobody knew I was alive in the first place, so when I *died*," she held up air quotes when she said died, "there was nobody to miss me and nobody for me to miss. Rome, the Sarge, and the Old Al was all I had anyway."

I wanted to ask her about that, but I didn't want to leave Tucker too long by himself. I filed it away as a topic to discuss with her at a later date.

"Well, hopefully, he'll be feeling better soon. I don't want to keep taking advantage of you guys' kindness."

They both waved that away. "It's no big deal. I need the excuse to get a break from the children anyway," Journey said.

I smiled; I'd met her little angels yesterday. Ms. Ayana

had helped her mother bring breakfast to us. She was just a doll.

I and the ladies chatted for another fifteen minutes before I told them I'd talk to them later. I went back in and after making a monster plate for his majesty, crawled back into bed. We ate, watched movies...made love, laughed, and joked. Heck, I even cried a time or two. We just took the time out to enjoy each other.

To me, it was the most perfect honeymoon. There was no place in the world I would rather be than closed up inside of our brand-new house, in our brand-new bedroom, and on our brand-new bed with the man that I loved.

But our little love cocoon was soon to come to an end. On the fourth day, Judah showed up at the door...

# Chapter 9

## The Training

### Free

I STOOD STARING with mouth agape at the giant angry man in front of me...or what I thought was a man. Now granted he had all the faculties of a man, two arms, two legs, a very muscled neck, a head... But there was something about the angles of his face and the chilling look in his eyes that made him look like an avenging angel sent here to cleanse the world of evil.

Don't know where all that came from, but Tucker had tried to warn me about his big brother, and I just assumed he was overexaggerating. However, I can bear witness to what everyone has said about this man. There was something savagely wild about him. Although his locs were in a neat ponytail, they didn't look as if they belonged that way. I could see them down, surrounding his face, making him look like a wild lion.

Yes…this man had the bearings of a lion.

"I need to speak with Tucker," he irritably grunted out when it appeared as if I was just going to continue to stand there like a loon and stare at him.

Snapping my mouth shut, I gave him a nervous smile. "Sorry about that. You just—"

*Dang it, Free, shut up! What were you going to say? Sorry about that. You just look like something I saw in a comic book once… Goodness! Get a grip!*

I cleared my throat to start again. "I'm sorry, Tucker isn't feeling well. Can I take a message?"

He frowned at me. And let me tell y'all, it was enough to make me take a step back. Goodness gracious! I think Naphtali was right about this guy; there were several things severely wrong here.

"What's the matter with him?" The way he grunted out his words let me know this guy wasn't a big talker.

"Well… He hasn't healed from his injuries. It's only been four days."

"What injuries?!" This he snapped. And yes, a little squeak left my throat as I was unable to hide the fact that he scared the heck out of me.

"The injuries he sustained—," was all I was able to get out before the wild man shoved the door open and began to come into the house. My first response was to step in front of him and demand he stop right where he was…But then I thought, *come on, who am I kidding?*

"Excuse me, sir! He's not feeling well!" I cried from a safe distance behind him. But I might as well have saved my voice. He took the stairs up to our bedroom two at a time.

In appalled horror, I watched as he pushed open the door without knocking. Tucker, who was lounging in the bed with only a pair of sweatpants that Journey had gotten from her husband, looked up in surprise.

"Judah! What are you doing here, man?"

"I sent Rome and Jo here every day for the last three days to tell you I needed to see you at headquarters. Did you get the messages?"

Tucker tiredly rubbed his hand down his face. "Yeah, I did. My ribs have been killing me; I think I may have broken or fractured—" He didn't get any more out.

A scream froze in my throat as Judah quickly drew a gun from somewhere in back of him. Tucker's eyes widened and moving faster than I've ever seen a human move, dove to the side of the bed just as his brother emptied the clip into the pillow he'd been resting against. I covered my ears to protect them from the loud sound.

Naphtali jumped to his feet. "What the f*ck is wrong with you?!" He clenched and unclenched his fists, the muscle in his jaw twitching uncontrollably. I could tell he was trying to keep himself from changing into that...*other fella*.

Judah wasn't bothered by his aggressive stance in the least. He slid his pistol back into its holster before glancing my way.

"Would you look at that, Doc? He's moving just fine. I must *also* have the gift of healing." His gaze went back to his brother. "Be on the training field in an hour. Don't make me have to come back." And then he turned and casually walked out of the house as if he did not just try and kill poor Tucker.

For just a moment all the both of us could do was stare after him. Slowly our stunned gazes reconnected.

"See? I told you. It's something wrong with that mutha f*cka..." The fact that my big, tough husband whispered that spoke volumes.

———

## Naphtali

"Just drive...don't say sh*t!" I growled as I pulled the car door closed behind me.

Jo grinned from the driver's seat, making me want to smash his head into the steering wheel.

"Good day to you too, brother. How are you? I'm fine; thanks for asking."

I didn't respond; I just stared out the window at my new neighborhood as we headed to the training field, whatever the f*ck that was...

"So, Judah came to visit you, huh?"

I shook my head. "It's something wrong with that mutha f*cka! He damn shot up my f*cking bed. Of course, my girl was ready to cut loose. I had to convince her that my life wasn't in danger and sh*t."

Jo chuckled shaking his head. "At least he paid you a visit. He hasn't stepped foot in any of our houses. Won't even come to the cookouts."

I grunted. "It's 'cause he's part silverback. Don't know how to mingle with real humans."

Jo had a good laugh at that, but sh*t, I was serious.

Judah's ass is feral. After he shot at me, I nearly popped a blood vessel in my head trying to keep the Bully from stepping into my shoes. The mutha f*cka beat at my soul, wanting to be let loose.

That was the last thing I needed. Free was already afraid and unsure of our future here. And it didn't help that I've been putting off meeting with the rest of the team and lying low in the crib. The real reason I've been ignoring Judah's summons is because I didn't know if fighting demons and giants…and whatever the hell else existed in the underworld was really for me.

Don't get me wrong, there is nothing I enjoyed more than bringing down drug dealers and mutha f*ckas like that. I lived for that sh*t. I understood that sh*t. What I'd seen in that cave was past my understanding. It was going to take more than my strength and brutality to defeat what I saw. It was going to take me becoming something I don't know if I had it in me to become.

As we headed to the training field, Jo pointed out the others' houses and spoke about the potential to add other things like a school or maybe even a clinic. He showed me another house that was still empty.

"Whose place is that?" I asked.

"Our brother, Levi's."

That was another thing that had been heavy on my mind. We were triplets. Y'all gon' think I'm bullsh*ting y'all, but I swear I used to feel them. At first, I thought it was just the Bully. But it wasn't; the Bully was dark… The feelings I used to get were different, like the time my eye started hurting really bad. For nearly a month, the pain was excruciating. My handlers took me to the doctor and everything; I could barely see out of the eye. Of course, the doctors could find nothing wrong, but it was so damn painful. And then one day, the pain just stopped.

"Where is he?" I asked Jo.

He shook his head. "Judah said out of the three of us, Levi is the hardest to keep up with. He moves like a ghost. Unlike you and me, he lives in the shadows and can easily disappear in a room. We won't be able to get eyes on him until he resurfaces, something Judah says he does every few years."

When he brought the car to a stop in the training field parking lot, we were met by the Old Man, Rome, and Nak, the rest of the team. Apparently, all of them had gone through what Free and I just went through and had to die to the world in order to keep themselves and their friends safe. They've all settled in quite nicely and were learning how to be a family. I didn't doubt that Free and I were going to settle in as well; I just worried that soon, she was going to start mourning for her precious clinic and her patients. I had no idea how I was going to replace them... She needed to be able to heal.

"Wow! You guys missed me or something?" Jo asked as he got out of his car.

Rome made a noise with his mouth that clearly said he didn't before he shook up with me. I liked Rome. Although he was a damn genius, he was down-to-earth, unlike my bigmouthed brother, whose head was way up in the clouds.

"Uncovered some more info on your boy, Judah; I figure I'll fill y'all in as we walk to the field," Rome told us as we all fell into step.

"You need to be careful, kid. What's he going to do if he finds out you're spying on him?" Al muttered.

"First of all, *Al!* My spy bots are undetectable. Nobody sees me unless I want them to. Second, you don't need to worry about me. Worry about my mother and making sure she stays happy."

Damn! It was beef between the Old Man and the young genius.

"Why you have to talk to him like that?" Jo hissed.

But Al put his hand on his shoulder stopping him. "Let it go… He'll come around."

Rome shook his head. "Naw, I probably won't."

I looked to see how Nak was handling all of this, but she wasn't paying attention. Her gaze kept shooting back toward the street.

Jo sighed. "What you find out, man?"

"Judah told you guys that his strength was intensified in that place because of Balaam's magic."

We nodded. That's exactly what he told us. After the chopper landed in Virginia, Jo asked him about his strength and how the hell he was able to catch that big metal-ass ball that should have squished all of us. He just shrugged and said he was only strong in that place because of Balaam's spells.

"What about it?" I asked.

Rome shook his head. "It's not true. I got ahold of a classified CIA document titled Project Samson. This thing dated back nearly six-hundred years. The first few cases documented were written in Portuguese and Spanish. It talked about a soldier named Yahya Ben Rabbi, also known as Don Yahya El Negro. He was a Sephardic Jew born in Cordoba Spain in 1115 A.D. He won so many battles for King Alfonso of Portugal that the king gave him a piece of land they named Land of The Negroes."

"Now there were two things that was exceptionally special about Don Negro. You see, he was also called Ha Nasi, which means the prince because it was a well-known fact that he was of the direct line of King David himself. But some of the Spanish called him Don Samson. There are eyewitness reports of him picking up and throwing horse and rider across the fields, punching through stone walls, and bellowing with rage loud enough to cause the earth to shake."

One of his eyebrows lifted. "Sound familiar?"

"Yeah, but why hide?" Jo asked.

"It wasn't long till the Spanish stopped looking at Don Yahya El Negro and his descendants who'd been born with his special abilities as heroes and began to see them as threats. They started writing laws banning the sons of David and putting bounties on their heads. The line was multiplying too fast, and they were having a hard time keeping eyes on it. Not all of the children born of this line have these superpowers...not even most. But the few that do is a few too many for certain power structures. They became prized game for flesh hunters."

"So, you're saying Judah is of this line?" I asked.

Rome smiled, but it didn't reach his eyes. "I'm saying you all are." The sound of a motorcycle filled the air.

Rome's eyes narrowed as his gaze fell on his wife. "What is he doing here?"

She shrugged. "What are you looking at me for? I didn't invite him."

The rider brought his bike to a stop right in front of us. He reached up and took his helmet off, and my day brightened. My man here was blew back. I damn near smiled. It had been a long time since that sweet smoke graced my lungs and I was long overdue.

As if he could sense my need, he grinned. "Damn, this nigga look just like Jo. I had to come see for myself."

"Man, what you doing here?!" Rome hissed. "You know if that dude see you, I'm gon' have to hear his mouth."

The kid got off the bike and walked toward me. "Aye, man, ain't nobody scared of him. It's a free country. I can go wherever the hell I want to go. Rob..." he said holding up his fist.

I touched my fist to his with a matching grin on my face. "Tucker..."

"I can tell me and you gon' be real cool, huh?" He shifted his eyebrows in a way that made me chuckle.

I nodded. "Oh yeah, you look like my kind of friend."

Rome grabbed him by the shoulder and snatched him away from me. "Tuck, man, I know you been in rehab and sh*t. Don't let my li'l brotha cause you to backtrack."

What the f*ck?

"Rehab?! I ain't been in rehab. I was doing some sh*t for the job. But since I ain't working that job no more, 'cause I'm dead, imma need you to mind yo' business."

"Yeah, mutha f*cka!" Rob mocked from behind him in a high pitched voice. "Mind yo' business..." Rome suddenly turned toward him, and the kid jumped two feet back, holding up his hands.

"I'm just playing, bro." When Rome continued walking, the kid fell into step with us. "I just came to watch y'all train; that's all."

"You better not be here to sneak Nak no more bullsh*t.

She's been complaining about her weig—" He didn't get a chance to finish that before she punched him in the arm.

"Nossa! Romeo…" she whined, sounding real girly, which was crazy as hell, seeing how damn deadly she is.

"That's private…you don't have to tell everybody."

"What?!" he asked holding up his hands. "Yeah, you gained a few pounds…it's sexy though." She went to try and punch him again, but he dodged her blow.

"You play too much." She laughed when he wrapped his arms around her to try and steal a kiss.

"Man, I'm done with that. I get it; she all about the vegetables. I ain't going to sneak her nothing else…it's over," Rob told him when his brother shot him an evil glance.

I had to grind my teeth to keep from laughing out though. The whole time the kid was telling him that, he was slipping a big-ass glazed honeybun to Nak, who took it and stashed it in the pocket of her cargo pants.

Yeah, me and Rob were going to get along just fine.

When we got to the training area, I was surprised to see other soldiers running various drills on the field. Judah stood with two men looking under the hood of an army green jeep. There were two other jeeps next to it. When he saw us approaching, they closed the hood as he picked up a towel to clean his hands.

"I see you finally decided to unattach yourself from your wife's skirt long enough to join us." The two fellas that stood next to him chuckled. My angry gaze fell on them and the smile left their faces.

"Didn't have much of a choice. An animal came in and shot up my wife's bed."

One side of his mouth lifted in what could be a grin. "Is that right?"

I nodded… "That's right." The Bully paced back and forth inside my soul. It could sense the threat standing in front of me who called himself my brotha.

"I guess you a tough guy, huh?" Judah continued.

I shrugged. "I can pull my weight."

That one-sided grin grew. "Is that right?"

I started to get a bad feeling at that point. Rome and Jo looked down at the ground as they slowly shook their heads. The grin on their faces said they knew some sh*t. But I ain't never been one to let nobody railroad me, so sh*t, I told him what the f*ck was up.

"That's right."

"Okay. Show me. Get in." He nodded his head toward the jeeps.

As we walked toward the vehicles, Rob fell into step next to me. "Hey, bruh, this sick bastard finna make you wish you were dead. You gon' need this when you done." He slid a beautifully rolled blunt halfway out of his pocket. I be damned if my mouth didn't water.

"Hey!" Judah bellowed when he finally spotted Rob. "Get the f*ck off my field, you little sh*t!"

"I'll find you," Rob whispered before he looked up at Judah and yelled, "Maaan, don't nobody want to be on the field with yo—" Whatever else he was going to say was cut short when Judah took a step toward him and he hauled ass the other way.

We all piled into the three jeeps and rode deeper into the woods. "What did I just get myself into?" I grumbled to no one in particular.

It was Rome who answered me. "I don't know, bro, but whatever it is…don't sound good."

"Naw, it don't," Jo agreed.

"The crazy part about it is, it sounds like he got us into it too," Nak muttered from where she sat on the back seat between her husband and Jo.

We rode for about another fifteen minutes before the jeeps came to a stop at a big rushing river that was surrounded on both sides by an intense-ass looking obstacle course. The sound of the water rushing down the slope was loud in the clearing.

Jo grunted. "Why does this remind me of Hell Week at BUDS training?"

"Because it is," Nak muttered.

"Learning to fight without your alters won't be easy, but it can be done," Judah began as he came to a stop in front of us. "The trick is making yourself stronger than them. Your will has to outpower theirs."

I frowned. What the hell was he talking about? The Bully can do sh*t I will never be able to do.

As if he could hear my thoughts, Judah's gaze fell on me. "What? Does your alter use a separate body, or does he borrow your body? It's a damn shame he knows how to use it better than you." He crossed his arms as he began to pace in front of us. I felt like I was at BUDS school; this dude was a drill sergeant.

"It's your body he borrows, your strength, your speed, your rage…" As he spoke, he stopped in front of each of us to look us in the eye.

"Today, you will learn how to make your will stronger than theirs." He held up his hand and gestured toward the obstacle course behind him. "What you see before you is an eight-hour obstacle course. For the next eight hours, I'm going to cause you intense pain. And I dare you to let those mutha f*ckas loose. I'll beat yo' asses and theirs."

Several of the other soldiers that had been running drills back on the training field had joined us; I wondered if they were going to do the course with us.

"The general goal of these trainings is teamwork, but today, I'm going to do something different. There is no secret you boys---" his gaze went to Nak, "and girl can hold your weight pretty good amongst civilians."

Jo chuckled as he rubbed his hand down the front of his shirt. "Bruh, we do pretty good at holding our weight amongst soldiers too."

Rome nodded in agreement. "And for once, he ain't bragging. He just speaking the truth."

"Yeah, you may be right," Judah spoke as if he was thinking heavily on something. "But I wonder how you'll stand up against each other."

"As a matter of fact," he continued, "I wonder how you three will stand up against Nak."

"Nak??" Rome, Jo, and I said at the same time. The Old Man chuckled.

"Meee?" The muffled voice came from next to us. We all turned to look at Rome's wife who was in the process of stuffing half a honeybun in her mouth. Judah's comment had surprised her just as much as it had us. I did chuckle then; she was busted red-handed. Rome narrowed his gaze at her, but since she was busted, she shrugged and looking him directly in the eyes, and went on and devoured the rest of the pastry, licking her lips when she was done.

"Yeah, Nak..." Judah continued. "I got money; say she beat all of you with time to spare."

Both Rome and Jo chuckled. "You are aware that Nak and I did BUDS training together. We both did this course. Not only did I beat her, I had to encourage her to make it to the finish line," Jo replied in his ever so arrogant manner.

Nak shook her head. "Naw, Sarge, I don't remember it going down like that."

"How much dough you talking?" Rome asked with a clever grin on his face. "I love my lady, but if the price is right, I'll get in that ass."

Judah nodded satisfied. "A hundred grand…"

Al whistled… "Yikes!"

"I'll take that bet," I told them. Hell yeah, I'll take that bet. I know Nak was tough for a girl, but haven't we just established that she was gaining weight from stuffing the honeybuns in her mouth? I mean, sh*t, if Judah was just trying to give money away, I'll take it.

"Me too…" Jo and Rome said at the same time.

Judah clapped his hands together. "Good! And I tell you what, boys… I'm going to make it even easier for you. Nak, you still remember your way around the course?"

She nodded. "Yep."

"All y'all have to do is keep up with her. You don't even have to beat her…just keep up."

"Bro, are you trying to insult me on purpose?" Jo asked. "I know back at that cave you said Nak was your best warrior. Surely you don't really believe that, do you?" he asked the question as if he felt sorry for Judah.

"Prove me wrong, little brotha."

Jo grinned. "I guess I'm going to have to."

"Now, as I was saying earlier, there are a few rules. The men you see standing before you today is going to assist you through the course. You are not to speak to them unless you're saying yes sir or no sir. Don't growl at them or threaten them, and you for damn sure better not touch 'em."

Side note: That should have been a warning for us that this thing was not going to go how we imagined. We should have stopped then. But now that I think about it, I don't think we had much of a choice.

"If you allow your alters to take over, I will hurt you. You better do your very best to keep them mutha f*ckas in check. Separate your mind from your body, boys!" He turned and walked back toward the jeep.

"Old Man, you're with me." He looked at us over his shoulder. "What the hell you waiting on?! Go!"

Nak took off, and so did we.

"We're just going to do a little warming up," one of the soldiers that had been standing next to Judah said as he ran alongside us. Because I don't know the mutha f*cka's name, for the sake of this story, I'll call him Blondie.

"But although we're warming up, it doesn't give you an excuse to slack off!" he yelled. "Move faster!"

The four of us pumped our legs and arms, sprinting across the forest floor. We leaped over logs and jumped across ditches.

"Move faster!" Blondie yelled! And that's when I realized this was going to be a long eight hours. If this mutha f*cka yelled at me again, I was going to trip his b*tch ass and step on his head.

"Naphtali! I'm watching you!" came Judah's voice from a megaphone. I looked over to see him standing up in the jeep that the Old Man drove on a trail alongside where we ran with the f*cking megaphone in his hand.

*If they wanted us to go faster, why the hell didn't they let us run on the trail instead of this bumpy-ass path?*

"Why are they jogging?" Judah asked. The soldier that ran with us shrugged.

"I told them to run faster, sir, but they've refused."

*Wait!* Oh yeah, me and Blondie was going to have a little chat.

"Sanders!" Judah called into the megaphone. "Let loose the dogs."

"What the f*ck?!" Jo growled when what sounded like laughter came from behind us.

Rome looked back. "Are those...hyenas?"

I glanced back and nearly ran into a tree. "Those the biggest hyenas I've ever seen!"

There had to be at least ten of the big bastards chasing after us.

"Those boys are hungry! They haven't eaten in days. You four look like big-ass, juicy turkeys running in front of them... Mmmmm! Good eating!" Judah laughed.

"Y'all thought he didn't have a sense of humor!" Rome yelled as he jumped over a log in his path. "He has one; it's just really f*cked up!"

The hyenas were gaining on us. When Blondie saw how close they were, he grabbed onto a tree and hauled ass up the mutha f*cka. My legs were beginning to burn, and my lungs felt like sh*t. I don't give a f*ck what Judah talking 'bout; if one of them big-ass, lab-grown dogs touch me, I'm going to f*ck them up.

The Bully began to pace restlessly in my soul. *Oh sh*t! Oh sh*t!* With my heart beating this fast, it was no way I could hold him off for long.

"Then let me loose, boy! You wasn't made to deal with sh*t like this."

I could now hear the breathing of the animals behind us. My gaze went to Judah. He was now holding a pair of binoculars, watching us carefully.

"This way!" Nak yelled as she suddenly went down in a slide and disappeared. Rome followed her and then Jo; I was right behind him. Somehow, she'd spotted a drop-off. All four of us hit the ground in a roll and got back to our feet. This bought us a few seconds as the hyenas had to find another way around the drop-off.

"Good job, Nak!" Judah called. Yeah, it was a really good job. That bought us enough time to finish the two miles with hyenas at a comfortable distance behind us.

Breathing heavily, we watched as the animals' handlers herded them up using big chunks of bloody meat.

The Old Man brought the jeep to a stop in front of us. "Good job," Judah said, stepping down out of it. "Didn't think you was going to make it, smoky bear." He slammed my shoulder, and I damn near broke a molar trying to keep the Bully at bay.

"Who does he think he's playing with? Let me f*ck him up! Let me loose!"

I wasn't going to make it…this wasn't going to work.

"Why don't you boys—" Judah's gaze went to Nak, "and girl have a little cooldown. Swim back to your starting point." He turned to get back in the vehicle, but Rome's voice brought him to a stop.

"Dude, you smoking! It's freezing out here!"

"Not to mention that violent current of the river. That's dangerous!" Jo added.

Judah exhaled. "You sound like two overgrown vaginas. Are you finished wasting my time?"

Remember when I told y'all earlier that I can sometimes feel my brothers? I was feeling Jo's rage right now. Like me, he was struggling to keep his alter at bay. I don't think he was going to make it either. Instead of responding, his hands balled into fists, and his nostrils flared.

Judah grinned and closed the gap between them, violating Jo's personal space big-time. "What? You got something you want to say to me?"

"No!" Jo bit out, but I'm telling you, this boy was pissed; I could feel his rage like it was my own.

"Then get yo' b*tch ass down the f*cking river." He stood for a moment daring him to act on his feelings. When Jo didn't take his bait, he turned and moseyed on to the vehicle. Seconds later the meaty tires of the jeep kicked up dirt as they headed back the way they came.

Nak shook her head walking toward the river. "Sarge, I think your brother is trying to test you, to see how much you can take before you let the Politician free. Don't give him what he wants."

She held her hand out for Rome. "Come on, meu rei; try and separate your mind from your body. Don't fight against the current."

Rome looked at her and nodded before his gaze came back to us. "I think Nak's right. He's trying to get under y'all skin. It's almost as if he wants you to let your alters free." He shook his head. "Don't let him." After that, he followed his wife into the cold, raging river. Seconds later they were being swept downstream.

Jo exhaled as he headed toward the river. "I don't think

I'm going to make it. I can't control the Politician. Twice he almost took over."

I nodded, falling into step next to him. "Yeah, me too. What do you think he's going to do if they take over?"

"I don't know...but I got a feeling we're going to find out," he said before he dove into the river.

*I got the same feeling...* I inhaled and followed him in.

# Chapter 10

## Face Your Fears

### Free

"THANK you for inviting me over for dinner," I told Journey again as she and I sat in front of our now empty plates enjoying an after-supper cup of tea.

She waved her hand. "It's no problem. If not for you I would be having dinner alone. The children have already eaten and are down for the night. I don't know why their training has run so late."

"Does it normally run late like this?"

She shook her head, but then she thought about it. "Well… sometimes. Nak says it's like that 'cause Judah doesn't have anyone to go home to, so he doesn't have any sympathy for his married soldiers."

I sat up a bit in my chair, very glad she brought up Judah. After what happened today, I was ready to leave, convinced this land was owned by a maniac. But Tucker assured me everything was okay, and that his brother had an unorthodox way of dealing with his men.

"So, about Judah... Is he okay? Should I be worried?"

Journey chuckled. "Nahhh. He has this rough exterior. But I think he's a big old teddy bear inside."

I looked at her as if she'd lost her mind. There were several kinds of bears I would have compared Judah to; teddy was not one of them.

"Doc, of all people, you should be able to see when someone is using gruffness as a defense mechanism."

"Defense mechanism? The man emptied the clip of his gun in a pillow on our bed, the same pillow my husband had been laying on seconds before."

She grimaced as she nodded her head a bit. "Yeah, I can see how that would come across as a bit savage, but I'm telling you, underneath all that barbarianism is a really sweet guy."

Well...she was young. The world hadn't jaded her the way it had me. And I couldn't bring myself to taint her, so I just responded with an, "If you say so, sweetheart."

She took a sip of her tea, thinking on something before she spoke. "Have you met my brother Rob yet?"

I shook my head. "No, I don't think that I have."

She laughed. "Don't worry; you will. Anyway, Rob is a very special individual. He can see things in people and capture it on canvas." As she spoke she had a smile on her face."It's like he can sense what makes them happy or would make them happy, even if they don't know it." She shook her head. "And I don't think there is anybody here that gets under Judah's skin as much as Rob."

"You see? Why would someone like that get under his skin? There's something wrong with that."

Journey's smile grew. "Well... Rob can also be a brat. And he's a pothead. I mean an *extreeeeme* pothead. The boy smokes so much weed he can never take anything serious. So out of all the folks here he could bug, can you guess who he chose?" She nodded. "Judah."

This brought a smile to my face. "How does he bug him?"

She exhaled dramatically. "Girl... First all, he knows Judah likes his privacy. So what does Rob do? Trespass at his place big-time. My brother is a brilliant artist, and he's decided that the most beautiful view he's ever seen is in back of Judah's place. So he sits out there staring at the view, smoking his weed. Then he'll get the munchies and break into Judah's garage where the grouchy man keeps a fridge full of beer and junk food and help himself."

That made me laugh. Rob had officially become my hero. If there is anybody who deserves that, it's the maniac that shot at my poor Tucker.

"If Judah was all that bad, why is Rob still alive?" she asked. "You've seen him. Does he look like a man that has a problem taking out an enemy?"

I shook my head. No, he did not look like a man that had a problem taking out an enemy. I would really hate to be that enemy.

"See... Why hasn't he killed Rob? He hasn't even hit him or anything. And get this... Rob, without asking Judah, started painting this elaborate mural on one of the walls in the grouchy man's garage. It's this crazy intricate piece. It doesn't make sense to anybody but Rob, and... apparently Judah."

"When he came out and saw Rob painting, his first response was to yell at him. But then he looked at the mural and I don't know...got lost in it. Rome say it's the darndest thing. He said the other day he went looking for Rob and found him in Judah's garage. He stood just out of sight when he heard Rob talking. Sometimes when my brother gets high, he has these thoughts that's really only deep to him. Well, anyway, Rome hears him going in on one of his tangents, talking about the stars and galaxies and possibilities." She gave me a silly look that made me laugh.

"Rome peeps around the corner and is surprised as heck to see Judah himself sitting there with a beer in his hand, watching my brother paint this mural and listening to his nonsense. Now granted, he had a frown on his face the whole time, but he listened. And when Rob gets done, Judah looks at him and says... *'That's the dumbest sh\*t I ever heard."* She and I both had a good laugh at that.

"You see?" she continues, "He's a hard man and very uncouth and extremely unsociable. But then he does things like put up with my twenty-three-year-old pothead brother. He says he doesn't like Rob, but his action shows differently. Rob says Judah gets extra beer and snacks now, and he's even broken into Judah's garage to find new cans of paint waiting on him. Now I ask you, does that sound like someone who is truly a bad guy?"

Before I could respond, a loud thump hit the front door. She and I both turned around just as the door opened and

Rome, Nak, and Al stumbled in supporting a badly beaten Tucker and Jo.

We cried out in unison jumping up to hurry to our husbands.

"What happened to him?" Journey demanded, but no one answered, too concerned with trying to get the men seated and then treated.

Tucker's face was severely swollen, he had cuts over both of his eyes that dripped blood, and his lip was split and bleeding badly as well. We got them both to the kitchen table as Journey hurried to get supplies.

I looked down in Tucker's face that although bruised pretty good, was still very handsome as I gently began to clean the blood away.

"Is this going to become a habit?" I whispered. He chuckled, but it was cut short with a hiss because of the pain from his cracked lip.

"What happened?" Journey repeated, now that their cuts were cleaned and bandaged. They really looked like twins now. Goodness!

"Lost a hundred grand," Jo grumbled through his swollen lips.

Tucker groaned. "Damn! Why did you remind me? I was trying to forget."

Rome frowned. "Do you think he wants it collectively or a hundred grand from each of us?"

"What are you guys talking about? And what does that have to do with your injuries?" I asked, completely lost.

"Well, nothing and everything. We got in a fight with our big brother and lost," Jo supplied.

Journey and my gaze met over their heads before she frowned down at her husband.

"Are you nuts?! Why would you fight him?"

Rome chuckled as he and Nak took a seat. "It wasn't them that fought and lost; it was their alters."

"Hey, kids, I'm going to get on out of here. I know my wife is waiting. I'll talk to you guys tomorrow," Al said before he touched Jo's shoulder. "You alright, son?"

Jo nodded. "Yeah, you know I heal quickly. I'm already feeling better."

"That's my boy," Al said patting him on the shoulder before giving us all a wave goodbye. As soon as the door shut, our gazes came back to Rome.

"What do you mean, their alters fought and lost?" I asked. This was a complete shock to me. I didn't think that there was anybody in the world who could mess with Tucker when his other personality falls on him.

Rome chuckled again shaking his head. "Man, I ain't never seen no sh*t like that a day in my life. Judah had us doing this eight-hour obstacle course. And I ain't gon' lie; the sh*t was hard as hell."

"Speak for yourself; it was easy to me," Nak told him as she stood to peek into Journey's pots. "Sis?" she asked.

Journey nodded. "Girl, you know you can help yourself."

Nak grinned big and began to make her and Rome a plate. Meanwhile the three men mean mugged her back.

"You do realize you helped him take a hundred grand from our house, from your precious horses. Don't know how I'm going to be able to buy feed for them now," Rome hissed with a petty frown on his face.

Nak laughed from the stove. "Yeah, right, you won't miss that little money. Pay up and stop whining." The frown grew on Rome's face, but I think it was the chuckle that escaped from Jo's busted lips that really pissed him off.

"That's a damn shame; your wife is more athletic than you."

"Mutha f*cka, she beat you too!" he yelled.

"Shush, boy! You going to wake up the kids," Journey admonished him.

"Yeah, shut up before you wake my kids. And she's not my wife, so I don't feel as bad as you're probably feeling right now."

Tucker chuckled shaking his head at them.

"Leave him alone, Sarge. He may not be as banged up as you guys are, but he's in pain too," Nak said sitting a plate in front of Rome that had no meat on it.

"I'm nowhere near as banged up as they are," Rome hissed before he began to fork food into his mouth. "Y'all should have seen it. Judah would get into one of these boy's faces, yelling at them, calling them b*tches and pussies while they were doing something strenuous like standing on a log while holding a log... for like an hour straight."

He pointed his fork at Tucker. "My man Tuck was the first one to lose it. His brother got to yelling at him, my man tossed the damn log to the side and jumped on Judah's ass." He shook his head while he chewed.

"Wasn't pretty. They looked like two wild-ass lions fighting over a bone. Couldn't have paid me to step between them and try and break it up."

"What happened?" I asked, now on the edge of my seat.

Rome looked at me with a grin on his face. "What do you mean, what happened? Judah beat his ass until the Bully retreated." He pointed his fork at Jo. "When this one saw how bad Judah was beating Tuck's ass, he lost it; Politician took over him, and then he jumped on Judah." He shook his head again, chewing another mouthful of food.

"Judah beat both of their asses at the same time."

Nak chuckled. "It was nuts. I felt bad."

"Not bad enough to assist a brother though, huh?" Jo grumbled.

"I said I felt bad, not crazy," she replied, taking a big bite out of her piece of chicken.

"I don't understand his method of training. How is beating you guys up helping?" I asked. They all seemed to be alright with what had happened, but I wasn't. There was nothing healthy about this.

Rome shrugged. "I don't know, Doc. Looks like his method may have worked. He beat them so bad, that to preserve their lives, they forced their alters to retreat while under extreme distress. As far as I know, they've never been able to do that before."

"Yeah, he's helping us to be able to control when our alters take over," Tucker said, still favoring his busted lip. I wanted to ask him if he was hungry, but I doubt he could eat anything with the condition of his mouth.

"I still don't understand how beating you will help anything."

He chuckled. "Well, every time the Bully took over, he knocked him back to where he belonged."

"It's kind of like shock therapy," Rome supplied before

he reached over with his fork and tried to steal the greens off Nak's plate.

She turned her plate to the side just in time to cause his fork to hit the table. "Nossa Romeo... Get your own."

"Can't you see this is all inhumane? When dealing with someone with Dissociative Identity Disorder, brute force trauma can cause setbacks rather than breakthroughs."

"Yeah, that would be true if we were dealing with the typical case of Dissociative Identity Disorder," Rome said, "Their situation is quite different. The doctor that splintered their minds used very similar tactics to create the alters; Judah is simply using the same tactics to reverse what was done. Kind of like the idea behind the hair of the dog that bit me. He's refracturing their minds…if that makes any sense. It's actually quite brilliant."

I shook my head. "It doesn't make any sense to me. It reminds me of the madness I read in my grandmother's medical journals about a doctor she worked for. He performed similar experiments on his subjects. It was plain brutality."

Rome froze from where he was harassing his wife to look at me. "Your grandmother left medical journals?"

I frowned confused. "Ummm…yes. She—wait! Do you know my grandmother?"

"I know of her?"

"What do you mean?"

"My bots found her name in a few odd places it shouldn't have been. And of course, because this information is always on the move, I haven't quite pegged her connection with all of this. However, if you have journals, they could be the missing link or get me that much closer to finding the missing link."

"I can't see how her information will help you. I've been doing a lot of digging myself trying to find out about my father."

Tucker's gaze came to me. "What's going on with your father?"

I exhaled, shaking my head. "Nothing…just something Angie had me looking into before we left." I quickly looked away before he could read more into that. I wasn't ready to share the news with anybody that I didn't know who my father was.

"Where can we find these journals?" Rome asked.

"Well, I had a few of them at the hotel with me in Vegas. Maybe if I can somehow get my things—"

"Let me handle that," Rome cut me off. "Where are the rest?"

"At my house. But how can we go back without—"

Rome grinned. "Leave that to me too, Doc. Come on, *minha anjo*," he said pushing back from the table. "We have work to do, my sweet lady."

Nak nodded as she got up taking her and Rome's plate to the sink.

"But they destroyed all of our homes. What makes you think the doctor's house is still standing?" Jo asked.

Rome's gaze came to Tucker. Whatever he was about to say was going to hurt.

"They've destroyed both Tucker's childhood home and his place on the lake. The doctor's house is still standing, probably because her late grandmother put the house in her son's name."

I reached for Tucker's hand, and he clutched it tightly, the only sign he showed that he was bothered by Rome's news.

"But we need to move fast before they realize their mistake. Those journals could be priceless," Rome continued.

I thought about Grapefruit and my friends. I wished there was some way that he could let them know I was alright. They can be trusted. They won't tell anyone that I'm alive. And I really missed my cat.

Before I could work up the courage to ask him about it, he and Nak were bidding us goodnight.

Damn it!

Although it looked like it hurt like hell, Tucker stood from his chair. He grabbed Jo's car keys off the counter before taking my hand and pulling me from my chair.

"I'm borrowing your car, bro," he muttered as he headed toward the door, pulling me in his wake. "Nice seeing you again, sis!" he called over his shoulder to Journey.

"Nice seeing you again too. Don't be a stranger," she called back. "I'll talk to you tomorrow, Free."

I waved at her. "Okay, thanks again for dinner."

"When am I going to get my car back?" Jo called

———

TUCKER BROUGHT the car to a stop in front of our house and killed the engine, but he didn't get out. He just sat for a moment staring down at the keys he held in his hand.

"What happened with your father, Free? I don't like it when you lie to me." His words were quiet.

I exhaled. I should have known he would catch that.

"Before we left to go to Vegas, Angie came to my house and informed me that the man I'd always knew as my father was not." I tried to swallow the lump forming in my throat.

Tucker's gaze came to me and I could see the hurt in his eyes. "Why didn't you tell me?"

I opened my mouth, but no words came out. I didn't have a good reason besides the fact that I was ashamed and a bit confused.

He turned to look out the front window before shaking his head. "I ain't never felt good enough to be your man. Which is f\*cked up because no matter how hard I try, I can't make myself stop loving you."

His gaze came back to mine. "Why can't I stop loving you?"

His whispered question tore at my heart. Tears came to my eyes. Once again I opened my mouth to speak, but no words came out.

"Come on, Doc, you're the smartest person I know. Why do I love a woman who won't love me back?"

I wanted to tell him that I loved him. I wanted to tell him just how broken I really am. I wanted to tell him so much.

*Then why haven't you?*

That question was as damning as the look of pain in his eyes. He leaned over and gently placed a kiss on my forehead before getting out of the car and walking into the house, leaving me sitting there staring after him, feeling as if my heart had been split in two.

*You're extremely vain, child.* The Preacher's words sounded loud in the quietness of the car. *If your patients could fix themselves, then why do they come to you?*

Why do I have to be the one to always have it together?

Why do I always have to be the doctor? Why can't I ever show people my scars?

*Are you better than them? If so, what makes you better?*

I flung open the car door and ran into the house. I didn't stop running until I stood at the bathroom door where Tucker was easing his bruised body down into a hot bath he'd ran for himself.

"I was ashamed," I told him. But my words came out breathy because my heart was beating extremely fast. I've never done anything like this. I've never shown my weakness to anybody.

"I was ashamed to tell you about my sister's wedding because I didn't want you to see how much they hated me."

Tears came to my eyes. "When we were young, I was too ashamed to tell you I lived in a home where nobody loved me, not even my father."

I wiped angrily at the tears underneath my glasses. "I hate crying; I hate feeling sorry for myself. I hate the fact that no one loved me!" The last of my words were barely comprehensible because I was crying so bad.

"And now I found out that I don't even have a father. I don't have anybody, I—"

He stood from the tub, crossed the floor dripping wet, and scooped me up in his arms.

"No, baby, that ain't true. You always had me; I've always loved you," he growled as he carried me back to the tub and stepped in, submerging us both in the hot water, him gloriously naked and me fully clothed. Water gushed out over the side, but he didn't seem to care.

Cradling me in his arms like a baby, he reached up and

dried my tears. "I knew that the twins picked fun at you, but I thought it was because they were jealous. I didn't know you were having a hard time at home with Angie and your dad."

I nodded. "After my mother died, my dad came and got me, bringing me back to Angie's house. But she never wanted me there, and she didn't keep that fact a secret. They gave me a bedroom in the basement away from everyone else's. I had to wear all of the twins' hand-me-downs. To pay for room and board and my schooling, I had to do all the cleaning and the cooking."

"At first I tried to do everything perfectly, thinking it would earn Angie's love, but it never did." A fresh wave of tears came with that confession.

Tucker dried them away. "What about your father? Why did he allow that b*tch to treat you that way?"

I chuckled without any humor. "I used to think it was because he was freeloading just like I was, but now I know the truth. He never felt a parental connection toward me. So why would he fight for me?"

Tucker's nostrils flared. "That mutha f*cka!" he hissed before his gaze came back to mine. "But why were you looking in your grandmother's medical journals for answers about him?"

"My fake grandmother, you mean." I shook my head. "It's a whole mess. Angie said something about me being Dorothy, my fake grandmother's investment. She said Dorothy had been so confident that she could plunk me down and I would be the perfect bait to capture the heart of the prince."

Naphtali frowned. "What the hell does that mean?"

I shrugged shaking my head. "I don't know. I don't know what any of it means. I've been trying to read through Dorothy's journals to try and find out. But I keep getting distracted with her studies on a patient she called Daisy."

"What's so special about Daisy?"

"I don't know…something about her calls out to me. Dorothy completely destroyed her life for the purposes of science. She was a beautiful soul, and Dorothy got her hooked on LSD just so that she could control her."

Tucker shook his head. "Kind of sounds like what they did to us and our dad."

I nodded. "Yeah, it does."

"How did Dorothy and her b*tch-ass son get ahold of you after your mother died?"

"I don't know; it's what I've been trying to find out. But it's so much information to go through. I just haven't had time to sort everything out."

He nodded. "Don't worry, once Rome get ahold of that sh*t, it's a wrap."

"Do you think he'll be able to do it?"

"What? Get the stuff from your place?" I nodded.

"Sure, why not?"

For a moment neither of us spoke; we just sat there in the tub enjoying being connected to the other.

"Tuck?"

"Hmmm…"

"Do you ever think about Jackson and Asher?"

"Yep, all the time."

"Me too; I think about Rachel and Oaklee…and I miss Grapefruit so much." The last of my statement made him growl.

"I hope he gets hit by a bus."

"Tucker!" I cried sitting up in the water to look at him.

He had the nerve to have a surprised look on his face. "What?!"

I laughed hitting him in the chest. "You know what! Why would you say that about that sweet little kitty?"

"That cat is as sweet as Satan."

I laid my head back on his chest, smiling. "He's not Satan; he's really nice when you get to know him."

He put his finger underneath my chin, lifting it a bit so that I was looking up into his eyes, our lips only inches apart.

"Do you feel better?"

My smile grew as I nodded. "Yeah…I do."

It was true. After talking to him I felt like a weight had been lifted from my shoulders. I'd never shared with anyone how I used to try and earn Angie's love or how much the fact that they refused to treat me like family had hurt. I've always presented a strong front to the world, including my best friends. I always made Rachel believe I wasn't fazed by the way they treated me and was just biding my time.

But now that I've confessed my pain, I felt like a new woman. Like now, I can truly heal.

"I'm sorry you were going through all that at home, only to come to school and have to deal with my dumb ass," Tucker muttered.

I gently touched his bruised bottom lip. "It's okay, you can't help that fact that you're the world's biggest jerk."

He kissed my thumb. "I guess we're two peas of a pod. Don't know where the f*ck we came from."

I laughed. "I guess you're right. But there is one thing I do know."

He reached up and dried away the last of my tears that still lingered. "Yeah...what's that?"

I didn't speak for a moment. I just sat and drowned in his intense gaze. How could I have missed the way it's always burned for me?

I gently caressed his lip again. "I know that I love you with my whole heart and soul..."

# Chapter 11

Finding Our Way

Free

SO DO you guys remember when I asked Tucker if him coming home bruised and battered would become a habit? Well, for the next two weeks it would be. Both he and Jo came home sporting new bruises on top of the old ones. The crazy men didn't even seem to mind. They laughed and joked like it was perfectly normal that their older brother beat the crap out of them every day.

Tucker seems to think he's getting better. He came home the other day ecstatic that for the first time in his life, he was able to control the Bully. He said his brother had attacked him with a sword, and instead of the Bully stepping forward to keep them safe, he defended himself.

I don't know. Maybe Rome is right and there was actually something to Judah's brute form of therapy. Tucker's spirits have really lifted from when we first got here. He even borrowed his brother's car to take me shopping for our place after he finished his training a few nights ago. Next week, we're supposed to go shopping for our own vehicle.

Rome being the hacker extraordinaire that he is, helped us to settle our affairs back home. We each made a will where we gave most of our savings to two mystery foundations that happened to be us. I gave Rachel my little book house with enough money to do the repairs that are needed.

Rome did some research and found two doctors that like me, Dr. Kimble, and Dr. Ross, sought to help the people in the community mentally kick the habits that were holding them back. One doctor was located in Tennessee and the other in California. Neither of them operated in their own clinics and was being limited to what they could do by all the red tape. The opportunity to not only be able to run their own clinic but to also have access to several huge grants that Rome somehow found, got them both to readily agree.

However, there were two stipulations. They had to keep on Oaklee, who knew that clinic better than anyone and give her a much-needed raise. And they had to agree to co-own the clinic with Dr. Ross and Dr. Kimble. The four of them should be able to better meet the workload that location receives.

Although I am sad that I had to leave my clinic, the fact that my absence brought it much- needed resources made it worth the while... I guess.

You know what? I'm just going to be honest with you

guys; it's been two weeks since we've been here and I'm *miserable!* I don't know how to be inactive. Outside of decorating our new home and baking, I have nothing to do.

Tucker had his training. At first, it was something he didn't want to do, but now, he's really into it. Journey has her greenhouse and her children. Sometimes I went over and visited with them, maybe watch her work with her plants for a little while, and although the greenhouse is extremely beautiful, it doesn't give me the joy the clinic gave me.

And it didn't help that Nak and Rome had left to get my grandmother's journals. I nearly cried when she told me it was time for them to go. But she said that Rome had just received a message from his friend named Hitter, the only man outside of us who knew he was still alive. Apparently Hitter was getting married to the Tea Maker, and he really wanted Rome to be there.

Before she left, I'd told her about my Grapefruit and how much I missed him, so she dropped off her Giant for me to babysit while she was gone, trying to make me feel a little better. While it's true that Giant had a lot of personality for one so tiny, he was no Grapefruit.

And if all that wasn't enough to make me blue...I'm late.

Yep, you heard right. I haven't gotten my period. This morning I confided in Journey, and she went with me to the drug store to get a pregnancy test. She came back to my place to sit with me as we waited for the results. Let me tell you, that was the longest five minutes of my life. I was excited and afraid at the same time. Excited because the thought of being a mommy warms my heart, and afraid because Tucker and I never talked about having children.

Does he even want kids? We haven't been using any protection, so surely he knew that there was a possibility this could happen. Although Jo and Journey seem to be raising children in this self-imposed exile pretty well, will we be able to step up to that challenge?

And then the five minutes ended, and the two of us were left staring down at the double-positive signs. I don't know what kind of expression I wore on my face, but whatever it was, it caused an uneasy, overly bright smile to come to Journey's.

"You're going to be a mommy, Free! This is excellent news!" she cried.

I nodded and tried to smile through my shock. *I was going to be a mommy.*

I was having my bully's baby…

Oh my God! I was going to be a mommy!!!

Journey left a couple of hours before Tucker was due to be home, giving me time to get myself together. Her sweet mother, Abby, continues to cook for us sometimes, even though we have a fully stocked fridge. I was warming up the smothered steak and potatoes she made when Tucker walked through the door, sporting less bruises than he did the day before.

"Mmmm, something smells good," he said, coming behind me where I stood at the sink, wrapping his strong arms around me pulling me close.

*God, I love when he does that.*

"How was your day?" he asked, turning me around so that he could look into my eyes.

I smiled. "Very good. Journey came over for a little while. You can thank Mrs. Abby for the delicious aroma you smell."

He leaned down and kissed my lips. "And who can I thank for the delicious aroma that's my wife?" His lips trailed down to my neck.

"You can thank God for that," I told him giggling because his beard tickled me.

"Guess what I did today."

I fingered a new bruise just above his eye. "Got beat up by your older brother."

He shook his head. "Besides that."

I stepped back to turn down the oven. "What?"

"I talked to Judah today about building you a clinic here."

I frowned. "Here?"

He nodded. "Yeah, our numbers are growing. Before long, this place will be a little town. A lot of his soldiers, their wives, and kids could use someone to talk to about some things. Someone that they won't have to worry would judge them or go back and tell what they've entrusted to them."

I clutched his hands. "What did he say?"

For the first time, the smile on his face faltered. "Well... he didn't say no."

"What exactly did he say?"

"He said it was probably a waste of time."

And just like that, my hopes were dashed to the ground. But Tucker's was not.

"But I have an idea," he said still excited.

I shook my head, turning back to the sink. "Forget it, bae; it's something wrong with that man. He's so tarnished he can't see hope and possibilities. He's broken!"

Tucker put his hands on my waist and turned me back to face him. "That's it! That's my plan!"

I pursed my lips, completely lost. "I'm confused... what's your plan?"

"Well, would you say it is in your professional opinion that Judah is mentally bogged down and should really see someone about it?"

I nodded. "Ohhhh! Hell yeah! If ever someone needed to make an appointment with a psychiatrist, it's him."

Tucker grinned from ear to ear. "Why don't you be that psychiatrist? If you can help him then he would be first in line to help build your clinic. Just think...he'll be the challenge of your career. You're Moby Dick."

Wow! With just a few words Tucker gave birth to a fire inside me that would not be quenched.

"Didn't you take an oath to help the mentally f*cked up?"

I frowned. "Tucker!"

Chuckling he shook his head. "My bad. I mean the mentally unstable?"

I nodded. "Yes, I did!" I puffed out my chest a bit, feeling like superwoman. I kid you guys not, in that moment, I heard superhero music playing in my head. Could it be that Judah was just a lost soul crying out for help?

Here I'd been feeling blue because I have no more patients. Inactivity had been closing in on me when the challenge of my life has just been sitting here under my nose the whole time, beating the crap out of my poor husband every day. Judah needed someone to get to the root of his anger. He needed someone to talk to... Someone to trudge through the sludge that is his emotion...

Y'all...Judah needed help! And I was just the person for the job. Dr. Robinson—wait, no, I mean Dr. Pelletier—wait, no! It wasn't Pelletier either. Tucker told me the other day that we were taking on his real family's name. Dr. Law to the rescue.

Yeeeaaahh...I liked the sound of that.

Tucker grinned. "That's right, Doc...own that sh*t!"

"Yeah!" I cried, nodding my head as if I was the quarterback walking toward my toughest game. "Yeah! I'm going to own that sh*******t!" I yelled.

Tucker wrapped his arm around my waist and pulled me close before kissing me to the point of distraction. The kiss got so hot I had to wrap my arms around his neck so that my knees didn't give out.

"Wow! What was that for?" I asked when he finally drew his lips away.

"Glad to see you feeling motivated again. You had me worried over these last two weeks."

I bit my bottom lip to try and tame the cheesy grin that wanted to break through. "I didn't know you noticed." I'd done my best to hide my feelings from him. I didn't want him to start feeling bad for us being here.

"Yeah...I noticed." He reached up and gently rubbed his knuckle just underneath my eye. "That spark that's there in your eyes now has been missing. It was breaking my heart."

Oh shucks! Sometimes my big jerk can be so sweet. I palmed his face and brought his head back down for a kiss.

After dinner I stood at the sink washing dishes, trying to figure out the best time to tell Tucker about the baby. I was contemplating if I wanted to do something romantic or maybe tell him at halftime during the Lyons' game on Sunday. He was supposed to be making up a pot of his famous chili. Looks like our place was going to be where all the sports-watching parties took place. Tucker put a lot of care into duplicating his theater room that he had at the Pelletier mansion, on a much smaller scale of course, in the basement.

Anyway, I was trying to figure out a good time to surprise him when I looked up to see Journey's little brother sitting in back of our house on a little stone table we have out there, smoking his drugs.

"Oh my goodness!" I cried out. "Would you believe that kid is back? And he's out there smoking marijuana! Did you tell him that you've quit, and he should really think about doing it too?"

Tucker angrily walked to the window to peer out. "That little bastard! Yes, I've told him I quit! He know I don't smoke that bulls*t anymore! He's f*cking with us like he's f*cking with Judah! Let me go get rid of his ass!"

He stormed out of the back door. I waited till it was closed before I burst out into laughter. Oh my God, that never gets old. Tucker is a hot mess. He actually thinks I'm buying his crap. He's been pulling the same song and dance for the last two weeks.

I shook my head as I continued to clean up the kitchen.

*What am I going to do with that man?*


TUCKER


"AYE, man! Damn! Be careful of the blunt!" Rob yelled when I snatched his little ass up off the table and dragged him out of the backyard. I keep telling him to wait for me out front. The little sh*t is getting a kick out of almost getting me busted with Free.

"What I tell you about coming around here with this bullsh*t!" I said loudly. "You need to get yo' life together, man!"

When I was out of earshot of Free, I released the little brotha and helped straighten out his clothes.

"Sorry about that, buddy…"

"Yeah, whateva, nigga," he growled, giving me the evil eye. "I ain't going to keep putting up with this bullsh*t."

"Shut up!" I told him, muffing him and taking the blunt from him. "What the f*ck else you got to do?" I took a nice deep pull from the brown beauty. It had been a long day. This training Judah was taking us through was kicking our asses. Sh*t, I thought I had it rough at the academy.

My man, Rob here been coming through for me though. Apparently I was the only other person here who smoked weed; so he and I have become buddies by default. Plus, he was weed and entertainment. I can sit and listen to the kid talk sh*t for hours. This mutha f*cka is a nut. He's helped to make the last two weeks here breezy for me.

Naw, you know what? I take that back. Although it's f*cked up that my previous life fell apart, and everything I thought I knew about it was a lie, including my parents, my time here has been good.

I feel like I'm at home. *Sh*t…at long last.*

I'm loving it. Everything about it, even the training. Learning to control the Bully makes putting up with all of Judah's sh*t worth it. He's been showing us that letting our alters take over when our adrenaline reaches a certain level is something we do out of habit rather than necessity. I've always thought that the Bully was something that I could not control. Whenever I'm upset or threatened, he takes over.

Apparently when we were kids, Father, *the sick bastard that did this to us,* put us through one traumatic event after the other until depending on our alters became second nature. And then he hypnotized us so that we didn't remember any of the trauma...or him.

Yeah, it's some wild sh*t, but for the first time in my life, I'm prevailing over my alter, and I can't tell y'all how liberating that is. Like I said, I'm loving my time here.

But my baby isn't. Yeah, she's been putting on a brave face for me and smiling when she sees me watching. But I know my girl. I know when she's the most happy. Naw, can't let her take one for me. If she's not happy, then I'm not.

Judah had a lot of soldiers and their families living here under his command. Most of them are sent here to be trained for some secret branch of the f*cking government while others had been assigned with him to complete a mission or two and just chose to stick with him out of loyalty. And then there were those the military wrote off as damaged goods or what they called retired and extremely dangerous. Them that cannot integrate back into normal society come here to find a home amongst soldiers. Nearly all of their asses had PTSD and needed help.

Sh*t, take Nak for an example. She was easy on the eyes, but that chick had all kinds of sh*t going wrong in that head of hers. I guess crazy as f*ck did it for my man, Rome. And then...there was my brother, Judah. Who in this mutha f*cka needed more help than him? He was what Free would call certifiably off. She could open her a clinic here and really make a difference.

Between you and me, I may have lied to her about what Judah said when I first brought the idea to him.

"*Man...get out of here with that p\*ssy sh\*t,*" was his real response.

"*My girl a doctor, bro. She need to be able to use her talent.*" I gestured to the soldiers that ran drills around us. "*Some of these mutha f\*ckas need help. They f\*cked up, up here,*" I told him pointing to my head.

"*Look at her!*" I gestured to Nak, who'd just thrown a metal bowl at one of the younger soldier's head because he'd been eyeballing her chest while she was trying to explain some kind of technique to him.

"*Nobody here needs your wife trying to get in their f\*cking heads. Everybody is fine. A mental clinic would be a waste of time and resources.*"

"*I'll pay to get it built.*"

He waved my words away and walked off. "*So does that mean you'll think about it?*" I yelled after him.

"Aye, mane," Rob said, bringing my mind back to the present. "You one of the goonish niggas I know, yet...you scared of yo' girl."

"What the f\*ck you say to me?" This was the problem when smoking good weed. It was always that one mutha f\*cka that got too high and let some wild sh\*t slip from his lips.

Although I was trying to frown at his ass, I ended up grinning. Sh\*t, he and I were both higher than a mutha f\*cka. I don't know where the kid got this weed from up here in these mountains, but it sure in the hell was a very good batch.

"I'm just saying," he continued, as he tried to get the last few pulls from the roach. "You a big tough-ass nigga, but you got to hide behind the tree in your front yard to smoke so yo' girl won't see you. I mean, what she gon' do? Whoop yo' big ass or some sh*t?"

The little mutha f*cka was having a good laugh at my expense. I moved suddenly toward him and he squeaked like a girl; the roach he held in his hand went flying as he damn near balled up into the fetal position.

"Tuck, man! I was just playing!" he cried.

"For your information," I told him puffing out my chest. How damn dare he insinuate that I'm some kind of punk b*tch? "I ain't scared of nothing breathing. I'm the paterfamilias in my house. I run that piece. I step outside to smoke out of respect for my lady. That's yo' problem, young buck. You don't know nothing about respecting a lady, which is probably why you ain't got no lady."

It was his turn to puff out his chest. "You crazy as hell. I can have any one of these dude's daughters. They be fighting to get my attention. Don't come at me 'cause you have to sneak and get high like a shawty."

"You got me f*cked up! I'm a grown-ass man; I don't have to sneak to do sh*t! My girl do whatever the hell I say. I told her…hey, baby, imma be right back. Imma smoke one with my little buddy. And she said… *Okay, sweetheart, thank you so much for not smoking in the house on my new furniture. Thank you, God, for blessing me with a big strong man that knows how to respect a woman.*" The last of that I said in a girlie voice, imitating Free.

And that's when I realized I was higher than I thought. It was time for me to bounce before I be out here arguing with his little ass over who had the better hair lining. That's what high mutha f*ckas did, sit around and argue over stupid sh*t.

"Hey," I told him tapping his shoulder. Of course, he flinched like I punched him. "Let me get that Visine up out you."

He laughed as he pulled the Visine out of his pocket. "What you need the Visine fo', Debo? I thought you said you told your girl you was coming to smoke."

I snatched the eyedrops from him. "Shut up! I do this so my eyes don't get irritated."

"You full of sh*t, man."

"What you say?" I growled from between clenched teeth after I finished putting in the drops. I was tired of his sh*t.

The grin left his face as he quickly broke eye contact. "Nothing." *Smart kid...*

"That's what I thought, chump." I tossed the Visine over my shoulder as I began walking back to my house.

"I should knock yo' big ass out..." I heard him grumble under his breath as he tried to find where it landed.

I walked real tough until I got around the side of the house, and then I deflated like a balloon so that I could sneak in without Free hearing me. By this time, she was upstairs soaking in her bath, which means I had time to get showered and changed into something that didn't reek of weed.

And yeah, I know what I'd just said to the kid. You and me both know it was a bunch of bullsh*t. I've been walking on eggshells around my lady since we've been here. Something was going on with her and I couldn't figure out what.

I know she wasn't completely happy here, and I know she's been missing her clinic and her friends and probably that crackhead-ass cat. But there was something else going on with her. She seems distant. I'm scared as f*ck she wants to leave me or some sh*t.

The last thing she needs to find out is that I'm smoking again, especially after I had her believe that the only reason I was smoking in the first place was because of the Bully. But now that Judah was teaching us how to control our alters, I didn't have that excuse anymore.

I guess the cat is out of the bag. I really am addicted to marijuana, something she and those other kooks at her clinic been trying to get me to see. It's funny how we make up excuses for our weaknesses. This whole time I'd convinced myself and tried to convince Free that I smoked to keep the Bully at bay, when in reality, I smoked because...well, because I liked it.

Hey...who knew?

I eased open the back door, carefully closing it behind me. Then I turned to head into the kitchen but came to a sudden stop at the sight of a shadowy figure in front of me blocking the way.

"Hey, Tuck!" Free yelled, flipping on the light, nearly scaring the sh*t out of me.

"Got damn, girl," I squeaked, sounding like Rob had just a minute ago. Hell, I was nearly balled up into the fetal position against the door as well. My damn heart was about to beat out of my chest.

"Why you lurking in the dark like a crazy woman?"

She bit her lip to keep from laughing at me. "Did I scare you? Only guilty people jump like you just did."

I straightened up a bit, fixing my clothes. "Naw, you ain't scare me."

"Really? 'Cause you just screamed like a girl." Now she was laughing.

"I didn't scream, Free… You know I'm a singer. I can hit high notes."

She narrowed her eyes and with her hands on her hip, began to walk toward me. I took several steps back until the door prevented me from taking more.

"So how did your talk go?" she asked, sounding like a f*cking detective. I don't know if it was the weed or what, but I felt like I was in the hot seat.

"What talk?" I asked, trying to make myself smaller, but she was crowding my space big-time.

"The talk with the young man who's throwing his life away getting high all day."

"Oh yeah." I tried to ease past her to the kitchen, but she stepped in my path preventing me. "I told him he's got to make some changes. Get his life together—"

"Bullsh*t!" she yelled in my face, pointing at me and laughing at the same time. "You are so full of sh*t. You told him no such thing. You were out there getting high with him."

I went to shake my head and deny it, but when I opened my mouth a chuckled escaped it.

"Let me tell you something, Mr.," she said poking me in my chest. "When I get my clinic—"

"*If,* baby… *if* you get your clinic," I corrected her. Judah still hasn't given us the go-ahead to start building.

She narrowed her eyes in a way that really did frighten me. "When," she growled.

I nodded. "Yep…you right. When."

She grinned again. "When I get my clinic, you and your little weedhead friend are going to be the first two that sign up."

"Alrighty," I told her, 'cause what the hell else was I going to say?

She poked me in my chest one more time. "And I tell you something else you and your little weedhead friend are going to do."

"Whatever you want, baby."

She nodded as if to say, damn right whatever I want. "You two are going to help me get close enough to Judah so that I can convince him how good of an idea it is to open a wellness clinic. Now get in the shower and come to bed! I want to cuddle!" she snapped before whipping around and heading back upstairs.

I stared after her. I probably should feel sorry for my brother. When Free gets her mind set on something she can be annoying as hell until she gets it. I grinned, thinking about all the hell he's put us through, and...well, he deserves whatever the hell he gets.

"Coming, sweetheart!" I called after my wife.

# Chapter 12

## I Have a Secret

### Free

WELL, guys, I've gotten myself in a bit of a pickle. As we speak, I'm sitting tied to my porch swing with duct tape over my mouth. Poor Grapefruit is on the other side of the door meowing his head off. And I know by this point you have many questions like 'how in the world did I get tied to my porch swing? Who did it? And...did I say Grapefruit?'

LOL!

The answer is I've finally gotten the go-ahead to build my clinic. Judah is the one that tied and gagged me. And Nak in trying to surprise me, kidnapped Grapefruit from poor Oaklee, who I'm sure is now racked with grief, but I'm going to come back to that.

So many things have taken place over the last two weeks. I don't know where to begin. But let me tell you guys this. I am extremely happy. No...I don't think you guys understand. Everything in my life is falling into place so perfectly, I don't know how I'd ever thought I was happy before.

Who am I kidding? I wasn't happy before. There, I said it. My life sucked before Tucker came back in it. Yeah, I had my clinic, but I had to put up with Angie's crap to keep it. I convinced myself that I was alright because I was doing something I'd always wanted. But the truth is, I was being drained. Angie, the clinic, the twins, and Dillion, were wearing down my soul.

For the first time in a long time, I actually felt free. And I owe it all to my beautiful jerk of a husband, his ornery, mean brother, my spontaneous friend and sister, Nak, who on a whim, kidnapped my cat from my grieving friend, my unborn child growing inside of my belly, and the bible the Preacher had given me, which Rome and Nak brought back with my other things they'd retrieved from the hotel.

Now settle back, and as I wait for my husband to return from his training so that he can untie me, I'll tell you guys just how all this came to be.

That next morning, Tucker and Rob had come up with a brilliant idea to get me to 'bump' into Judah. We staged it so that Tucker and I were going for a casual stroll just as Judah was working in his garage on a motorcycle that Rob says is one of his prized possessions. The other he says, Judah keeps behind a padlocked door that he's tried on several occasions to break in with no success. Of course, I admonished Rob for invading his privacy. Yes, it is true that Judah is a major asshole, but even major assholes deserved some privacy. It was bad enough Rob had taken over his garage and was painting that beautiful mural that we'd used as an excuse to stop and have a little chat.

Judah looked up from what he was doing and when he saw Tucker, he frowned, but when his gaze fell on me, the frown turned into a scowl.

"Hey…look, J. There's Tucker and his beautiful wife," Rob cried turning away from his mural. The kid was barely holding onto his laughter. Judah grunted and went back to working on his bike.

"Yes, I brought Free up here to see the view you're always going on about," Tucker responded. Judah grunted again without looking up.

"And what a view it is," I said, reciting my lines just as we practiced. "So peaceful and serene."

"Hey, Judah, I don't think you and Free formally met," Tucker said, steering us over to where the grumpy man was working.

"We met," Judah muttered once again without looking up.

Goodness! He was rude.

I plastered on my schoolteacher smile. "Not formally. The last time we talked, you tried to kill my husband by emptying a clip into our bed right where he lay." A snicker came from behind us from Rob.

Judah grunted. "If I wanted him dead, he would be dead." He placed a tool in the box next to him and grabbed another.

"So, you just wanted his attention?"

His gaze rose then. It landed on me for a moment before it settled on Tucker. "Really?"

"Really what, dear brother?" my husband asked. By

this time, he and Rob were struggling to keep their laughter in check. Judah stood and amazingly made my Bully of a husband feel like a little brother. This was going to take some getting used to. For as long as I could remember, Tucker was the big man on the set. It was just outright odd seeing one that exuded more power than him.

"Do I look like I have time for this sh*t?" Judah growled.

Tucker blinked innocently at him. "Whatever do you mean, dear brother?"

Judah exhaled, rolled his eyes, threw the tool he was using into the box, and then turned and walked back into his house slamming the door behind him.

"I think that went really well," Rob said into the quietness, causing Tucker to have a good chuckle at that.

It didn't go well. But if Judah thought his gruff manner was going to discourage me, he didn't know me very well. I didn't make it as far as I had in spite of all the hurdles that had been in my way by happenstance. If nothing else, I have tenacity and determination.

We would go on to stage several more encounters between Judah and me. It didn't take long till I became something of a hero amongst the group, because I was fearlessly taking on the grumpy monster that they all feared.

When Nak and Rome returned from Hard Hitter's wedding and retrieving my grandmother's journals, they quickly jumped on board and were more than willing to help us in our endeavor. To Judah's dismay, I began to show up everywhere, in the cafeteria where he liked to eat lunch and dinner, on the training field under the guise of providing moral support for Tucker.

Rome took all of the journals to his computer lab at headquarters. He said it will take him a couple of days to get everything scanned into his system that he called the Equalizer... Yeah, I know...super corny, right?

Please don't get me started talking about this group's genius and all of his idiosyncrasies. Sometimes I sit and I watch him work, utterly amazed at his abilities. I would love a chance to examine Rome's mind. I've never in my life seen one as brilliant as him, and I've studied with the best and the brightest of them. None of them could hold a flame to him.

Anyway, don't let me get distracted; I was telling you guys how we conquered Judah. Well, at the very least, got him to agree to let us begin construction on a new wellness clinic.

Where was I?

Oh yes... Rome and the Equalizer.

He said it will take a couple of days to get everything scanned in. But once it's done, the Equalizer would be able to sort everything into categories that will make it easier for us to cipher through the information.

To get me closer to Judah, Rome had me come to the lab with him to help scan in the journals. Of course, I got distracted and often wandered to Judah's office where I would try and spark up a conversation. I felt that if I could just get him used to talking to me, it would be a great segue into him actually agreeing to sit for a session.

However, it never went well. The first time I showed up, he left. The second time I showed up, he asked me very kindly to take three steps back. Me thinking that because he was being kind, we were making leeway, took the three steps back with a huge smile. But the smile quickly left when he slammed the door in my face.

The third time I cornered him in the library, and that's when I think we had our breakthrough.

"Why are you harassing me?" he asked when he looked up to see me searching for a book that just so happened to be in the area he sat in.

I pretended to be startled that he was even there. "Oh! I didn't see you there."

"Do you think that because you're my brother's wife I won't kill you?"

That question would have frightened me a year ago. I slid into the empty chair at the table he was using.

"Let's talk about that."

"Let's not." He stood, and I stood right with him.

"Don't you think it's a little strange that you find it hard to commingle with people?" I asked, following him as he hurried out of the library.

"No. I find it strange that my brother's bug of a wife won't leave me alone."

"Excuse me, sir? Did you call me a bug?" I was now practically running to keep up with him.

"Yes. You're like a gnat, buzzing in my ear." He waved his big hand at me. "Scram and leave me be, woman!"

"Why do you hate happiness?" I called out when we made it to his office door. My question stopped him in his tracks as he turned to look at me with a frown that said he thought I was the one who needed help.

"What?!"

"Why do you hate happiness?"

"I don't hate happiness. In fact, I strive to be happy all the time. And what makes me happy is to be left the hell alone. So, scram, flea…I mean Free. And leave me alone!" And then he slammed the door in my face once again.

I heard laughing and turned to the side to see Rome, Jo, and Tucker peeking around the corner, spying on us. That wasn't the first time, and I'm sure it won't be the last. They were getting a real kick out of me harassing their older brother.

However, as I was staring at the closed door, I realized my husband was not as big of a jerk as I thought he was. His big brother was a far bigger jerk than he'll ever be. Even still, I didn't let that deter me. In fact, I doubled down on my efforts until finally this morning, after finding out Judah and Rob stayed up late last night drinking beer in his garage, had the bright idea to bake him some cookies and show up on his doorstep.

Rob said whenever Judah gets drunk, he always wakes up late with a killer hangover. The fellas say he shows up for training late and grouchier than usual. So, the way I figured, that was the time to strike. I'll never find him as weak as he is then. After Tucker left for training with Jo, I rode my bicycle to Judah's place.

He opened the door, clearly hungover. When he saw me, he scowled so fiercely that if I didn't know for a fact that Journey was right, and his bark was bigger than his bite, I would have ran for my life.

"Good morning!" I told him, smiling brightly before holding up the plate of cookies. "I heard you were feeling under the weather, so I made you a plate of my famous peanut butter fudge cookies."

He narrowed his eyes at me. "Tell me, Doc, have you ever been shot?"

I blinked but still kept my smile in place. "No, I don't believe that I have. Why?"

"Because I'm really thinking about grabbing my gun and shooting you in both knees."

"That is a very hurtful thing to say," I told him, my smile still there.

"Imagine how much more hurtful it would be if I took out your knees," he grumbled.

"I know you don't mean that. You're speaking from a place—"

"Okay, Doc…you win," he said, cutting me off.

My eyebrows lifted in shock. "I have?"

He nodded. "Yep…You win. Let's go back to your place, and I'll tell you all about my f*cked up life."

I couldn't believe it. This had been way easier than I thought. Journey was so right. Judah just needs someone not to give up on him. I went to turn around to head back to my bike, but he stopped me.

"Doc?"

"Yeah," I asked, turning back to face him.

He held out his hand. "The cookies?"

"Oh! I almost forgot." I laughed, handing him the cookies.

He even surprised me by smiling. "Okay…I'll meet you at your place."

I rode the bike back to my house on cloud nine. I couldn't wait to tell the rest of the team how with a little determination and a fresh batch of peanut butter fudge cookies, I'd defeated the grumpy monster they were all afraid of.

By the time I pulled my bicycle into the gate, he was bringing his Hummer to a stop in front. I noticed he held rope and duct tape in his hand, but I didn't think anything of it. I was just ecstatic that he agreed to talk to me. I couldn't wait to delve into that darkened brain of his and see if we could shed some light in there somewhere.

"Hey, Doc, why don't you have a seat on the swing," he said, gesturing to the lovely wicker swing.

"Oh...okay." I took a seat and then began my spiel. "I'm so glad you finally agreed to talk to me."

"Mmmhhhmmm..." he said, going down to one knee next to the swing.

"I think that you will find that once you talk about some of your past traumas, a weight will be lifted from your chest, making life appear brighter and not as bad as we thought it to be."

"Mmmhhhhmmm..." was his only response as he lifted one of my hands and began to tie it to the bench.

"What are you doing?"

"You want me to be vulnerable and tell you what's going on in my head. I will feel safer if you were tied up."

Ooookay...strange. But okay...he's willing to talk.

"I want to first begin by saying there is no need to feel vulnerable. We can move at your pace. This is a safe space for you—"

After tying up my other hand, he quickly stood and slapped a piece of duct tape over my mouth.

"For the love of God...shut up. You've caused my ears to bleed," he said before he bent down to look me in the eye. "You are a terrifying woman. And I hope that after today, I never have to see you again."

I frowned at him. "That's not nice," I mumbled behind the tape, but I doubt he understood it.

"If I give your husband permission to start construction

on your clinic so that you can terrify anybody else but me, will you promise to leave me the hell alone?"

And that, my friends, is how it's done. With a huge smile on my face behind the duct tape, I crossed my fingers and nodded my head.

"Okay... You got it. Build your clinic. Do whatever the f*ck you want to do. Just please...please never speak to me again." And then he stood and walked down the stairs, taking his duct tape with him.

"Hey!" I yelled at him through the tape. "Aren't you going to untie me?"

He looked back at me with an evil grin on his face. "F*ck no! You're on time-out."

So yeah... that's how I got my clinic. I'll leave him be for now. But once those doors are open, I'll start harassing him again. That man really needed help. And as Tucker pointed out, I have a sworn duty to help him.

Anyhow, as you guys know, Rome and Nak have returned. I was surprised beyond words when they showed up at our door at 2:30 in the morning holding two boxes. When they had first rung the doorbell waking us up, Tucker had grabbed his gun out of habit. I had to remind him that it was probably family at the door because I doubted if anyone that wished us ill would had made it past Judah's security.

Yeah, his land is up in the mountains, but Rome said he had eyes on every inch of it. *Paranoid much?!*

"Sorry to bother y'all so late," Rome said as they stepped into the house so that Tucker could close the door behind them. "We would have waited till morning to bring you your things, but my wife, who suffers from Impulse Control Disorder, decided to go behind my back and break into your friend's house and steal your cat. But there is something wrong with this cat, and I refuse to allow it in my home."

My hands flew to my mouth as pure joy rushed through my veins. "Grapefruit is here?"

A groan left Tucker's throat. "Please tell me you guys did not bring back that devil cat?"

Rome chuckled shaking his head. "Man, I ain't never in my life seen nothing like it. I don't think it's well. It looks like it's been chewed on by a dog. And I'm pretty sure it's got some mental issues."

"There's nothing wrong with him," Nak cooed as she set the box on the floor before reaching in to take out my kitty. "He's a precious little angel."

A sound left Rome's throat. "Fallen angel, you mean. That little mutha f*cka tried to claw my face off when I tried to take him back to where she'd found him."

Nak chuckled. "You shouldn't have tried to take him back. He doesn't like men." Before she handed him to me, she gave him a little kiss on his nose. "He has the cutest little mohawk."

Both Rome and Tucker frowned as if it was a big rat she kissed.

Tears came to my eyes. "You have no idea how much this means to me," I told her as she placed my little spitfire in my hands.

She gently kissed me on the forehead. "Don't worry about it. We're sisters…"

Smiling at her through tears, I nodded before greeting my little Grapefruit. "Hey, baby! Mommy has missed you sooooo much! Did you miss me?" He rubbed his little rumpled head under my chin meowing loudly.

"I think he has," Nak said as she gently stroked his back, clearly falling for his charms.

Tucker's head dropped back on his shoulders. "Why, Nak? Why would you bring him here? You should have tossed his little ass over a bridge or something," he groaned to the ceiling.

Nak rolled her eyes at him. "Nossa! Stop acting like a baby and get over yourself."

Rome shook his head. "You get over *your*self. Did you even think about how her friend must feel now? He was the last thing she had left of Free. But now she doesn't even have that because you stole him."

The smile left both Nak's and my face. Her gaze came to me. "Oh sh*t, Free! I'm so sorry. I didn't think of that."

Rome shook his finger at her. "You never think about stuff like that. And what did we discuss about you going on recon missions anyway? All that sh*t is over for you for the next year." Her angry gaze whipped to him.

Yikes! If looks could kill, he would be dead. "We didn't discuss anything. *You* discussed it... I didn't agree to nothing!"

He pointed at her. "You not scaring nobody, so put away your claws. I'm done arguing with you about it! Case closed!"

Her face turned red as she slowly turned toward him fully. Tucker's, Grapefruit's, and my eyes widened as the impending explosion filled the air with tension. Her hands balled into fists at her sides, and then she began to fire off what I was more than positive was a very colorful tirade in rapid Portuguese. She was so angry the veins were bulging out of her neck as she laid into him. Whatever she was saying wasn't pretty, because Rome's face went through a wide range of emotions, anger, shock, back to anger, and then finally humor.

"Yeah, right. You ain't gon' do sh*t. You love me, girl!" he told her, laughing at her, which only made her angrier. Cool resolve settled over her before her mouth snapped shut, and she stormed past him out the door.

"What's going on with your lady?" Tucker asked.

Rome looked out the door after his wife before shooting us a huge smile. "We're having a baby."

Both Tucker and my mouth dropped. "Nak's pregnant?" we asked in unison.

Rome nodded. "Yep, we just found out."

Right then the sound of a car starting and the tires peeling out the driveway filled the night. Rome rushed out the door. A few seconds later he popped back in.

"Hey, bro, can you give me a lift home, so I can stop this crazy-ass girl from taking her bat to my computer?"

Tucker chuckled. "Yeah, let me grab my keys."

"I'm going to take the other boxes with your grandmother's journals in them to headquarters. The Equalizer will be able to sort through them in record time."

I grinned. "The Equalizer?"

He returned my grin, nodding. "Oh yeah! You'll see…"

Tucker made his way back and they hurried out the door. Chuckling I shut it behind them and carried Grapefruit upstairs.

"Mommy has missed her Grapefruit so much," I cooed as he continued to rub his head under my chin.

Poor Oaklee; I know she was probably racked with grief right now. There had to be a way I could put her heart at ease. If only I could talk to them…at least once. I know my friends; they won't tell anybody that I'm alive. We can trust them with our secret, just like Rome trusts his friend, Hard Hitter. Maybe I can talk to Rome and see if he can find a way for me to send a message to them.

The sound of Tucker coming back in caused me to scoop up Grapefruit, who had started to snooze on the bed in Naphtali's spot.

"Now you need to be on your best behavior, and squash whatever this beef is you have with Tucker. The three of us are going to live here together… happy. Have I made myself clear?"

Grapefruit looked at me through lowered lids before opening his mouth in a wide yawn that clearly said he had no intentions of being on his best behavior.

"We may want to call somebody. I think Rome and Nak are going to have a domestic dispute, and I fear for my boy; I ain't gon' lie. When we pulled up, she was standing on the porch with that golden bat of hers. As soon as she saw him, she took off inside the house. He jumped out the car before I could even bring the mutha f*cka to a stop and chased after her." He chuckled as he pulled off his t-shirt.

"Why are they fighting? They just found out they're going to have a baby. Shouldn't they be happy?"

"They are happy. They're fighting over the fact that he's grounded her for the next year—" He paused as he thought of something.

"What's the matter?" I asked, sitting up in the bed.

"This means she beat us in that f*cking obstacle course pregnant. Ain't that a b*tch?"

After he kicked off his shoes, he made his way to the bed, but Grapefruit wasn't having it. He stood with his back arched ready to pounce on Tucker.

"Get out of my bed, you little sh*t!" Tucker hissed,

crouching low as if he was really going to try and fight a kitten.

Grapefruit let out a loud meow and was getting ready to lunge when I scooped him up.

"None of that," I told him before sitting him down on the floor.

Tucker jumped in the bed and hurried to my side so that he could look down at Grapefruit. I laughed because he nearly toppled me over, being silly.

"Yeah! None of that you, little mutha f---" I put my hand over his mouth before pointing at him.

"None of that."

Grapefruit meowed as if to say, *yeah, right back at you.* Before going down in a stretch and then moseying his way out of the room to explore his new home.

Tucker plopped down on the bed next to me. "That cat is the devil; I'm telling you."

I distractedly played with the string to his basketball shorts as I thought of how cool it was that Nak and I were both pregnant at the same time.

"Hey, Tuck?"

"Hmmm…" he said as he scrolled through his phone.

"What do you think about kids?"

He lifted an eyebrow without looking away from his phone. "I don't know…never really thought about it."

"Well," I said, taking his phone out of his hand. "Think about it."

He turned towards me, studying my face closely. "Why?" I bit my lip.

He sat straight up in the bed. "Why, Free?"

"There's something I've been meaning to tell you."

A huge smile broke out on his face as he once again

came to his knees in the bed nearly knocking me over because his body was so big.

"What? What have you been meaning to tell me?"

"I ummm… I'm preg—"

I didn't get a chance to get the rest out before he let out a loud whoop and shot out of the bed and the room.

"Oh sh*t! We're having a baby!" he yelled in the hall, causing me to erupt in laughter.

He ran back in the room snatching me up out of the bed and into his arms. "We're having a baby!"

Around and around he turned us. At that point, I was laughing so hard at his silliness my throat hurt.

"I knew something was up. I said…I said, something is up with you." He let me slide to my feet. "And the other night when we were making love, I thought to myself, damn, my baby got a little thicker. Girl, I was about to take you to the gym."

My mouth popped open in shock. But he closed it back. "Naw, I'm just kidding."

"Are you calling me fat already?" That really hurt. I mean real tears came to my eyes. I did notice I had gotten a little thicker. My doctor's appointment wasn't until the week after next. So, I didn't know how far along I was, but apparently I'm already as big as a house.

"Noooo, bae, nooo! I was just playing," Tucker said, taking my hand and guiding me to sit back on the bed. He came down to one knee next to me. "Don't go getting sensitive on me. You know I can be a jerk."

I nodded, trying to fight away the tears. "I know you can. But it's true…I'm faaaat!" I wailed.

The look of agony on his face was priceless. "No, baby, you're not. I like my girl with a little meat on her bones.

You were way too skinny in high school. I like to be able to grab ahold of my women like this." He grabbed my thighs and pulled me so that I fell back on the bed, causing my nightgown to raise just enough to give a peek of the peach panties I wore underneath.

His heated gaze fell to them as he licked his lips. Goodness! I nearly groaned.

"Do you know how much I love your thighs?" he asked, settling his big body between them.

My breathing picked up. I had to bite my bottom lip to keep from crying out. Slowly I shook my head no, my hurt feelings a thing of the past.

His gaze went from heat to outright hunger. "You're so damn sexy to me, Free. Everything about you do it for me. Your breasts, your stomach, your thighs..." As he spoke, he ran his big hands up my hips, causing my nightgown to raise above my panties.

"So sexy..." he moaned, licking his lips again. "I love the way you feel wrapped around me."

He lowered his head and open mouth kissed me just above my panty line before carefully removing them.

"I love your taste..." When his hungry lips lowered again, I was lost. My moans filled the room as my hands fisted the covers. Right when I thought my world was getting ready to shatter, he entered me.

That night he made love to me as if I was the most precious thing he'd ever held. But what I'll never forget was his words to me before my world exploded into a million pieces.

"Free..." he whispered in my ear as he drove into me. My body was on fire; the pressure inside me was building to a point that I thought that maybe I would die.

"Free…" he whispered again.

I don't know where I got the strength to answer him. "Hmmmm…" I moaned.

"I have a secret," he said as he continued to artfully stroke the fire that was killing me.

"What secret?"

"I got you pregnant on purpose…"

And that was it… The next thing I knew, I was clawing at his back as a million stars exploded behind my closed eyelids.

Whew! Yeah… I know right? Intense. That's my Naphtali, intense.

Anyway, so, that about catches you guys up to this moment. And just in time too. Tucker, Jo, and Al just pulled up in our driveway.

"Bae! What happened?" Tucker asked, jumping out of the car hurrying to me. He went down to one knee in front of the wicker swing I was tied to and carefully removed the tape from my mouth.

I smiled. "We got the go-ahead to start construction on the clinic."

He returned my smile, but it didn't reach his eyes. There was something wrong with him. "That's my girl. I knew you would wear him down."

"Yeah, I did. You would have been so proud of me. He told me I made his ears bleed."

That caused him to chuckle a bit as he removed the rope from my arms. As soon as I was free, I threw my arms around his neck and held him close.

"We should go out and celebrate," I cried.

He shook his head; the look on his face was beginning to worry me. "Maybe later. For now, we have to go meet

Rome at headquarters. He says he found something in your grandmother's journals that he thinks you should know."

"Is it bad?" I couldn't help but ask. I didn't want any bad news right now. For the first time in my life, everything was perfect, and I wanted to at least hold onto this feeling for a whole day before I was brought back to my reality. My reality being that just maybe I wasn't meant to hold onto happiness for long.

He exhaled. "I don't know, baby. But he says he needs to see, you, me, and the Old Man right now. Jo's nosey ass is coming too."

I nodded. "Okay, let's go," my mouth said.

But my soul wept with the dread it now felt…

# Chapter 13

## Who in the World is Subject B?

*And so, the Plot Thickens…*

### Free

"DAMN, CAN YOU HURRY UP?" Jo snapped at Rome, who had not turned away from his computer since we all took a seat in his lab.

Nak said he'd been so immersed in the journals over the last few days that she'd had to force him to eat and to come to bed. She said when he left the lab at headquarters, he came home and closed himself inside of his office still sorting through the madness that was the woman who posed as my grandmother.

"Jo, nobody invited you. So why don't you shut the hell up," Rome grumbled, not looking away from his computer as his hands flew over the keyboard. My gaze went to Judah, who stood across the room leaning against the wall with his muscled arms folded. The frown on his face said he was irritated with all of us. I was beginning to think it was a permanent fixture.

"I'm just a—bou—t…finished!" Rome said before suddenly turning to face me where I sat next to Tucker. For a moment he didn't speak. He just studied me with his elbow resting on the arm of his seat and his finger under his chin.

"What's up, man?" Tucker asked him. "The suspense is killing us."

"Free, what do you remember about your mother?" he finally spoke.

But I must admit to being a little shocked by his question. "Ummm… everything. Her favorite food, her favorite color. What specifically do you mean?"

"Well…do you ever remember seeing or meeting her parents? Any family for that matter?"

"Ummm…" I had to think about that. "I remember my mother telling me that her mom died when she was a little girl. I don't remember what she said about her dad. And no, I never met any of her other relatives, just her friends that she hung out with."

He nodded before turning to click a few buttons on his keyboard. "I believe this is your mom."

On several of the big screens in front of us, all the notes my grandmother took on Daisy began to flash across them.

I frowned. "Daisy?"

He nodded. "Yep, at one point, Daisy had a child. A little girl."

I stood and walked closer to the screen that had the journal entry that was dated July 1, 1979… my birthday.

"Today, Daisy gave birth to a beautiful baby girl," I read out loud. "And although the father wasn't who I'd hoped he would have been, I'm praying that Dr. Baxter finds her acceptable and worthy to join his collection of extraordinary individuals. Maybe if he does, he won't punish me for what I've done. But if he doesn't, I'm going to have to take Daisy and her daughter and run for our lives. Today is the day that will make or break my lab. If God is merciful, he will find all that I've sacrificed earnest and deserving of recognition."

I frowned down at Rome. "What makes you think this is talking about me?"

"Well, outside of the fact that this baby girl was born on the same day as you, there are these group of journal entries here." He clicked a few buttons and on one screen, about thirty journal entries appeared. "I'll give you the quick version."

"She basically says Dr. Baxter not only rejected the child but flew into a rage and beat her within inches of her life. She fled into the night, taking Daisy and the child with her. She later pulled her son, who was away in college, out of the school, giving him, herself, and Daisy new identities."

"By this point, I think there is love in her heart for her subject because she takes great care in relocating and hiding Daisy and the child in Detroit. However, she has one problem. She's gotten Daisy addicted to opioids but can no longer supply her with the drugs she needs now that she's in hiding. It breaks her heart to see Daisy turn to street drugs, but she continues to do what she can for you guys. She made sure your rent was paid and that you were taken care of by convincing her son to claim you as his own."

"How did she convince him?"

"By promising to help find him a wealthy wife that will at long last give him what he craved above all else. A place at the table with the black elite. Just like his mother, he wanted a name."

I eased back into my seat, dumbfounded. This all made so much sense, my mom and I always having a place to live although she was never really able to keep a real job, the bags she kept in our closet. Daisy was obsessed with her travel bag. It was important to her that she was ready when it was time to go. Although my fake grandmother kept her heavily drugged, she was only at ease if her bag was around. I don't remember my mother ever telling me why she kept the bags in our closet, but thanks to the journals, I know why.

*Dear God! My mother is Daisy...* And yes, she was a very extraordinary individual.

"Now at first, I thought grandma relocating everybody to Detroit was a random act." Rome shook his head. "It wasn't."

"What do you mean?" Nak asked.

"She had another agenda. By this point, she has a vendetta against Dr. Baxter and wants revenge for him never taking her work seriously. What better revenge than to perfect his gene manipulation experiment by creating the perfect specimen without his help. It's too late for Daisy, and even Daisy's child, who was missing the superman gene. But what about Daisy's child's, child?"

Sounding like the mad scientist, he had all of our heads

spinning, trying to keep up with him. All except for Judah, who signaled for him to continue.

"This is just my theory. Grandma is the reason why Dr. Baxter was forced to pull the plug on his research. She'd drawn too much attention to what he was doing. She finds out that one of the subjects he'd been experimenting on ended up in a small Michigan town. So, she manipulates a few things in order to plant Daisy's daughter in said subjects' path in hopes that he will see the daughter and want to procreate."

"She's in a good place. She already set herself up as Free's grandmother, which would mean she would have access to whatever child comes from the union. Only she dies before Free makes it to childbearing age." His gaze came to me and Tucker. "Congratulations on becoming pregnant by the way."

Ummm... I didn't know how to respond, and neither did Tucker, who now wore a confused look on his face to match mine. If what Rome said is correct, Tucker and my baby were plotted out before the two of us ever thought about the other that way. That was kind of freaky...right?

But I was saved from saying anything by Judah, who finally spoke. "This all sounds viable...but can you prove it?"

Rome smiled big. "Why, of course, fearless leader. If I'm correct about what I'm saying, we should be able to discover just who Daisy's baby daddy is."

He turns to his computer and types something into his keyboard. "Please take a look at the screen to your left."

We all did as he said. Several journal entries came upon the screen. "This is what grandmother did that caused Baxter to fly into a rage."

"Can you give us the short version?" Jo asked because there were at least twenty journal entries on the screen.

Rome shook his head at him. "You continue to amaze me with how stupid you are."

Jo didn't get offended, in fact, he grinned. "I was smart enough to bust your ass."

Before Rome could respond, Judah signaled for him to continue. After giving a long exhale, the kid went into his spiel.

"Grandma had been trying to get Baxter to allow who she calls subject A, to mate with Daisy. She was convinced that Daisy carried the gene that was needed to combine with subject A's gene and make a super baby. But Dr. Baxter refused. Soooo, grandma went behind Baxter's back and using his technique hypnotized subject A, bringing him to a heavily drugged Daisy, who by the way, was only sixteen, and had him mate with her. Nothing came from the mating. So, she began to look at subject B, whose genes were similar but not quite like subject A's, but similar enough to manipulate into a very lethal machine in his own right. After hypnotizing subject B and drugging Daisy, she got them to mate, and voila! Daisy ends up pregnant."

"Damn! That's f*cked up..." Nak muttered, shaking her head as she sliced into an apple with her blade.

"If I'm correct about my theory," Rome continued, "Free and subject B have the matching DNA of a father and daughter." He typed something into his computer and two DNA strands appeared. I held my breath as he carefully lined them up, showing that they were a match except for a few slight differences.

Rome turned to face me with a grin on his face. "Look at that, Free, we found yo' daddy."

The breath whooshed out of my lungs, making me feel lightheaded. "Ho—how is this possible? Who in the world is subject B?"

Rome's gaze fell on Al, who'd been sitting quietly, taking in all of this.

"Wait!" the Oldman cried. "Me?"

Rome nodded. "Yes sir, you are our Free's biological father."

That was the last I heard...Everything went black.


Naphtali


MY ARMS SHOT out to catch Free before she hit the floor, lifting her slightly so that her head rested against my chest. This was all too much for her. The whole time we thought the experimenting and sh*t only happened to me. Now she was finding out that her whole life had been manipulated as well. And not only that, Ol' Al here is her dad.

His gaze met mine before it fell to Free. Poor fella, it looked like he was going to hit it next. Jo must have sensed the same thing because he grasped the Old Man's shoulder, no doubt holding him up.

Nak grunted as she cut off another slice of apple, stuffing it in her mouth. "She'll be alright. She fainted. We pregnant girls have to go through so much. I nearly fainted the other day myself." We all turned to stare at her. Nobody in the room believing her sh*t. Even pregnant, she was as tough as nails.

"What?!" she cried with a mouth full of partially chewed apple. "I faint sometimes."

"So, Baxter's our man?" Judah asked, bringing everybody's attention back to the matter at hand.

Rome nodded. "Baxter's our man. Track him down, and he will lead us to your long lost sister."

"But if the grandmother changed everybody's names in her journals, what makes you think she didn't change Baxter's?" I asked.

Rome grinned. "Because she hated him. Subconsciously she wanted him to be exposed."

Judah gave him a look that said he was going to need more than that. Rome chuckled, turning to his computer where he typed something in. On the screens, several images of a building popped up.

"And plus, I ran a cross-reference for doctors with the name, Baxter, with information for Jo's handler, the senator, and this is what I came up with."

An image appeared on the screen of two men, but----

"Aggghhh!" I yelled as a sharp pain pierced my head. Securing Free in my arms so that she didn't fall, I went down to my knees, trying to stop the pain.

"Turn it off!" Judah yelled, clutching his head...

Rome whipped back to his computer as his hands frantically shot across the keyboard, causing the picture to disappear. Only then did the ringing in my head stop and the pressure release. I lay with Free on the ground, trying to catch my breath.

*What the f*ck just happened?!*

"Nossa!" Nak gasped, looking down at us with a look of shock on her face. It was then I noticed that the picture had not only affected me, but also Jo, The Old Man, and Judah. We were all on our knees clutching our heads…

"What happened?" Judah asked, slowly getting to his feet.

Rome shook his head. "I don't know, but I'm going to find out. You all looked at the picture and then freaked the f*ck out. We have definitely found our man. Now the question is, what the hell did he do to y'all heads, and how do we fix it?"

Judah lifted his phone. "Send me the address; we're going after him."

"Naw…can't do that, boss."

Frowning, Judah hung up the phone. "Why the hell not?!"

Rome typed something on his computer, bringing the empty building back up on the screen. "This is the last known address we have for him before he went under. According to my records…this building has been empty since 1979."

———

### Free

I opened my eyes to see that I was lying in my bed. Tucker must have started a fire in the fireplace because it cast a warm glow over the room. Just outside our window, the moon sat high and full in the sky. After giving my limbs a good stretching, I sat up in the bed to see my husband asleep in the chair next to it.

Hmmm… My mind wasn't quite firing on all cylinders yet, so I had to really think hard on how I got here in my bed without me remembering. However, it didn't take long for everything to come back to me.

Daisy was my mother. Dorothy or whatever her real name is, who pretended to be my grandmother, had plopped me down to be tortured by Tucker in hopes that he would fall in love with me and get me pregnant.

*God! Who does these types of things?*

And then there was Al… my real dad. I put my face in my hands and tried to stifle the whimper that came from my throat. But it did no good, the sound woke Tucker.

"Hey, bae…how are you feeling?" he asked, sitting up in his chair. I shook my head, still trying to fight the tears that gathered in my throat.

"No, don't cry, Freebie…" he cooed before he eased into the bed next to me, lifting me so that I lay in his arms. The feeling of his protective embrace was like a green light to my tears. I cried for my mother, whose parents misunderstood her demeanor and put her into the hands of a wolf who destroyed her just to get access to her head.

Dorothy drugged her and manipulated her into having sex with two men all because she wanted a super baby. She wanted my mother to give birth to one of Tucker's siblings. And when that didn't work, she set it up so that I could give birth to a super baby.

Suddenly a real worry came over me. I sat up on Tucker's lap drying my tears.

"Our baby is in danger. They won't give up. They're going to try and do what they did to you guys to our--"

"Shhh…" Naphtali said, shaking his head, cutting me off. "My hand to God, I'll tear this place down if they try. Nothing is going to happen to our children. We're going to find the man that did this to us. And then we're going to kill him. Period."

The look in his eyes had turned so deadly I wondered if the Bully had joined us. "You and the baby will be safe here. They'll have to get through a lot of killas to get to you, Freebie. Trust me..."

I nodded. I did trust him. I'd seen them training. Tucker, his brothers, Nak, and Al were a force to be reckoned with.

"What about Al? How did he take the news that he is my father?"

Tucker grinned. "I think it made his day. Like you, he was a bit shocked at first. But then he started warming up to the idea. He and Abby were here for a while trying to wait for you to wake up so that you guys could talk. But after the sun went down, I told them to go on home and that we will come by their place tomorrow for breakfast."

He gently rubbed my cheek. "He said he always wanted children of his own. But his first wife was sick, and they never had any. He's excited about the baby and wishes that all this could have happened under different circumstances."

I nodded. "Me too. It's just not fair what they were allowed to do to us. So many people have suffered at their hands."

He brought my head back to his shoulder. "I don't want you to worry about any of that. As long as I have breath in my body, I'm going to do all that I can to make them pay. But most importantly, I'm going to do all that I can to make sure you are happy so that our babies can have a different beginning than us. "

I clutched his hand, bringing it to my lips. "Yes, I want them to be surrounded by happiness."

"And they will, baby. That's my word. I'll do anything I have to do to make sure of it."

He lifted my chin so that our eyes met. "Freebie."

"Hmmm…"

"I know I haven't been the perfect friend or the perfect boyfriend…" He grinned. "Or the perfect husband. I'm sure I probably won't be the perfect dad. But I want you to know that you are loved."

I smiled at him through tears. That is the same thing the Preacher wrote to me in the bible he left me, the bible that was on the nightstand next to our bed, the bible that had miraculously found its way back into my hands.

*"Yes, baht, there is always something else there. Although you can't touch it, taste it, see it, hear it…it's still there."*

The Preacher's words came back to me. A sudden feeling of safety came over me. Not the safety in knowing that my husband was a very vicious man and could do much damage with his own two hands, not to mention the others that were here just like him.

No…

The safety that I felt was knowing that something else is here. It's always been here, moving and shaping our lives. It brought us together to this place and at this time. And I'm not afraid anymore.

Reaching up, I gently ran my fingers through my husband's beard. "You're wrong."

He frowned. "Wrong about what?"

"You're wrong about you being perfect." I raised up, kissing his lips. "You're absolutely, positively, equivalently, perfect for me…"

# The Epilogue

### Naphtali

"SORRY I'M LATE, everybody. My daughter had a craving for cotton candy ice cream, and she asked her old man to pick her up some," Al said, coming into the impromptu meeting Judah had just called.

Using my elbow, I lightly jabbed Jo, who sat next to me on the bench. He chuckled, shaking his head as the Old Man took a seat. I'm telling y'all, this dude is so proud to be a father. It's been five months since he and Free found out they were father and daughter. And I swear he's tried to make up for all the years they'd lost in that short time.

Several times I had to flat out kick him out of my house. I ain't really used to her doting on another man. It was bad enough I had to share her with that hell cat. All she had to do was look like she needed something and Ol' Al was there to supply it for her, and Free was loving it. She'd been deprived of a father's attention her whole life, so she was in heaven right now. That's really the only reason I put up with as much of Al as I do.

But I ain't going to lie, I liked being the only man Free depended on to make sh*t happen for her. Now it's '*My dad this…*' and '*My dad that…*' '*Look, my dad got this for the baby,*' and '*Can you believe he actually found a pair of these for me?*'

I have to bite my tongue to keep from just outright telling her not to ask him for anything; just ask me. Yeah, I know. That's childish and petty as hell… Well, I don't give a f*ck! Free is mine, and I don't want to share her with Al's old ass.

"Okay, good… you're all here," Judah said, striding into the room. "Rome, pull up that information for me."

Rome went to work on his computer. On one screen a picture of Scarlett Amherst, the princess of R&B, popped up, and on the other, newspaper articles of random killings.

"As you know, I've been searching for Levi, to pull him in," Judah began. His gaze came to Jo and me. "Unlike the two of you, he doesn't care much for the limelight. He likes the shadows. So keeping tabs on him is a real pain in the ass. He'll fall off the map and be gone for years with no trace. But every now and again he resurfaces…"

He looked down at his hand. "I believe he knows I watch him, and that the few times he resurfaces, it's to let me know he's alright."

"Levi knows about you?" I asked, wondering why the f*ck he didn't reach out to me and Jo sooner. He must have noticed the bite in my voice because he chuckled.

"It's not what you think. Levi is…" He paused as he tried to search for a word. "Different from us."

"What do you mean, different?" Jo asked.

"He sees things…you know? Always have. When you guys were kids, it was him that got you two out of the most trouble. By nature, the two of you are charging bulls. Some of the things Father put you through the two of you often responded with anger, which often distorted your view of the situation you were in. Levi was always able to just look at a problem and know how to work his way through it."

He shook his head as a proud grin appeared on his face. "He's…he's spectacular."

If there was a soundtrack to my tale, this is where the loud record scratch would be inserted. Me, Jo, the Old Man, and Nak exchanged confused looks. We'd never heard Judah compliment anyone before.

"You feeling alright, boss?" Nak asked, her belly round and protruding in front of her. Although Rome had grounded her till after she gave birth, Judah still wanted her to be at meetings and some training sessions.

Ignoring her question, Judah gestured toward the beautiful Scarlett. "He's been working security detail for the last nine months for this woman."

Rome typed something in his computer and the footage on several of the screens changed to show Scarlett coming out of a building being swarmed by the paparazzi. Walking next to her with his arm possessively around her shoulders, guiding her through the crowd, was Jo's and my doppelganger. Although he wore shades, it was clear he was one of us, his height, his build…his haircut. Everything was the same.

One of the cameras got close enough to him to see a scar running along his cheek underneath his shades.

"There have been several deaths in Hollywood and other areas where this woman inhabits with his stamp on them," Judah continued.

"Stamp?" I asked.

Judah nodded. "Yeah...Unlike the two of you, Levi's bite is way deadlier than his bark."

*Did this bastard just insinuate that me and Jo sell wolf tickets?* I have broken mutha f*ckas' jaws for less.

"My guess is Ms. Scarlett here got herself in trouble and Levi was brought in to clean it up," Rome supplied. "He moves like a ghost. All of these kills were clean and swift. He slit one man's throat and when the cops found him, the body was still standing." As he spoke, he pulled up an article that headline read,

**"California Man Gets His Throat Slit While Looking in the Fridge for a Drink. Cops Find the Body Still Standing with His Hand on the Fridge Handle."**

"Damn!" the Old Man said. "Is that even possible?"

Rome nodded. "All his kills are like that. The murder scenes are left so clean, many of these kills were not ruled out as suicides. No fingerprints, no footprints, not even dust particle prints. This dude is a f*cking ninja."

Judah chuckled. "You're not too far off. While the two princesses here were coming up in their plush mansions, Levi was brought up by a Tibetan monk, high up in Mount Everest."

Yep, that's all the sh*t I was going to take from him. "Alright, bruh...you gon' keep coming at us and—"

"And what?" Judah growled, cutting me off.

Rome grinned. "Yeah, Tuck...and what?"

"Me and Jo gon—"

Jo shook his head. "My wife said I can't come home

with no more bruises. You on your own, bro." That made us all laugh.

"Nap…I need you and Jo to go get him," Judah picked up when our laughter died down.

"What if he doesn't want to be gotten?" Jo asked…

I nodded. "Very good question."

Judah grinned. "That's why I'm sending you two smooth-talking brothas to do the job. I figure once he gets a look at your faces and you tell him what's going on, he won't give you a hard time about it." Both Jo and I frowned. That didn't sound too reassuring.

"And if all else fails," Rome picked up, "you can always tell him that his girl is in danger, and if he wants to keep her safe, he will come back with you."

"His girl?" Jo asked.

Rome clicked a button and Scarlett popped up on all the screens. "The Sexy Scarle—"

"Watch it, Romeo…" Nak purred sweetly, as she used the blade of her wicked-ass knife to pick dirt out of her fingernails.

Damn! I still ain't got used to seeing her belly swollen with child. She sat here wearing army fatigue cargo pants, her boots that have stomped the life out of many unfortunate fools, a black t-shirt, while holding that wicked blade that I'm sure has cut its fair share of throats, with that golden bat that was never too far from her, leaning against her chair. Can y'all imagine what kind of mommy she was going to be?

"Yeah, Rome…you better watch it, little brother," I told him.

Chuckling, he tried again. "I believe your brother is sleeping with the Princess of R&B."

"What makes you say that?" Jo asked.

Rome typed something else in his computer and the screens all showed different scenes of Levi guarding Scarlett. In a couple of scenes, he was carrying her. It looked like maybe she was either drunk or tired from a show. But the way he carried her was definitely that of a lover.

"Yep, I think you're right, Romeo," Jo told him. "That's how were going to get him to come back with us."

"Well…Okay," the Old Man said coming to his feet. "If you don't need me, I promised my Abby cat and my daughter that I was going to take them—"

"I need you and Rome to go and look into another situation for me," Judah said, bringing Al's little show to an end. I couldn't help the smile that came to my face when he slid his ass back in his chair.

As Judah went over what he had for Al and Rome to do, I shot a text to Free, telling her to meet me back at the house. She's been crazy busy these days over seeing the building of her clinic, between that and shopping for the baby.

This wasn't the first mission Judah had sent me on. But this will be the first one that will require me to stay gone away from home for a while. Who knows how long it was going to take Jo and me to convince Levi to come back with us? But one thing I did know, my daughter was coming in three months. Our brother, Levi, had three days to make up his mind or else, we were gagging him and his broad and throwing them in the trunk.

No way was I staying away from my girl any longer than that.

"I sure do hate to leave my wife and baby girl here by

themselves while I travel all the way to Texas," Al muttered as we headed back to our cars.

That was it! I'd had enough of his sh*t!

"Damn, Al! Give me a f*cking break!" I snapped. "Your baby girl got a husband. A big strong one that look after her just fine. She don't need you always clucking around."

He put his hand on my shoulder, giving me a sympathetic look. "When your daughter...my granddaughter, is born, you'll know how I feel." And then the mutha f*cka chugged me under the chin and walked off to his car.

The only thing I could do was stand there in shock and watch him go. Jo came to a stop next to me.

"You alright?"

"He acts like he's been there all her life and not just the last five months. I'm getting sick of his ass!" I growled.

Jo chuckled, clapping me on the back. "Bro, you might as well get used to it. Whether you like it or not, the Old Man is your father-in-law. Hell, if we can get rid of in-laws, don't you know I would have stashed Rome's ass somewhere by now? Unfortunately, they come with the package. Come on...let's go get *he who walks on water.*"

Although I laughed at that, I couldn't help but wonder what the hell we were getting ready to walk into...

## Bonus Epilogue

*One Year Before the Flare Hit...*

## Free

"Doc! Doc! Wake up!" Oaklee whispered as she shook me awake.

"Hmmmm," I moaned, cracking open my eyes, but when I saw the urgent look on her face, I woke up with a start. Tucker and the others had been away for nearly four weeks. The last time I'd talked to him he said they were landing in New York, but that was two days ago. I'd been worried sick, because I haven't been able to get in contact with him since.

"Is everything alright?!" I asked Oak, throwing back the cover. "Is it Tucker?"

She shook her head. "Tucker's fine…but they need you to go to the clinic quickly. Here, let me get your coat for you. I'll stay here with the kids."

I started to slide on a pair of jeans, but she shook her head. "You don't have time Doc…you have to go quickly!"

I stepped into my shoes as Oaklee draped my coat over my shoulders. I didn't get my arms in the sleeves before she was pushing me out the front door. Quickly I jumped in my car and sped to the clinic. My headlights shined on a young man covered in blood, holding two knives in his hand. He looked like a caged animal.

Tucker and the others surrounded him, trying to calm him, but they were having the opposite effect, the boy was afraid and was ready to lunge with those knives at whoever came close to him.

Rome ran to me as soon as I got out of the car. "Doc, we need your help."

"Who is it?" I asked as I hurried to them.

"Calm down, kid, we're not going to hurt you," Tucker told him. "Here, this is my wife, she's a doctor…she can help you."

The boy had to be no more than eighteen. His eyes

showed signs of acute Dementophobia. Something very traumatizing had happened to him.

"What happened?" I asked Rome in a soothing voice while keeping eye contact with the kid.

"We found him in the devil's den. He had to fight and kill other kids to entertain some very evil people. I don't know how long he's been there, but he and the other children were being kept in cages and fed like dogs. They only let them out to fight."

"Do you know his name?" I asked as I motioned for Tucker and the others to step away.

"When we found him, he was holding a little girl in his arms...I think that maybe it was his sister. She was being eaten by a hybrid demon dog for the entertainment of those sick bastards. He killed the dog but couldn't save her. Before she died...she said, Amir, it hurts."

I nodded and took another step towards the kid. "Hi, Amir. My name is Free..."

## The End...

Whew! Chile...What a ride this was. And I wish I could give y'all a break. But I can't. The saga continues. We're getting ready to delve into the world of Sex, Drugs, and Rhythm and Blues. Y'all hold on now 'cause as they say, the plot thickens... May I present to you, SAVE ME – Levi's and Scarlett's Tale...

# SWEETEST REVENGE

## EDWINA FORT

## The Prologue

I SAT on the basketball court bleachers forcing myself not to pull at the little skirt that barely covered my butt. I was going to lose my nerves. What I was attempting was so far past crazy I began to doubt myself.

Oh goodness! If I was caught my Nana would never see me again! My death would probably be bloody and painful! I couldn't do this! What was wrong with me? I was getting ready to get myself killed!

I stood clutching my book bag to my chest which had enough rock cocaine in it to get me sent to prison for a long time. But then a memory of my big brother by one year, Man-Man, surfaced. He was smiling down at me as he handed me one of Nana's honey buns that were stashed up high in her closet. She thought we didn't know about them. She busted us and he took all the blame. Boy, Nana tore him up!

I eased back down to the bleachers, remembering why I was doing this.

My brother was dead! Murdered!

And the man responsible was down there standing on the sideline, larger than life, watching his younger brother play in a four-on-four hood tournament. Although this event was big in the hood, and Rasheed, his younger brother was something of a hood legend, being the biggest and most violent drug dealer on this side of town, the groupies were not here to see Rasheed.

No, they were all here to see Kaleb. If Rasheed was the prince around these parts, then Kaleb was the king, who rumor has it, was not only the power behind Rasheed, but also had his hands in everything from prime real estate to being the money behind several big named record labels here in the Chi. But what he was known for was The King and Sons' Classic Car Restoration Shop.

The story goes, their father, whose name was King, was this big-time drug dealer in his day. And to hide all the money he had coming in, he opened a classic car restoration shop in downtown Chicago. Anyway, the shop got so big it is said that it was bringing in just as much money, if not more than his dope empire. Needless to say, King did well with the business.

Kaleb however, has taken it to another level. Their shop had become the place to take your classic car amongst our people, and not just hood rich folks either. Big time rappers have shot their music videos at the shop. They rapped about driving their fresh whip off the lot. Hell, even the mayor joked about having to leave a press conference early, because he was going to pick up his '69 Cutlass that had been restored at The King and Sons'. They say the waiting list is like eight years out to even get a quote.

Hmm! Yeah, the women were not here like this to see

Rasheed. He was a regular on the block. His older brother was not. So, whenever Kaleb was spotted in the neighborhood, folks surrounded him as if he was a king. And tonight, there was going to be a party at his place. So yeah, the chickens were out.

I looked around at all the women who were here dressed like I was, hoping to be picked by one of the party promoters, who believe it or not, were moving around the park handing invites to certain girls. Certain girls that looked like they were down for whatever. Pretty girls. Scantily dressed girls. And they were cheesing and smiling as if they had just won the damn lottery.

Silly women!

I on the other hand, was dressed like a whore because I was getting ready to bring down the untouchable. And trust me, being dressed in a mini-skirt that left most of my legs and thighs exposed, and a crop-top that exposed my stomach and hung low on one side exposing my shoulder was not easy. And to top it all off, I was not wearing a bra. I let my long locs fall to cover the side of my face.

I'm not going to lie. I was hiding behind them, letting my body do all the work for me.

Hell yeah, I was ashamed that I was using my body this way. I could only imagine what my Nana or big sister Stormy would say if they saw me dressed this way.

*Come on, Mon! Remember, you're just playing a part. This is not real. It's acting.* I told myself.

And like Madame Queen, the woman who had been my acting coach for the last ten years had always said, "To convince the world that you are a certain character, you must first convince yourself." Today, I was not Monica. Today, I was Toya, hoochie mama extraordinaire. A gold-digger, whose every dream would come true if only Kaleb, Drug Lord, King Pin, would just choose me to come to his big party tonight. And as I watched his goons continue to move around the crowd giving exclusive invites, I almost threw up in my mouth.

I just wanted this to be over. I had to get revenge for my brother. I could not let his death go without somebody paying for it. Then I can have peace. Then I can focus on graduating high school in a few months, and then on to Juilliard. I had been accepted there on a dance scholarship. My Nana was sad that I was going to be moving to New York, but she was thrilled about me being accepted at Juilliard. She herself has been one of the first black women to dance on Broadway behind the late, great, Ms. Janet Collins, who had in fact been the very first black prima ballerina of the Metropolitan Opera House. Her and my Nana were my role models.

I too wanted to dance on Broadway. Ever since I was a little girl, it had been my dream. Before Man-Man got turned out to the streets, he would help me practice by lifting me high in the air, twirling me around in my little tutu. I had hoped that he would one day come back to us. That he would turn back into the Man-Man me and Nana loved instead of the gangster he was so determined to be. I used to tell Nana that it was just a phase, and he would snap out of it and be normal again.

But he never will. He will never do anything else, because he was dead. I angrily wiped away the tears that began to well up in my eyes.

No! I will not cry! I will not!

Instead, I will get revenge for my brother. And then I

will leave town and become a prima ballerina like my grandmother.

I looked back down at the man who was responsible for the death of my brother, and pure hatred shot through my veins. He had messed with the wrong girl's brother. And if it was the last thing I do, tonight, he was going to pay for it!

However, later that night I found myself in a bit of trouble. Everything had gone so smoothly at first. While most of the girls at the park had been loud and obnoxious to get noticed, I had taken a different approach for two reasons. First and foremost, I was terrified and ashamed of showing off so much of my body! The last thing I wanted to do was to draw too many eyes. I just needed to draw the eyes of those that mattered, Kaleb's goons.

The second reason was something Madame Queen had always told me. "You don't have to be loud to be noticed. In fact, use your body language to speak. Speak with the arch in your back, the curve of your hand, the grace in your step, the swan-like dip in your neck. Let your grace speak for you. It is more noticeable than any voice."

And so I did. I sat there reading a book, not speaking to anyone. Every now and again I would flip my hair. When I reached for my water bottle next to me to take a sip, I curved my palm so that my long slender fingers gracefully lifted the bottle to my lips. When I drank, I sat straight up with just a slight arch to my back. I elongated my neck as the cool water ran down my throat, and then when I was done, I licked my lips.

Seconds later, I had my invite. I was handed a card with the address to Kaleb's Gold Coast penthouse condo by some guy that was very proud of his looks. I know this because every now and again he would stop and take a selfie of himself talking to someone, or shaking their hand or something. And he was proud of his car. He made sure everybody knew he was driving the candy red Lexus. Every now and again he would point his keys toward it and click a button to turn it on.

"Got to keep the air conditioner blowing, you know what I'm saying!" he would say to whoever was standing by him before laughing and looking around the park— probably trying to make sure everybody was watching him. Anyway. The clown handed me the card, and instructed me to give it to the guards in the downstairs lobby of Kaleb's condo.

"You need a ride boo?" he asked. I flinched.

"Oh no, I can get there. Thank you for the invite though!" As he made his way back down the bleachers, I breathed a sigh of relief.

Now that I was in, my plan was to fade to the background while I try to find a place to plant the drugs. I know you're wondering about the drugs. And to make a long story short, I found them in my brother's room. I know my brother sold this crap for Rasheed and Kaleb, so I figure I will just return their product and just maybe, make an anonymous call to the police, saying that a white woman was about to be murdered by a group of black thugs while at the same time making sure the drugs were somewhere that the police could see.

I know the white woman part was low. But hey, it will get the results I needed for this to go off as planned.

When I got to the penthouse, I was pleased to see that the place was packed, which was perfect. I found a seat in a dark corner where I could go unnoticed while I staked out the joint. Kaleb's penthouse was huge, I mean life of the rich and famous huge. I sat in what I assumed was the parlor, which was good, because it kept me close to the front door and it opened into the rest of the condo, giving me a great view of the sunken living room. You had to walk down a few steps to go into it. Wait staff came in and out of the kitchen. There were a full bar and a DJ table. One whole side of his place was glass windows. Outside of them was a big pool area with an Olympic size pool. There was a full bar out there as well.

The other women that had been invited were doing their jobs fabulously. They were all dressed in tiny dresses and high heels. I kind of felt underdressed. Most of them had gone home and changed into something far more glamorous than what they had been wearing at the park earlier. I still wore the tiny jean skirt and crop top that I was going to burn on my grill after tonight. Oh well, I wasn't here to be noticed at this point.

I heard a girl scream by the pool. Some guy had snatched off her bikini top and tossed her in the water. Oh, my goodness! I held my breath, waiting for her to emerge from the water and yell, "Rape!" Except when she came up, it wasn't her bare breasts she was squalling about, it was her hair.

Em, Em, Em…

Welp! So, like I was saying with all that kind of activity going on, who would pay attention to little old me in a dark corner, right? Right.

Okay, so this is where things started going wrong. You see, I had planned on being out of this place by now. But neither Kaleb nor Rasheed was here, and timing was everything. I needed to plant the drugs at the right time and make my call. Hopefully when they find Man-Man's drugs they will go ahead and search the premises for more drugs. Now granted, from what I've researched on Kaleb, he's nobody's dummy. So chances are he won't have any drugs here at his house. But I bet he had a gun or two. Plus, Man-Man had enough drugs to put anybody away for a good while. I don't care how it happens, just as long as the bastard goes to jail. Him and his psychotic brother.

The guy that had given me the invite sat down on the wide circular chair next to me. I had to force myself not to stiffen at his nearness. I was playing the role of a whore after all.

"The book reader," he said leaning in close to me. He had on so much cologne I almost choked. I smiled at him.

"Yep, I like to read," I told him, wishing he would just get up and leave me be.

He held up his hand and one of the serving girls came over carrying a tray with two shot glasses of alcohol on it.

Oh crap! I was getting ready to panic.

"Thank you, baby," he said to her as she put the glasses down on a table next to us. When she turned to leave, he smacked her on her butt. Goodness, what a savage!

"You drink Tequila, boo?" He turned to look at me while handing me one of the glasses. "It's Patron; only the good stuff for the sexiest girl at the party." Everything in me screamed for me to say, "No," but I would draw too much attention to myself saying no to a drink. With a very forced smile on my face, I nodded.

"Oh, yeah, I like Patron," I told him. He smiled before he turned his glass up and swallowed the contents in one swoop. Oh crap. I have never drunk a thing in my whole life. Oh crap! "I am playing a part," I reminded myself, before I lifted the glass to my lips and duplicated his action.

I almost died! As the fiery liquid washed down my throat, I began to choke. It was taking everything within me to keep it down. Oh goodness! It was horrible! I'm pretty sure I just drank rubbing alcohol.

"You okay, boo?" The creep said, patting me on my back. I nodded.

"Yeah!" I croaked. "It's just been a while."

"Girl, the way you took that, it looks like it's been never." He frowned at me.

Even though it almost killed me, I forced myself to stop choking. The last thing I needed was for this guy to start asking questions. The less anybody knew about me here, the better. Tonight I was supposed to be a phantom.

The drink was beginning to warm me up on the inside. I took my foot and scooted my backpack underneath the chair out of sight. The alarm system was going off inside my head and I didn't know why.

"So," he said, putting his arm on the chair behind me, "what's your name, boo?"

What is with this guy and the "boo" thang? I cleared my throat.

"Toya," I said, clearing my throat again. Something was wrong. I was beginning to feel warm on the inside, and my throat felt scratchy. It was probably just the shot. I guess that's what it was supposed to do. I mean why else would anybody drink such vile tasting stuff?

"Toya. Em, that's a pretty name, just like you." He put his hand on my thigh, and for the third time tonight I almost threw up.

"Thank you," I said, turning to look around at the other

party goers. "Please leave!" I screamed in my head. I began to fan myself with my hand. Somebody must have turned on the heat, because it was really getting hot in here.

"I was thinking me and you can get out of here and go for a little drive in my Lexus." He winked at me, and oh my goodness! I could not stop the laughter that erupted from my mouth. I don't know why, but that wink coupled with his words was hilarious.

"What's so funny?" he asked.

"You, boo!" I told him, before I erupted into another fit of laughter. This dude was trash and so was his game. Dang, was I drunk? Why did I just find that so funny? Was it possible to get drunk off of one shot?

"Can you get drunk off of one shot?" I asked him. He smiled then, very wickedly.

"Yep, if it's Liquid Ex." I frowned at him.

"Is that Tequila?" He shook his head.

"Nope." Those alarm bells were getting louder.

"What is it then?"

"It's new... just hit the streets." My eyes widened. Oh no!

"Don't worry, baby. It's just a little something to help you loosen up a bit, that's all." He opened his mouth to say something else to me, but right then the front door opened and Rasheed walked in. Behind him were several guys that I had seen standing with Kaleb. Either they were his main boys or maybe even his bodyguards. Behind them walked in Kaleb.

My breath stalled in my throat. I don't know if it was because of the drugs or just the general impact of seeing this man up close for the first time, but it felt as if I had been sucker punched right in the stomach. You see, I had not gotten a good look at his face earlier.

What a face!

He was extremely good looking, in a very rugged kind of way. He was good looking without even trying. He wore his beard low as if it hadn't been cut in a few days. However, his fade looked fresh as if it had been cut today. He didn't have a friendly face. You know the kind that welcomed people to approach you?

His face said loud and clear, "Don't mess with me, because I'm not in the mood." He frowned. In fact, he looked as if he was irritated with us all.

That, added with the fact that he was big. I mean *really* big. He wore a button-up shirt with the top three buttons opened that gave a sneak peek at the immense chest underneath it. The material hugged his arms just enough to see that they too were gigantic. He could probably snap me in half like a twig if he chose to. And him being dressed in all black—black jeans, black shirt, black Gaiter boots—only added to the fear I was feeling right now.

This fear I couldn't blame on the drugs. If anything, the drugs were keeping me from getting up and running for my life. I have a confession to make. I may have a slight problem of getting an idea in my head and running with it before I could think it all the way through. My Nana and Stormy say my little condition was probably going to get me in trouble one day. And I think that today just may be that day.

I am so stupid! Why did I just assume that Kaleb was going to be like Rasheed? Yeah, Rasheed scared a lot of people on the streets because he was a murdering thug. Him, I could have handled. But this force that was his older brother was a different story. He was... dangerous. I felt way out of my element. He was above anything I had ever encountered. Power and experience just seemed to radiate from him. Everybody felt it. I could tell by the way they all stared at him with a look of awe on their faces.

And to top it all off, I had been drugged. Even as we were speaking, I could feel it making changes to my body, or at least how I felt about my body.

The shame I had felt earlier for exposing so much skin was gone. And although I know I was afraid right now, my brain wasn't sending the proper signals to my body, like..."Run!"

"Welcome home, Boss," the man who had been sitting on the couch next to me said, getting up to approach the group. His voice boomed over the music so that all of us that sat in the front parlor heard.

"Jamie, I don't need you to welcome me to my own home," Kaleb spoke sounding tired. His voice was deep and raspy.

"Sit your goofy a$$ down!" Rasheed said shoving Jamie in the head, causing a bunch of people to laugh. "Why do you keep this chump around?" he asked his brother. Kaleb chuckled, shaking his head a bit. As the men passed me, I prayed to Stormy's God, Yah, that I went unnoticed. My heart was beating so loud in my ear it was louder than the music. I wanted to fan myself because I was extremely hot now. I could feel beads of sweat pooling up on my temples, but I sat perfectly still as not to draw attention to myself.

But right as he passed, Kaleb looked down at me. At first his eyes just seemed to skim over me. I was just about to exhale when they flew back to me. And Oh! My! Goodness! He stopped dead in his tracks and turned to look at me fully. The heat had turned into an inferno! I was burning alive!

Please floor, just open and swallow me, this chair and my brother's drugs through you. I began to breathe heavily. At least it seemed like it to me. My chest rose and fell with each panic breath I took. *This was not the plan! This was not the plan!*

"You the shorty with the book," he said, and a quiver went through me as his deep voice washed over me. I almost moaned. His voice felt so good. What the world was happening to me?

I just froze in fear. If Madame Queen could see me now, she would shake her head and say, "Well, you were born to be a dancer. This acting thing just comes in a strong second to that." I opened my mouth to speak but nothing came out. I don't know if it was the drugs in my system or just the power that seemed to ooze from him, but I felt terrified. Having his full attention was like having the attention of an oncoming, speeding Mac-truck. I bit my lip, more nervous than I've ever been in my life. His eyes lowered to my mouth.

"Boss, she ain't nobody. I brought her here for me. *This is what I have for you,*" Jamie said turning to gesture towards two very voluptuous women dressed in brown bikinis that matched their brown oiled up bodies perfectly.

Dang! They looked like two bars of chocolate. The mouths of Rasheed and the other men that came in with him fell open as the women approached Kaleb. They both wore inviting smiles on their faces as their hungry eyes took in all that was Kaleb. Kaleb looked at them for a minute. His eyes slowly traveled up their bodies and back down again. I eased my hand down on the side of the chair and pushed the bag back to the wall so that it could not be seen at all. My heart was racing so fast I was finding it hard to breathe. I needed to get away from this force that was Kaleb.

I eased to my feet. While everybody's attention was on the two chocolate drops, I would just ease myself out of this situation. With my head down, I quietly slipped away. I had taken five, maybe six steps when I felt a strong, warm hand come around my waist and palm my flat, bare stomach.

Oh! I closed my eyes as a feeling I had never felt before shot through me. Oh! What was happening? I think I was feeling pleasure; pure, intense pleasure. How could this be? How could I feel pleasure for a man I hated? He pressed his front so close to my back I could feel the outline of his strong body.

"Where you going, Shorty? I'm not finished talking to you," he spoke quietly, his lips brushing my ear as his deep voice and warm breath caressed my lobe. I closed my eyes and suppressed a moan that tried to escape my lips. It had to be the drugs. Oh no! That jerk slipped me a Mickey!

"I..." my voice quivered as I spoke. I cleared my throat. "I was just going to get some air, that's all," I told him.

"Good idea. Let's go together." He took my hand and began to pull me across the huge parlor. With panicked eyes, I looked back at Jamie. I would rather deal with him and his buffoonery over this power force any day.

"Boss, what's up?" Jamie yelled after us. Kaleb came to a stop. As he inhaled, his nostrils flared and the muscle ticked in his cheek. He didn't turn around. He just stood there for a few seconds, breathing angrily while staring straight ahead. Right then, two of the big goons that had come in the door with him, stood from where they had been sitting with a girl on their laps. Rasheed, who had been whispering something in one of the chocolate drop's ears, stopped and approached Jamie.

"Man, what the hell you just say?" he growled at Jamie, who now wore a look of terror on his face.

"Nothing. I just wanted to tell the boss to enjoy my treat to him." Kaleb grunted then continued walking. I was doomed. He led me through the crowd and up the sleek stairs that sat in full view of everyone. I let my hair fall to cover my face, so embarrassed. Everyone was looking at us. Some of the women looked as if they wanted to claw my eyes out. I wanted to beg someone to take my place. Please!

Two big men with guns sat in the open space that was at the top of the stairs.

"Boss," they said as we passed. Kaleb didn't speak. He just slightly nodded his head. We walked down a long, dark hallway, passing a few rooms to a pair of wooden double doors at the end of it. He opened one and pulled me through it.

And yes, he was pulling me because I was dragging my feet.

"Umm, I should go back to the party," I told him, trying to pull my hand out of his. I couldn't even pretend that I was not afraid, and yet the drugs were making me feel something else. I was trying to fight them, but the feeling was getting stronger and stronger.

"Naw, Ma. I ain't in the mood for all that out there. It's been a long week, and I just want to chill with you, okay?" I opened my mouth to say, "Not okay," but then I got my first view of his room and my words just seemed to die away. Just like the rest of his place, his bedroom was humongous and very masculine. On his big bed was a very plush looking black comforter with matching pillows. All the furniture was made of mahogany wood.

His room smelled like him; a mix of his spicy cologne and soap, and maybe even laundry detergent. He walked to a pair of glass double doors that were across the room and opened them to a beautiful modest size balcony.

"Wow!" I said as I crossed the floor with feet that seemed to have a mind of their own. He had the most amazing view of the lake.

"Best place to get some air." He spoke so close to my ear, I jumped. I didn't hear him come up behind me. I walked away from him to the rail and looked out across the dark lake. The gentle breeze felt so good blowing against my warm skin. I held my head back and let the wind blow my locs around my body and face. It felt amazing. I closed my eyes and moaned as the wind caressed my skin that seemed to be inflamed ever since Kaleb first looked at me.

Giving in to the caress of the wind was all the drug needed to take over. I could no longer fight it. I wanted to feel good. I wanted to dance.

And as if on cue, the DJ began to play something slow and sensual. I lost track of reality. In my mind, I was dancing in the night, in the streets of Paris or across the sands of Arabia. I was slightly aware of Kaleb watching me. He felt like a king and I his harem girl, dancing for his pleasure.

He sat on the edge of his bed and watched me move through lowered lids. I can tell he liked what he saw because of the hungry look on his face. Funny, his look didn't repulse me like it should. No, quite the opposite. It made me feel good, sexy, and empowered.

I went up on my toes and came down in a simple balance, which is a rocking sequence of three steps.

"You're a ballerina," he stated quietly as if he was speaking to himself. I stopped dancing and looked at him.

"You don't know me," I laughed. "I'm the phantom of the opera." One of his eyebrows lifted.

"The opera?" he asked, his deep voice washing over my body, causing everything within me to want something I had never wanted before. Well, at least not like *this*.

"And where is this opera?" I opened my arms wide.

"Here." His gaze lowered to my stomach and probably the underside of my breasts that I was revealing with my raised arms. He licked his lips, watching me like a wolf watched a small deer. I snatched my arms down and laughed.

"You look hungry," I told him. Slowly he nodded.

"I am, baby. I want to taste you so bad it's taking everything within me to keep my hands to myself right now." I closed my eyes as pure uncut pleasure shot through me at his words.

"How old are you?" he asked. I opened my eyes and looked at him.

"Eighteen."

"Damn, you're young," he said looking miserable. I giggled.

"How old are you?"

"Twenty-nine. I'll be thirty in a few months." I shrugged my bare shoulder.

"Why does my age upset you?"

He shook his head. "I don't mess with young women.

They get attached because I make them feel something they have never felt before. Next thing you know, they're in love and don't know how to go home when it's time."

I lifted one side of my mouth in a grin. "Baby, you ain't never got to worry about me falling in love with you. And as far as going home, that sounds like a great idea. I'll just let myself out." I turned to head for the door. Damn, that was easy.

I had only gone a few steps before I found myself lifted off my feet and into a pair of strong arms. My startled breath whooshed out my body. I looked at him in shock. He smiled at me.

"I see you a sassy young lady. What's your name?" he asked, carrying me back to his bed. I was so befuddled by suddenly being in his arms that I opened my mouth and uttered the truth.

"Monica!" I closed my eyes as soon as my name escaped my lips. Damn it!

"Well, Monica, if I don't have to worry about you falling in love, then I want a taste."

When we got to the bed, he tossed me in it. I giggled, trying to fight my way out of the plush blanket. Before I could, he was on the bed. He wedged his big body between my legs and was holding himself up over me with one hand. His other hand was coming towards my face. I laid there paralyzed. I know I should be stopping him. My mind said I should. But my body... my body wanted to know how it felt to be touched by a man.

And I ain't gon' lie. The fact that this powerful man was looking at me like that... like I was something he craved... He lifted a finger to my lips and gently rubbed across my bottom lip.

"So soft," he whispered. "Can I taste you?"

*Say, No! Say, No!*

I slowly nodded. *What am I doing?* I thought, as he slowly lowered his head. When his lips first touched mine, it felt like electricity. I inhaled. He lifted his head, looking down at me. I touched my lips with fingers that shook as I stared up into his searching eyes. He had felt it too. His eyes fell on my lips and he lowered his head again, but this time when he took my mouth, he ravished.

Oh! Goodness! He was so hungry, I—

I clutched his shirt in my fist, trying to hold on for dear life.

"You taste so good... so sweet," he said low in my ear before his mouth was on my neck.

His big palm lay flat against my belly, feeling each quiver he caused to go off there. Slowly his hand lifted, and with it, my shirt. He broke his lips away from mine and looked down at my flesh he had just exposed. He moaned.

"Beautiful, baby," he said, before he slowly lowered his head—

Okay, yeah. So, I'm going to do a little editing at this point. But for the sake of my story, I'm going to fill you in on a little more detail. At one point, at that very moment he made me a woman, a look of utter surprise crossed his face when I screamed out in pain.

"You're a virgin?" he whispered. His surprise turned into confusion. His confusion turned into a look of utter... possession?

"You're a virgin," he whispered in my ear as he slowed down, and then very gently continued to awaken my body in a way that will forever ruin me to the touch of any other man.

Now, I want to say that after we finished I felt ashamed and got my clothes and left. But then I would be lying. We made love two more times before we both passed out in an exhausted sleep.

When I woke up, I was in bed alone. I sat up and looked around the dark room confused.

Where was I? For a moment, I was completely lost. And then the last few hours came back to me. And yes, for the fourth time that night, I felt as if I was going to be ill. I scrambled out of bed.

"What have I done?" I whispered as I quickly put my clothes back on. Oh, man! This was not good. This was not good! I stopped when I looked down at the condom wrapper on the floor.

*One wrapper*!

My hand flew to my mouth. Oh, goodness! One wrapper!

The last two times we made love had been unprotected. No! No!

*Okay. Get it together, Mon. You need to get out of here!* Yes, that's what I needed to do. I had to get out of here. Now was not the time to think of anything else outside of getting revenge for Man-Man and getting on with my life. I had to see this through. I had already botched it something terrible. And I had to move quickly before that bastard came back.

I eased the bedroom door open, listening. It was quiet. It sounded as if the party had died down.

Okay, you can do this!

I took a deep breath, then walked out of the door and

down the long hallway. I didn't even look at the men that were still in the opening before the stairs. I just quickly made my way down them. There were only a few stragglers still here. Kaleb stood with his back to me out in the pool area talking to a few guys. What a bastard. He was probably telling them he was ready for me to be out of his bed. I almost laughed out loud. You don't have to worry, Mister. After today, you ain't gon' never see me again.

I made my way back to the parlor. I could see that my bag was still under the chair I sat in earlier. Quickly, I pulled it out and carried it across the room to a closet that I had scouted out and figured would be the perfect place for the cops to find dope.

With hands that shook, I took out the drugs and stashed them on the top shelf. And then without looking back, I slipped out the front door.

An hour later, I stood outside with the small crowd that was forming and watched as the police came out with a handcuffed Kaleb as well as a few other people. Unfortunately, not Rasheed. But I was fine with that. Like Bob Marley said, "I shot the sheriff. I don't need to shoot the deputy." I pulled out one of Man-Man's Cuban cigars, his prized possession, that he had more than likely stolen. And as the police car that carried Kaleb rolled past me I lit it, and put it to my lips. When his angry eyes connected with mine, I winked at him with a smirk on my face.

Got you, bastard!

# More From Edwina Fort

Falling For Rome

Falling For Rome 2

Coming For What's Mine

Coming For What's Mine 2

Mean Tucker

Hitta's Tea Maker

Hitta's Tea Maker 2

Redemption: Earth's Cry

Redemption

---

Thank you

---


Thank you, guys for coming along Kaleb and Monica's journey to finding love for the

Heavenly Father Yah and for each other.

Like them, we all must learn how to put Yah first. And then, he in his loving commitment will provide our every need.

I am Edwina Fort, The Hebrew Griot...

If you liked this story, please leave me a message letting me know and don't forget to

check out my Hebrew Griot YouTube page for many more stories just like this one...

Hebrew Griot YouTube Channel:
youtube.com/channel/UCN2wo3cuLpM20So1SUpyXzA

Facebook Page:
www.facebook.com/hebrewgriot

Edwina Fort Facebook Page:
www.facebook.com/AuthorEdwinaFort

Edwina Fort Twitter:
twitter.com/Edwina_Fort

Edwina Fort Website:
authoredwinafort.com

Edwina Fort YouTube Channel:
www.youtube.com/channel/UCSKCjVKwFB-
rWq_uHUuqE4Q

# the griot's garden
## IS LOOKING FOR AUTHORS.

*Do you have a story to tell?*

*Submit online:*

GriotsGardenPublications.com/submissions

# About the Author

*Author Edwina Fort is a writer who writes with a passion and purpose. She was born and raised in Chicago, but now resides in the South. Although she is new to many, this author has been writing for many years and has given her unique style of writing away freely at no cost to those who would receive. Her passion for writing came about at an early age and developed into what it is today based on her experience and life lessons. With her stories, she wants to redefine all that we've been taught to believe and shed light on our truths and potential. Writing is her calling and she wants to share that gift with you through the pages of her work. Each book will take you on a memorable journey you will find hard to forget.*

facebook.com/AuthorEdwinaFort

twitter.com/Edwina_Fort

instagram.com/author_edwina